ADVANCE PRAISE FOR *THE SEVENTH SUN*

"With a rich world and even richer characters, Lani's
The Seventh Sun will pull you in and keep you wanting more."
–KARA BARBIERI,
author of the Permafrost series

"This vivid, historic tale will transport readers to an ancient culture and,
along the way, will capture their hearts, as well."
–MERRIE DESTEFANO,
award-winning author of *Valiant*

"Lani Forbes delivers lush storytelling, vivid characters,
and heart-pounding drama in her compelling debut novel…Lani Forbes
now joins Leigh Bardugo and Alwyn Hamilton
in the ranks of the most talented fantasy authors of today."
–MARGO KELLY,
award-winning author of *Who R U Really?* and *Unlocked*

THE
SEVENTH
SUN

THE
SEVENTH
SUN

LANI FORBES

**BLACK
STONE**
PUBLISHING

Printed in the United States of America

First edition: 2020

ISBN 978-1-982546-09-0

Young Adult Fiction / Fantasy / General

1 3 5 7 9 10 8 6 4 2

CIP data for this book is available
from the Library of Congress

Blackstone Publishing
31 Mistletoe Rd.
Ashland, OR 97520

www.BlackstonePublishing.com

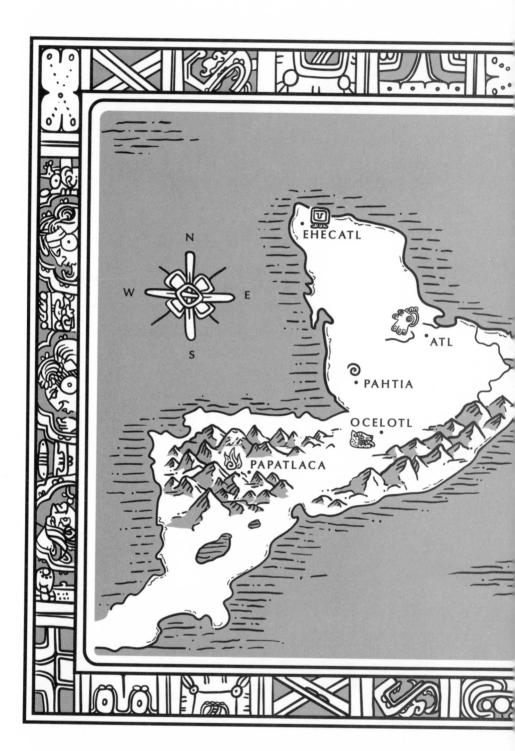

MIQUITZ MOUNTAINS

•OMITL

MILLACATL
•

TOLLAN

PART 1

CHAPTER

1

The Great Star was fading.

Most of the palace slumbered, enjoying a respite from the daily routines that secured the favor of the gods. Prince Ahkin, however, splayed his hands across the surface of a carved stone table with a heavy sigh. Charts of star movements and accompanying religious texts lay strewn before him, detailing the knowledge the Chicome people had collected since the time of the Second Sun. Muted light from the moon, forever jealous of its glorious brother, filtered in through the palace window along with the stifling humidity of the jungle beyond.

He slammed his fist against the table. Why were the heavens being so secretive tonight? His calculations were accurate; he had repeated them several times just to be sure. The Seventh Sun had set much earlier than it should have last night. And just after the first stars had blinked awake, a comet appeared in the heavens. A comet the color of blood. If the gods painted their warnings in the skies, then what were they trying to tell him? There must be an answer.

"M-m-my lord?" came a tremulous voice from behind him.

"What is it?" The prince refused to lift his gaze from his calculations. The servants usually knew better than to disturb him so late into the night.

Shuffling footsteps grew louder. "I am so sorry to interrupt, but you are needed to … to … raise the sun."

A stone seemed to settle in the pit of his stomach. The sun was not his responsibility—not yet.

He whirled to face a familiar middle-aged man dressed in traditional white cotton cloak and loincloth. Olli. White feathers crowned the top of his head—a symbol of his status as one of his father's most loyal servants. Olli's face gave the impression he had seen a spirit wandering in the land of the living. The hair on the back of Ahkin's neck rose.

Ahkin's eyes narrowed. "Why is my father unable to perform the ritual?"

"Emperor Acatl has begun his journey through the underworld." Olli dropped his chin to his chest.

Ahkin lunged from the table and grabbed the servant's shoulder, a sound like rushing water filling his ears.

"Coatl. Summon Coatl. What are you waiting for?" The command poured from his lips with the power and authority of the emperor—which he realized, with a start, was a title that might actually belong to him now.

"We summoned the healer immediately, but it was too late. Your father is gone, my lord."

The prince stumbled back. Folding his hands behind his head, he paced in a small circle, urgency racing through his veins along with the blood of the god of the sun.

"When? How?"

"We do not know how. Your mother discovered his body when she awoke." The wretched servant held his hands over his face.

Air rushed from Ahkin's lungs as if he'd taken a blow to the stomach. If his father was gone, then that meant ...

"And my mother?"

"She is preparing to fulfill her duty to the emperor as we speak."

"No ..."

"My lord, there is nothing you can do. The codex stipulates that she must take her life so that she may accompany your father on his journey. If she does not, she will dishonor the emperor and the gods themselves."

Ahkin ignored him and sprinted from the room. The Eagle warriors standing guard outside of his room called after him in concern.

Shadows of night still clung to the dark hallways of the palace. He removed the obsidian dagger from his waistband and sliced the blade across his thumb. The moment the blood of the sun god oozed through the cut, the power of his ancestor coursed through him. He threw out his hand, calling every trace of light from the palace torches, even the reflected rays of the moon itself. The light obeyed his command, pouring into the hall and illuminating the path ahead.

His heart threw itself against his ribcage, almost as if it could escape and run the distance faster on its own. The wailing of servants filled his ears as he passed one of their residential halls. Though many emperors before had been ruthless and cruel in their reigns, his father had been as well-loved as he was respected. Several servants fell to their knees and prostrated themselves before him as he passed. He traded the anguish rising up inside him for numb disbelief. He didn't have time to feel. He had to get to her before it was too late.

Ahkin rounded the corner into the emperor's chambers. The light that had followed the calling of his blood flooded into the room behind him, but it did little to ease the dark shadow that seemed to hang over the room like an otherworldly presence.

The empress of the Chicome stood before a small group of Tlana priests, her yellow-and-gold robe glittering in his summoned light. Ahkin took in the body of his father, unmarked and peaceful, resting upon the bed mat as though he were sleeping. Even in death, his father's lightly lined face seemed far too young. Had something internal been plaguing him without their knowledge? Had the gods simply decided it was his time and taken him? Only the healer would be able to answer those questions, and Ahkin would ensure he did. The image didn't seem real, as though his father would sit up at any moment and greet them with a beaming smile. But if what the servant said was true …

Had the signs in the heavens been a warning?

His mother's coal-dark eyes found his own, and he swallowed hard. "Mother …" But Ahkin couldn't think what to say. He couldn't ask her to stop, especially given the pointed stares of the priests surrounding her like spirits waiting to escort her to the depths of Xibalba. He clenched his teeth, restraining the beast within him that longed to fly across the room and pry the obsidian dagger from his mother's fingers. This was not right, no matter what the codex demanded.

"My lord prince." One of the priests stepped forward, the many beads and ornaments hanging around his neck rattling like bones. "The blood of Huitzilopochtli must be shown the respect it deserves. It is not to be summoned merely in lieu of finding a torch to light a hallway."

Condescension dripped from the priest's tone and crawled underneath Ahkin's skin, but he bit his tongue and returned his attention to his mother.

"You can't leave me. I need you. The Great Star is fading and ..."

The empress swept forward, a ray of sunlight penetrating the gloom. She placed a hand against his cheek. His throat tightened in response. No matter what had happened in his life, she had always been that continual source of comfort, a steadfast presence that never wavered.

"You will be fine without me, dear boy. You are the emperor now, and you will not be alone. It's your turn to select a wife who can stand by your side, one who will fill your world with vibrancy and life and color. Someone to complete your duality."

"It's too soon. I'm not ready. There's still so much I need to observe, to study, to learn ..."

His mother gave a soft laugh. "You always think that knowledge gives you power, but you will never learn enough to feel ready. There are some answers in this life that will elude you, Ahkin. Sometimes, there are none to be found. Those are the times where you must trust the will of the Mother."

"What about Metzi?" he threw out in a pathetic attempt to change her mind.

"There is not enough time for me to say goodbye to her. We don't know how long ago your father entered Xibalba, and I must accompany him. That is my duty and my honor."

"But—"

"Please tell your sister that I love her, and remind her that she must do her duty to the family." Her watery smile betrayed no fear or regret.

"Mother—please wait ..."

"Honor the rituals, Ahkin. It is your job to protect our people now, and you must not anger the gods." She spoke with such finality that Ahkin knew better than to argue. His mother's faith never faltered. It was as steady as the mountains. Her strength and dedication to the gods had always earned their favor in the past. How could they demand this of her now? Demand her very life?

"I will," he choked out. His throat was thick, as though he had swallowed cold honey. A vicious battle waged inside his heart. He knew the rituals kept his people safe, that there was nothing more important than pleasing the gods, but despite that knowledge, part of him raged against their cruel demand. How could they take her away from him?

His mother's smile widened. "I will always hold you in my heart."

And she plunged the dagger beneath her breastbone.

Ahkin spread a hand across his chest as if the dagger had pierced him as well. Blood drenched his mother's fingers, flowing down her dress in a river of scarlet. She slowly lowered herself to the floor as the priests surrounded her and blocked her from view—separating them forever as the last of her life force faded. The smell of the holy incense burned his nose and the chanting prayers of the priests faded against the rushing in his ears.

Where he was supposed to feel pride in his mother's dedication, he instead felt a hollow emptiness, as though a torch had been snuffed out leaving only a darkness. *Honor the rituals*, she had said. *Honor the rituals*. The rituals that protected their empire, pleased the gods, and kept the sun aloft. The same rituals that had just taken his mother away from him.

Olli's hand touched his shoulder lightly and he jerked away, numb with disbelief.

"My lord ... the sun. Please."

He rose to his feet and rubbed his eyes with a thumb and forefinger. His parents were both gone. A weight like a cumbersome cloak settled onto his shoulders, making it hard to breathe. How could this have happened so suddenly? How could everything change in the course of a single night?

Shoving down the suffocating pressure building in his chest, he tried to focus on the jobs that needed to be done—to honor the gods, protect his people, follow his mother's final wish. As usual, the rigid boundaries of the codex's holy texts quelled the chaos in his mind. Despite how he felt, at least he knew what he had to *do*. That was part of the beauty of the rituals.

"Are we prepared for the morning ceremony?" He willed his voice to remain strong and calm.

"Yes, my lord. The sacrificial papers are waiting for you on the altar."

This day would've come eventually. He'd prepared for this moment his entire eighteen calendar cycles of life, but he always imagined there would be more time. His father dying in his sleep—not even Coatl, the healer, could have prevented that. His father hadn't been ill, at least not that anyone knew of. Perhaps he had hidden his condition because he didn't want to appear weak? Or had his body failing really been a silent surprise? The will of the gods was sometimes as baffling as it was terrifying.

He crossed the lush gardens of the central courtyard, his sense of purpose growing stronger with each step. The heavy scent of the night-blooming flowers washed the incense from his nose. Fountains trickled through the snaking pools, their joyous music feeling out of place. Monkeys chattered and darted between branches as if spreading news of the new emperor's approach. All around him, the palace began to rouse. Servants that had not yet learned the terrible news busied themselves in the storerooms, preparing the day's first meal. Birds twittered in their wooden cages, greeting the aviary with their morning songs.

The entire Chicome Empire now relied on him. Hundreds of thousands of lives depended on his blood. He and his twin sister, Metzi, were now the only two surviving descendants of the sun god. Dread filled his stomach at the thought of waking her after the ceremony. She would be devastated. Still, he wanted to be the one to tell her. She was the only family he had left—until she left for Ehecatl to marry the oldest son of the Storm Lord. A wife would soon replace his sister at his side.

Becoming emperor. A wife. Children. How could he endure so much change without his parents? He would never again seek his father's wise counsel. His mother would never know the joy of grandchildren.

Reaching the foot of the Temple of the Sun, he gazed upward at the hundreds of steps ascending the sloping sides of the tiered pyramid. The temple loomed like a golden mountain atop the volcanic plateau, casting its massive shadow over the capital city in the pale light of the glowing moon. Behind the distant mountains and the miles of dense jungle that separated them from the city, a pinkish glow hinted at the sun waiting just below the horizon.

Waiting for him.

He turned to the servant, Olli, who had been trotting along in his wake.

"Notify the matchmaker Atanzah and send representatives immediately to the six other city-states to inform the lords of the noble families that Emperor Acatl is dead. They are to send their chosen daughters as soon as possible. I want to begin the ritual of selecting an empress in no more than a week's time."

"Yes, my … my emperor."

The prince squirmed a little at the new title. "I am your emperor in spirit, but not in name until I find a wife."

"Yes, my prince. Please forgive me." Olli paused, seeming to chew on a question before continuing. "Should we anticipate any resistance? The noble families are all aware of … of … what happens to the daughters who are not chosen?"

"They will not question what the gods have ordained, or they risk bringing another apocalypse upon us all."

"Even Ehecatl?"

Ahkin pursed his lips but did not respond. Ehecatl, City of Storms, was still under his rule, and the tension there would hopefully ease with the upcoming wedding between his sister and their oldest son.

Olli inclined his head before rushing back to the palace.

Ahkin took a deep breath and straightened his spine. He wasn't ready for this—for the responsibility, the title, even to be married. How had he missed the warning signs of such a life-altering event? He should have been able to divine the answers from the stars.

He would consult with the high priest after the sun had risen.

His sandaled foot slid onto the first smooth golden step, and he began the climb toward his destiny. A low-level Tlana priest waited at the top, bouncing nervously on the balls of his feet. Giant feathers protruded from the priest's elaborate headdress, and his bloodred ceremonial robes glittered with beads and adornments of various gemstones. Wrinkles like tiny bird feet creased the corners of his ancient eyes, but there were more creases on his brow than usual.

Ahkin crested the final step, panting slightly from the exertion of so many stairs, and greeted the priest with a small nod.

The priest returned the greeting with a slow, sorrowful incline of his head and gestured toward the altar, darting an anxious glance to the dim glow on the horizon and back to the prince. So many depended on the timely ritual that brought the sunrise.

Standing over the strips of maguey paper scattered across the altar, Ahkin drew the blade of the ceremonial knife across his palm, a far larger and deeper cut than the one on his thumb. The image of his mother's blood flashed before his eyes and he blinked furiously to remove it. The gods demanded blood, and it was blood he must give them. With a wave of his hand, red stained the papers like raindrops the color of cinnabar. He gathered them together before throwing them into the massive brazier that burned atop the temple. The heat of the flames rushed against his face, and he released a breath. He had watched his father perform this same ritual thousands of times, never thinking the burden would fall to his own shoulders so soon.

Clenching his injured hand into a fist, he ignored the sting of the cut. Coatl would heal the skin later. A feather of smoke from the burning papers curled into the air, and the city was bathed in light. Fed by the blood of Ahkin's ancestor, the god Huitzilopochtli, the sun's glowing face greeted him and began its journey across the sky. Ahkin let its warmth creep across his skin, savoring the feeling and thanking the Mother goddess for the light of the Seventh Sun—that the Chicome Empire even had a sun at all.

Their sun had been destroyed six times. First by water, then by fire, then famine, sickness, beasts, and storms. After each apocalypse, the creator goddess Ometeotl allowed one of her divine children to sacrifice themselves to save civilization. The gods paid their blood as the price for the lives of the people, and the people owed them blood in return. The compulsion to repay that debt was ever present in their culture, even though it had been hundreds of calendar cycles since the last sun was destroyed. And there was an undercurrent continually whispering at the edge of Ahkin's mind …

When would *this* world end?

CHAPTER

2

Mayana never looked forward to the days when her family must sacrifice their blood to bring the rains, especially when it was her turn. The sacrifice took place every three months, but with so many family members, Mayana had years before she'd have to pay her tribute again. She just needed to make it until sundown. Taking a breath, she gently sliced the palm of her hand with a long, thin shard of obsidian. The sharper the blade, the more painless the cut, and there was nothing in this world sharper than obsidian fire-glass from the volcano at Papatlaca. She didn't even flinch this time.

She shook her hand over the bone-white strips of paper and sprinkles of her blood dotted them like crimson drops of rain. Her father, Oztoc, the lord and high priest of Atl, nodded his approval, enormous blue and green feathers on his headdress quivering in response. The ceremonial beads and ornaments draped around his neck rattled against one another like dried beans in a gourd.

Other members of the noble family hovered around the altar dressed in the jewel-toned feathers and fabrics of their ceremonial costumes. They reminded her of hummingbirds. Mayana bit her lip to suppress a laugh at the sight of her youngest brother, Tenoch, wearing a headpiece designed to resemble the head of a toucan. Tenoch's excited eyes peeked out from under the large orange beak that extended from his forehead. Laughing in the middle of a bloodletting ceremony was sure to trigger a stern reprimand from her father.

She approached the great stone bowl where a large fire burned and dropped the speckled papers into the flames. They turned brown and then black, curling into a pungent smoke that dissipated into the hot, humid air. A sense of pride coursed through her, and every muscle in Mayana's body relaxed—at least until she noticed the look of immense relief on her father's face. Had he really doubted her that much?

When she had been younger, Mayana had cried to no avail when it was her turn to sacrifice her own blood. The sting of piercing her own flesh, the rust and salt smell of her life's essence seeping out of her—she hated everything about it. But now that she was older, she did a better job of hiding it.

The lord of Atl's commanding voice rang out across the plaza like the call of a howler monkey, echoing down the steps of their stone temple pyramid. "The Mother goddess is now pleased. Our sacrifice of blood honors the sacrifice her daughter, Atlacoya, made to save us after the first sun was destroyed by water. Her blood, which lives on through our family, can continue to pay the price for our survival. Never again shall the waters sweep the Chicome away, nor shall Mother Ometeotl withhold the rains that nourish our lands."

The mass of people gathered below cheered so loudly that flocks of birds took flight from the jungle canopy. Mayana focused her gaze toward them, trying very hard *not* to think about the ritual that would come later that evening—the ritual she dreaded above all others.

A solitary flash of red splashed against the blue of the sky and distracted her from the twitching shadows of the birds. It looked like a comet, barely visible on the horizon, but with a tail that glowed the color of blood. A shiver crept down her spine. She had never seen anything like it before. White stars falling in a burst of light across the heavens—those were not uncommon. But red? In the middle of the day? Could it be some kind of omen?

The noble family chorused "never again" in unison, drawing her focus back to the ceremony. Mayana gave her head a little shake. Her brothers began their descent down the steps to partake in the festivities with the rest of Atl. She tore her gaze away from the bleeding star and joined them. She knew better than to disrupt the ceremony.

Great waterfalls gushed on either side of the steep staircase, muffling the sounds of the celebrations below. Music swelled through the plaza and dancers emerged from a smaller temple in the shadow of the great stone pyramid, taking the crowd's attention away from her family's slow march down the side of the temple. Panic sent her heart thudding against her ribcage harder than deer hooves against the earth. Mayana always had a terrible fear that she would trip on one of the impossibly narrow stone steps with the entire city-state watching and plummet to a painful and very public death.

After all, as a descendant of the goddess Atlacoya, goddess of drought and patron of Atl, her blood was a precious treasure.

The muscles of Mayana's legs burned by the time she reached the plaza floor. Her eyes found her father, and she shrank back, feeling utterly insignificant.

He looked like a true descendant of the gods, a tall stone pillar of serenity. How could the man walk down hundreds of stairs in this heat and not perspire? Not a single drop. She gripped her aching side, a clumsy impostor in comparison. All five of her brothers at least panted along with her, sweat pouring down their faces and tanned chests.

Mayana's crown of blue-and-gold feathers slid down her forehead, pulling strands of her long, dark hair into her face with it. She reached up with one hand to push it back, the blood still seeping through the gash in her skin. She longed to use the divine power of her exposed blood to summon a mist from one of the many rivers and waterfalls that cascaded through the ancient city, but she could already imagine her father's face if she were to ask for permission.

The lord of Atl glanced back at his family, and Mayana and her brothers all straightened up, attempting, unsuccessfully, to hide their fatigue. He waved his hand, beaded bracelets of jade sliding down his wrist, before dismissing them to enjoy the festival.

"You will all return to the palace before sundown for the feast," he called after the retreating backs of his five sons. His brow creased when they didn't respond and he let out a familiar grunt of disapproval. Before he could call them back, servants arrived with an elaborately carved wooden throne suspended between them on thick poles. They dropped the chair beside him and he paused, as though deciding whether a lecture was warranted or not, before he fanned his multicolored cloak out behind him and took his seat.

"Mayana." Her father's ebony eyes narrowed, and her stomach dropped as though she'd missed a step on the side of the temple. "You will obey the rituals exactly as they are written in the codex this time." It was a command—and a warning.

"Yes, Father, exactly as they are written." Her mind's eye flashed to the stacks of folded sheets of paper filled with colorful hieroglyphs that contained the detailed instructions for every Chicome ritual. The headdress slipped again and she bowed her head to catch it.

He sighed, shaking his head. The servants lifted the poles onto their shoulders, hoisting him high above her head. Mayana's cheeks flooded with heat. Sometimes it was impossible not to disappoint her father. She threw back her shoulders with an air of determination. Maybe if she did everything else right, he'd let her forgo the final ritual tonight. Maybe.

Her father disappeared into the crowd, and she turned to find the hunched, wizened form of Nemi, the royal healer of Atl, pushing toward her. The old healer rummaged in the folds of her red cotton dress and withdrew a single stingray spine. She plunged the barb into the tip of her thumb, exposing a tiny crimson drop. Royal healers like Nemi hailed from the city-state of Pahtia and used the power of the divine blood in their veins to repair the human body.

The old woman grabbed Mayana's hand rather roughly and yanked it toward her. Nemi was, ironically, not known for her gentleness.

"Would it be alright if I use the blood first?" Mayana pulled her arm back, cradling it against her chest.

Nemi threw her hands into the air with an exasperated sigh before wiping the small drop of blood off her thumb. Her only response was an incoherent grumbling.

"I'm sorry, I didn't mean to make you waste—" Mayana began, but Nemi turned on the spot and waddled away, her hunched shoulders disappearing into the suffocating mass of bodies without so much as a backward glance. Mayana smiled. The healer could be surlier than her father sometimes, and that was not an easy task to accomplish.

She pressed herself into the swelling crowd, a servant chaperone silently trailing along behind her. The sounds and jostling of the celebrations were disorienting. The plaza was a great sprawling marketplace, but every three months the entire city of Atl celebrated her family's bloodletting ritual. There were dances, costumes, dramatic performances, and ball games—all culminating in the great feast at sunset.

Impersonations of toucans, jaguars, eagles, wolves, and deer twirled around Mayana in a blur of color. The loud music of drums and flutes vibrated within her chest. She knew the river was close, but the chaos of the festival made it difficult to gauge her surroundings. So, she held her injured hand out in front of her and closed her eyes—feeling for the quickest path to the river. A cool awareness across her skin told her that the river rushed to her right, not far away. She opened them, and through a gap between what looked like a blue crocodile and a feathered serpent, she finally found the small bridge she was searching for.

Waterfalls flowing from the top of the temple fed the river that framed the plaza. It circled around and through the city before plunging deep into the aqueducts that supplied water to every fountain, bath, and canal in Atl. Mayana approached the flowing river, anticipating the cool water against her flushed, overheated skin. Crouching low and partially hidden by the shade provided by the small stone bridge, she removed her feathered headdress and placed it beside her foot. Her hand reached toward the water, willing it toward her with a beckoning finger.

The water rose like a shining silver snake poised to strike. Molding the water into a transparent sphere, Mayana let it hover between her hands for just a moment, enjoying the light sparkling and reflecting off its shining surface. She never tired of seeing the power of her divine ancestor coaxing the water to obey her every whim. Lifting it high above her, Mayana released it to splash over her head. The relief was cool and sweet and—

A throat cleared loudly behind her.

She spun to find Nemi with arms crossed over her massive, sagging bosom and a frown of disapproval etched upon her face.

"Alright, alright, I'm done. I just wanted to cool off." Mayana thrust her hand out to the healer. Her father forbade the family from spilling any blood unnecessarily, so she rarely got to use her abilities. She tried to take advantage every time she got the chance.

For the second time, Nemi pricked her own finger and moved a hand slowly over Mayana's injured palm. The skin knit itself together like a weaver working thread—leaving fresh, healed skin where the gash had been moments before. Even the sting had vanished along with the blood.

Mayana took back her hand and sighed. Now that it was healed, she would have to get water from the river the common way.

So much for enjoying what little she could before the sacrifice.

CHAPTER

3

Ahkin closed his eyes and savored the warmth of the newly risen sun. It felt like a gentle embrace from his father, a reminder of the long line of emperors he descended from. He wished he could hide here all morning, enjoying the last connection he had to his father. But he could avoid reality for only so long. He now had an empire to manage.

Making his way down the steep steps of the temple, he took a deep breath and turned to Olli. "Summon the council to meet. I want every advisor and elder ready to discuss our plans to move forward."

The servant jogged along beside him, trying to match Ahkin's long strides with his own stubby little legs. Ahkin couldn't help but notice that the man's short stature would make him a terrible warrior. "The elders are already waiting for you."

A jolt of panic shot through him like an arrow. "How long have they been waiting?" He increased his pace. Olli had to nearly run to keep up.

"They convened as soon as news of your father's death spread throughout the palace. They knew you would be busy with the morning sun ceremony, so I assure you they will not mind your lateness, my prince." The smaller man panted like a dog as they crossed the main plaza of the palace. The light of the newly risen sun reflected off the golden pillars and pyramids of the royal residence. The effect of its brilliance was almost blinding.

Tardiness would not be the best start to his first meeting with his advisors. Ahkin needed to make a good impression upon the collection of religious, noble, and military leaders. He flung the curtain aside, and the deep rumblings of male voices silenced at his sudden appearance.

The men seated on benches and cushions in the large meeting room all clambered to their feet and bowed, headdresses and ornaments flashing and clattering at their swift movements.

Ahkin adjusted his own golden chestpiece to make sure it hung straight across his shoulders. He felt like a child interrupting one of his father's important meetings.

A low wooden table stretched between them bearing platters of grains, bowls overflowing with brightly colored fruits, and drinks spiced with chilies and honey. The smell of the food drew Ahkin in, and his stomach rumbled.

Pushing his hunger away, Ahkin strode to the head of the low table and settled himself on the largest bench, facing the men he had always looked up to and admired as a boy growing up in his father's shadow. The vibrant red columns surrounding them reminded him of the gravity of the circumstances and the burden of the blood in his veins.

"Your Highness. I am saddened to hear of your father beginning his journey to the underworld so unexpectedly." Toani, the high priest, inclined his head and folded his hands in front of his chest. Bright-red feathers extended several feet from his elaborate headpiece. His matching red cloak gave the impression that he had been soaked in blood, and a necklace of fire-glass beads with matching earrings glistened against his tanned, wizened skin. Though Toani himself was not a descendant of the gods, no man in all of the Chicome Empire had studied the codex as extensively or knew it as well. Ahkin valued him as a member of the council.

"Thank you, Toani. We were definitely surprised. His health gave no indication of failing."

"Do we know how it happened, my lord?" growled Yaotl, leader of the empire's elite Jaguar warriors and Ahkin's personal mentor.

"We do not." Ahkin took a sip of cacao sweetened with honey. "It happened as he was sleeping and the body was unmarked, so Coatl believes it was something internal." His mind flashed to the memory of his father's body lying peacefully upon the bed mat, his mother's blood seeping across the stone tiles of the floor. He shook his head slightly to dislodge the image.

"The healer has already inspected the body?" Yaotl shifted his massive shoulders.

"He has. Do you have suspicions, Yaotl?"

The mountainous man shrugged. His voice rumbled like an active volcano.

"I just know the Miquitz have been more active at our borders than usual. I enlisted as many naguals from Ocelotl as possible to fend off attacks."

"I can honestly say that I do not suspect Miquitz to be involved in my father's death. They fear and respect our duty to ensure the sun rises. The death worshippers may capture our warriors for their sacrifices, but they would not dare to threaten the royal bloodline of Tollan."

"And what of Ehecatl? They continue to challenge Tollan's authority to oversee the empire."

"Ehecatl should be appeased by my sister's match to the eldest son of the Storm Lord. Our peace with them is tenuous, but it is peace nonetheless."

Yaotl grunted, but did not elaborate.

"Shall I begin preparations for Emperor Acatl's burial?" Toani interrupted. He sounded like what Ahkin imagined the earth itself would sound like if it had a voice. Ancient, wise, deep, and endless.

"Yes. After the mourning period, I would like my father's burial to be as worthy of his memory as the life he lived." Ahkin fought back the pressure settling on his shoulders again. He was not supposed to be so saddened by his father's death. It marked the beginning of his journey through the underworld, his father's chance to earn a place in one of the paradises by proving himself worthy through completing several trials set by the god of the underworld. He struggled to force his heart to submit to what his head already knew.

"The crafters are already working on his effigies. I would like to sacrifice a large dog for the burial, to guide Emperor Acatl through the layers of the underworld. A dog will make a wonderful companion," Toani said thoughtfully, as though he were planning what to have for the midday meal. "We will also sacrifice a servant, of course. His wife has already joined him, so that spares us that worry. I think I will also send priests to the city-states to collect tributes of fabrics, choice foods, and treasures to take with him. And the royal builders finished the tomb several years ago, in anticipation, of course ..." Ahkin blocked out the man's musings and signaled for a servant to bring in the royal matchmaker.

Atanzah, like all professional matchmakers, was an elderly woman, round and soft like a ripe mango. As one of his mother's dearest friends, she had always been a presence in his life. Her white-and-gold shawl was hung with tiny golden bells and bright feathers, making her resemble a flamboyant finch as she strode in with purpose, completely at ease in a room full of the most powerful men in the empire. She immediately flourished a hand in an elegant bow, and Ahkin tried not to wrinkle his nose at the cloud of pungent floral perfume that washed over him.

"My dear Prince Ahkin." Atanzah enveloped him in color and sound and smell as she drew him into a bone-crushing embrace. "I wondered when you would be requiring my services. It was such a pleasure to arrange your sister's match."

"Thank you for coming, Atanzah," he said, choking back a cough and taking a step back. As a child, he always avoided his mother's friend for this very reason. Thankfully, she did not pinch his cheek or ruffle his hair in front of his advisors. "I am officially beginning the empress selection ritual so that—"

"—I can select the best wife and ensure the wedding ceremony is the most lavish the empire has seen this age." She smiled widely as her eyes misted over, already lost in her visions and plans.

A nervous flutter tickled Ahkin's stomach. This woman would embarrass him in front of the entire empire. "I have already sent word for the daughters of the noble families to come to the city. Can you see that the rooms are prepared for our arriving guests? I will also need your help in selecting some ... tasks, I believe?" Atanzah nodded encouragingly. Ahkin continued. "Tasks to help us discern who will be most fit to serve as empress. I admit, I am unfamiliar with the process."

"Of course, my lord. I remember your mother's selection so clearly. It would be my pleasure."

A sharp stab shot through Ahkin's chest at the mention of his mother. She should be the one helping him select a wife, not Atanzah. The sudden anger and bitterness that swelled through him caught him by surprise, followed by a deep sense of shame. The gods would not appreciate his resistance to their demands. He dismissed the matchmaker with a heavy sigh to begin her likely ostentatious preparations, then turned back to the others.

"I believe that is all for now. Yaotl, please keep me updated on the status of the borders and our interactions with …"

"My lord, please wait," Toani interrupted again. "I wish to discuss some troubling matters with you before we adjourn."

Ahkin didn't know what could possibly be more troubling than the pressure to live up to his father's legacy, all while marrying a complete stranger and sentencing five others to die, providing descendants as soon as possible, protecting his people from the Miquitz Empire, and making sure the sun itself rose each morning. The image of his mother driving a dagger into her own heart kept flashing before his eyes. How could she have left him at such a crucial time? He needed her comfort now more than ever. He needed someone to believe in him.

"I have seen troubling signs in the stars. A comet with a tail as red as blood has appeared in the heavens, and the Great Star has faded."

He had intended to speak to the high priest about the Great Star fading, but the events of the morning had pushed the thought from his mind. What were bleeding stars compared to the bleeding body of his mother?

A sense of foreboding warned him against asking Toani to elaborate, but he had to. What was one more burden to add to the enormous load he already carried at this point?

"What do such signs indicate?" He ran a hand through his short hair. The air in the room was heavy with anticipation.

"I am not entirely sure yet, but I fear the coming turmoil to be dangerous to the well-being of the Chicome people as a whole."

"Another apocalypse?" Yaotl asked the question everyone else seemed too afraid to voice.

Ahkin swallowed hard, his mouth dry.

"Let us hope the signs do not point in that direction. I will continue my studies and inform you as soon as I can." The old priest hesitated, fixing sad eyes upon Ahkin. "But I fear that Emperor Acatl's sudden death is not a good omen."

Were the gods angry at him for his lack of faith? Of all the burdens that could exist in the world, an apocalypse was not one Ahkin's shoulders could bear.

CHAPTER

4

"See? This isn't so bad. You've done every ritual so far without a single problem." Mayana's oldest brother, Chimalli, flicked the back of her hair playfully. He had already seen twenty-three cycles of the calendar, and like all her brothers, with the exception of Tenoch, who had only seen eight calendar cycles, he towered over her, especially with the crown of blue feathers sticking up from his messy dark hair.

Mayana set down the basket of corn flatbread she had just blessed. As the designated bloodletter for the festival that day, Mayana had led dances, signaled the start of the ball games, and blessed food at various smaller gatherings throughout the city with the prayers her father had taught her since she was a child. The feast for the royal family and gathered guests would be held later at their stone palace.

Mayana furrowed her brow at him. "I don't mind these rituals, it's the sacrifices I hate."

"I don't see what the big deal is." Chimalli grabbed a flatbread out of the basket and shoved the entire thing into his mouth.

"That's disgusting. You'll never find a wife if you eat like that in front of her."

Chimalli opened his mouth and showed her the wad on his tongue.

"You're a beast."

Chimalli chuckled and chewed a few more times before swallowing.

"Seriously, Mayana. I know you want to make Father proud more than anything, and you know the best way to do that is to just do the sacrifice."

Mayana grimaced and turned to walk away. "Of course I want to make him proud. But forgive me if I don't enjoy butchering animals because some ancient ritual says it protects us from—"

Chimalli grabbed her by the upper arm and pulled her back rather roughly.

"Chimalli!"

"Don't ever let Father hear you say that. You have a tender heart, but you need to learn to silence it and do your duty to your people."

Mayana yanked her arm back, her cheeks burning again. "I know. Believe me, Father's already made his thoughts on the matter clear."

"So why won't you just do your duty without such a fight?"

Something hot and angry writhed in her gut. "I *am* doing my duty. I am leading the prayers, the dances …"

"And you will lead tonight's sacrifice to appease the gods."

"Why don't you go jump off the temple, Chimalli?"

Her brother gave her a long warning glare before wiggling his eyebrows and disappearing after a group of giggling merchant daughters. She crossed her arms and stuck out her tongue at his retreating form.

The anticipation of the evening's coming events soured her against any kind of frivolity. Her twin brothers, Achto and Aquin, each twenty cycles old, tried to get her to pole fly with them—a request she quickly rejected. Dressed as birds, with ropes tied around their feet, her brothers jumped from the top of the high pole and swung in circles around it, suspended by their ankles. Exactly fifty-four revolutions in honor of the calendar stone. She shook her head with a shudder, imagining the pounding in their skulls from being upside down for so long. All the gold in the capital would not be enough to make her join them. At fourteen cycles old, her other brother, Mati, should be busy playing with his friends or older brothers too. But Mayana guessed he was probably busy lurking around the temple reading and memorizing any codex sheet he could get his curious little hands on.

By the time the sun began to set and the shell horns signaled the return to the palace, she had followed the rituals exactly as the holy texts instructed. Her relief, however, was temporary. The real test of her conviction would take place before the feast.

"Mayana," the lord of Atl greeted her when she took her seat on a cushion beside him. "How did today go?"

She could hear his hidden meaning: *Did you follow the codex?*

"I did my duty." Mayana looked down at her knees.

"Your duties are not yet finished." He dipped his chin and fixed her with a meaningful glare.

Her stomach churned. *I have to do it*, she told herself. *It will be over soon.*

Every member of the royal family, both immediate and extended, filled the central botanical garden of the palace. Mayana's five brothers sat circled around her and her father, while her aunts, uncles, and cousins branched out in rings like those on the sacred calendar stone. The empty space beside her father drew her attention for the briefest moment and her throat tightened—Mayana didn't want to think about her mother.

"Did you see the red comet in the sky?" a voice whispered close by. She turned to find the source of the comment, but with so many voices chattering, she couldn't tell who had spoken. Goosebumps rose on her arms.

Royal guests from other city-states lounged on Atl's finest cushions, sprinkled among the crowd like the drops of her blood on the sacrificial papers. Ceremonial feasts were as much a political event as they were religious—a chance to show her family's power and prestige. A man from the city of Ocelotl lounged nearby, the skin of a jaguar draped across his expansive shoulders.

Her palms grew moist, so she wiped them on the fabric of her skirt.

Servants meandered through the loud, sweaty crowd carrying small bowls of pulque, a fermented drink made from the sap of a maguey plant. Those too young for the pulque received a drink made of cacao. The codex dictated exactly what and when the Chicome could eat and drink during the ceremonies. The rest of the food would not be brought out until … well, until she fulfilled the next ritual.

Her father stood, and the babbling voices around them quieted. He spread his arms wide, embracing the crowd. His many ornaments rattled into the sudden silence. Mayana could smell the roasted meat and corn cakes waiting just out of view and her mouth watered in anticipation.

"My family and honored guests." He nodded to the man from Ocelotl and several others. Mayana took a sip of her cacao drink and tried to stop her hands from trembling. "We are safe from floods and drought for another three months." The room exploded into excited yells and exclamations before the lord of Atl hushed them.

"Let us now honor the Mother Ometeotl and the sacrifice her divine children made with a sacrifice of our own to bless the food we are about to eat. The great city of Ocelotl has brought to us a beast in honor of the month of the bird."

Mayana's father gestured to the visitor with the jaguar pelt. The man rose gracefully to his feet before gouging his palm with an obsidian blade much larger than Mayana's tiny knife. He waved his bleeding hand in a great arc, and a flock of birds erupted through an open window. This did not surprise Mayana in the slightest. Royal naguals from the city-state of Ocelotl used their divine blood to possess and control the spirits of animals.

Birds swirled around the courtyard like a black-and-yellow raincloud, singing their hauntingly beautiful melodies. Their music stirred something deep within her heart. Tears pricked behind her eyes, but she held them back, knowing they would accomplish nothing. The crowd clapped and squealed in delight. Her little brother jumped to his feet and batted at the birds with his hands, but one look from their father quelled his excitement. He quickly returned to his cushion, head bowed in respect.

Lord Atl slowly paced toward the burning pit sunk into the center of the courtyard and motioned for Mayana to follow. She rose—still shaking slightly—and tightly gripped the wooden handle of her obsidian dagger. Holding onto something solid gave her strength. Saying a silent prayer to the Mother goddess, Mayana begged to be spared from the ritual, from causing a scene and disappointing her father again.

With the flick of the royal nagual's finger, a single black-and-yellow bird broke away from the flock, landing delicately on her wrist. Mayana cupped the tiny creature in her other hand. The bird stared up at her with a glassy black eye, tilting its head as though asking a question. Her stomach dropped. She couldn't do this.

Mayana looked at her father, tears building despite her best effort, and silently pleaded for him to stop her.

"Mayana." The lord of Atl barely moved his lips. "You must."

"Father—" Her voice broke. "Please."

"If you do not, you risk the safety and well-being of the entire Chicome Empire," he growled through gritted teeth.

"I did everything else. I did it all perfectly, Father."

"We are not doing this again. You *will* do your duty this time, or so help me Mayana …"

She sucked in a breath. She hated sacrificing animals even more than sacrificing her own blood. At least her hand would be healed … unlike the bird's throat. Her empathy toward the small creature was overwhelming, especially when she thought of her dog Ona and what her father had done to him. But she couldn't refuse. Her mother wasn't here to save her anymore.

This was her duty, no matter how hard her heart screamed in protest. Her father would force her hands to do it, just like he had last time. Hot tears slid down her cheeks, but she slowly lifted the blade of her knife toward the bird's neck. She hated this ritual. *Hated* it.

At that moment, a man burst through the woven tapestry covering the main entrance. Mayana dropped the hand with the blade to her side, exhaling the breath she was holding. The newcomer was dressed in a white cotton cloak that glittered with golden thread. The flaps of his loincloth hung to his knees and jingled with tiny bells. Upon his dark hair sat a headband of small yellow feathers, reminding Mayana of a cockatoo with yellow plumage.

Everyone in the room recognized the colors at once. This man was from Tollan, the golden capital born from the first darkness—the City of the Sun.

He gripped the stone frame of the doorway, leaning against it and panting hard. The crowd waited, the silence in the room thicker than corn cakes. A feeling like cold water rose in Mayana's chest. She felt as though she was drowning.

Whatever news he held, it would not be good.

The glittering golden visitor from Tollan took several gasping breaths and fixed his eyes upon Mayana's father.

"The Lord of the Sun is dead."

The silence that had filled the room shattered with a sudden buzzing like angry bees. Mayana looked to her father, unsure how to proceed. He stared at the man from Tollan, his mouth hanging open slightly. She took her chances and loosened her grip. The bird fluttered out of her hand and through the window it had come from, but the lord of Atl was too distracted to notice.

"Emperor Acatl is … dead?"

The man pushed himself off the doorframe and stood straight, meeting her father's gaze with a sorrowful nod.

The lord of Atl fell to his knees and ripped the many necklaces from around his neck. The beads clattered onto the floor and rolled out of sight, scattering like ants on the jungle floor. The guests in the room continued to whisper as the lord of Atl bent forward and cradled his head in his hands.

"That is not the only reason I am here," the newcomer said.

To Mayana's surprise, her father lifted his head and looked, not at the golden, glittering man from Tollan, but at *her*. His face suggested he had seen a night spirit. His fear seeped into her like something contagious and her heart began to race. Why was he staring at her like that?

"The prince ... he is to become emperor?" His voice sounded strained.

"Yes, Lord Atl. You know what that means."

"I do." He rose slowly to his feet. "Hona, I need you to finish the sacrifice and begin the meal. I wish to speak to my sons and daughter alone."

Mayana's uncle rushed forward to finish the ritual while the nagual summoned another bird. If her father was going to have her uncle perform the ceremony instead, something was seriously wrong. Mayana was grateful she would not have to witness the sacrifice, let alone perform the ritual herself, but that now seemed to be the least of her worries.

Her father strode purposefully from the room and her brothers followed, their eyebrows pulled together. Mayana jumped and ran after them, leaving the buzzing of the crowd behind her.

The lord of Atl marched them through the palace, through curtain after curtain, until they reached the great stone room where his throne sat—a room reserved for politics. He stopped, facing her in the midst of the richly decorated chairs and benches overflowing with animal furs. The trickling fountains that dripped water from the ceiling into jade bowls along the back wall usually soothed her, but not tonight.

Why had he brought them there?

"Mayana," her father said, the words coming out in a rush. "The codex stipulates that the prince cannot rule until he has an empress by his side. Do you know how the empress of Tollan is chosen?"

"N-n-no." Mayana shivered despite the suffocating heat. She had never heard that part of the codex. She'd assumed it did not apply to life here in Atl. Chimalli covered his mouth with his hand, eyes wide with shock.

"The empress is chosen from one of the other city-states, a way to encourage unity and to keep the divine bloodline strong. Each city must send one noble daughter to the prince. The matchmaker helps the prince choose a wife," her father explained.

"That doesn't sound too bad," Tenoch said.

Mayana studied the expressions of her brothers and father. She was the only daughter. The lord of Atl would have to send her to the prince.

"Well, I'll just go and do my best to not be chosen. It shouldn't be hard." She crossed her arms. It was a simple solution, so why did her father and oldest brother still look like someone had died?

"Mayana …" Her father's eyes swam with uncharacteristic tears. "The princesses not chosen are sacrificed to Ometeotl … to bless the emperor's marriage and reign."

Oh. The hair on Mayana's arms stood. She must not have heard him correctly.

Tenoch started to cry. Her four older brothers all shifted uncomfortably. Their actions verified the truth Mayana was struggling to grasp.

After a minute of silence, everyone refusing to meet her eyes, the tears finally started to build.

"Father." Her voice cracked for the second time that evening. "You can't let this happen. Please, you must do something."

"There is nothing I can do. This is the ritual and we must respect it."

His words were firm, but Mayana could hear the pain in his voice. He did not like this, but he would not challenge the codex. Anger flared hot within her chest like a flame. She was sick of the stifling and suffocating shackles of the rituals. She had fought against her heart for years to submit to them, constantly wrestling between what she wanted to do and what she *should* do. They had stolen the joy from her life. Now, they demanded her actual life.

"Would you see me die to uphold some ancient ritual?"

Her father's eyes flashed, and he clenched his fists.

"You must learn to respect our way of life, Mayana," he said. "You, born into a time of privilege, do not know the pain of drought or famine. You have not watched your family be swept away by waves of fire or water. You have not seen whole cities succumb to sickness or fall to the jaws of ravenous beasts."

"Neither have you," she mumbled, glaring at her feet. It had been hundreds of years since the Sixth Sun perished.

"Thank the gods I have not," he roared. "But I can imagine. And I understand the importance of the rituals, of honoring the gods who protect us and making sure I never do have to know that pain." He slammed his fist against the wall.

Her tears spilled over.

"This can't be the will of the gods," her scream ripped through her throat. "I don't believe they would want this. And I *do* know pain. We lost Mother. All the rituals in the world did not save her." The words tumbled out before she could call them back. Shame bit at the back of her mind like an irritating wasp, sudden and sharp.

The lord of Atl did not answer. The shadow of a grief far worse than her own crossed his face. He did not like to think about her mother any more than she did. When he spoke again, his voice was softer, more understanding.

"The rituals protect us as a people, not as individuals. Had Nemi been there, she could have saved your mother, but she was not. We cannot change the past, Mayana, we can only affect what happens in the future."

"I may not have a future." She sniffed.

"Then you must be chosen," her father said with finality. "There is no other way."

Tenoch wiped his nose, a watery smile on his face. "Of course the prince will choose Mayana. She is so beautiful!"

Mayana gave him an appreciative smile.

Her oldest brother, Chimalli, was not so hopeful. "Is there someone else we can send? Surely Mayana is not our only option."

"Mayana has seen seventeen cycles of the calendar. The next oldest female blood relative who is not already married has only seven. She is our only daughter of marriageable age." The lord of Atl rubbed his temple as though a headache were forming.

Chimalli tried to speak out of the corner of his mouth. "But ... she will sabotage herself."

"What do you mean, I will sabotage myself?" Mayana narrowed her eyes at him.

"Well, you tend to follow your heart above your duty. You are beautiful, yes, but I worry your compassion will get you in trouble. It can make you seem ... disrespectful to the gods, like you follow your own will above theirs."

Mayana curled her hands into fists and suppressed the urge to slap him. Her father would scold her if she did.

"That's enough, Chimalli. I am confident Mayana can rein in her rebelliousness for the sake of saving her own life."

"Rebelliousness? Just because I won't ..."

"Now is not the time, Mayana." He silenced her with a look. Mayana bit her lip and did not respond.

"So, what happens now?" Tenoch asked, tugging at his father's hand.

"Mayana will leave at first light with the servant from Tollan. She will impress the prince and the matchmaker and become our empress." Her father said the words so firmly it was as if he were attempting to force them to become reality.

"And if not, she dies," Chimalli added in frustration, but Mayana knew her oldest brother. She reached out and placed her hand on his arm.

"I will not be sacrificed," she told him softly. Jerking his arm away with tears gleaming in his eyes, he turned his back to her.

"We must return to the feast and show the proper respect Ometeotl deserves. Tomorrow, we will say goodbye to Mayana and pray every day that she is chosen." The lord pulled the curtain aside to lead them back.

The festival would now feel less like a celebration and more like a farewell.

For the rest of the evening, Mayana could not eat. The tamales tasted like sand and stuck in her throat whenever she tried to swallow. Her eyes were drawn, continually, to the servant with the white-and-gold cloak. Tomorrow that man would take her away, to a glorious future or a gruesome death.

Normally, the Chicome saved human sacrifices for the beginning of a new calendar year, or for major events like a looming battle, and even then, the victims were captured enemies. Outside of the New Fire ceremony that took place every fifty-four years, she had never heard of sacrificing a noble before. She couldn't imagine the power contained in the blood of five noble young girls. Maybe that was why it was reserved for the coronation of kings.

The ritual didn't feel right either way. Five innocent young women killed for nothing more than the use of their blood? She knew she was supposed to see it as an honor, but how could gods who supposedly loved the people enough to die for them demand so much pain and suffering?

After the feast ended, she wandered the labyrinthine halls of the palace, aimlessly searching for some kind of distraction. The towering columns cast ominous flickering shadows in the light of the flaming torches, the engraved faces of the gods following her with uncaring eyes. Several servants rushed past with baskets full of animal furs. They averted their eyes as she passed, their pity hanging in the air like a foul stench.

Mayana ended up in one of the steam-bath rooms, curled in a ball in the corner. Not able to bring herself to cry again, she let the sweat run off her skin in place of the tears she could not shed. Her heart drummed a rhythm so deep it pounded inside her ears, making her wonder how many beats it had left. Would they cut it from her chest and burn it on an altar? She shuddered, pressing her hand against it as though she could shield it from such a fate.

Chimalli peeked around the corner.

He did not speak. Instead, he inched over to her, waiting for her to decide she was ready. Mayana appreciated the gesture. After several stubborn minutes, she finally found her voice.

"I don't want to be an empress." She rested her head on her knees and refused to meet his eyes.

"I know." He chuckled. "You'll be terrible at it. You can't even sacrifice a bird. How are you supposed to follow all the rules and rituals in Tollan?"

She groaned loudly. "Is this supposed to be helping?"

"No." His eyes danced with humor. "But this might."

He handed her a small, beautifully woven bundle of cloth. She ran her fingers over a hard bulge beneath the folds.

Chimalli smiled encouragingly.

Mayana pulled aside the detailed fabric to reveal an obsidian dagger. Unlike her simple ceremonial knife with the wooden handle, this dagger's handle was made of an almost translucent green jadeite. The blade was the size of her hand, and the edges were impossibly sharp.

"You really think stabbing the prince will make him like me?"

Her brother snorted a laugh.

"No, if you stabbed the prince of the sun, I imagine the power in his blood would cause the sun itself to burst and rain fire down upon us all."

She sighed. "Which would defeat the whole purpose of trying to save myself from him." Her forehead dropped back down to her knees.

"I want you to have something to remember your family by, and something you can use to summon your power if you need to."

She turned her head to look at him.

"My dagger can bring forth blood just fine." She showed him her healed palm for emphasis.

"Yes, it can. But it is the plain dagger of a lord's daughter. You need a dagger beautiful enough for an empress of the Chicome."

Just when she thought she had no more tears to shed, her eyes pricked again and she choked back a sob. Throwing her arms around her brother's neck, she whispered "Thank you" in his ear.

"Just promise me you will try to follow the rules while you are there? If you do, I don't see how he could refuse you."

She laughed into his shoulder. "I can promise, but that doesn't mean he'll choose me."

"He has to." Chimalli hugged her tighter. "I can't lose you too."

A fine line existed between laughing and crying, life and death. She now walked between both on a knife blade sharper than obsidian.

Mayana wandered back to her room long after everyone else had gone to bed. She didn't expect that she would actually be able to sleep, and she was right. She tossed and turned on her bed mat all night, burying her face into the soft rabbit skins to no avail. Her father had told her to rest so that she would be refreshed and beautiful, that first impressions were important in politics. Mayana argued that choosing a wife was a personal decision, not a political one, but her father had just laughed.

"Everything is political, Mayana. You will do well to learn that now," he had said.

She continued to stare at the ceiling, willing herself to fall asleep. It looked as though she was going to disappoint him again. The night seemed to stretch on far longer than usual. When the glowing face of the sun peeked above the horizon, Mayana gave up and decided to find something to eat.

She had taken barely two steps toward the doorway when a flock of aunts and female cousins wrenched the curtain open and flooded into the room. An explosion of sound threatened to shatter her eardrums as the older women squawked like a bunch of parrots, grabbing her by her upper arms and marching her out into the hall.

Before Mayana could object, they stripped her naked and threw her into a temazcalli steam room like the one she had hidden in the night before. Her aunt splashed water against the blazing hot wall and mist filled the room with a hiss. Mayana tried not to dwell on the fact that she was being cleansed for a wedding—or a sacrificial ceremony.

"I always wondered if you possessed the proper curves to entice a husband under all those modest dresses." Her aunt gave her a teasing wink, and Mayana's face burned hotter than steam. She certainly flaunted those curves now.

A cousin brought in a clay basin, and Mayana's head was immediately forced into the water. She bit her lip to keep from crying out as her aunt rubbed her skin raw and plastered her hair with some kind of conditioning concoction. Once her hair was rinsed, she could smell the black clay mixed with acacia bark that would be used to dye her hair even darker than it already was.

"Can we please be a little gentler?" Mayana asked her aunt.

"No, we don't have time. You will reach Tollan before sunset, and you have many people to impress." The large, motherly woman smeared yet another cream of some kind across her cheeks.

"What is that?" Mayana wrinkled her nose at the putrid smell of the cream.

"Combination of senna, yarrow … and pigeon droppings."

"Pigeon what?" Mayana shrieked.

"Makes your skin shine and glow." Her aunt shrugged.

Her well-meaning family finally dragged Mayana out of the steam room. She was now thoroughly cleansed and, in her opinion, smelled like the floor of the aviary. She hoped the prince would not get too close to her face.

They hustled her to one of the common rooms usually reserved for women, and Mayana's mouth dropped open at the collection of potions and ornaments. Necklaces, headdresses, bracelets, and feathers were draped across cushions and baskets. Small pots of auxin, charcoal, paints, and pastes sat waiting upon the floor. She didn't know the ingredients in most of them, and probably didn't want to.

Two of the older cousins set to work on braiding Mayana's dark hair and securing it in some noble fashion that would communicate her important royal standing. They reminisced about their own weddings, giggling together and ignoring her completely. Mayana's stomach dropped as she realized she would never have a wedding if she did not marry the prince.

Her breathing grew shallow and frantic. *Relax*, she reminded herself.

Several of her aunts began bickering about which headpiece would be most impressive, while Mayana remained silent, praying desperately that they would avoid the heavy golden helmet shaped like a half sun. The younger cousins dashed in and out carrying different fabrics and pieces of jewelry.

At least the flurry of activity distracted her from focusing too much on how hard her heart was hammering, or the dizziness she feared would overtake her at any moment. She wondered vaguely what her aunts would do if she keeled over face first into the pot of bright-yellow paste.

"I think a dark-red stripe, right across her eyes," someone said. There were excited murmurs of consent before the cold tip of a paintbrush pressed against her eyelid.

Mayana felt like a piece of pottery they were decorating to sell in the marketplace.

Her aunts painted designs onto her arms and face, finally deciding on a feathered headpiece that framed Mayana's face with long, curving, bright-blue feathers. Jade earrings hung from her earlobes, and a gold and jadeite pendant that matched her many bracelets dangled around her neck. The Chicome considered jade a symbol of water, so Mayana understood their significance. Someone secured feathered cuffs with tiny golden bells around her ankles and slipped her feet into simple sandals.

"Do I need to be showing so much skin?" Mayana asked, turning on the spot and looking down at the outfit they had chosen for her.

"Absolutely." Mayana's aunt surveyed her work and grunted in approval.

Narrow strips of blue fabric crossed her chest to form a strategically placed *x*, while her stomach was entirely bare. The skirt looked more like a long loincloth than a woman's skirt, and the skin of her legs was visible right up to her waist. Mayana gritted her teeth—her fingers itched for her new dagger, which was, unfortunately, back in her room. She longed to summon the water from the steam baths and drench herself, washing away everything that was not *her*.

"I'm really not comfortable …" No one was listening. She sighed and allowed the preparations to continue. She would never be able to replicate this look by herself in the capital. She had asked about bringing a female servant with her, but her father assured her that all of her needs would be taken care of in Tollan.

Mayana's thoughts drifted to Tenoch. Her heart ached as she thought of leaving her youngest brother, but an idea came to her as she fingered the strips of fabric discarded upon a cushion. She grabbed a small strip and filled it with a fluff of wool. She tied it closed with a cord and set it aside, a secret little present to give him a positive memory of today.

By the time her aunt deemed her "ready," Mayana had been sufficiently buried beneath ornaments and potions. She looked at her reflection in the surface of a water jug and did not even recognize herself. Her face looked more like that of an ancient goddess—beautiful, terrible, and utterly perfect. She splashed her hand against the surface to make the goddess disappear before it devoured her, like the stories of the Tzitzimimeh star demons.

"Mayana, you will meet your father in the palace courtyard in several minutes." Her aunt handed her some leftover tamales from the night before. Mayana's stomach grumbled and she took them gratefully.

"May I go back to my room for a moment? I have something important I want to take with me." Mayana was already shoving the tamales unceremoniously into her mouth.

Her aunt nodded her approval and chuckled as maize crumbs fell from Mayana's face. Running back to her room, she noticed the sun rising higher through a window. Either way, this would be her last day in her home. She took one last look around her small room. It was unusually bare. Someone had packed most of her things during her cleansing and preparation.

But there, on a small stone table, the colorful bundle from Chimalli sat next to her old ceremonial knife. Mayana opened it and removed the new dagger, admiring the sharpness of the jet-black blade. It matched her freshly dyed hair exactly.

Mayana hesitated for a moment, her eyes darting back and forth between the old knife and the new, and then turned her back on the dagger with the wooden handle. It was part of an old life, one to which she could never return. Several tears escaped and traced their way down her cheek, and she swiped them away with a finger. She mustn't ruin the face paint, or her aunt would never forgive her.

Having no place to hide a dagger in the scant clothing, she managed to wedge it into the cuff around her ankle. The jadeite handle protruded like an additional turquoise feather.

Mayana hoped no one would notice.

"Mayana!" Tenoch's high voice carried through the courtyard. "She looks beautiful, doesn't she, Father? Like a bride."

"Indeed, she does." Her father rarely smiled, but Mayana took the twitching at the corners of his mouth as a good sign.

"What is today?" her brother asked.

"The sign of the monkey." The lord of Atl failed to conceal his exasperation.

"A favorable day for a wedding." Tenoch bounced up and down like a jumping bean.

"Mayana will not be married today," her father reminded him. "Today, she will travel to Tollan. Tomorrow, she and the other princesses will be presented to the prince. Then, the matchmaker will choose several tasks for them to complete to prove their worth and dedication to the rituals."

Their dedication to the rituals? Mayana shifted uncomfortably on her feet.

"When will he make the decision?" she asked, curious exactly how long she had to live.

"It depends. The union must ultimately be approved by the matchmaker, but some princes have taken days, and for others, it's taken weeks."

"Let's hope the prince is indecisive," Mayana muttered.

"It will be before the Nemontemi, so within two weeks," her father said. Of course, the prince would not want a wedding to take place during the last days of the calendar, the five unluckiest days of the year.

Tenoch's face fell, so Mayana reached out a finger and tickled him under his ribs. She couldn't stand seeing him in pain.

"Here," she whispered to him, pulling out the small sack filled with wool she had made during her preparations that morning. It fit perfectly in his hand as he grabbed and squeezed the small, soft bag.

"What is this?" he whispered back.

"Something to throw at the girl you think is prettiest and get her attention," Mayana teased, ruffling his hair. The mischievous grin that spread across his face suggested he already had the perfect girl in mind. She smiled to herself as he scampered away to find his victim. At least he would have a happy memory of today. Mayana prayed his pretty girl had a playful spirit.

"You are encouraging him to throw things at other children?" Her father watched Tenoch disappear behind a curtain, frowning slightly.

"It's a soft little pillow of wool. It won't hurt anyone. Besides, he needs something happy to distract him," she said.

Her father pinched the bridge of his nose with a thumb and forefinger.

"If the matchmaker approves of you, it will be a miracle."

His words struck her heart where it was most vulnerable. "Thank you, Father. Your confidence in me is overwhelming." If she couldn't even make her father proud, who would choose her for his empress?

"I will pray and bloodlet every day for the Mother goddess to bless you. You must do your part, Mayana, to impress them. You must be willing to give to the gods as much as you give to the family. Please, promise me you will try."

"I will." Her cheeks burned. Did he have so little faith in her?

The lord of Atl turned away as the servant from Tollan arrived, accompanied by a small crowd of well-wishers. Her brothers were among them, each taking a moment to hug her in turn. Mayana could see her extended family watching and waving from nearly every window and opening in the palace face. A lump formed in her throat at such a loving farewell.

Mayana glanced toward the mass of green shadows waiting in the distance and groaned internally. All day in this heat—if she couldn't wash everything off, maybe she would at least sweat it off as they hiked through the jungle. She was fortunate Atl was one of the closer city-states to Tollan. The poor princess from Papatlaca must have had to leave the volcano last night to reach Tollan in time.

To her surprise, her father waved his hand and several servants appeared. Three of them carried large packs on their shoulders filled with various items for her to take to the city. Two more carted a smaller version of the throne that had carried her father back to the palace during the celebrations yesterday. A plain wooden chair rested on poles that two men alone could carry instead of four. Mayana eyed the chair apprehensively. She generally walked or rode in boats everywhere she went.

Compared to most of the woman in the noble family of Atl, Mayana weighed hardly more than a feather. Her aunt—the same one who was so shocked that she possessed the "proper curves" after all—always lamented that Mayana didn't look properly fed. Regardless, she didn't like the idea of being carried all the way to Tollan. The poor servants would be exhausted, even with her small frame.

"I want you to look rested and beautiful when you arrive," her father said, seeming to read her thoughts. "Please sit in the chair, Mayana. We don't want to ruin the work your aunts did this morning."

Mayana frowned but nodded in consent. She clambered awkwardly onto the seat and the servants lifted her off the ground, balancing the poles on their shoulders. Sure enough, they acted as if she weighed no more than a quetzal feather.

"Um … let me know if it gets too heavy for you," Mayana said, but her seat just vibrated with the servants' laughter.

"They will be fine, Mayana." The lord of Atl waved an impatient hand.

Mayana adjusted the blue fabric of her skirt as best she could, but it was no use. Her bare legs were visible no matter what she did. Her stomach clenched in panic. She looked down at her father, sure the fear and sadness were written as clearly on her face as the inscriptions in the temple. Her throat tightened, and she could not find her voice.

He placed his hand over hers. It was warm and strong, but soft. She wondered wildly for a moment if he used pigeon cream to keep his skin so smooth.

"This will not be the last time we see each other," he told her. "And when I see you next, I will be even more proud of you than I am now. Your compassionate heart may hold you back at times from doing what is necessary, but it is also your greatest gift. You see what others see, you feel what others feel. Use that, Mayana. It can be a strength if you let it."

Her heart must have swelled to twice its normal size. Her father was proud. He thought she had strength. Sort of. Mayana had never heard him say something so encouraging, but she needed his words now more than ever. They quenched a thirst in her soul.

Mayana didn't say anything in response, afraid she would cry. Instead, she placed her other hand over his and squeezed, hoping the gesture communicated everything she could not say.

Her father nodded and pulled his hand back, clearing his throat uncomfortably. Mayana almost laughed out loud. The lord of Atl had never been good at expressing affection. Such a reaction was the best she could have ever hoped for from her father. She prayed to Ometeotl that she would see him again.

∴

CHAPTER

8

"Have you ever been to the golden City of the Sun?" the servant from Tollan asked. The yellow feathers of his headdress bobbed as he walked along beside her.

Mayana wasn't much for polite conversation. She often found that silence was less dangerous than voicing her thoughts, especially around her father.

"No, I've never left Atl," she told him.

His round, boyish face broke into a wide smile, but Mayana didn't know how to interpret it.

Their little caravan made its way through the palace gates and toward the canal. The rivers that flowed through Atl not only provided abundant water, they also served as conduits of transportation. The sparkling water crisscrossed the city like a massive blue spider's web dotted with hundreds of wooden boats like dewdrops.

The servants lowered Mayana into a boat and took their seats beside her. The rivers would take them to Ehecatl on the coast, but not to Tollan. They would only need to take the boat to where the trade road through the jungles began. The boatman launched off the side with a large wooden pole, sending them into the traffic navigating through the heart of the city. Mayana dug her nails into the armrests of the wooden chair as the boat rocked violently to the side.

Every face in the city followed their progression as they passed. Traders and merchants paused in the middle of unloading their goods, children looked up from their games, and women's conversations silenced, their gazes filled with silent concern. Mayana kept her eyes firmly on her knees, and a blush rose high in her cheeks. Was she imagining the looks of pity and grief? Were they all convinced that she would fail to be chosen?

Apparently, the memories of her last day of sacrifice, when she had only seen twelve cycles of the calendar, still burned fresh in everyone's minds. Mayana scowled. Only yesterday she'd managed to get through the entire day without a huge, tearful fight with her father in front of the entire city. Well, minus the mishap with the bird, but no one in the city would have heard about that yet. The situation with the emperor dying covered that whole debacle anyway. Mayana heaved a great sigh and resisted the urge to throw her head into her hands.

"Are you nervous, my lady?"

She didn't respond. Of course, she was nervous.

"You may call me Xol." He leaned toward Mayana with a warm, reassuring smile. She kept her mouth shut and merely nodded. Feeling slightly sick, she worried that opening her mouth was not the wisest of decisions.

"You will be amazed when you see the city, my lady." The words came out in a rush as he nearly bounced up and down on his cushion. "Your temples and palaces are made of stone here in Atl, but in Tollan"—his eyes glazed over as a dreamy expression crossed his face—"the buildings themselves are made of gold. The aviaries and zoos managed by the naguals have the most unique and mysterious creatures. The botanical pleasure gardens are like nothing you've ever seen. Even farmers from Millacatl cannot believe how beautiful they are. I'm sure you would appreciate the fountains that run down the terraces of the gardens."

"You ... aren't from Tollan originally, are you?" Mayana guessed, finally deciding it was safe to speak without being sick. His unbridled enthusiasm betrayed that he was new to the city.

"No, my lady. I am originally from Millacatl."

"Oh, are you descended from the gods too, or ...?"

"No, no." He laughed, lounging back against the side of the boat. "I am only a commoner. I *have* seen our noble family use their blood to grow crops with my own eyes, though. Absolutely incredible. Even though my blood has no traces of the divine within it, I will always have an appreciation for the gardens and the beauty the Millacatl royal family can create." He certainly was an excitable little man.

"Have you met their princesses?" She let her curiosity get the better of her.

"The lord of Millacatl has many daughters. Seven, if I remember correctly. I have been serving the Lord of the Sun for several years now, so my memories of them are not perfect. My best guess is that they would send Princess Teniza. She is by far the most beautiful of the seven, and I once saw her raise an entire field of maize with just a few drops of blood. The green sprouts shot right through the earth at her beckoning." He slapped a hand on his thigh for emphasis.

"That's … that's nice." Mayana fidgeted, wringing the fabric of her skirt in her hands.

Were the other princesses allowed to use their divine blood on a more regular basis? She only got to experiment when she accidentally tripped and sliced her knee open, or, of course, when it was her turn to bloodlet for the gods. She hoped she was not at a disadvantage.

The cold blade of the obsidian dagger sat against the flesh of her ankle, still hidden by the feathers of the cuff. Maybe she should practice? Or would she upset the gods by spilling her blood for such a selfish reason? Maybe she shouldn't practice. How important would their divine abilities be in the decision-making process? She had no way to know.

"Can you tell me about the prince at all?" They had reached the outer edges of the city. Across the river lay the wild jungle. Somewhere along the bank was a path that would lead to Tollan.

"What do you want to know?" Xol said.

"What is he like?"

"I think Prince Ahkin will make an even better emperor than his father, which will be a difficult task to accomplish. Emperor Acatl was …" His voice caught in his throat. Mayana could see tears glistening in the man's eyes. The burly servants sitting beside her shifted their shoulders and looked determinedly away. Obviously, such a blatant display of emotion embarrassed them. She frowned at their insensitivity.

"It's alright. I'm sure you miss him very much. From what Father always said, he was a kind ruler." Mayana tried to keep her voice calm, reassuring.

"Forgive me." He dabbed the corners of his eyes with his white-and-gold cloak. "The emperor always treated those of us who served him with extraordinary kindness and generosity. You would expect with making sure the sun rises every single day, he would be arrogant, but that was never the case. He will be missed by many more than me."

Mayana let him hiccup himself into silence, not wanting to pester him for more details. He hadn't told her anything about Prince Ahkin. She prayed silently that the prince took after his father. If by some miracle he did choose her, she didn't want her future husband to be cruel.

And what of the matchmaker? How much of a role would she play in the process?

Usually if a groom was interested in a potential bride, his family would hire a professional matchmaker to oversee the courtship and determine compatibility. If the wise, elderly matchmaker approved, she would approach the bride's father with a proposal of marriage. But Mayana had no idea how the process would work with *six* possible brides.

The boat finally reached the muddy bank and they disembarked. The servants lifted Mayana between them again, and she gazed up at the expansive canopy of trees. From the windows of the palace, they had not seemed so tall, so intimidating. The shadows between the vines and shrubbery quivered with life. The sounds of birds and the calls of monkeys echoed all around them. Wild beasts and spirits lived in the jungle. Apprehension settled over her, creeping across her skin and giving her goosebumps. Thank Ometeotl she did not have to go in alone.

Xol directed the group to the right path, and Atl's towering temple pyramid disappeared behind the greenery. Mayana swallowed hard and pressed both hands to her chest. It did nothing to stop the ache. She said a silent goodbye to her home.

Hours passed by in boring, blurred-green monotony. The canopy above grew suffocating. Mayana almost wished for some wild beast to attack or a spirit to appear just for something different. Gratitude overwhelmed her when Xol announced they would be stopping for a short break.

Mayana rose from her chair after the servants set her down, and she swore her muscles had forgotten how to function properly. She felt even worse for the men who had carried her. Their bare chests heaved and dripped with perspiration. A twinge of guilt settled in the pit of her stomach for thinking her own discomfort in any way compared to theirs.

"Is it safe to look around?" she asked Xol.

"As long as you stay close to the path, my lady. Traders and merchants use the roads often and so animals usually avoid it, but you can never count on an animal's behavior." He shuddered at the thought.

Mayana stepped behind the vine-covered trunk of an ancient tree and reached down for her blade. She hovered the tip of her finger over the knife's point for several seconds before she finally squared her shoulders and made a small cut.

As soon as the crimson drop appeared, a cool awareness across her skin told her water was nearby. Mayana closed her eyes and moved her hand slowly in front of her, feeling for which direction she should go.

A small stream trickled across the jungle floor a few yards from where she stood. Looking back over her shoulder at the group of men lounging on the ground, she had a sudden idea. She could practice her skills in a way that also benefited her travel mates. Surely the gods would not oppose her using her blood to be of service to others.

Mayana summoned water from the stream and formed it between her hands into a transparent sphere, just as she had at the edge of the river during the festival. Rising slowly to her feet, she concentrated on keeping it suspended. The task proved easier than she anticipated, and she sighed with relief. Maybe she wouldn't be at a disadvantage after all.

Mayana made her way over to Xol and her father's servants, trying not to giggle at the wide eyes and open mouths.

She pinched her thumb and forefinger together and pulled a small fist-sized orb away from the larger one. It floated above her hand like a small hummingbird and she offered it to Xol.

"For ... for me?"

"Yes, for you. You looked like you could use some water." Mayana couldn't help it, a small giggle escaped anyway. This was too much fun.

She had forgotten that seeing the power of the gods so blatantly displayed would be a rarity to commoners. Nemi usually reserved her healing for the royal family, and they didn't often mingle out in the city. Her father used his power to keep the waters in Atl flowing and would occasionally visit other city-states to address water-related crises, but other than that, her family did not flaunt their power. The royal family of Tollan displayed their ability every morning to wake up the sun, but seeing the power to control water would be new to Xol.

Xol cupped his hands and Mayana directed the small sphere so that it splashed into them. His eyes stretched wide like an owl's and he brought his hands to his lips. She created spheres for the other servants and dropped them one by one into their hands. She purposely gave a little extra to the men who had been carrying her. They lapped it up like a pair of dogs, water dripping from their smiling faces. Her heart swelled with pride, partly because she had used her power so effectively and partly because of their gratitude.

"I can get a little more," Mayana said, already rising to her feet. She skipped behind the large tree, her focus entirely on relocating the little stream.

When she found it, Mayana froze. Her pulse quickened, and her stomach dropped into the dirt at her feet. She was not the only one who had found the stream.

Every hair on her skin stood on end as she gazed into the golden eyes of a jet-black jaguar. The cat was larger than any she had seen the animal-controlling naguals flaunt through the city during festivals. Mayana could see the faint characteristic spots of its kind blended into the midnight-black fur. It drank lazily from the stream on the opposite bank, its pink tongue creating small ripples on the water's surface. Her sudden appearance must have surprised it, but the shock seemed to be wearing off. It crouched low with its eyes fixed upon her and shifted its shoulders up and down as it prepared to pounce.

Mayana stumbled back and tripped over a branch. Her hands flung out behind her to break her fall and rocks and sticks instantly gouged into her palms. Before she could stop herself, she screamed. The cat's pupils dilated, and its muscles tensed. It leaped.

Her arms flew up to cover her face as she braced for claws and teeth.

The stream exploded.

Massive amounts of water burst from the small brook and condensed, forming something like a battering ram that plowed into the jaguar, knocking it to the side. The black body skidded across the jungle floor, leaves, dirt, and water flying into the air.

The great cat flailed its limbs and clambered back onto its feet. Golden eyes found Mayana's brown ones and it shrank back, tripping over itself to get away from her. The jaguar disappeared into the underbrush as quick and silent as a shadow.

Mayana choked out a dry sob. Her pulse pounded behind her ears. She jumped to her feet and grabbed the trunk of the nearby tree to steady herself. Had that really just happened? The jaguar almost attacked her, and the water had knocked it aside like a powerful punch from one of her brothers.

She stared down at her injured hands—at the red blood of the gods mixed with the dirt and bits of dead leaves. Never had so much of her blood been exposed before. That explained the explosion of water anyway. Mayana had no idea her power was strong enough to do something so ...

damaging. She leaned heavily onto the trunk, still breathing hard, and dropped her gaze to the mud splattered across her skirt. It was stupid, but tears built behind her eyes. Her aunt would kill her. Was she completely incapable of honoring her father's instructions? The urge to cry nearly overwhelmed her, but she forced it back down.

After several steadying breaths, Mayana straightened and turned. Xol and the other servants stood shoulder to shoulder where the line of trees ended. Their eyes were wide, either from fear or awe, she couldn't tell. Spears lay on the ground under their slack, open hands.

"Uh, there was a jaguar," was all she could think to say. A blush rose in her cheeks again, making them burn. Mayana hastily tried to wipe her hands off on her skirt—smearing bloodstains into the mud already clinging to the fabric.

The men continued to stare at her with their mouths slightly open. None of them moved.

Mayana picked a leaf out of her feathered headdress and flicked it aside.

"Would it be alright if we left?" she asked Xol. Did they have to stare at her like that?

He shook his head as though clearing his thoughts.

"Y-yes, my lady." He swept his arm to the side to allow her to pass. She ducked her head and rushed by him, noticing their eyes following her as she went.

Mayana took her seat on the little wooden throne and smoothed out the folds of her ruined skirt just to give her hands something to do. The servants finally followed and hoisted her back into the air.

As they resumed their trek along the path toward Tollan, Mayana ran over what happened at the stream again and again in her head. She couldn't believe what she had done, and neither, it seemed, could anyone else.

Well, one thing was for certain. She definitely had gotten the chance to practice. Hopefully it would be enough to impress the prince.

CHAPTER

10

"Why is the sun setting so early?" Ahkin stood at the window of his throne room, watching the Seventh Sun dip toward the mountains and tinge the sky with shades of pink. Along the distant ridges, the red tail of the comet stood out like blood splattered across the altar.

"Is it, my lord?" Atanzah adjusted her shawl and the tiny bells tinkled into the silence. The matchmaker didn't seem too concerned about the sun's schedule. But then again, she was not as educated as Ahkin when it came to the heavens. Well, aside from knowing the compatibility of prospective match-day signs.

"It is not the correct time for the sun to be in that position." Ahkin returned his gaze to the books and sheets of papers spread out across the table before him, his brow furrowed. Charts of star movements and accompanying religious instruction gazed back at him.

Studying them gave him a sense of control over the universe, that maybe he wasn't as powerless as he sometimes felt. Maybe by studying them, he could obtain the secret knowledge the stars held. The patterns suggested an impending eclipse in the next month, and although eclipses were incredibly dangerous, they were not *apocalyptically* dangerous.

Unfortunately, other than a flaming red comet and the odd timing of sunset, the skies remained entirely silent. It was equally maddening and terrifying.

The comet suggested life-altering instability in the layers of the heavens. Changes in the sun's patterns meant bad luck, but they gave no specific hints that an apocalypse was imminent. Ahkin could predict the movements of the celestial bodies down to the very moment they would appear or fade. He could complete complicated mathematical calculations using the unique number system developed by his ancestors, but he could not figure out how their world would end. How could he protect his people if he didn't know what to protect them from?

Was the high priest right? Could it really be another impending apocalypse? The same signs Ahkin saw hinted that something was wrong, that cataclysmic danger and chaos loomed on the horizon. But world-ending chaos? They had to wait for more indications. Ahkin rubbed the back of his neck in frustration. Why couldn't the stars be more specific?

"I'm sorry. You wanted to speak to me?" He reluctantly pulled his eyes away from his charts and focused on the matchmaker.

"Yes, my prince. The rooms are prepared, and the princesses are all on their way. The daughters of Millacatl, Ocelotl, and Pahtia have already arrived. We are still awaiting the daughters of Atl, Ehecatl, and Papatlaca."

"Thank you, Atanzah. Please make sure they are comfortable for the duration of their stay."

"Of course, my lord." Atanzah inclined her head respectfully.

Ahkin cleared his throat, his cheeks warming. "What are they like? The ones who have arrived?" Suddenly the ornaments around his neck felt tight and he wanted to rip them off.

"They are beautiful, from what I can tell. Well," she paused, scratching under her chin. "Most of them are beautiful, anyway. I do not think the lord of Pahtia sent his most gracious offering."

Ahkin frowned and busied himself with putting away the charts. "Beauty eventually fades for everyone. The spirit is what lasts forever."

The matchmaker did not seem fazed in the slightest by the reprimand. "Of course, I know this better than anyone. The tasks will help us determine which of the girls' spirits is most compatible with your own. But a little beauty in this world never hurts." She winked at the prince with a heavily kohled eye.

Ahkin's neck grew warm again. Coatl, the palace healer and his friend, was always the one who impressed women, not him. Ahkin himself was too sullen and quiet to hold their interest for long. "Speaking of the tasks, what does the codex require?"

"Usually, the ritual begins with a ceremony to demonstrate that each daughter is a true descendant of her city's patron god or goddess. Then the codex suggests you and I together decide what tasks to assign that will allow the daughters to demonstrate their resourcefulness, their ability to influence, and, of course, their dedication to the rituals. These also help us to assess their personalities. Once you have a daughter selected, I will hopefully give my approval and notify the bride's parents. There will be a luxurious four-day marriage feast followed immediately by the coronation. The event culminates in the sacrifice of the daughters not chosen."

"And we have to complete all of this before the Nemontemi?" Only two weeks to make such an important decision? Ahkin fidgeted with his chestpiece and breathed deeply.

"We do not have to select an empress before the last days of the calendar, but I cannot pretend it would not be ... risky to enter such an unlucky time without a crowned emperor. The people are usually so fearful during that time. The city-states will appreciate going into the inauspicious days with the knowledge that their leadership is secure."

"I just—" Ahkin swallowed hard. "Atanzah, may I ask you something personal?"

"Of course, my lord. I live to serve you however I can."

The heat from his neck spread to his cheeks. He needed to voice his concerns to someone, and who better than the old woman who made arranging and planning marriages her purpose in life?

"How will I know which girl's spirit is most compatible with my own? What if she isn't impressed with me?"

Atanzah chuckled and flourished a wrinkled hand, as though dismissing Ahkin's worries as childish. "From what I have seen, my dear, you take everything so seriously. I would love to see you choose someone who can lift the weight of the world off your shoulders with only a smile. Someone who can show you that there is more to life than rules and responsibilities."

Ahkin narrowed his eyes. "I don't understand what you mean."

Atanzah threw her arms in the air in mock frustration.

"Good gods, Ahkin. I helped your mother birth you into this world, and from the moment you opened your eyes you have always been such a sour little thing. Find someone who brings you *joy*. Someone who can bring color and light into your rigid black-and-white world."

"That sounds unrealistic to me. Shouldn't I find someone who is the most sensible, who will best fulfill the duties required of her?"

"Of course. But these are all daughters of the noble families. I am sure any one of them would make an excellent empress to the Chicome people. I want to see you happy. I want to find the daughter that makes your soul sing. One who completes the other half of your duality." Atanzah grinned and poked a withered finger at the golden symbol of the sun hanging on Ahkin's chest. "You are the descendant of the god of the *sun*. Don't be so dark and dour."

Ahkin frowned even deeper, convinced Atanzah was much too romantic for her own good.

The matchmaker sighed in a motherly sort of way.

"Just listen to your heart, dear boy. You will know which girl is right for you when you see her."

CHAPTER

11

The sky faded to a dull orange glow as the sun set behind the mountains ahead. Mayana's chin, which she had been resting on her fist, slipped, jerking her out of a half-awake state. Heart pounding from the sudden shock, she shook out her arms in an attempt to stay alert. Gnats buzzed around her face. She flinched and pawed at the side of her head as one entered her ear canal. She was definitely ready to be out of the jungle.

"Almost there, my lady." Xol pointed ahead to where the path curved sharply to the left. Mayana sat straighter and her muscles tensed. As much as she wanted this journey to end, she dreaded what would happen when it finally did.

"I thought we would arrive before sunset," Mayana said.

"So did I, my lady. We must have traveled more slowly than I thought." He frowned up at the setting sun.

They rounded the curve and the City of the Sun came into view. Mayana sucked in a sharp breath. It was like nothing she ever imagined.

Tollan sat high upon a volcanic plateau. Numerous waterfalls cascaded down the cliff faces into the dense green jungle below. Golden pyramids reflected the light of the sunset in such brilliance that she held up her hand to shield her eyes. Tollan dwarfed her own city-state not only in size but in splendor. Mayana immediately understood Xol's smile when she told him she had never visited before.

"Well? Was I right?" Xol sounded breathless.

Mayana nodded her head in silence, eyes wide. She was supposed to impress the prince who lived *there*? In a city of gold set high in the sky with the prince who could raise the sun itself every morning with the power of his blood? Her hope set along with the sun as darkness fell over them. She was probably going to die in that shining, glittering place.

Mayana didn't think she would have been able to force herself to take another step forward, so she was grateful the servants carried her. As it was, she leaned as far back against the wooden chair as she possibly could, pushing herself away from her impending fate.

She pressed a hand against her heretical heart as it fluttered in panic beneath her fingers. Would they cut it from her chest and burn it on an altar? Would they throw her down the side of the temple, her divine blood painting the steps? She contemplated for a moment whether or not the servants would stop her if she leapt from the chair and bolted for the jungle.

The caravan marched up the carved path along the plateau, snaking around one of the sloping cliff faces toward their destination. Darkness continued to gather, so by the time they reached the gates inlaid with hieroglyphs, night had completely fallen. Despite the darkness, giant flaming torches reflecting from the golden buildings kept the streets as bright as day. Mayana couldn't even see the stars, only the misshapen moon rising into the sky like a deadly smile. How did people sleep here?

Apparently they didn't, because hundreds of people had gathered along the avenue that connected the main city gates to the massive palace looming over the rest of Tollan. Beside the palace stood the Pyramid of the Sun, the temple where the Mother goddess supposedly gave life to the first people. That must be where the prince did his morning rituals to awaken the sun. If Mayana was exhausted just hiking up and down the steep steps of the temple in Atl, she would die before reaching the top of the temple of Tollan. She wondered if Emperor Acatl had suffered heart failure from trying to climb that monstrosity.

Like Xol, most of the common people of Tollan wore white cotton embroidered with golden thread. Men and women sported golden necklaces, bracelets, and earrings. Many of the women held the hands of small children as they balanced baskets on their heads or hips. Mayana pretended not to notice the children gawking and pointing at her or the women raking her over with their judgmental eyes before turning to whisper in the ear of a neighbor. She assumed she was not the first princess to arrive, and she worried they were comparing her to the competition.

One young woman about her own age blatantly shook her head and laughed with her fellows, as though to say, *Oh, surely not her.* Mayana's gaze fell to her scraped hands and muddy skirt. Her throat constricted. She could almost hear her father's disappointed sigh.

Snippets of conversations floated back to her ears: "Blue and jade"; "She must be from City of Water"; "A daughter of the goddess Atlacoya." She blocked the voices out before she heard something she didn't want to and turned her attention to her traveling companions.

Xol reveled in the attention. He puffed out his chest, looking more like a cockatoo than ever as he strutted along the avenue ahead of them. The servants carrying her belongings trailed him slowly, turning in every direction with mouths agape.

Their march toward the palace through a great sprawling plaza felt as though it took several cycles of the calendar, but they finally reached the entrance and passed beyond a hanging curtain. Mayana's heart beat like a drum at the bloodletting festival. The servants lowered her to the ground.

She had just gotten shakily to her feet when another glittering servant, tinkling with many tiny bells dangling from her shawl as she walked, came into the room.

"Whom do we have the pleasure of welcoming this evening?" The plump older woman folded her hands neatly in front of her chest and gave Mayana a warm smile.

"I bring you Lady Mayana, daughter of the lord of Atl," Xol replied. "My lady, this is Atanzah. She is the royal matchmaker."

Mayana tried to keep her eyes from going wide at the almost indigo shade of the old woman's hair and the vibrantly colored feathers hanging from her shawl. If Xol resembled a cockatoo, the matchmaker was a brilliant macaw. This was the woman who must approve her match to the prince? Her stomach twisted as she forced herself to meet Atanzah's curious eyes.

"Was there a problem on the journey?" Atanzah asked, appraising her appearance with deep-red lips puckered in concern.

"The Lady Mayana was attacked by a jaguar," Xol said.

Atanzah gasped and fanned herself. "You poor dear. How did you ever escape?" she whispered dramatically.

Mayana didn't know what to say. She looked to Xol for some kind of direction, panic flooding her veins. Was she supposed to tell the truth?

"We managed to scare it away before any lasting damage was done. Lady Mayana fell, but other than receiving some scrapes, she is perfectly well," Xol said.

Mayana mouthed *Thank you* to him, and he gave her a small nod in return.

"If she has been injured, you should take her to see Coatl."

"I certainly agree. Lady Mayana is a rarity, and I want her to look her best," Xol said.

Mayana's cheeks warmed and she reached out a hand to Xol to thank him. He grabbed it momentarily in his own and gave it a small squeeze.

Atanzah looked her up and down several more times with a look of obvious concern before waving them on. Mayana began to tremble.

Xol guided her out of the room and through multiple curtains, down more brightly lit hallways, and across a large, beautiful courtyard. Mayana was glad he knew where he was going, because she would have wandered through this palace for days before ever finding a way out.

The palace bustled with frantic activity. Servants and guards darted back and forth, giving Mayana glimpses into the rooms beyond. Luxurious sitting rooms boasted colorful textiles, courtrooms loomed cold and imposing, and armories glistened with obsidian weapons and warrior costumes. Food stores overflowed with maize and beans and fruits of every color, and an aviary twittered with hundreds of birds. The aroma of baking bread and corn cakes mixed with the perfumes of nobles as they marched purposefully past. Her eyes darted around, hungry to take in every new sight and smell. Usually the Chicome imposed strict curfews because of deeply held superstitions about being out at night, but the constant light that shone through Tollan and the excitement of the arriving noble daughters must have rendered the curfew temporarily obsolete. That, or the city and palace just never slept.

They arrived at an alcove with a crimson curtain, the color of the city of Pahtia, draped across the doorway. Coatl was obviously the healer for Tollan. Mayana imagined a hunched, male version of Nemi who would silently heal her hands with a scowl on his face. She certainly did not expect the incredibly handsome young man who opened the curtain. He couldn't be any older than her brother Chimalli. Mayana's stomach clenched the moment his dark eyes found her, and a seductive smile played across his lips.

"Hello," he purred.

Mayana was pretty sure the sound she made sounded more like a squeak than anything else. She forced herself not to stare at the tanned, highly defined muscles of his chest. Her mouth went dry.

"I'll wait outside until you're finished, my lady, and then I will see you to your room." Xol inclined his head and then left her alone with the glorious creature in the doorway.

Coatl disappeared into the depths of his alcove and Mayana followed with shaky footsteps. The large room smelled strongly of herbs. Shelves bearing various ointments and salves covered the walls. It was much dimmer than the rest of the palace, with a single torch burning in the back corner. She tried to speak, but again, all that came out was a strange high-pitched sound.

"Well, little mouse, how can I be of service?" His eyes appraised her in a way that made Mayana acutely aware of how much of her skin was showing. She wished she could somehow cover herself better.

"I need to heal the scrapes and cuts on my palms." She stood a little straighter.

"What happened?" he asked, drawing out his words in a bored, disinterested voice.

"I tripped."

"A clumsy little mouse, are we?" He ran his fingers through his dark curls.

"No, I fell escaping from a jaguar." She tried to sound as casual as he did, as though escaping from jaguars in the jungle was a typical daily occurrence.

He cocked an eyebrow.

"So the mouse ran away from a cat?"

"Actually, the cat ran away from *me*," Mayana said, narrowing her eyes at him. Who was this healer that thought he could speak to a lord's daughter in such a way?

Coatl snorted with laughter at her proclamation. He may have been handsome, but the healer appeared highly aware of that fact.

"I'll need to clean the wounds before I heal them," he said.

Coatl sauntered away with an effortless grace toward the shelves sagging with various stone bottles. He selected a little pot with some kind of yellow paste crusted along its edges and a hollowed gourd bowl.

Coatl gestured for Mayana to sit on one of the many cushions that lined the floor of his room. He sat directly in front of her, and Mayana instinctively scooted back several inches. He placed the bowl beside him and reached out to jingle the bracelets on her wrist. She yanked them out of his reach.

"Jade. You're from Atl." It wasn't a question. "Since your blood is exposed, why don't you bring some water over for us?" He inclined his head toward the back of the room, where a large painted jar sat against the wall. Mayana could sense the cool water within it.

She heaved a sigh and held her hand out to the jar palm-first. A small stream of water rose from the jar and wriggled toward them before landing in the bowl.

"Well done, little mouse."

He cleaned her hands with a strip of cloth dipped into the water and then smeared them with the yellow paste. He rubbed the paste into her skin with long, lingering strokes. The way he moved his fingers across her hands was much too intimate, especially when he attempted to catch her eye as he worked the salve. She looked determinedly at the back wall.

"You should be a little nicer to me. You know the healers have the most important job in the empire," he said with a smirk.

"And why is that?"

"Well, think about it. Without me, your ability would be unsustainable. We wield a tremendous and holy power through healing."

Mayana's response stuck in her throat. She had never thought about

that before, but what he said was true. Healers from Pahtia were necessary
for the continuation of the rituals. Without them, how could the families
continue to use their divine abilities without severe consequences?

Coatl finally withdrew a blade from his beaded belt. The ruby handle
glinted in the light of the flaming torch as he pricked his finger. Waving his hand over hers, he healed the gashes and scrapes that covered her
palms, returning her blood back where it belonged.

Mayana withdrew her hands as fast as she could and rose. She gave
him a curt "Thank you" and turned to leave. Before she even made it two
steps, Coatl grabbed her wrist and turned her roughly back to face him.

He pulled her in close to him and tipped her head back as though he
were going to kiss her. Instead, he reached up and tapped Mayana's nose
with his forefinger.

Her newly healed palms shot to his bare chest and Mayana pushed
him away from her with all the strength she could muster. He was taunting her.

Coatl doubled over laughing.

"Oh, you should've seen your face." He gasped for breath between
peals of laughter.

"What is wrong with you?" Mayana hissed at him.

"Little mouse." He gave her a wicked smile full of mischief and held
the curtain open for her to leave. "Relax. You might as well have a little
fun before you die."

CHAPTER

12

Mayana sputtered as Coatl closed the curtain in her face. She wondered how someone that full of himself could possibly be related to her healer back home.

"Let me show you where you will be staying for the time being." Xol took her attention away from the infuriating healer behind the curtain and gestured down the hall.

For the time being? Oh. He meant until she either moved into the emperor's rooms ... or until she no longer required a room. She suppressed a shudder.

They arrived at a long hallway hung with different-colored curtains. She chanted the names of the various city-states to herself as she passed. Green for Millacatl, purple for Ehecatl, black for Papatlaca, yellow for Ocelotl, red for Pahtia. Sure enough, he led her to the second curtain on the left, a tapestry dyed a dark blue with a woven hieroglyph of Atlacoya. Mayana found the color comforting, a little reminder of her identity.

She tried to catch glimpses of the other girls, but their curtains were pulled closed. Either they didn't want to be seen, or they had not arrived yet. The black curtain of Papatlaca gave no indication of life behind it. Mayana assumed the room was still awaiting its occupant.

A pair of eyes like tiny dark cacao beans peeked out from behind the red curtain of Pahtia. Coatl's impression still clung to her like a bad taste in her mouth, so Mayana had no desire to greet the princess from his city. Instead, she thanked Xol once more and practically ran to isolate herself in her room.

Once she entered, Mayana halted in surprise. The room stretched out to twice the size of her room back home and the large chamber danced with the light of several torches. Blue weavings with feathers and jade ornaments covered the walls, and a large fountain trickled reassuringly in the corner. Mayana loved the sound of the dancing water.

On the far side, there was no wall at all. Instead, the room simply opened out onto steps that led down to a lush tropical garden. Vines served as the only curtain across the opening. The sounds of monkeys scurrying through the foliage outside kept Mayana from exploring the garden further. She had not had many good experiences with the frisky little creatures, no matter how lucky they were supposed to be.

Her bed mat overflowed with thick animal furs, and beside them sat the baskets her servants had brought from Atl. She rummaged through the clothing that had been packed for her, searching for a familiar blue cotton dress and shawl, but much to her dismay, her aunts knew her too well. They had packed more of the same highly revealing outfits. Mayana silently cursed them all straight to the depths of the underworld.

She stood there glaring at the thin strips of fabric in her hands for several minutes. How was she supposed to tie these by herself?

"Do you need some help?" a soft, nervous voice said behind her.

Mayana spun to find a young woman dressed in red, and she instantly stiffened. This must be the princess from Pahtia, the City of Healers. The girl was much shorter than Mayana and slightly thicker around her middle, making her seem more blocky than curvy. Her dark eyes sparkled with kindness but her rather large nose, unfortunately, dominated her face. She hovered near the doorway and rubbed her arm nervously up and down.

"Or I can leave, I just …" She turned, but her nervousness struck a chord in Mayana's heart. She looked exactly how Mayana felt.

"No, actually, I would appreciate some help if you're willing." Mayana motioned for her to come in.

The princess gave her a meek smile and stepped back into the room.

"I'm Yemania. The princess from …"

"Pahtia?"

"Yes," she laughed, slightly breathless. "You're from Atl, right?"

Mayana nodded in confirmation. "I'm Mayana."

"Is it true you have waterfalls and rivers that run through your whole city? And you travel from place to place in boats?" She reached for the clean fabric and helped Mayana tie it around her chest.

"Yes, we do," Mayana said, slightly taken aback. She never thought of their canals and boats as anything other than ordinary. Apparently she took them for granted.

"Who is the healer in Atl?" Yemania asked, politely turning away as Mayana changed out of her muddy skirt.

"An older woman named Nemi."

"She is my great-aunt." Yemania chattered away like a parrot. "Isn't she the grumpiest little thing?"

"Absolutely." Mayana rolled her eyes, remembering Nemi's disapproving frowns. She let herself relax in Yemania's company until her father's words floated back to her. *Everything is political, Mayana.* As friendly as Yemania seemed, Mayana still needed to guard herself.

"How is Coatl related to you?" she asked, carefully avoiding Yemania's gaze.

Yemania bit her lip. "You met him already?"

"I met him, yes." Mayana hoped her voice didn't sound too cold.

"Coatl is my brother. Please don't think poorly of me because of him. He can be very ..."

"Full of himself? Inappropriate?" She shoved her dirty clothing into a basket a little more roughly than she meant to.

Yemania flinched.

"My father and Coatl do not ... get along. Usually immediate family members are kept at the main palace, to perform our rituals to prevent plague, but Coatl and my father always argued about the role of healers in the empire. I think that's partly why he asked to go to Tollan instead of staying home. He really isn't as bad as he seems. He was always very kind to me."

Guilt flooded Mayana's veins. It was not Yemania's fault her brother had teased her, and maybe she hadn't really given him a chance. "I'm sorry ... but why are you being so nice to me, if you don't mind me asking?" She hoped Yemania wasn't playing with her too.

To her surprise, tears built up in Yemania's eyes. "Well, look at me." Yemania gestured to her nose and pudgy stomach. "Do you think the prince will choose someone like me?"

Mayana didn't know how to respond. She hoped the prince was not so shallow, but she also couldn't pretend that Yemania's appearance hadn't given her a little bit of hope. Mayana instantly shamed herself for such a thought.

"I'm no fool. I know why my father sent me instead of one of my sisters. If another princess is chosen, I will not be a loss. I am expendable." Yemania refused to look up, but tears flowed freely onto her sandaled feet.

Mayana took in Yemania's pain as the truth of her situation sank in. Yemania's father had sent her instead of one of his other daughters because he would rather lose her. He had already written her off as a sacrifice to the emperor. Tears fell from Mayana's eyes too. Without thinking about what she was doing, Mayana rushed forward and hugged Yemania tightly. She put everything she could not put into words into the embrace.

Yemania broke down into anguished sobs that Mayana could tell she had been holding back for some time. Mayana cried with her. If anyone knew what it felt like to be a disappointment, to not live up to what others thought you should be, she did. The agony and fear churning within her from the moment her father told her about the empress-selection ritual bubbled up and escaped as she cried. Their tears washed them both clean from their misery. It took a long while for either of them to regain her composure.

"I'm s-s-sorry, Mayana. I j-j-just can't stand the idea of dying alone, and you were the first princess I've met that s-s-seems as shaken as I am."

Mayana wiped her eyes and took a shuddering breath. Apparently looking disheveled with mud all over her skirt had been a recommendation.

"You don't need to be sorry. None of us deserves to face death alone. I promise we can die together," Mayana assured her. Yemania must have been a gift from the gods. She was the first person Mayana felt comfortable with since yesterday. She hadn't realized how much she needed an outlet.

"Do you mean that? We can die together?"

"Absolutely. I know the prince will never pick someone like me. So, I promise you will not face this alone." Mayana held Yemania by her shoulders and let her gaze bore her seriousness into the daughter of healing. Yemania pulled her in for another embrace and whispered a tremulous "Thank you" in her ear.

Mayana gently pulled away. "It makes me feel better to not face it alone too."

"Do you know how they will …?" Yemania's words trailed off significantly, but Mayana knew what she was asking.

"I don't. Maybe it's best we don't know."

Yemania nodded and looked down at her hands as they twisted in her lap. Mayana personally couldn't handle thinking about how she would die, so she changed the subject.

"Yemania, I know why your father sent you," she said. Her voice rang with the authority of her godly heritage. Yemania lifted her head, still sniffling.

"The codex instructs the city-states to send the most beautiful, and he did. Your beauty shines through every inch of you."

Yemania gave a weak, half-hearted smile. She didn't believe her, but Mayana meant what she had said. The true core of a person encompassed their whole being. Now that she saw Yemania's heart, the girl radiated beauty.

Mayana hoped the prince would see Yemania's beauty as she did, but at the same time, she realized that if he did, it would seal her own fate. How was she supposed to hope for Yemania without dooming herself? Mayana threw her anguished thoughts toward the heavens. She didn't know how, but she prayed for Ometeotl to find a way to save them both.

CHAPTER

13

Mayana slept better that night than she had in days. Her father probably wouldn't approve of her trusting Yemania, but he also had told her to use her heart. She often struggled with following the rituals exactly as the codex instructed, but her compassion did give her the ability to read others better than most. Yemania's pain was sincere. Mayana did not doubt it for a moment.

The next morning, she woke up to maidservants scurrying around her room. They pulled her off the bed mat and proceeded to touch up the primping job her aunts had done the day before.

"You will be presented to Prince Ahkin before breakfast in a ceremony to prove your royal standing. Each of you will display the power of your divine blood in the manner of your choosing," a servant girl with a long dark braid told her.

"The manner of my choosing?"

"You may request any supplies you will need, and I will see that they are provided for you."

Her father had told her there would be tasks to complete. This was the first task ... and her first impression. She had to make sure it was memorable. The room started spinning and the voices around her sounded garbled, as though the servants were speaking through water.

"My lady?"

Mayana gave her head a little shake.

"Yes?"

"What supplies will you require for the ceremony?"

"Um." She swallowed hard. "Some water?"

"How much, my lady? A bowl? A jar?"

Her palms started sweating again. Mayana wished more than anything she could run home and hide behind the waterfall gushing off the temple pyramid in Atl. It was one of her favorite places in the world, listening to the roaring water, watching the rainbows in the mist dancing on the stone wall. An idea hit her like a ball from a ceremonial game.

"I just need a bowl."

The servant dipped her head and left the room.

"You look beautiful, Mayana." Yemania appeared in the doorway.

Her red skirt and top did not reveal as much skin as Mayana's, but it flattered her figure. The designs painted in red on her cheeks distracted from her nose.

"You look beautiful too." Mayana gave her a sad smile.

"Do you know what you are going to do to display your power?"

"I have an idea. But it's a little risky," Mayana said.

"I wanted to know if you'd help me with mine." Yemania shuffled her feet and didn't meet Mayana's eyes.

She needed to display her ability to heal …

"That depends." Mayana involuntarily leaned away from the princess of Pahtia. She could barely handle pricking her own finger to bring forth blood. A sudden image of Yemania driving a spear through her stomach and then healing her to great applause popped into her head.

"It won't be much. If you go before me, just let me heal your hand. I'm not trying to impress anyone. I just need to show that I am a descendant of Ixtlilton."

Mayana's instinct to avoid pain warred with her instinct to help. Yemania's eyes opened wide to implore her.

"As long as you promise to heal it as fast as you possibly can." Mayana gave a great, exaggerated sigh.

Yemania beamed.

"I mean it. Have your blood ready the second I make the cut." Mayana smiled and the relief on Yemania's face was tangible.

"Ladies, it is time." Atanzah's voice echoed down the hall, her hands clapping a quick little beat.

"Are you ready?" she asked Yemania, squeezing the other girl's hand for a moment.

"No." Yemania gave her head a quick little shake.

"Me either, but it's happening whether we like it or not." Mayana swept the curtain aside and they took their places at the end of the line of princesses waiting in the hall.

Mayana immediately scanned the faces of the other noble daughters, taking in their postures, their expressions, anything to give her a clue as to what to expect from them. Yemania took a step behind her as though she were hoping Mayana could conceal her.

The princess in green chatted animatedly with another of the girls. Mayana assumed the first was Teniza, from Xol's home city. He had not exaggerated her beauty. Her long dark hair flowed freely down her back, set with small pink flowers at regular intervals. The blooms, paired with the bright-green color of her form-fitting dress, made her resemble a fresh jungle flower shooting right up through the earth. Her willowy height intimidated Mayana more than anything. She towered over the rest of them, a tree over sproutlings.

The princess of Ocelotl exuded a wild energy. She wore bits of a jaguar pelt that barely covered her most intimate secrets, and her long dark hair was pulled up into a severe style that accentuated the pronounced features of her face. A thick black stripe of paint covered her eyes and ran across the bridge of her nose, but the way her eyes darted back and forth reminded Mayana of a predator scanning for easy prey. She certainly didn't seem to mind showing as much of herself as possible.

Behind her, lounging against the wall, was the daughter of Papatlaca, City of the Volcano. Her dark hair was cut to her shoulders with a short harsh fringe across her forehead. Shiny black beads of obsidian dangled from a black toucan-feather headdress and blended almost seamlessly into her hair. The effect cast a shadow over her dark, brooding eyes. She was dressed in all black and twirled a long shard of fire glass between her fingers. A ring of polished obsidian pierced her bottom lip. She fixed Mayana with a glare, and Yemania squeaked behind her. Mayana stiffened and tried to hold her gaze without blinking. The corner of the girl's mouth ticked up in a slight smirk before she turned away.

Mayana wondered where the last princess was. Then the purple curtain next to them fluttered. A tiny wisp of a girl, a full head shorter than Mayana, took her place in line ahead of Mayana. She looked as though a single gust of wind might carry her away like a feather, which Mayana guessed was appropriate, considering she hailed from Ehecatl, the city of wind and storms. Shells from the sea dangled around her neck and encrusted the headpiece she wore, a nod to her city-state's location on the coast. Mayana felt an urge to protect her ... until she saw her face. The girl's delicate features betrayed a fierceness Mayana had not expected from one so small. Mayana took an involuntary step back the moment their gazes collided. Lightning crackled from her eyes, and the hair on Mayana's arms stood up. She held her head high with a sense of regality bordering on condescension, as though the other girls were beneath her notice entirely.

Mayana took a deep, steadying breath. All of the princesses exuded a sense of confidence, though whether true or staged she could not tell. She pitied poor Yemania. No wonder she had approached Mayana instead of one of the others. At the same time, did that mean Mayana seemed weaker? Softer than the others? She hoped that wasn't true.

"Yemania, what do you know of the princesses?" Mayana whispered over her shoulder. She assumed that because Yemania's family visited the other city-states so frequently as healers that she would know a lot more about them.

"Just what I've heard from my aunts and uncles." Yemania scooted a little closer so that her lips were nearly at Mayana's ear. "Ocelotl is horrible, from what I can tell. They value strength and power, like animals do, and they train their children in gladiatorial combat from a young age. They are required to fight to weed out the weak. I heard that Zorrah killed her own older sister in one of their competitions."

Mayana's heart leapt into her throat as she took in the lean muscle and feral energy of the animal princess walking in front of her. She hadn't noticed before, but now she could see an abundance of scars marring the girl's beautiful tanned skin. Mayana felt a stab of pity. How awful to grow up in such a world. This girl must have faced competition her entire life, and here she was in another competition.

"I don't know much about Teniza, the princess of Millacatl, other than the fact that her family is incredibly wealthy," Yemania continued. Mayana snorted at that. Everyone knew Millacatl practically bathed in their wealth, not to mention used it to gain as much influence as possible. Her father said they were always bribing the royal family of Tollan for favors.

"I also don't know much about the princess from Papatlaca. I don't even know her name, to be honest, and seeing her in person, I'm not sure I want to."

"Why is that?" Mayana asked.

"Well, look at her."

Mayana frowned at that. The princess from the mountain of fire did seem intimidating, but something about her drew Mayana in. She exuded a sense of protected sadness that made Mayana want to reach out and take her hand.

"My uncle Ataro said she always kept to herself. That she was very isolated and didn't like to mingle. I think something happened to her as a child, but I don't remember what. But they're vicious out there in the mountains. He told me that they are a little overzealous about the sacrifices, that they keep him busy with how much he has to heal."

Mayana's stomach turned at the thought. She turned the topic of conversation away from sacrifices. "What about the princess from Ehecatl?"

Yemania's face went dark at the mention of the City of Storms. Her eyes narrowed at the back of the tiny wind princess marching ahead of them. "Surely your family is familiar with the issues surrounding Ehecatl."

"Well, I know they challenge the authority of Tollan. They're extremely pious, aren't they? That's what I've heard my brothers discussing, anyway. They are obsessed with preparing for the return of Quetzalcoatl." Mayana had always longed to visit Ehecatl and walk along its legendary beaches, to see the ocean, but her father would never allow it. He didn't trust the royal family of Ehecatl at all.

"Their attitudes will get us all killed by the gods, if you ask me. Sanctimonious fanatics. I hope the marriage arrangement they announced with the prince's sister will do something to help smooth the tensions." Yemania shook her head slowly back and forth.

Mayana didn't respond. She wondered if the prince's advisors would promote this opportunity to strengthen the relationship with the City of Storms with yet another marriage. Hopefully the prince wouldn't let politics influence his decision as much as his heart. She could practically hear her father's laughter in the back of her head at the thought.

A thought suddenly occurred to her. "If the princess of Tollan does marry the storm prince, wouldn't their child also have the power to control the sun? Doesn't the ability of the more powerful god always dominate over the lesser when our bloods are mixed?"

"Yes," Yemania answered. "But Ahkin is older and his children will continue to sit on the throne in Tollan, even if Metzi has children."

Mayana lapsed into thoughtful silence. Could it really be wise to match a descendant of the sun god with Ehecatl? If the rebellious city also had someone capable of controlling the sun … She shook her head. Surely the council had already discussed such a scenario.

Heads poked out of doorways and windows to watch their procession through the palace. Atanzah stopped just before entering the room where the feast would be held and gathered them close around her with short frantic motions.

"You will wait here until called," she whispered, her cheeks pink and eyes sparkling with excitement. "I will introduce you to the prince and his guests before you perform your demonstrations. After, you will join the prince on one of the empty cushions around him. He will lead us in a sacrifice before the feast begins."

Mayana's heart dropped at the mention of a sacrifice. At least she wouldn't have to do it herself. Atanzah disappeared behind the hanging tapestry across the doorway and for the first time, the daughters of the noble families were alone together.

The tension in the air hung heavy, like the suffocating moisture of the jungles below Tollan's volcanic perch. What did one say to the other young women determined to steal the heart of the prince and sentence you to death? Because that was the truth. Every set of eyes that met hers wished her dead. Yemania was, perhaps, the only exception. Part of Mayana wanted to curl in on herself like a scared dog, submissive and cowed in the face of superior beasts.

But a larger part of her refused to be viewed as a frightened little animal. She was the daughter of a lord, the descendant of an ancient and powerful goddess. No matter how she felt, she was not inferior. Mayana lifted her head high and squared her shoulders. She would not be intimidated by anyone.

CHAPTER

14

Ahkin was already supposed to be in the throne room waiting to greet the princesses, but instead he stood before the polished obsidian mirror in his chambers fidgeting with his father's gold chestpiece. He longed to shrug it off his shoulders and throw it in a corner. It was a stupid, heavy thing. He considered going bare-chested to the welcoming feast, but he needed to make a good impression. A heavy sigh escaped through his lips. His mother would have known how to fix it.

Shame burned away his frustration. He had to stop questioning the will of the gods. His mother had done her duty and would be disappointed in him if he couldn't do his. He was not supposed to miss her this much.

The beads dangling over the curtain to his room clattered, announcing the arrival of some unknown visitor. Ahkin finished positioning his golden adornments before turning to find his twin sister stretching herself out lazily along a wooden bench.

"Do we have to go?" she asked him, pouting out her lower lip.

"I know the feeling." He rolled his eyes. "I'm sorry you have to sit through this too."

"Well, at least you get to decide who you are going to marry."

"You've never even met the storm prince. Atanzah thinks you would be an excellent match."

"Except that I had no say in a decision that determines the rest of my life."

"Metzi …" An argument was the last thing Ahkin wanted to deal with moments before meeting his future wife.

She waved a flippant hand in his direction. "I know, I know. Spare me the lecture about how my marriage will save the kingdom." Her sweet smile eased the tension that had started building in his chest.

Metzi was technically older than he was by about six minutes, but he was as protective of her as if she were a much younger sister. It didn't help that her beauty was legendary throughout the kingdom. Ahkin frequently found himself glaring at warriors and servants, even council members, who let their gazes linger too long on her feminine curves. She was his sister, not an object of lust for the men of the kingdom to salivate over.

The long dark waves of her hair fell almost to the floor as she tipped her head over the edge of the bench. She looked at Ahkin upside down with a teasing smile.

"It's alright. I'm used to doing as I'm told, even if I don't like it. Maybe I'll make a new friend. After all, one of them is going to be my new sister."

Ahkin smiled warmly in return. He was happy to see her maintaining her innocent playfulness in spite of losing their parents and her own impending marriage. He had worried that the spark of mischief and joy within her might have been snuffed.

"Would you be terribly opposed to seating me by Yaotl at the feast? I love throwing corn kernels at him when he isn't looking and watching him look around stupidly."

"Metzi …" Ahkin arched an eyebrow at her.

"Oh, alright." She flipped and propped herself up on her elbows, chin in her hands. "Seat me by Coatl. Then, at least, I can listen to his commentary. I'm sure he will have much to say about the noble daughters."

"That I don't doubt. When we were younger I swore he would get us whipped for his tongue. I haven't spent as much time with him lately." Ahkin yanked at the chestpiece again. "He's been so busy since Father appointed him High Healer."

"Leave it alone, it looks fine."

Ahkin frowned at his sister.

"It does not look fine. All the gold makes me feel like I'm going to suffocate under it, and the weight keeps pulling it down too far."

Metzi trilled a laugh like the song of a canopy bird. Springing to her feet, she wrapped her arms around her twin brother and nuzzled against his neck.

"I love when you are so cheerful," she teased.

Ahkin grumbled an incoherent response.

"Do you think you'll fall in love with one of them at first sight?" Metzi leaned back and looked at him, but her eyes were distant and dreamy.

"I don't know." He shrugged out of her hug and she pouted again.

"Fine, I am going to find someone else who will be nicer to me."

"No one is nicer than I am." He crossed his arms across his chest and deepened his frown at her.

She broke into another peal of laughter at the look on his face before kissing his cheek and skipping from the room.

"Whoever she is, I hope she likes her husband grumpy," she called as she went.

Ahkin rolled his eyes and returned to fidgeting with his infuriating chestpiece.

"Your highness?" Toani, the priest, appeared through the curtain.

Ahkin gave up on the chestpiece and decided he didn't care about it anymore.

Sighing, he turned to his advisor. His stomach dropped at the worry lines creasing the old man's face.

"I have read some most interesting signs and am honestly disturbed by what I am seeing. Are you reading the signs as well, my prince?"

"I'm trying to. The stars are being rather reluctant to divulge their secrets."

"I have found the same to be true." The dark crescents under Toani's eyes suggested he had been up all night studying.

"I keep seeing signs that chaos rises like the sun—that danger waits for us. But I cannot tell what kind of danger it is." Ahkin threw himself down onto the bench Metzi had just vacated. He rubbed a hand over his chest, under the golden jewelry.

"Did—have you—noticed the sun seems to be setting earlier than usual?" Toani sounded nervous. Ahkin stopped rubbing his chest and looked up.

"I have."

"You know the sun dies each night and travels through the layers of the underworld. Each morning, your blood brings it back to life and nourishes it so it may continue on its journey."

"Yes, yes, I know." Ahkin waved his hand impatiently. Toani had lectured him for years on the journey of the sun and the emperor's role in that journey.

"Perhaps the sun is getting tired?" Toani suggested. "Your family is many generations descended from the sun god himself, and your blood has become mixed with the blood of other gods. Maybe it is losing its strength?"

Ahkin could do little to quell the panic that raced through him. His heart thudded so hard he was surprised the chestpiece did not twitch in response. Was Toani suggesting he wasn't strong enough to raise the sun?

"What could we do if that were true?"

"Let us not panic just yet," Toani said, placing a reassuring hand on his shoulder. "We do not know for sure. If darkness is, in fact, the next apocalypse, the signs will become clearer."

Ahkin shrugged out from under the older man's hand.

"The emperor is dead. I am about to have the daughters of our noble families sacrificed. The Nemontemi is in ten days, an eclipse is set to happen next month. Now you tell me the sun may be dying because my blood is not strong enough—and you ask me to remain calm?"

The priest gazed at Ahkin with sorrow in his eyes.

"I am afraid you will go down in history as one of our unluckiest emperors. There is nothing that can be done except follow the codex and wait for the gods to decide our fates."

"I will not give up so easily. I will find a way to stop this and save our people. Mark my words."

Toani sighed.

"You are so young, and your spirit speaks to the warrior within you. But some battles cannot be fought on our layer of creation."

"You said yourself we can't be sure what the signs indicate."

"That is true. I hope for all of our sakes that I am wrong. In the meantime, let us continue on with what we know for sure, and we know you need a wife."

Ahkin growled, wishing more than anything that his parents were still here to guide him down this dark and difficult path.

At least he would soon have a wife to stand beside him, so he would not have to trudge the path alone.

15

"Just as the creator Ometeotl has both male and female aspects, the joining together of our emperor with a wife will ensure we are in cosmic balance with the gods." The matchmaker addressed the banquet hall with impressive dramatic flair. "Through their children, we can ensure the blood of the sun god will continue to nourish the Seventh Sun for many more generations to come. I would now like to present the six noble daughters. Each has been sent to represent her city to bless the rule of our future Emperor Ahkin and ensure the well-being of the entire Chicome Empire."

Mayana's legs felt like heavy stone. Thankfully, Yemania's sharp prod in the small of her back forced her forward. The crowd roared with excitement as the daughters filed in before them. The large room was surrounded by multihued pillars carved with glyphs depicting the gods. Hundreds of nobles and warriors seated on reed mats strained their necks to catch glimpses of the princesses as they walked up the cleared walkway. Mayana kept her head held high. They needed to see an elegant empress, not a terrified child.

Which one was the prince? Her eyes scanned the crowd of nobles lounging across the cushions and furs before a raised dais at the head of the room, but Prince Ahkin immediately caught her attention. He was the focal point of the entire gathering, seated on a golden bench with a tall backrest—sharp points of gold protruding from it like rays of the sun itself. Mayana would be lying to herself if she didn't admit the first thing she noticed was the highly defined contours of his chest beneath the chestpiece. He leaned against the side of his gold throne, and her gaze raked along the strong sinews of his forearm, up to where his head leaned against his curled fingers. His eyes were dark chips of fire glass, his brow furrowed in deep thought. He looked almost troubled, as if his mind was somewhere else entirely.

Ahkin's youth was evident—he counted perhaps only a year or two more than her own seventeen calendar cycles—but a shadow dusted his defined jawline. And his lips. Oh, his lips. Mayana wanted to touch them and see for herself whether they truly felt as soft and as full as they appeared. What a blessing it must be to come from a long line of emperors that selected the most beautiful wives.

The prince wore a golden headpiece with white feathers that contrasted sharply with his short dark hair. An emblem of the sun glittered from the striking golden chestpiece that dangled from his shoulders. Gold bangles etched with hieroglyphs encircled his taut biceps.

Was the light that seemed to radiate off him an invention of her mind? Or just a result of the amount of gold he wore? Were they sure he was a descendant and not an actual god himself?

"Lady Teniza of Millacatl. Descendant of the goddess Xilonen, who sacrificed herself to create the Fifth Sun and save us from famine." Atanzah's voice drew her out of her observations and back to the ceremony that was about to begin.

Teniza stepped away and entered the large open space in the center of the room that had been cleared for the demonstrations. Around the space sat hundreds of spectators, sprawled across the ground on cushions, mats, and low bench seats. The faces of the audience lit with excitement. A shiver of anticipation slid down Mayana's spine at the prospect of seeing the power of so many gods displayed in one place.

A servant rushed forward with a large clay bowl filled to the brim with soil. Teniza withdrew a cactus spine and plunged it into the tip of her forefinger. Making a fist, she thrust her hand upward. In synchrony with the motion of her hand, a cornstalk broke through the surface of the soil and shot skyward, taller than the princess herself. She slowly opened her curled fist, and several ears of perfect, ready-to-harvest corn burst from the stalk. Mayana's jaw dropped. Teniza strode forward to pluck them free and laid them at Ahkin's feet.

"For you, my lord prince." Her voice danced with mirth and playfulness. Mayana's heart sank. How could she compete with such a demonstration?

Teniza of Millacatl gave a small bow, and he nodded in thanks, watching her take a seat on one of the pillows arranged near his throne. Coatl rushed toward her to heal her skin, his focus and dedication to his calling evident in the proud set of his shoulders. Mayana contemplated what he had said about his gift being able to sustain all others.

Yemania must have seen her brother too, because she let out an anguished whimper.

"Lady Yoli of Papatlaca. Daughter of Xiuhtecuhtli, who sacrificed himself to create the Fourth Sun and save us from an eruption of the Great Volcano."

Yoli took a breath that rattled with impatience before strolling into the open. The shimmering black fabric of her dress caught the light of the sacrificial firepit in the floor and she glowed like a living ember. She lifted the shard of obsidian she had twirled between her fingers in the hallway, so long it resembled an arrow, and drove the tip into the flesh of her forearm.

Mayana gasped along with everyone else. Was she trying to prove she wasn't afraid of pain? The dark ring through her lip showed that by itself. Her face remained cool and bored, as though spearing herself in the arm was a perfectly natural way to bring forth blood. Mayana shivered and instinctively grabbed her own forearm.

Blood oozed down Yoli's wrist and dripped from her fingers as her face broke into a wide, haunting grin. Holding her arm above the flames of the pit, she made a bloody fist. The flames shot up and engulfed her hand. Mayana waited for Yoli's flesh to char as black as her dress, but it didn't. The fire covered her hand and she pulled it toward her lips. Yoli gave the prince a seductive smile and blew him a flaming kiss. The tongue of fire that had followed her breath dissipated into the air.

The crowd cooed in delight.

Mayana jerked her gaze away from the fire princess and toward the golden throne. The prince shifted his shoulders uncomfortably. His eyes darted to the side as if he was afraid to look at the princess on display right in front of him. Atanzah looked as though she were suppressing a laugh.

Coatl healed her arm and Yoli took her seat on one of the empty cushions surrounding the throne.

"Princess Zorrah of Ocelotl, descendant of Tezcatlipoca, who sacrificed himself to save us from wild beasts and create our Third Sun."

The naguals in the room straightened at the mention of her name, eyeing their princess. Zorrah bared her teeth. Mayana thought it was supposed to be a smile, but to her it looked more like a growl. Zorrah was almost completely naked except for the tiny shreds of jaguar pelts woven together across her chest. A matching loincloth barely covered her backside, and Mayana blushed on her behalf. Thank the gods her aunts hadn't tried to dress her like that. She was sure she would have exploded every fountain in her father's temple if they had tried.

Zorrah prowled to the center of the room, her long ponytail swinging behind her like the tail of a beast on the hunt. She removed a wooden dagger inlaid with shark teeth from her ... actually, Mayana had no idea where she had been concealing it. So much of her skin was bared, there weren't many places left to hide a weapon of any kind. Zorrah ran her finger across one of the sharp white edges.

The crowd's eyes focused on the doorway behind Mayana, so she followed their stares. She had to restrain herself from jumping back. A servant led a large black jaguar into the room and Zorrah held out a welcoming hand toward it. Something about the beast seemed familiar ...

As it padded its way past the remaining princesses, it locked its golden eyes on Mayana and skittered back several steps. Zorrah made an impatient sound and gestured again for the cat to come to her. Mayana pressed her mouth into a thin line and slowly met Zorrah's eyes, righteous indignation burning through her as if she had swallowed an entire bowl of pulque. It was the same jaguar from the jungle. Their meeting had not been an accident.

Zorrah met her gaze with equal ferocity and did not blink. She showed her teeth again in a vicious smile, as if to say, *What are you going to do about it, daughter of water?*

Mayana breathed heavily through her nose and clenched her hands into fists, but Zorrah turned to face the prince, the jaguar now waiting obediently at her side.

Zorrah nudged the cat toward the firepit with her foot, and the beast walked slowly, purposefully, toward the hot coals. Mayana's fists relaxed in shock, momentarily forgetting her rage. What was Zorrah going to have the beast do?

Yemania sucked in her breath as the realization hit Mayana. *No.* Zorrah wouldn't have it walk into the fire, would she? What would that prove? With a sickened feeling in her stomach, Mayana answered her own question. It would prove her ability to control the animal to the point that she could make it torture itself.

Mayana stiffened, her eyes darting frantically around the room. Someone had to stop her. The faces of the crowd did not look sickened. On the contrary, they learned forward with greedy, expectant expressions.

Its paws were inches from the edge. Mayana's heart twisted in on itself. Yemania grabbed her arm and her nails dug into Mayana's skin. She didn't think Yemania would be upset for the same reason. Perhaps this was reminding Yemania how she was going to be sacrificed like this beast.

It placed its first paw into the coals and pulled back, but Zorrah growled and thrust a red-stained finger toward the pit. The beast slowly lowered its front paw back into the flames.

"Stop!"

The scream ripped through Mayana's throat before she could call it back.

The silence in the room was thicker than the air on the most humid day of summer. The jaguar's paw still remained in the fire, its yellow eyes contracting in pain.

Mayana yanked her dagger from the cuff around her ankle and sliced deep into her palm. She had never drawn so much blood within so few days in her life. She sensed the water placed along the walls in clay jugs and she summoned it toward her.

All of it.

PART 2

Mayana threw her hand out in front of her, clenching it into a fist. Silver streams of water rushed from every corner of the room, meeting over the sacrificial fire and condensing into a giant, crystal-clear mass. She opened her hand.

The water crashed over the pit in a great wave, extinguishing every ember that burned within it. Steam and smoke filled the room in a great hiss while the audience sputtered and coughed it out of their lungs. The smell of burnt flesh and wood overwhelmed Mayana's nose.

Without any warning, a gust of wind rushed through the room and carried the suffocating clouds out the nearest window. Mayana looked around, confusion clouding her thoughts worse than the smoke. The tiny princess from Ehecatl stood beside her, a bloody gash on her outstretched palm.

"You idiot," she hissed at Mayana. "What were you thinking?"

Surprisingly, she didn't look angry. Instead, her eyes were wide with fear and she spoke so low that only Mayana could hear her.

As the shock wore off, every eye in the room fixed on Mayana. Some were wide with awe, others narrowed in indignation. Several naguals had actually leapt to their feet, nostrils flaring with anger. If she thought her heart had been pounding before, it was nothing to how it hammered now. Had she offended the prince? Had she just sentenced herself to death for the sake of a beast that had almost killed her?

Zorrah's flashing eyes betrayed her desire to tear Mayana to shreds faster than a wolf devouring a deer. Mayana's eyes searched for Prince Ahkin's. His response alone would tell her what to expect.

Ahkin was already on his feet. His shrewd, calculating expression now focused on her. He frowned slightly, as though he could not decide what to make of her. The matchmaker's eyes were also narrowed in suspicion.

She was dead. So very, very dead.

"Is there a reason you interrupted the ceremony?" His voice rang with an authority worthy of his position. Mayana didn't sense any anger in his question ... not yet, anyway.

She couldn't make her mouth move. Her body froze in place. The prince cocked his head slightly to the side, waiting for her answer. His dark eyes bored into her own, but her thoughts were as disjointed as a flock of frightened birds.

An idea burst through her consciousness as she thought of birds. Birds. It was the month of the bird ...

Yemania nudged her slightly forward. For the second time, the touch gave her courage. Mayana shook her shoulders and raised herself to her full height. She still wasn't as tall as Teniza the tree, but she met the prince's gaze with blazing determination.

"My lord." Mayana swept out her arms and dipped her head in a bow, forcing her voice to remain steady. "It is the month of the bird. I did not wish to insult the Mother goddess. The sacrifice of a jaguar should be saved for the month of the jaguar, lest we bring ill fortune upon us all."

Prince Ahkin's eyebrows shot up beneath the rim of his headpiece. Clicking her tongue impatiently, Zorrah rolled her eyes and turned her head.

Out of the corner of her eye, Mayana saw the tiny wind princess give a half smile.

The prince and Mayana held each other's gazes for the length of an eternity. *Please, Ometeotl, let him believe me.*

He dipped his chin, continuing to appraise her with his dark eyes, until finally, *finally*, an exasperated smile crossed his face.

"Th-thank you." He cleared his throat. "The codex does not stipulate regarding animals sacrificed for events other than meals, but thank you for caring to observe the calendar rituals with such"—he paused, obviously searching for the right word—"devotion."

Mayana's heart skipped a beat, filling with gratitude at his graciousness.

Ahkin did seem to be a merciful ruler—that much was clear. A sudden rush of affection toward him flowed through her. The feeling scared her as much as it thrilled her. She was supposed to make *him* want *her*, not the other way around.

"Since you are standing anyway, daughter of Atl, why don't you show us your power? I think you've already proven you are indeed a daughter of Atlacoya, but I'm sure you had something else planned." Ahkin settled himself back into the throne, crossing his ankle up onto his knee and thrumming his fingers against the armrests.

"I—um—alright ..." Mayana absently wiped her sweating hands onto her skirt as a servant rushed forward with a small bowl of water and placed it on the floor.

It held only several handfuls of water, probably much less than what the crowd would expect for her to use to demonstrate the impressiveness of her divine abilities.

Zorrah's lip curled.

Ahkin's attention was devoted entirely to her. She had to impress him.

"Actually, your highness"—Mayana inclined her head—"I was wondering if you could assist me with my demonstration."

He cocked an eyebrow, but his mouth curved into an amused smile. "How may I be of assistance?"

Mayana held up a finger, silently asking him to wait while she prepared.

Her hand was still bleeding, so there was no need to bring forth more blood. Mayana held her stinging palm over the bowl and the water rose, forming a small orb. She willed it up past her hand until it glittered high above her head. Taking another steadying breath, she hoped with every fiber of her being that her plan would work.

Ahkin's eyes studied her with an intense curiosity.

Mayana focused all of her energy into blasting the orb apart. The particles of water separated from each other until a cloud of fine mist hovered above her. She lowered her eyes from her creation, relief spreading through her and extinguishing the fear as effectively as she had extinguished the fire.

"My lord." She smiled, bringing her attention back to the prince. He leaned forward on his throne, his attention devoted to her. "Would you be so kind as to direct a beam of sunlight through the mist?"

He paused for the briefest moment before removing a dagger from the belt around his waist. He pierced his thumb and waved his hand toward the nearest window, where rich morning sunlight poured into the room. The beam of light followed the movement of his hand and shot directly through the center of Mayana's mist.

The water particles bent the light into a thousand tiny rainbows that sparkled against every wall of the banquet hall. They bounced off the delighted faces of the audience, who reached up to touch the little bursts of color splattered across their faces and chests.

Mayana twirled her finger and the cloud of mist spun, making the tiny rainbows dance. She smiled at the memories of sitting behind the temple waterfalls back home, watching the colors refracted onto the cold gray stone. Ahkin's expression was as filled with awe as the spectators'.

"When water and light are joined together, it creates something beautiful," she said finally. Ahkin's eyes locked with hers again, something fierce and hopeful burning within them like lit coals. Even Atanzah glanced between them, her expression curious.

Mayana bowed deeply and dissipated the mist. The crowd groaned as the colors vanished, and the look of pure hatred etched upon Zorrah's face told her she had accomplished exactly what she had hoped. Pride burned across every inch of her skin, making her feel like a true descendant of a goddess.

But the look of heartbreaking misery upon Yemania's face plucked the joy from her heart faster than a feather carried off by the wind.

CHAPTER

17

Mayana chose a cushion as far from Zorrah as she could get. "Well done, little mouse," Coatl's voice purred into Mayana's ear the moment she was settled. He reached for her hand and she pulled it out of his reach.

"Don't heal the cut yet," she whispered.

"Why? Planning on putting out more fires?" His eyebrows wiggled teasingly at her.

"I have a purpose." Mayana turned her body away from him, hugging her hand to her chest, as Atanzah announced Yemania to the crowd.

"Yemania of the city of Pahtia, descendant of Ixtlilton, who sacrificed himself to create the Sixth Sun and save the Chicome from a terrible plague."

Yemania slowly walked forward, stumbling a little on the hem of her long skirt.

Coatl suddenly stiffened, his eyes wide and full of concern as he took in the sight of his younger sister.

"I knew he would send her." The anger in his voice surprised Mayana as he slammed a fist against the cushion beneath him. "He's never appreciated her."

"On that we can agree," Mayana said.

Coatl gave her a sad smile.

Yemania's eyes nervously peeked up at her brother and then back down to her feet. Her shoulders trembled, and Mayana rose to her feet again. Yemania hadn't summoned her to help yet, but the daughter of healing needed her, just as she had needed Yemania's prods in her back.

Mayana took her place silently beside Yemania and held out her hand with the crimson gash. Yemania sniffed loudly but took out a stingray spine and pricked her finger. Just as her great-aunt had done back in Atl, Yemania moved her hand over Mayana's and the skin knit itself back together. Yemania's display of power had easily been the least interesting so far. She had no confidence, no showmanship. Mayana's heart ached for her, but also for herself. How was she supposed to encourage Yemania when doing so doomed her own chances? Mayana felt like a carcass caught between the jaws of two crocodiles pulling in opposite directions.

She flashed her healed palm to the prince so that he could see the new skin. He nodded his approval and thanked Yemania for her demonstration before dismissing them. The back of Mayana's neck tingled. Was she imagining his eyes following her back to her seat?

"Lady Itza of Ehecatl, descendant of the god Ehecatl, the wind aspect of the god Quetzalcoatl, who sacrificed himself to create our current Seventh Sun." Atanzah's voice spiked slightly with excitement, and Mayana found herself instinctively leaning forward in anticipation of the final demonstration.

Itza swept forward, the rich purple fabric of her tunic billowing as though the wind itself was carrying her.

A servant scurried forward and littered the ground around her feet with white flower petals. White, the color of the god Quetzalcoatl. Mayana's eyes focused on the cut across Itza's palm. It still bled from dispelling the smoke and steam from the fire incident. The wind princess moved her hand in a small circle and the petals rose from the floor, twirling around in a miniature cyclone of her own creation. The white of the petals contrasted sharply with her dark hair and rich purple dress. Itza stepped into the funnel of wind and flowers and spread her arms wide, embracing the chaos around her with a look of pure serenity upon her face. The cyclone grew in size until it engulfed her, trapping her within her own private windstorm and whipping her hair and dress around her delicate frame. The fierceness in her eyes, the steadfast way she endured the tempest around her, sent a shiver up Mayana's spine. She was *powerful*.

All too soon she lowered her arms and the petals fell softly back to the stone floor. Itza gave a quick bow to the prince. His eyes were wide, but he nodded and motioned for her to join the other princesses. The matchmaker leaned over to Ahkin and whispered something in his ear. Itza took a seat on the cushion at Mayana's other side, opposite from Yemania.

Prince Ahkin stood, and the chatter in the room silenced.

"Welcome, daughters of the noble families, direct descendants of the gods who gave us life." His deep voice reverberated around the feast.

"I will now lead us in a sacrifice to bless our meal. May Ometeotl bless this selection process and help me choose the empress who will make you most proud."

The room filled with cheering and he made his way toward the still-smoking pit where Zorrah had tried to burn the jaguar. He paused at the edge, an amused smile pulling at the corner of his mouth.

"Daughter of Papatlaca, would you mind assisting us with the sacrificial fire?"

Yoli's stomach-churning smile made Mayana look away. She squeezed her eyes shut, not wanting to watch her spear herself in the arm again. The fire princess must have pulled the flames from some nearby torch because by the time Mayana deemed it safe to look again, the embers of the sacrificial fire had been relit. A young man wearing a jaguar pelt, a relative of Zorrah's, had materialized beside the prince with an elegant toucan perched upon his arm. The bird held itself with a peaceful grace, the glossy black feathers glinting in the reflected light of the fire.

Prince Ahkin took his knife out from his waistband and lifted it toward the bird's throat. Mayana sucked in a breath.

Zorrah's eyes shot to her.

Mayana ducked her head, tears filling her eyes, and blinked furiously, trying to force them back where they came from. The strangled cry of the toucan was cut short and the sputtering of flames told her the prince had finished the sacrifice. Mayana brought her eyes back up and took in two things that sent her stomach plummeting to her feet. Blood dripped off the prince's hand onto the smooth stone floor, and Zorrah was looking at her with a deadly smile that curled with an air of triumph. She had obviously noticed Mayana's reaction to the sacrifice.

⸻

The meal seemed to drag on forever, especially as Mayana tried to avoid Zorrah's taunting stares throughout most of it. She knew the princess of beasts was trying her hardest to intimidate her. When the servants finally cleared away the last of the bowls and serving vessels, the noble daughters were asked to remain in the hall while the rest of the guests filed out.

"You will have the rest of the day to explore the city and make your-selves at home in the palace," Atanzah told them, picking at her teeth. "The next task will be assigned to you tomorrow at midday. Please make sure you are back inside before curfew." She dismissed them with a wave of her hand.

"What are you going to do?" Yemania asked, gripping Mayana's elbow in panic. Mayana quickly turned them around the corner and away from the prowling eyes of Zorrah.

"I haven't decided yet. Someone told me about the beautiful pleasure gardens of Tollan. I'd probably like to see those before I die." Mayana meant it to be funny, but she regretted her frankness the moment Yemania blanched.

"Sorry, I didn't mean to upset you." She put her hand over Yemania's.

"I don't know how you can speak so bluntly about your own death," the other girl whispered. Her eyes darted back and forth.

"It's probably just my way of handling the stress." Mayana shrugged. "I promise I am just as terrified as you are."

Yemania gave her a watery smile.

Strolling arm in arm, they walked absently through one of the large courtyards. Innumerable rooms used for various administrative needs encircled several expansive courtyards, while at the far end of the main courtyard, raised high above on a towering set of steps, sat the mazelike residence of the royal family. As in her father's main palace, the lower-level rooms were used mainly for political purposes: meeting rooms for nobil-ity, courtrooms, armories, storage areas.

Mayana didn't even know where to begin to explore.

"Let's ask a servant where the gardens are," Yemania suggested. "Or we could see one of the aviaries."

"No birds ..." Mayana said, rubbing her eyes with her free hand, trying to dispel the memory of blood dripping from Ahkin's hands.

Yemania stopped walking and yanked Mayana backward by her arm into an alcove between two towering pillars painted the color of jade.

"Yemania! What—?"

"What happened with the jaguar, really?" She crossed her arms across her ample bosom, reminding Mayana so forcefully of her great-aunt Nemi that she had to stifle a laugh.

"I—told everyone. It is the month of the bird, so ..." But she couldn't meet Yemania's eyes.

"Then why couldn't you even watch the prince sacrifice the toucan? You looked like he was about to murder a member of your family."

Mayana bit her lower lip. Had it been that obvious? She knew Zorrah had noticed, but not Yemania.

Flicking a rock on the ground with her foot, Mayana looked determinedly away.

"I just—I couldn't—its *eyes*, couldn't you just see the pain in its eyes?"

"It was a sacrifice," she said matter-of-factly.

"I know. It's just ..." How did she put into words what she was feeling? "I hate sacrificing animals. I can almost never do it myself back home." Mayana hung her head in defeat.

"But the gods demand blood. Our divine power comes from exposing our blood." Again, Yemania's voice was flat, as though Mayana was stupid for not understanding.

"Haven't you ever wondered why, though?"

Yemania's eyebrows shot up.

"Because the codex tells us. The gods sacrificed themselves to save us. We *owe* them blood. You should know this better than anyone, Mayana. You are a noble. Your blood itself is from the gods." Her voice sounded almost pleading.

"Exactly. They already paid the price to save us. Why do we have to keep paying? If they loved us enough to die for us, surely they wouldn't—"

Yemania held up a hand to silence her.

"What you are saying disrespects the gods and everything that we believe as a people. Do you think you know better than the codex? The holy texts *given* to us by the gods thousands of years ago?"

Mayana dropped her chin. Yemania sounded exactly like her father. Exactly like everyone else in her life that she had ever had the courage to voice her opinions to. Everyone except her mother.

"Have you studied the codices themselves, Yemania? I mean, physically held the folded sheets of paper in your hands?"

"No, our tutors taught us."

"My mother encouraged me to study them for myself and—" Mayana hesitated. She had never shared her reasons for questioning the rituals with anyone since she voiced her concerns to her father once as a young girl. He had not exactly responded well.

"Stop." Yemania's eyes were wide with fear. "I don't know where you are going with this, but I recommend you stop there. You sound like a heretic from Ehecatl. If you are questioning the validity of the codex …"

"No." Mayana crossed her own arms over her chest. Her traitorous eyes suddenly blurred with tears again. "I believe in the gods, that the Mother loves us and let her children die for us. But I guess I just struggle to believe she would demand blood in return. Love does not hold grudges or demand payment. What if the rituals are just our own superstitions? To make us feel like we have some kind of control over our own fate? I don't know. I only know what my heart tells me. I can't help it."

"Your heart is yours. You control it, not the other way around."

"Well maybe they can cut it out of me, Yemania, and burn it as a sacrifice when they kill us both." Anger and frustration seeped into her tone.

Yemania stepped back as if Mayana had slapped her, tears swimming in her eyes.

"Don't!" She stomped her foot in frustration. "I can't stand thinking about …about …" She threw her head in her hands and her shoulders shook with heart-wrenching sobs.

Mayana immediately regretted her defensiveness. She wrapped her arms around Yemania, longing to correct the effects of her outburst.

"I'm sorry," Mayana whispered in her ear. "I didn't mean that."

Yemania continued to cry. Several servants carrying baskets eyed them nervously as they passed the alcove. Mayana waved them on with silent gestures.

"Yemania." Mayana tried to soothe her by rubbing her back gently. "I have been reminded by my family every day of my life how I disrespect the gods, how my heart does nothing but cause trouble—" Her voice broke. "It just hurt me to hear it again. I try so hard, and it never seems to be enough. *I* am never enough."

"I don't want to die, Mayana, but I believe in the rituals. I believe they protect us. My heart fights as much as yours, but I am here. I will do what needs to be done. You think it requires bravery to question the rituals, but it takes just as much to obey them when everything inside you doesn't want to."

Mayana froze, Yemania's words piercing through her. Did she struggle with the rituals because she didn't like them? Or because of a fear of doing what was necessary? Was she questioning their validity out of selfishness? Mayana honestly didn't know the answer to that.

"Come on, let's find the aviary." Mayana bent down, trying to peek at Yemania's face between her fingers.

Yemania lifted her head, eyes red and swollen.

"I think I'm going to go back to my room. I need some time to myself."

Mayana's smile faltered.

"Maybe we can go to the aviary together later this afternoon," Yemania added. The daughter of healing squeezed her hand for reassurance before turning and slumping her way toward the royal residences.

Mayana let out a huff of breath and ran her hands through her long hair. Her mind was jumbled, and thoughts stuck to the inside of her skull like flies caught in a pitcher plant. Mayana needed to wash them out. *Water.* She needed to find water.

She wandered down a hallway in a daze, trying to decide which way to go.

"Daughter of Atl," called a sweet, melodious voice.

Mayana turned to find a young woman immaculately dressed in the traditional white cotton of Tollan. She was no servant, though. Golden jewelry dripped like honey from her wrists, neck, and earlobes. A headband encrusted with pearlescent gemstones held back her thick, dark hair. Mayana recognized the beautifully angular features as one of the faces that had been seated close to the prince at breakfast.

"I'm Metzi," she said, inclining her head in a smooth graceful bow. "Ahkin's twin sister and princess of Tollan."

Mayana swallowed hard, trying to find her voice. Metzi was as beautiful as Ahkin was godlike. It was an otherworldly beauty that should not have been possible for mere mortals. She moved with an effortless grace, and a hint of light hung about her, making her skin glow like the moon. Her hair flowed down in ebony cascades across the sultry curves of her body. Jealousy pricked like sharp bee stings in her chest before Mayana realized that as Ahkin's sister, she posed no threat.

"You look lost," she said, cocking her head slightly to the side. "Can I help you find whatever you are looking for?"

"The—the gardens," Mayana managed to say.

"Ah. I imagine you want to see the fountains." Metzi gave her a warm, knowing smile. Mayana's frantic heartbeat slowed slightly.

"I do." Mayana couldn't help it, she returned the smile.

"They are behind the royal residence halls. Go around this way." She flourished a graceful hand down an adjacent hallway. "And follow the courtyard back behind the high walls. You can't miss the gardens. They encompass the entire back wall of the palace."

"Thank you, my lady." Mayana gave her a small bow in gratitude.

Metzi considered her thoughtfully for a moment. Mayana fidgeted nervously with the bracelets on her wrist, refusing to make eye contact.

"I think you were incredibly brave this morning," Metzi finally said.

Mayana's heart swelled, overflowing with hope. "Really? You don't think I was disrespectful?"

"On the contrary. I found your dedication to the calendar inspiring. You were quite right to ensure that a proper sacrifice be given in accordance with the signs in the stars. Even though it was not a designated ritual in the codex, it should be held to no lower standards than a ritualistic sacrifice. Lady Zorrah should have chosen a bird for her demonstration."

Mayana's smile became fixed. Her cheeks ached with the effort of keeping her face from falling in disappointment. Metzi thought her *overly* dedicated to the rituals. Was that what everyone else thought too? Prince Ahkin included?

Not Yemania and Zorrah, unfortunately. How was she supposed to keep up a facade like that?

"I think my brother would be lucky to find another soul as devoted to our rules as you seem to be." Metzi gave her a teasing wink that she obviously thought would be encouraging.

The back of Mayana's neck grew hot and she longed to run. Yes,

Mayana had managed to turn her mishap with the jaguar around to her benefit, but she seriously doubted she would be able to hide her dislike for the sacrifices much longer. Could she ignore the pull of her heart-strings? Cut them free and submit herself to the supposed will of the gods? Her brother doubted her ability. So did her father. Could she prove them wrong? Did she even want to?

"Well, we all must honor the rituals." Mayana shrugged her shoulders. She hoped she didn't sound as fake to Metzi as she did to herself.

"My mother also dedicated herself to the rituals with impressive devotion. Unfortunately, that is why she is no longer with us to meet you herself." Metzi's tone was causal and light, but Mayana's ears pricked at the slight hint of sadness.

"Your mother took her life to join your father in the underworld?"

"Yes," Metzi said simply, her attention suddenly focused somewhere off in the distance.

"I'm sorry," Mayana said.

Metzi sniffed and blinked several times in quick succession before turning her attention back to Mayana. "Well, women in positions such as ours are left with little choice. Our paths are often determined for us."

Mayana didn't really know how to respond. She knew exactly how it felt to have her choices taken away from her. After all, given the choice, she would be back home in Atl swimming in the rivers and not worrying about how she was going to be sacrificed to the gods.

"I'm sorry for distracting you," Metzi said. "Enjoy your time in our gardens."

And with that, she was gone.

Mayana stood alone for several moments, trying to gather her thoughts before following the hall Metzi indicated. When she finally came around the last corner, her jaw dropped open. Never in her life could she have imagined a view like this.

The rear of the palace sloped down steeply in great rocky terraces, each level overflowing with more greenery and blooms than even the jungle surrounding them. Orchards of trees sagged under the weight of their sweet-smelling fruits. Along the rocky side walls hung more plants in various pots, re-creating a feeling of the jungle canopy. Flowers arranged in boxes and planters painted the landscape with violets, reds, and whites, like her rainbows had painted the banquet hall.

In addition to the plant life, ponds and streams interconnected and flowed into one another and small waterfalls rushed down the terraces onto rocks until the edge of the garden plunged out of sight in the distance. Mayana assumed that was the end of the plateau, recalling the cliff stretching down to the jungle floor.

Birds twittered around her, flitting from bush to bush, and monkeys scurried around the branches of the tallest trees. Numerous bathing pools were tucked into rock-cut terraces, fed by the flowing water that wove through the garden like a shining snake. The pools were plastered and tiled with intricate masonry, and more beautifully decorated tiles created a winding path through the foliage. The pool closest to her teemed with fish and water birds.

The garden and everything about it breathed life, renewal. She found herself thanking Ometeotl for such a beautiful creation—and that no one else was here to disturb her. Finally, a few moments alone.

An overwhelming sense of peace overtook her as she made her way into the paradise, drawn to one of the bathing pools surrounded by rock walls hung with vines and a single waterfall cascading from a rock ledge above. How she loved the sound of water. She didn't even realize what she had been planning to do until her toes kissed the water at the tiled edge of the pool.

Mayana checked her surroundings and made sure she was alone before stripping off the fabric tied around her chest and shimmying out of her skirt. She yanked the feathered headdress off, hissing as a few stray tendrils of hair caught and were pulled out with the feathers. Dark strands hung in a mess over her eyes and she blew them out of her face while her feet pushed the feathered cuffs off of her ankles. Mayana's obsidian blade from Chimalli clattered onto the tile. She pulled off every bracelet, every necklace and earring, and piled the entire collection of belongings by a rock at the pool's edge.

Mayana's stomach twisted as she thought she heard a rustling sound behind her. A chirping bird escaped from a nearby bush and she relaxed.

Her face split into a smile as wide as a crescent moon as she observed her rippling reflection in the pool's surface. Her soul was light, free, for the first time in days. Easing into the water, she descended the stone steps that led deeper until the water lapped around her bare waist.

Mayana let her feet fall out from underneath her, and she slipped under the water's cool surface.

The sounds of the birds and flowing water silenced all at once. She let her arms float out in front of her, enjoying the sensation and wishing her heart could feel as weightless as her limbs. Mayana didn't ever want to re-surface, to return to the real world of pain and princes and blood dripping from knife blades. Maybe Ometeotl would allow her to become a fish and stay in this pool forever.

All too soon, her lungs began to sting in protest. Mayana let out the last of her breath in a great bubble. Bringing her feet back to the stone bottom of the pool, she stood so that the water lapped around her mid-dle. She brushed her hair off her forehead and leaned her head back into the waterfall, watching the way the droplets dashed themselves to pieces against the few large rocks jutting out from the terrace wall.

Mayana closed her eyes and let the water beat against the top of her head and shoulders, as if the water goddess herself was working the ten-sion from her muscles with pounding fists.

A low, distinctly *male* voice shattered the peace of her solitude.

"I thought I'd find you in one of the pools."

Mayana's heart leapt into her throat and she plunged into the water up to her chin. Her arms instinctively covered her chest.

"Your Highness," she squeaked in alarm.

Prince Ahkin leaned casually against the trunk of a cypress tree, watching her with his dark, calculating eyes.

Except for the golden bands around his upper arms, he had removed the ornaments he had worn to the welcoming banquet. White cotton draped around his waist, but his chest was bare. He was now a mere mortal like the rest of them, no longer a personification of the sun god. Although—Mayana sucked in a little water and coughed—he still took her breath away.

"I'm not exactly appropriate, my lord ..." she started, squeezing her arms around herself even tighter. How could her cheeks burn so hot in the cold water?

"Don't worry, I didn't look when you got in."

Mayana was shocked the water around her didn't burn into steam as she flushed deeper.

"I—thought I was alone."

"You were. I just got here." He pushed himself off the tree trunk and strode over to the edge of the pool. He stepped onto the top stone stair but sat himself on the side instead of joining her in the water.

"Metzi said you were heading toward the gardens. There is something I want to ask you."

Mayana pushed back against the side of the pool, forcing herself as far away from him as possible. She didn't answer, feeling naked and exposed in more ways than one. Thoughts swirled in her mind like Itza's flower petals caught in the whirlwind. He was going to ask about the jaguar. About the toucan. About her supposed "dedication" to the calendar rituals. And she was going to disappoint him just like—

"What's your name?" He tilted his head to the side.

Mayana flinched, but then slowly relaxed. That was the last question she was expecting.

"My name?"

"Yes, I do assume you have one." The corner of his mouth quirked up into a half smile. "Your rather unconventional introduction skipped over the announcement of your name."

"Mayana," she whispered, her lips hovering inches above the water.

He still waited, leaning slightly forward in anticipation. He hadn't heard her.

Mayana cleared her throat and tried again, slightly louder and with a little more strength.

"I am Mayana, descendant of the goddess Atlacoya, who sacrificed herself to save us from a flood and began the age of the Second Sun."

"Mayana ..." he mused, as if he was trying the name on his tongue.

"I'm sorry about the fire," she blurted out before she could stop herself.

"Why would you apologize for honoring the calendar stone with such devotion?" He raised an eyebrow.

Mayana dropped her eyes, refusing to meet his gaze.

"Oh. Yes. I mean, I'm sorry I did so with such ... such a scene." She floundered in the shallows of her explanation. She knew she should tell him the truth, but the words stuck to her tongue like tree sap. The shame of her inadequacy coupled with the knowledge that she was lying to the prince made her wish she could sink below the surface and never come back up.

"I thought your courage was admirable. I wish I had a faith as devout as yours."

Mayana swallowed a large gulp of water, and the future emperor gave her a glowing smile.

"My only wish is to serve the gods, my lord." *Except when I don't have the stomach to do what they ask of me.* She hoped the Mother did not smite her on the spot.

"I must admit, I'm amazed you can swim." Ahkin changed the subject, lifting a foot and dropping it back into the water with a small splash.

Mayana was torn between awe that he was taking the time to speak to her and horror that she was completely naked as he did so. Part of her wished he would leave so she could enjoy the water in peace, but another part of her wanted him to stay and keep talking—to give her his attention.

"We all know how to swim in Atl, my lord." Mayana shifted her arms slightly so that she wasn't squeezing her chest as tight. "My mother taught me to swim when I was a little girl. With all the rivers and canals in our city, it's safer to know how."

Ahkin's face crumpled and he dropped his gaze the moment she mentioned her mother. Mayana sucked in a breath through her teeth. She forgot that he would have lost his mother not even days before.

"Do you miss them?" Mayana's voice was quiet, and she wished she could reach out a hand and touch him.

Ahkin's eyes shot back to her face.

"No one has asked me that." The calculating expression was back, as if she was a complicated star chart he was struggling to understand. His voice sounded full of restrained emotion.

"I just know how I felt after I lost my mother. No matter how many people told me to celebrate the beginning of her journey, it still tore my heart to shreds."

Ahkin pursed his lips. "You lost your mother? Doesn't Atl have a healer?"

"She ... she fell. Down some stone stairs. By the time we found her, it was too late." The pain of the memory washed over her again, as though her father had come into her room to tell her only yesterday. It had been a full cycle of the calendar since her mother had died, but some wounds ran too deep to heal in the course of a single year.

"Too late ..." Ahkin's voice trailed off as he contemplated her words, his gaze distant and unfocused. "I guess even the holy power given to us by our ancestors cannot protect us from everything."

"No. I guess it can't." Mayana sighed.

"I'm sorry." Ahkin suddenly rose to his feet as though a lightning fish had shocked him. "I imagine you'd like to finish your bath. I should probably get back." He ran a hand nervously across the back of his neck, careful not to meet her eyes. "Mayana, daughter of water. It has certainly been a pleasure to meet you."

"And you, prince of light."

Ahkin stumbled out of the water and back onto the stone path. He took a moment to straighten himself and inclined his head toward her.

"I will see you this evening at dinner."

Mayana inclined her head, her heart aching for the obvious pain he worked so hard to hide.

The moment he disappeared around the edge of the rock outcropping, Mayana let out a large sigh and sank beneath the water. Prince Ahkin was not what she had expected at all. He radiated power and a quiet, stoic strength. At times he almost seemed to border on grumpy. Yet, beneath his prickly exterior, she sensed he craved more. Like a cactus hiding luscious fruit. She didn't want to admit it to herself, but she liked him. It warmed her heart to reach beneath his rough shell and see the core that waited just below, like a secret he was sharing only with her.

Ometeotl, why do you have to make this so hard? It's one thing to fear for my life, it's another to fear for my heart now too.

CHAPTER

20

"This task will test both your resourcefulness and insight." Atanzah held out a basket full of small bundles tied with cords. "You will be given a bag of cacao beans to buy a wedding gift for Prince Ahkin. He will judge his favorite."

Mayana exhaled with relief. She hadn't been sure what to expect for their next task, but it didn't seem too difficult. Buy the prince a present? At least no blood would be involved ... any blood that she knew of, anyway.

The noble daughters and Atanzah stood in the large courtyard beside a massive blazing firepit. Mayana had survived the evening and morning meals with grace, making more of an effort to hide her distaste for the ritual sacrifice that blessed the meals than she had the first morning. Back home, animal sacrifices were saved for feasts. Here, however, they performed them at every meal. The thought of so many animals losing their lives churned her stomach.

Zorrah had watched her with hawklike attention throughout the blessing rituals at both meals, and Mayana tried to be careful to give her nothing to notice.

"How are you feeling this morning, daughter of water? You looked a little unwell after this morning's meal blessing," Zorrah had said. Mayana didn't believe the look of concern on her face for a moment.

"I'm surprised to see anyone from Ocelotl feeling compassion," Yoli cut across, saving Mayana the necessity of responding. "Don't you host regular gladiatorial games to weed out the weak members of your society? I thought all your people cared about was proving who is superior."

"All life has value in the eyes of the gods. Thank you, Quetzalcoatl, for your gift of life," Itza chanted, her voice flat and emotionless. The other princesses stared at her in silence for several seconds, unsure if she was actually speaking to them or just to herself.

"Even beasts feel and can sense when others are in pain, daughter of fire," Zorrah finally purred, turning her attention back to Yoli.

The princess of Papatlaca threw her head back with a husky laugh. "Yes, I'm sure your concern for the princess of Atl is entirely genuine."

Mayana had just ignored them both. She ate her atolli and maize and pretended not to see how Ahkin's gaze continually lingered upon her. She had also pretended that it did not make her skin flush or butterflies flutter around in her stomach every time she caught his eye. Perhaps this task might give her an indication of his feelings toward her.

"Is this all we have to get the prince a worthy wedding gift?" The light and airy voice of Teniza of Millacatl turned slightly panicked. She held the bag of beans in front of her with a look of indignation etched upon her features. Mayana figured that since her family could literally grow cacao beans with a slice of their skin, she was used to having as many as she pleased.

She opened the small bag and dull black beans spilled onto her palm. They smelled like sun and earth. Teniza was right. There were only ten beans. That would hardly be enough to buy a single eagle feather, let alone a gift worthy for the prince.

"Ah, you have noticed," Atanzah said, positively beaming with mischief. "This is where the challenge comes in. You are being given very little to work with, so you must be creative in how you obtain this gift. A true empress can do much with only a little, and she can take what she is given and multiply it. Be resourceful, look at the city around you. Sometimes the true worth of a gift is in its significance instead of its value."

Mayana frowned at her hand. Significance instead of value? What was that supposed to mean? Her eyes flitted around the circle, and she was relieved to see the other girls furrowing their brows in confusion as well. A twinge of jealousy shot through her as she looked at Teniza. The princess of Millacatl could multiply as many as she wanted. But then again, that would be too easy, and surely Teniza wasn't foolish enough to use such a simple solution. Mayana relaxed slightly.

"Tonight at dinner you will present your gifts to the prince, so I pray you choose wisely."

Zorrah narrowed her eyes at Atanzah, but the animal princess did not question her. She might be as wild as a jungle cat, but Mayana had seen her pupils contract in fear. Perhaps she was not as fierce as she pretended to be.

"Off you go, ladies." Atanzah shooed them out of the courtyard and toward the main gate of the palace. "I recommend trying the shops and booths along the main plaza, though you are of course welcome to explore beyond that if you wish. We only request that you do not leave the confines of Tollan itself."

"Like we'd want to anyway," mumbled Yoli from Papatlaca, again twirling her long shard of obsidian between her fingers and looking bored.

Mayana inched slowly away from her and toward Yemania.

"Scared, daughter of water?" Yoli chewed the ring of obsidian protruding from her lower lip and lifted her eyebrows up and down tauntingly.

"No." Mayana's tone was as cold as the water in the river back home. "I would think that fire should be the one to fear water anyway."

Yoli's face broke into that same smile from yesterday that made the hairs on Mayana's arms stand on end.

After a moment, Yoli tipped her head to the side. "You are stronger than you look."

Mayana didn't respond. Why did everyone here have to tease her and play with her, as if she was a monkey performing for their entertainment?

"Good luck," said Atanzah. "I look forward to seeing what you can come up with."

Yemania rushed to Mayana's side the moment they were through the main palace entrance. Mayana slowed for her to keep up.

"Any ideas?" Yemania's eyes were wide and full of concern.

"Not yet." Mayana's thoughts buzzed around her head like bees, still frazzled and irritated from her interaction with Yoli.

They turned a corner that led them to the main cobblestoned avenue of Tollan. Yoli herself materialized out of the shadows and walked right behind them.

Mayana jumped, trying not the spill the precious beans onto the gold and stone tiles under their feet. "What are you doing?"

"Following you." Yoli shrugged. The fire princess had a resonant, almost husky voice. "You two seem more fun than the plant princess or the crazy one wearing dead animals. I can't even find the wind princess, she disappeared so fast. Probably rushing off to pray or something."

Yemania squeaked, but Mayana grinned. She appraised Yoli, taking in her sharp, severe hairstyle and dark, intimidating clothes, and couldn't decide what to make of her. Frankly, Yoli had terrified her at the welcoming feast, but now she wasn't so sure.

"So, you are from the volcano? What's that like?" Mayana tried to at least make polite conversation. Perhaps it would be better to have one less enemy here in the capital, even if they were still competing to sentence each other to die.

"Hot." Yemania and Mayana both waited for her to elaborate, but Yoli didn't.

She smirked with a look of satisfaction at their confused faces, like she enjoyed being difficult.

"Your city-state makes our weapons, doesn't it?" Mayana pressed. "I know obsidian comes from the liquid fire in the volcano."

"That's us." Yoli curled her lip mischievously. "So what's Atl like, daughter of water?"

"Wet." Mayana teased, playing Yoli's game of being irritatingly vague.

"I knew I liked you." She gave her a genuine smile this time.

Mayana couldn't help it, she laughed. This terrifyingly morbid girl from a mountain that oozed fire wasn't as scary as she seemed.

"So, what are we supposed to do with these beans?" Yoli held out her own small bag.

"We could put them together, perhaps?" Yemania suggested.

"How would we each get gifts then?"

Yemania's shoulders sagged.

"Too bad we aren't friends with the plant princess," Mayana said. "Or else we'd be able to grow more and just buy whatever we want."

"Good point, maybe I should have followed her after all," Yoli said. "Never mind. I think I'd strangle her with her own vines before she got the chance to sprout a single cacao pod."

Mayana snorted.

"Maybe we should split up and see what we can find?" Yemania nervously chewed her lip. Mayana had a feeling she just wanted to get away from Yoli but couldn't think how else to do it.

"Alright," Mayana said. "We probably should do this task on our own anyway." She winked at Yemania when Yoli turned her head.

Thank you, Yemania mouthed behind Yoli's back.

Poor Yemania. Mayana couldn't think of a way for the two of them to stay together without excluding Yoli. She actually didn't mind the company of the fire princess now that she had seen a little more of who she was, but if Yemania was still scared of her, she would do what she could to help her friend.

They split their separate ways, and she sighed, unsure of where to go or even how to start. Water could not earn her more money, so she would have to do something with the ten beans she had. Or maybe she could trade one of her jade bracelets?

The plaza in Tollan was twice the size of the market in Atl. Thousands of citizens from all over the empire milled about between the wooden stalls. Everything was on sale, from freshly grown produce to blankets and clothing, dyes and herbs, basic clay pottery and delicate ceramic serving vessels. Live monkeys, birds, and dogs in wooden cages filled the stalls with noise. Baskets overflowed with animal pelts and freshly caught fish, while racks and shelves boasted jewelry and bright feathers from exotic jungle birds.

She rolled the fabric bag around in her hand and bounced a little on her toes, anxious to go somewhere but not sure at all where that somewhere might be.

Out of nowhere, something heavy fell onto her shoulder. The warm, musky scent of fur enveloped her before the beans were snatched out of her hand. She threw her arms up to dislodge the creature, but it leapt off her as quickly as it had appeared.

Straightening, she batted the hair that hung disheveled across her face. Tan-and-white fur covered the long, lanky body of a squirrel monkey, its bright yellow hands clutching the small bag of cacao beans. Little beast. This was exactly why she hated monkeys.

"Give that back." She lunged for the monkey and it danced out of her reach, a small pink tongue protruding from between its dark lips. The liquid brown eyes taunted her as it let out a screech and disappeared over the straw roof of one of the nearest houses.

Mayana's pulse pounded behind her ears as her chest heaved. She wanted to hunt the little creature down and steal her beans back, but she would never catch it. The monkey was acting on *someone's* behalf. She did not have to think hard to guess who. Zorrah had found a way to use her ability with beasts to increase her earnings. She prayed Yemania and Yoli would not become the monkey's next victims.

"Next time, hold the beans a little tighter," a gravelly voice said behind her.

An older woman with a face as creased as mud cracks in a riverbed hobbled down the pathway. She was short, much shorter than Mayana, and her shoulders hunched over a crooked, spindly walking stick. The crone was dressed in a tunic dress and shawl that swirled in contrasting colors of white and black, matching her hair exactly. Strands of light and dark were pulled together into a knot that perched on the top of her head like an owl on a branch.

Mayana reached out and caught the frail woman as she stumbled forward, tripping over the uneven pavement. The cane clattered onto the stones and Mayana bent to retrieve it for her. Her heart lurched in pity.

"Thank you." The old woman exhaled and leaned heavily on her walking stick while Mayana helped to steady her. "Are you lost, young one? Why are you wandering the streets of the city alone?"

"I'm not lost. I was just trying to ... find a gift. For a friend. Someone important. But that monkey just ..."

"Stole every bean you have." Her face split into a toothy grin.

"Yes." Mayana let her breath out in a huff and resisted the urge to stomp her foot in frustration.

"If it is a gift you are searching for, I might be able to help you." The old woman picked at a spot on her wrinkled chin.

"I don't have any way to pay."

"Nonsense. You show kindness to an old woman and she will show you kindness in return." She grabbed Mayana by the elbow and led her away from the crowds toward a wood-framed doorway in a squat stucco building. A massive ceiba tree towered over the structure, casting it in dark shadow.

Mayana's instincts told her to run, but the bony fingers were strong and firm.

"No really, I don't—"

"Yoco," the woman said. "You may call me Yoco."

"Alright. Thank you, Yoco, but I need—" Mayana's mouth dropped open as she crossed the threshold into a low, small room that smelled like freshly cut herbs. Every surface was covered in dolls. Dolls as large as her forearm down to dolls as tiny as a fingernail. Some were woven from wool, others were made from folded and colored paper. The clothes they wore were as varied as a rainbow. Her eyes widened at the abundance of color and patterns.

"What are these?" Mayana picked up the nearest doll made from wool. She fingered the geometric patterns woven into the bright blue-and-yellow dress. It had slanting black thread for eyes and a tiny little red mouth like a chili pepper.

"Worry dolls," Yoco croaked. "Does your friend have many worries?"

Mayana laughed a little hysterically.

"Don't we all?"

"Indeed, we do." Yoco sighed. "The legends of the first people speak of a princess presented with a gift from the gods. It was a doll said to be able to solve any problem or worry a human could have."

Mayana nodded, not looking up. She had heard the story from her mother many times as a child. She even had a worry doll once. She had been a rather nervous and sensitive child and her mother thought it would be good for her. Her heart skipped at the memory of the tiny thumb-sized doll she had grown up with. She wondered what had happened to it.

Yoco gave her a knowing smile.

"Would you like one for your prince?"

Mayana's stomach twisted and she dropped the doll she was holding. She immediately stooped to pick it up again.

"My prince?"

"I know who you are, daughter of Atl, princess of water and descendant of Atlacoya." Yoco listed her head to the side, appraising her.

A drop of sweat ran slowly down Mayana's spine, making her shiver. She licked her dry lips before answering. "How do you know who I am?"

"I saw you arrive. You were covered in mud and looked like a skittish little deer running from hunters. My heart broke for you."

Mayana swallowed, her vision swimming with traitorous tears. The people watching her arrive *had* judged her. They thought she was weak, disheveled … destined to be sacrificed.

"I should go." Mayana placed the doll back onto the basket she had picked it up from and turned to leave. She didn't need this woman's pity.

"That is your choice, but I think this is exactly what you are looking for." Yoco drew her shawl tighter around her stooped shoulders.

Mayana paused midstep and turned to face her. How could this woman have any idea what she was looking for? She didn't even know herself.

"I don't think the prince would want a doll made for a child."

"The choice is yours to make, my dear. But who says my dolls are made for children? You do not have worries, princess? Do you think the prince himself does not have burdens?"

Mayana picked the doll back up and contemplated it. Maybe the best gift to give wasn't going to be something grand and expensive. Maybe the prince needed something personal, something that would speak to his heart. The pain within his eyes as he spoke of his parents was obvious. She knew of his responsibilities to raise the sun, to protect their people from Miquitz, and now to choose a wife and doom the other princesses to death. If it were her, she would drown under such a flood of worries. The longer she gazed into the plain, loving face of the doll, the more certain she felt. Yoco was right. A worry doll was exactly what she was looking for. Though the doll was only the size of her thumb, its demure little face looked hopeful, like it was already taking care of your deepest worries.

Her intuition flickered and suddenly she knew without a doubt. "I will take a doll after all."

"A wise choice, my dear. Now we can discuss the method of payment."

Her stomach dropped. Payment? Hadn't the old woman said that she would show her kindness?

"Oh, I thought …"

"Helping you choose the gift is a kindness. You still have to pay for it."

"How am I supposed to pay for it? You saw the monkey took every bean I had."

"Let's just say you will owe me a favor." Yoco winked. Mayana hesitated, rankling at the request. But what choice did she have at this point? She could either return with a doll or nothing at all, and she highly doubted the prince would appreciate nothing. Besides, she didn't want to return a failure.

"Alright." She pinched the bridge of her nose and hoped she wasn't making a promise she'd later regret.

Ahkin paced the length of the room three times before returning to the golden throne. He jostled his knees up and down and slapped the armrests impatiently. Where were they? Shouldn't they be back by now?

"Good gods, Ahkin, you are making me nervous. Just sit still." Metzi dug her teeth into the creamy flesh of an avocado. The crowd of nobles and honored guests gathered below the dais chattered away in anticipation of the night's meal and the princesses' gifts.

Ahkin placed his hands on his knees and pressed them down, attempting to quell the energy coursing through him. He was going to see her again. He couldn't *wait* to see her again.

"I've never seen you like this," Metzi said through a full mouth, leaning back on her cushion. "Could my brother have a favorite already?"

Ahkin glared at her and leaned over to grab the avocado out of her hand.

"Hey, that's mine." Metzi shoved him back playfully.

Ahkin raised an eyebrow and took a large bite out of the fruit before tossing it back to his twin with a smirking grin.

She clucked her tongue in mock disgust.

"You ruin everything."

"It's a brother's job."

"It's also a brother's job to provide his sister with a sister-in-law," she teased.

Ahkin rolled his eyes.

"Are we ready, my lord?" Atanzah strode into the room with her hands neatly folded in front of her. "The daughters are almost ready to present their gifts."

Ahkin's hands tapped against the armrests again, a short, fast rhythm like rain upon the palace roof. *Finally.* "Yes, I am ready."

"Hurry and bring them in before my brother bruises his hands," Metzi drawled lazily.

Atanzah nodded and readjusted her shawl before leaving to fetch the princesses. When she returned, they followed behind her like ducklings in the wake of a brightly colored mother duck. Ahkin shifted in his seat and leaned forward, his gaze immediately drawn to Mayana.

Mayana. The daughter of water and rainbows. The girl who had blazed into his life like the flaming red comet in the heavens. She demanded his attention with her outspoken dedication to their calendar, with such devotion to their rituals. The kind of devotion his mother had had. He could not forget her look of fierce determination as she summoned the water to douse the sacrificial fire, or the joy that had radiated from her as she watched the rainbows dance. *Light and water make something beautiful,* she had said.

But then, not only had she emanated life and spirit, she had the courage to rip away every pretext and speak straight to his heart. No one, not even Metzi, had asked him if he missed his parents. The empathy and compassion that had shone within her eyes stirred something within him he didn't quite recognize. He only knew he was drawn to her, like a moth to the flame of a torch. It was almost enough to distract him from the worries that incessantly tugged at his consciousness. Almost.

"Ladies, you will, in turn, present your chosen gifts to Prince Ahkin and explain the reasoning behind your choice."

He hadn't been sure what to expect from this particular trial. Atanzah had suggested it, arguing that whatever wedding gift the girls chose to give him would say a great deal about their characters. Ahkin had suggested adding the difficulty of limiting their funds. He wanted to see how creative they could be. One of his great-grandfathers had selected his empress after seeing her create a beautiful cloak after having been given only scraps to work with.

"Please continue." Ahkin waved a hand to begin, and Metzi gave a giggle of excitement. Cups clattered against wood as the many gathered nobles put down their drinks of pulque and cacao, attention now turned toward Ahkin. The princesses had formed a line up the center of the room before his throne, waiting to make their presentations.

"Lady Yemania of Pahtia," Atanzah announced, and the plump young woman with a rather unfortunate nose stumbled forward. Ahkin had hardly any memory of her from the night before, except that she had healed Mayana's palm. His focus had been on the daughter of water, not the daughter of healing. In Yemania's hands, she held a small plant in an equally small clay pot.

"That's Coatl's sister," Metzi whispered in his ear. A twinge of sadness pricked at his throat as he realized he might have to sentence his friend's sister to death.

Ahkin shushed his twin and batted her away like an irritating fly. Metzi stuck out her tongue at him and flumped back onto her pillow, crossing her arms.

"Fine, I can be quiet."

"That, I seriously doubt." But he lifted the corner of his mouth into a half smile.

He turned his attention back to Yemania, who stood frozen before him, her cheeks as red as her tunic dress. She looked nothing like her handsome brother. Was Coatl afraid for his sister? Could that be why he suddenly seemed so distant?

"I … I … bring my lord leaves of aloe," she said, her voice barely above a tremulous whisper.

"Thank you, daughter of Pahtia. Why have you chosen aloe as your gift to your future emperor?" His voice sounded deeper than usual from the formality of his address.

"Aloe has many known healing properties, especially for … sunburns. And as the lord of the sun, one never knows when aloe might be handy."

Ahkin smiled appreciatively as the crowd tittered and snorted in laughter. Even Coatl smiled in relief, though the healer wouldn't meet his eyes. What a clever gift. Not that sunburns were ever an issue for him, but he appreciated her thoughtfulness. His eyes wandered to Mayana, who gave Yemania a smile that glowed with pride. She seemed genuinely happy for the princess of Pahtia. A surge of warmth spread across his skin. Mayana's compassion was as evident as the sun was bright.

Atanzah announced the tiny storm princess. "Princess Itza of Ehecatl."

She was pretty, her small stature giving almost the impression of a bird, delicate and fragile. Her face spoke the opposite. He admired the warrior-like strength emanating from behind her eyes.

"I bring you a feather, my lord. In honor of the god Quetzalcoatl, who gave us all life and will someday return to the world he helped create."

Atanzah nodded approvingly, a wide smile crinkling her already wrinkled skin as she studied the princess of wind. He suspected Atanzah had already selected *her* favorite. Ahkin ground his teeth together at the thought. He had no desire to be so intimately connected with the city of Ehecatl, even if his father had arranged such a marriage for Metzi.

The presentations continued. Ahkin found himself distracted, waiting for the moment when Mayana would present her gift to him. He had to remind himself to be gracious as he received a glittering geode from the princess of fire, a headpiece of multicolored feathers from the animal princess, and a beautiful gold pendant inlaid with jade gemstones from Teniza of Millacatl. Teniza must have used her gift to acquire more cacao beans. Couldn't the princess have been a little more creative? Leave it to Millacatl to flaunt their excessive wealth.

He couldn't explain it, but none of the other princesses held the same interest for him as Mayana did. He hadn't really given the other girls much of a chance, but something about the princess of Atl drew him in. Perhaps it was her courageous commitment to their rituals, or her obvious insight and compassion toward those around her? Either way, something about her seemed to emanate passion and conviction in a way that inspired him to do the same.

Finally, it was Mayana's turn. She stepped forward, eyelashes turned down. He couldn't stop his eyes from roving over her slender yet subtle curves. His pulse thrummed at the way the skin of her legs peeked through the sides of her long blue loincloth skirt, and the way her long dark hair hung to her waist like a waterfall of obsidian. The way she moved even reminded him of water snaking around stones in a river—smooth, grace-ful … sensual. He shook his head as his thoughts wandered to places they shouldn't, and he reminded himself to focus on what she held in her hands.

One of his eyebrows twitched. It was a doll. A doll? He blinked and forced his eyes to look harder, but no, he had not made a mistake. A tiny doll no larger than a finger with a delicate little dress made of patterned blue-and-yellow fabric. It had a little blue shawl wrapped around its or-ange face and slanting black eyes made of thread. He heard a snort come from one of the other princesses, but he couldn't see which one. At that, a sliver of doubt at his choice pierced through his heart like a dart. Was she making fun of him? Was this some kind of joke to her?

"I present to my lord a worry doll."

Something about the name "worry doll" tickled the back of his brain, like a memory that danced just out of his reach.

Metzi took in a breath beside him, understanding dawning on her a little faster that it did for him. "Oh, I loved those as a child," she breathed.

Ahkin stood suddenly. Mayana's eyes went wide with shock and she took a small step back, biting her lip.

"What is a worry doll?" he demanded, probably more harshly than he meant to.

"I—they—there is a legend from the time of the first people that a princess was gifted with a doll that could solve any problem. It was a gift from the gods. So—" She hesitated, rubbing the fabric of its skirt between her fingers. "Worry dolls are said to possess magic from the gods. When you tell them your worries, the dolls help to fix them while you sleep." Their gazes collided across the short distance. Her eyes were deep and endless, pleading with him to understand her meaning. He sat back down.

"I know that the prince must have many worries, many burdens on his shoulders. It is hard to find joy when the pressures of the world threaten to crush you with their weight. So, I wanted to give Prince Ahkin something that would help relieve his burden, if only a little."

With those words, she had ripped the dart of doubt right out of his heart. There was no present she could have gotten that could possibly be more appropriate. He did feel like a little boy, a little boy attempting to wear his father's headpiece that was much too big for him, a little boy that craved the warm hand of his mother against his cheek. His worries were as heavy as the volcano of Papatlaca. He worried for his kingdom, for the dying sun, for the thousands of lives that now depended on him to keep them safe, for his lack of faith in trusting the will of the gods. Some powerful emotion tightened his throat as he took in the small doll from Mayana's hand. The gift said, "*I know you are burdened, and I wish to help relieve you of your sufferings.*" Ahkin immediately forced the emotion down and away—he just couldn't handle it right now.

He lifted a fist to his mouth and cleared his throat.

"Thank you, Mayana of Atl. Your gift is more appreciated than you know."

He could see the relief spread across her face at his words. Her shoulders relaxed and she gave a small bow before taking a seat on one of the cushions to his left.

He turned to address his guests.

"Thank you for joining us in the next step of this sacred selection ritual. Before the meal, I need to make an announcement. As you know, the Nemontemi approaches. It is a dangerous time when the layers of creation are unstable. We will begin our preparations and rituals tomorrow to ensure that we are protected from the evils and spirits that will be roaming the earth at that time. I encourage each of you to do the same in your homes as well, that you may be protected from the bad luck of the last days of the year."

There was a general rumble of concerned agreement.

"Let your minds rest at ease. I intend to have a new empress selected for you before that time comes. Now, let's enjoy the festivities of the evening and the gifts the gods have given to us."

Ahkin lifted his bowl of pulque and signaled for the high priest to commence the sacrifice that would begin the meal. He tried to ignore that fact that the sun was already much lower in the sky than it was supposed to be.

After the meal, Ahkin's stomach bulged with deer meat and tortillas. Servants meandered through the rooms with additional bowls of cacao and smoking pipes while the dancers and musicians prepared for the night's performance.

"Can I see the doll?" Metzi asked, picking it up before Ahkin could give her an answer. Their gourd bowls lay empty aside from several leftover crumbs, waiting for servants to come and remove them.

"Go ahead," Ahkin said. "I always love how you ask before you take things."

"Where do you think I learned it? It's not like you ever ask my permission about anything."

"Will you two stop bickering?" Atanzah chimed in, though she gave them both a good-natured grin. "Now that your mother is no longer here to tell you that, I feel it is my responsibility as her oldest friend to keep the both of you on your best behavior."

Ahkin chuckled and tilted his head toward the old woman. "You do realize, Atanzah, I could choose a different matchmaker to oversee the selection ritual?"

"But no one will oversee a wedding like the one I have planned for you." She patted Ahkin's cheek in a loving way before removing his empty bowls. Ahkin rolled his eyes at the old matchmaker.

"Oh, it's charming," Metzi cooed, smoothing back the threaded hair of the worry doll. "And I love how it is so small, you could carry it around with you all the time."

Ahkin grunted an acknowledgment. He didn't want to let his sister know how touched he had been by Mayana's gift. An accomplished warrior should not be happy to receive a doll, after all.

"Just imagine, you could tie it to the end of your macana sword. General Yaotl would be so impressed." She thrust the doll into his face and shook it, her laughter filling his ears.

Ahkin snatched the doll away from her and tucked it under his leg. Metzi's lower lip jutted out into a familiar pout.

The rapid beats of the drums suddenly filled the room, accompanied by the hiss of rice- and bean-filled gourds.

"Just enjoy the festivities, dear sister."

"Dance with me." Metzi's face lit up like the temple in the light of the newly risen sun. She gripped his hand and shook it up and down in short, jerky movements.

"I don't dance."

"You must show the daughters of the noble families what a terrible dancer you are."

"*I don't dance*," Ahkin repeated, all teasing drained from his voice.

"What is a battle but a dance between warriors? Come on, *dear brother*, if we are lucky, several of the girls may volunteer to be sacrificed rather than marry you. Besides, once you ship me off to Ehecatl to marry their boring, pious prince, we won't have as many chances to irritate each other."

Ahkin growled but reluctantly let his twin drag him onto his feet.

Mayana looked up as Ahkin let his sister pull him into the center of the room. The look on his face clearly said he didn't want to be there. The music of the drums and shaking gourds intensified, and the dancers in costumes welcomed the prince and princess into their midst.

Metzi seemed to be halfway dragging the prince through the first few drumbeat cycles before he joined her in the choreographed movements of the dance. Mayana couldn't help but notice how lithe and light on his feet the prince was. He jumped and spun and stomped his feet as well as any of the dancers on the floor. Mayana leaned her chin on her hand and lost herself in the movement of the muscles of his legs ... of his wide shoulders.

"Careful, daughter of water, or you are going to start drooling all over your sandals." Yoli nudged Mayana with her shoulder.

"What?" She jerked her chin up.

Yoli laughed. "You're as pathetic as Teniza. Fawning over the prince like he's Quetzalcoatl himself come back from the underworld."

"I am not." Mayana rubbed her elbow where it had slipped and hit the wooden table.

"Teniza fawns over the prince?" Yemania leaned across Mayana to get a better look at Yoli.

The fire princess absently bit at the obsidian ring on her lip and shrugged.

"Yeah, the cornstalk spent the whole hour before the feast going on and on about how handsome he is. I wanted to gouge my eyes out." Yoli lifted the tip of her obsidian shard toward her eyes.

"Let's refrain from any eye-gouging during the feast, please." Mayana placed her hand gently on Yoli's wrist and lowered the shard away from her face.

"Fine," Yoli said. "But I can't make any promises about after the feast."

Mayana gave a quick laugh but Yemania looked nothing short of terrified. She obviously didn't get Yoli's humor at all.

"Don't *you* think Prince Ahkin is handsome?" Yemania eyed the obsidian shard like it was a snake about to bite her.

"I'd definitely rather look at him than the backside of a capybara, if that's what you mean."

Mayana snorted into her cacao drink and then sputtered as she choked on it. Yemania thumped her on the back and glared at Yoli.

"Relax, daughter of Pahtia. I am no competition to either of you. I know the prince will not choose me. I'm not afraid to begin my trek through the underworld."

Yemania's eyebrows shot up.

"Aren't you afraid of the pain of how they will kill us, at least?"

Yoli's expression went flat as she tilted her head down to survey Yemania.

"Really?" She twirled her weapon between her fingers again. "You think *I* would be afraid of the pain?"

Yemania leaned back so that Mayana blocked their view of each other.

"There's something wrong with her," Yemania whispered, shaking her head slowly.

"There's something wrong with all of you." Zorrah sneered and leaned over from Yoli's other side.

"Nice gift," Mayana said, narrowing her eyes at the animal princess. "How did you ever afford to buy such an expensive headpiece with only ten beans?"

"Oh, you know, I found some extra ones that some careless person must have left lying around." Zorrah widened her eyes innocently.

"You're just scared the prince will pick Mayana." Yoli flicked a kernel of corn at Zorrah, but she batted it away with a hiss.

"Careful, fire princess." Her eyes flashed dangerously.

"Why? The worst you can do is send me to the underworld, and I'm going there anyway. You'd just speed up the process."

"Don't you have any sense of self-preservation?" Zorrah brushed her long ponytail over her shoulder as she spoke.

"Like you, you mean? You are a beast yourself, princess of beasts. Your determination to save your own skin is evident to us all." Yoli waved a dismissive hand and laughed.

Zorrah glared, obviously seething with a fury that could rival the bloodlust of a wolf. Mayana understood Zorrah's anger, her desperation. Competition was a way of life to her. She just didn't want to lose—that was a feeling Mayana could relate to. Mayana simply had entirely different methods of winning the prince's heart.

She took another bite of meat, chewing it thoughtfully as she watched Ahkin dance with Metzi. Her heart swelled with admiration as a smile broke across his face, finally allowing himself to get swept up in the passion of the music. He was so serious and calculating at times that she loved seeing those moments when he softened. Mayana made it a personal mission to see as many of them as she could before … well, the end. One way or another.

"I'm surprised you can handle eating meat without crying," Zorrah's voice said casually.

Mayana swallowed as Yoli and Yemania both turned to face her. Yemania's lip trembled while Yoli cocked her head to the side.

"I don't know what you mean, Zorrah." Mayana tried to keep her voice steady.

"I think you do, and it will be interesting to see how long you can keep your particular … *aversion* a secret from the prince."

"What aversion?" Yoli raised an eyebrow.

"I have no idea what she's talking about." Mayana tore a tortilla in half and shoved it into her mouth. Yemania looked determinedly at her lap as she twisted her hands.

"Mayana, would you like to dance?" said a low voice.

Mayana swallowed the tortilla before it was fully chewed, making her throat ache. Why did his voice already sound so familiar? Her pulse pounded behind her ears as she lifted her gaze to meet Prince Ahkin's. He stood above her, hand outstretched and waiting. She glanced sideways at Yemania, whose mouth formed a perfect circle of surprise, and then at Yoli, who nodded her head toward the prince as if to say *Well? What are you waiting for?* Mayana imagined every eye in the room fixed on her as she slowly slipped her hand into his and rose to her feet.

Mayana followed him toward the other dancers, sure she was going to trip and land in the brazier. Her stomach churned as if she had swallowed snakes. She focused on her feet, making sure that they functioned properly, and on the warm, soft hand that was wrapped around hers.

He must use pigeon cream on his hands. She smiled at the thought.

When she lifted her gaze, he was smiling at her. Her face flushed warmer than the brazier fire.

His feet began to move in quick stomping motions in time with the almost impossibly fast drumbeats that pounded within Mayana's chest. He released her hand and spread his arms wide as he moved with the beat, kicking out his legs in time with the other dancers. She took a deep breath and let the music sweep her along with him.

Mayana thought the biggest risk would be getting hit in the face with feathers from one of the enormous headdresses of the nobility and dancers twirling around her like giant, wild turkeys. Some of them were literally taller than the person wearing them. Many of the dancers carried instruments rattling with dried beans, jingling bells around their ankles, and shields adorned with feathers. She secretly thanked Ometeotl that her father had made sure she learned the fast-paced footwork of the celebratory feast dances.

The tempo of the drums picked up to a near frenzy and Mayana's heart beat its own frantic rhythm from the exertion of the dance. Yells and cheers from those around her called out between rhythms. It was easy to get lost in the intensity of it all, in the haze of herb smoke from the pipes hovering around them and the throbbing in her head from the fermented pulque drink.

The Chicome viewed their dances as a form of prayer, a way to communicate with the gods. Mayana completely understood—the emotion of the music and the movements brought literal tears to her eyes. When the music finally stopped, the prince reached forward and wiped a tear from her cheek. His chest heaved, and his breathing was as heavy as hers. As his thumb brushed across her skin, she reached her hand up and held it briefly over his.

It was as if the world around them did not exist. She was alone, alone with this sun-god-made-flesh whose gaze bored into her eyes with a look of such intensity she feared she might burst into flame. His hand was against her cheek, so warm, so close. Ahkin took a step toward her, closing the distance between their bodies until he stood only inches from her. Mayana didn't think she could breathe any harder and faster than she already was.

A series of excited, earsplitting yells shattered their isolation as one of the dancers moved through the crowd holding a bowl of fire in his hands. He placed the bowl on the ground and motioned for the drums to begin the next dance, the dance to honor the god of fire.

As if she had been doused in cold water, awareness of her surroundings cleared Mayana's mind. Her gaze focused over Ahkin's shoulder and settled on the tear-stricken form of Yemania, fear and heartbreak painted as clearly on her face as the paint swirling across her cheeks.

And next to her, the murderous glare of Zorrah chilled Mayana to her bones.

23

Mayana removed her headdress and placed it on one of the baskets her aunts had packed for her. Her soul seemed to grow lighter with each piece of jewelry she discarded.

She threw herself onto her bed mat, not even bothering to change her clothes, and burrowed into the rabbit furs. She had tried to talk to Yemania after the feast ended, but the daughter of healing ran back to her room before Mayana got the chance.

She had hovered outside of Yemania's curtain for a good ten minutes, debating whether or not to go in, but Yemania's sobs could be heard even out in the hall. Mayana didn't know if she was crying because the prince obviously favored someone other than her, because this meant the selection and her death were drawing near, or because Mayana might not be there with her when she did die. Maybe it was a combination of the three.

While Yemania was the type to dissolve into tears and accept the cruelty of her fate, Zorrah was not the type to give up without a fight. And this made her more and more dangerous. She had already sent a jaguar after Mayana and tried to ruin the trial of the gifts, and Mayana didn't doubt for a moment that Zorrah would try again. Her only hope was that the protection of the prince would deter the animal princess, but she wouldn't count on that.

Her stomach tightened as she remembered Zorrah's taunt about the deer meat. The prince currently thought her an example of dedication to the rituals, not someone who questioned and fought against them.

Mayana grimaced into the furs, not wanting to think about what Zorrah could possibly do to her.

A clatter came from the garden just beyond the vines draping her room's opening to the outside. She lifted her head, straining her ears for a sound. *Clack. Clack—clack—clack.* Her eyes fell to the floor, where a pebble rolled to a stop against the stones.

Throwing off the furs, Mayana scrambled to her feet. She stooped over and picked up the small lopsided stone, turning it over in her fingers. It was probably the stupid monkeys in the garden. Another stone clattered in and landed inches from her foot.

Fuming at the memory of the monkey stealing her cacao beans, she tightened her hand around the stone and threw it as hard as she could through the vines. It sailed through the hanging plants. A male voice grunted in pain.

Mayana's hands flew to her mouth in surprise. She threw the vines apart and found Prince Ahkin standing at the foot of the small flight of stairs leading into the botanical garden below her room. He was rubbing a spot just above his left eye and squinting up at her.

"Oh gods! I am so sorry." She flew down the steps, but stopped a few paces from him, hands still covering her mouth.

"I wasn't expecting you to throw the stone *back*." He lowered his hand and studied it as if checking for signs of blood.

"I don't think it's bleeding." Mayana reached out and fingered the small bulge above his eyebrow.

Ahkin winced at her touch and pulled away. "It's alright, I've had worse."

"What are you doing out here?" Mayana rubbed her arms up and down and looked around to make sure they were alone.

"I—" Ahkin rubbed the back of his neck uncertainly, frowning down at his feet. "I just wanted to see how you are doing."

"How I'm doing?" The corner of Mayana's mouth ticked up. She could tell he was nervous. It was endearing to watch his internal struggle.

"Yes—um—how is your room? Is it arranged to your liking? I made sure to ask Atanzah to—"

She giggled.

Ahkin's face fell into a frown.

"My room is fine, my lord. Why don't you tell me the real reason you are here throwing pebbles?" She wondered if she was being too forward, so she gave him a reassuring smile. Ahkin's sheepish grin and flushing cheeks told her he did have different intentions.

"Would you—want to take a walk through the gardens with me?"

"At night? Alone?" The many flaming torches that reflected off the hundreds of gold surfaces kept Tollan as bright as day at all hours, but the gardens? They wouldn't be as bright ... and night was when spirits and demons roamed the jungles.

Ahkin lifted a small blade and waved it back and forth in front of her nose.

"You will be with one of the Chicome's best-trained warriors, who also happens to have the power to bend light and raise the sun itself if necessary."

Mayana pushed his hand back toward him. "Who also happens to be exceedingly modest?"

"I'll do what I have to if you'll agree to come with me." His eyes turned pleading.

"If I get eaten by a star demon, I am holding you personally responsible."

"Does that mean you'll join me?" The hope and joy radiating from his face warmed her heart, almost as if he had truly feared she wouldn't want to.

"Yes, I'll join you."

Ahkin held out a hand and she reached for it, lacing her fingers with his. It was entirely new and foreign to Mayana, holding the hand of someone who was not family. She would often hold Tenoch's hand back home, though he would bounce up and down with excitement about wherever they were going. The prince's hand was solid and steady, and Mayana suddenly worried that her palms would start sweating. Was she squeezing his hand too hard? Not hard enough? Why had her father taught her every important ritual and rule under the sun but not how to hold the hand of a prince? Surely that would have served as a helpful lesson given how the codex dictated the selection of the Chicome's empress. Then again, Mayana tried to imagine her stoic father giving her such a lesson and she had to bite her lip to stop from laughing.

"I enjoyed watching you dance this evening." Ahkin walked slightly ahead of her, leading the way through the small garden and then into labyrinthine halls toward the rear of the palace.

Blood rushed into her cheeks. "I enjoyed watching you dance as well."

The prince let out a disgruntled snort. "I—don't usually dance."

"Why? I thought your dancing was … moving."

Ahkin smirked. "Isn't all dancing technically moving?"

"You know what I meant." She gave him a playful smack on the arm.

"You dare to hit the prince of the sun and your future emperor?" He raised an eyebrow.

Shame and fear flooded Mayana's veins. Had she gone too far?

"I'm sorry—I didn't—"

But to her surprise, Ahkin roared with laughter and squeezed her hand tighter.

"You will need to learn not to take me so seriously," he said. "You should see the way Metzi and I tease each other."

She would need to learn? Was that a promise for the future? Mayana's heart fluttered like the wings of a hummingbird. But she still couldn't shake the feeling she had overstepped a boundary with her playfulness. She dropped her gaze to their pacing feet and refused to meet his eyes.

"Mayana." Ahkin stopped and turned to face her. "Please don't ever hide yourself from me."

He pinched her chin between his thumb and forefinger, forcing her to look up at him. "So far, what I have seen of your spirit and courage and compassion has done nothing but recommend you to me. Your dedication to the gods reminds me of my mother's own devotion. Your joy and appreciation for beauty, the way your face illuminated as you watched the rainbows we made together. The way you sensed my own"—he swallowed hard—"difficulty with losing my parents. You even gave me a present that showed you understand the worry I have found overwhelming me since they died."

Mayana's heart swelled at his words and yet she couldn't help but feel a little sad at the same time. He was obviously lonely and hurting. It likely had to do with losing his parents and being afraid of the responsibilities thrust upon him, but she feared he was idealizing her. He was seeing what he wanted to see and trying to lose himself in the distraction of choosing a wife.

That, or he just wasn't looking as hard as he should. He wasn't seeing how her compassion could get her into trouble. How she hated sacrifices and even questioned why the gods demanded blood in the first place. She was starting to fear that what Yemania had accused her of was true. She was selfish. What if Mayana couldn't stand to deal with pain or see it in others and that was what drove her to compassion? What if her empathy was a form of self-preservation just like Zorrah's? She hated herself for even thinking it ... but what if it was true?

" ...and more than that, the way you did not care about anything but making sure we pleased the gods by not sacrificing that jaguar. That was so brave. The way you gave yourself over to the worship of the gods through your dancing. Your devotion to them shames even my own and makes me want to strive to worship them with the same ... reckless abandon."

Ahkin's words pierced her heart like a spear. He was definitely only seeing what he wanted to see. Mayana's eyes roved over his face, taking in the curve of his lips and the shadow across his chin. She longed to reach up and see if his cheek was as rough as it appeared. Would it be so bad if he held her up to an idealized standard? As long as he chose her, her life would be spared. Did he have to choose her for the right reasons?

With his fingers still holding her chin, he leaned toward her. She should stop him—he was trying to kiss the Mayana he had made up in his own mind because of how he thought he felt toward her—but she didn't. She wanted to kiss him too, because she was beginning to feel the same way. This beautiful, glorious warrior prince whose dark, calculating eyes she alone could soften.

Their lips met for the briefest of moments, like the brush of a moth's wing. He pulled back, searching her eyes for a response, and Mayana shuddered. She didn't care anymore. She would be whatever he wanted her to be in that moment, as long as he kissed her again. He must have seen the desire in her eyes because he crushed his lips to hers.

He pulled her toward him, one hand pressed against the exposed skin of her lower back. His other hand moved from her chin to cup the back of her head. The warmth of his palm against her skin sent a shiver up her spine, and she leaned into him, spreading her hands on his chest, thankful he had removed his golden jewelry so that her fingers could trace his flesh and not the carved metal.

Mayana had never held hands with a boy before, let alone kissed one, and she immediately wondered why she had rejected the advances the boys of her city had offered her. This was *wonderful*. Ahkin smelled of xiuhamolli soap, a fresh herbal scent she loved. His lips were as soft and full as she had imagined the first moment she saw him, and they were firm but gentle as they moved against her own. He was pure, radiant sunlight, warming every inch of her skin …

A clatter of wood against stone echoed through the hallway, and they broke apart. Ahkin closed his eyes and bit his lower lip, breathing hard, before turning to glare at the servant who was sweeping up the wooden bowls she had dropped onto the floor.

"S-sorry," the servant girl whispered. She quickly gathered the bowls and backed around the corner, her face aflame.

Mayana sucked in a shuddering breath, longing to pull Ahkin back into their embrace. Instead, when he turned back to face her, he gave her an amused grin and jerked his head down the hall.

"We were going to see the gardens, weren't we?"

"If you say so," Mayana breathed, lightheaded.

Ahkin brushed another quick kiss across her lips and pulled her down the hall toward the back of the palace.

Would it be so wrong to pretend to be the girl he wanted, to be overly dedicated to the gods? But as she looked down at his hand, which held so tightly onto her own, her mind imagined those same hands dripping with the blood of the toucan he had sacrificed. She heard the memory of the strangled screech before it went silent forever. An image flashed in her mind of the tiny black-and-yellow bird in her own hand back in the palace of Atl, the bird looking up at her with its glassy, bead-like eye as she lifted her knife toward its throat. She could still see the disappointment mixed with rage in her father's eyes as he waited for her to prove she could do what was necessary.

Maybe she needed a worry doll of her own.

CHAPTER

24

"What's at the end of the gardens?" Mayana pointed to where the trees and shrubbery dropped down into blackness. The red comet still flared against the night sky, but Mayana was too distracted to think much on it. Their footsteps on the stone tiles of the garden path were the only sounds aside from the waterfalls dashing against the rocks in the bathing pools. Mayana assumed most of the animals had sensed them coming and were hiding in more secluded parts of the pleasure gardens.

"That's the end of the city's plateau." The muscles in his neck tensed, and Mayana sensed there was something he was not telling her.

A raised stone platform hugged the cliff's edge. Intricate hieroglyphs were carved into its surface. What kind of ceremony was performed here? Curiosity got the better of her and she led them toward it, wanting to see the details for herself. A small set of stone stairs led up to the platform's surface, and up close, she recognized the histories of the gods depicted in the stone. She pulled Ahkin up to the top, though his hand tightened slightly, as if he was fighting the urge to pull her back. His gaze focused over the side of the cliff, and she carefully leaned over to see what lay below.

It was a sinkhole larger than any she had seen before, scarring the landscape like a gaping open wound. It looked big enough to swallow the Temple of the Sun whole. Vines and plants dangled precariously over the sinkhole's lip. The blackness within it seemed endless, pulsing with an energy bordering on sinister.

Ahkin draped an arm across her shoulder and drew her closer to him, as if to protect her from the drop.

His voice was tense. "That's the sinkhole that leads to Xibalba."

A sudden chill swept across her skin.

"Are you cold?"

"No, I just ... didn't know you had an entrance to the underworld here in Tollan." She nestled in closer to him, wrapping an arm around his waist. The chill subsided. She was tempted to trace her finger along one of the defined muscles of his stomach, but she resisted. Good gods, he was beautiful. His constant battle training left his body fit and lean and absolutely breathtaking.

He turned away from the sinkhole and led her back down the stone steps toward the gardens. "Well, technically it isn't *in* Tollan, more *under* it."

"Directly under it?"

Ahkin shifted his shoulder uncomfortably. She wondered if he was thinking about his parents' souls residing somewhere down there.

"Not literally. I haven't studied the layers of creation too extensively, but Xibalba is a different plane of existence altogether. The sinkhole is more of a gateway that leads there than a physical place, if that makes any sense."

Mayana had heard enough about the underworld. She tickled a finger against his side and he grabbed her hand to stop her. He lifted her fingers to his mouth and pressed a kiss against them. Mayana's stomach fluttered.

Ahkin gave one last look over his shoulder. "Ours and the doorway in Miquitz are the only two I know of."

"Miquitz has an entrance to the underworld too?"

"How else do you think the spirits of the dead mingle with the living?"

"I guess I never thought about it. Father doesn't talk about the Miquitz Empire much, and I'm honestly too afraid to ask. They terrify me."

"To be honest, they terrify me as well."

Mayana dropped her voice to a whisper.

"Is it true they allow the spirits of the dead to possess them during their religious rites?"

Ahkin gave a slow nod, his brow furrowed.

"Yes. They celebrate the dead and welcome them during the few days a year the dead spirits can roam the earth. Not many know, but the Miquitz priests even have means to possess the spirits of the *living* and control their bodies."

Mayana gasped. The thought raised goosebumps over her skin.

The rival empire was only about half the size of their own, but they had been enemies since the age of the Seventh Sun began. The Miquitz captured Chicome soldiers for their sacrifices, sometimes staging battles purely for that purpose. They were obsessed with the dead and the underworld. There were even rumors that their warrior costumes were not modeled after animals like those of the soldiers from Ocelotl, but skeletons.

"Have you ever battled with the death demons?"

"I have." Ahkin turned and showed Mayana a pale scar that crossed the length of his upper left arm.

She reached out a finger and trailed it down the puckered skin.

"What happened?"

"I caught the edge of a spear during a battle where they were doing a sacrificial raid outside of Ocelotl. I was lucky though." He ran a hand over his bicep. "Usually the Miquitz poison their blades with the secretions of poison dart frogs. Coatl thinks the blade had stabbed so many times that the poison had been mostly wiped off. Scared my mentor, Yaotl, half to death when he saw me take the blow."

Mayana stared at the prince, her jaw slack.

"Isn't that dangerous? For you to be on the battlefront? I mean, your blood is so important …"

"Well, when my father was still alive, it wasn't as crucial. Plus Metzi is still alive, and she can raise the sun as easily as I can. But it is essential for a leader to be a warrior. I've been training with Yaotl since I was a boy, and he is the greatest warrior in the Chicome Empire. Our soldiers will not respect me unless I earn that respect."

"I can respect that." A playful smile returned to her lips.

They reached the pool where she had been swimming yesterday morning, and Ahkin pulled her to a stop, his gaze wistful.

"I wanted so badly to go in the water with you yesterday, but I was too much of a coward."

"You can face the Miquitz demons of death with their poisoned blades and you were too afraid to ask to swim with me?" Mayana brushed her long hair over her shoulder. She kind of liked this idea of him being nervous. It made her feel less so.

"Is this pool deep?" He ignored her playful jibe.

"No, you could stand. You don't need to know how to swim."

"Good." The smile upon his face sparkled with mischief. And then Ahkin pushed her into the water.

With a shriek, she toppled in. The water that covered her head was much colder now that it was night, but she quickly regained her footing and stood, the water level just below her chest. What was he *thinking*?

She pushed her sopping hair out of her eyes as a large splash beside her told her that Ahkin had joined her in the pool. The wave of his entry buffeted her to the side before his head broke through the surface.

"There are much easier ways to get me into the bathing pool, you know." She splashed water at his face. What fun it was to tease him.

"I know, but I'm the kind who likes to jump in once I've made up my mind." He prowled toward her like a caiman in the river.

"I've noticed." Mayana didn't move, mimicking an unsuspecting deer in a caiman's sights.

He lunged and caught her against the stone wall of the terrace, his hands and muscular arms on either side of her head. With his body, he pressed her back against the wall. She didn't protest. His lips found hers. At first, they were cold and slick from the water, but they slowly warmed from the heat of their bodies.

Mayana wrapped her legs around his waist and deepened the kiss, her head swimming as if she had had too much pulque to drink. His tongue traced the corners of her mouth and her lips parted, meeting his tongue with hers.

Her hands slid up his chest and along his face, until her fingers dug into the short, wet strands of his dark hair.

Their mouths broke apart and she gasped as his kisses trailed along the side of her chin and down her neck. She shivered again at the sensation and his arms left the rock walls and wrapped around her instead, encircling her with their heat and strength.

She didn't know how long it lasted, only that she never wanted this moment to end. His hand snaked up under the fabric of her top and she grabbed his hand to stop him.

He broke their kiss and rested his forehead against hers.

"I'm sorry," he said, his chest heaving.

"Believe me, I don't want to stop you, but I also don't want to tempt you into defying the gods."

"Hmm?" he said, still distracted as his lips moved along her collarbone. Her skin was on fire and her body ached for him, but she also knew the strict nature of the codex. There were certain … practices that would have to wait until after a wedding ceremony. And Mayana feared that if she didn't stop them now, they would both lack the willpower to stop later.

She took his face in her hands and turned him to look at her. She could feel the rough stubble of his cheeks under her fingertips.

"I have to stop you." She planted another soft kiss on his lips to show him that she didn't want to.

"I know." Ahkin pulled back. Without the warmth of his body against her, Mayana suddenly realized how cold the water was. Her teeth started to chatter, and her body began to shake.

"Come on, we should get you in a steam bath." Ahkin directed her attention to a small stone bath house several yards down the path.

"I had a servant light a fire in it earlier," he admitted, looking slightly sheepish.

"You knew we were going to go swimming?" It was Mayana's turn to arch an eyebrow. So, he had planned this from the start.

"Well, I hoped." He winked at her, heaving himself out of the water and soaking the path around the pool. Mayana followed, careful not to slip on the slick stones.

The carved face of the goddess Tlazoltéotl watched over them with suspicious eyes from the wall of the steam bath as they entered.

"You know, Tlazoltéotl is also the goddess of passion and lust." Mayana moved her eyebrows up and down at Ahkin, trying to look serious. Her mouth twitched with suppressed laughter.

"Good thing we are alone then." Ahkin wrapped his arms around her shoulders and planted a kiss on her cheek. Her pulse quickened, but he removed his arms and grabbed a jar of water from beside the wall. He splashed the water across the glowing hot wall of the steam bath and the water turned to steam with a loud hiss, engulfing them in a warm cloud of moisture. Ahkin moved to lounge upon one of the low stone benches encircling the perimeter of the small room and patted the space beside him. Mayana self-consciously tucked her hair behind her ear and went to join him, her grin as wide and bright as the moon outside.

"Do you know what's amazing to me?" Ahkin's finger traced little patterns across Mayana's palm.

"What?" She wished she could wrap her arms around his neck, but it was much too hot in the steam bath to do more than hold hands.

"I've only just met you, and yet I feel like our souls know each other already."

"I know what you mean." Mayana was surprised by the strength of her attraction to him, but something buzzed in the back of her mind, like a pesky mosquito that she had to keep batting away.

Buzz. He is grieving and desperate for a distraction. *Buzz.* He only knows the Mayana he wants to see. *Buzz.* He will eventually discover you aren't as pious as you are pretending to be. *Buzz. Buzz. Buzz.*

But the adoring look in his eyes and the knowledge that being chosen would mean she wouldn't be sacrificed to the gods kept her from giving the thoughts the attention they deserved.

"What's your day sign?" Ahkin asked, pulling Mayana away from her internal battle.

"I was born on the day of the flower."

"Hmmm, so that means you are creative, you appreciate beauty, and you like to dream. It also means you can be idealistic and stubborn."

Mayana shrugged. "You know your day signs well, my lord."

"I have studied the day signs and the stars since I was a child. Our priest, Toani, says that our destinies are written in the stars."

"What's your day sign?" Mayana asked him.

"Metzi and I were born on the day of the earthquake."

Mayana squinted in concentration, trying to remember what the codex said about the sign of the earthquake. "So you are most dominated by intelligence and practicality. You have a tendency to put your head above your heart?"

She peeked at Ahkin, waiting for his confirmation.

"Usually, yes. But for some reason, I've been giving my heart the most attention lately." Ahkin scooted toward her and put his head in her lap. Mayana's breath hitched.

"Well, I believe that if you ignore the heart for too long, when it finally does grab your attention, it often screams and demands that you listen." She ran her fingers through his hair and he closed his eyes at her touch.

"Spoken like a true flower. I feel like mine is definitely screaming at me to listen." His voice was soft and sweet like melted cacao as he nestled the back of his head against her thighs.

Mayana continued to run her fingers through his hair, studying the features of his face. The dark circles under his closed eyes hinted that he hadn't been getting much sleep, but the soft lips were curled up in a pacified smile.

"What do you like to do with your time back at home?" Ahkin asked her.

Mayana drew her eyebrows together.

"Nothing as interesting as studying the stars," she said.

"I'm interested."

"Well, mostly I help take care of my younger cousins. I help with cooking, cleaning. I spend a lot of my time swimming in Atl's bathing pools. My favorite place to be is in the water."

"That doesn't surprise me." His body rumbled with laughter.

"And ..." Mayana hesitated, wondering if it would be dangerous to tell him her favorite thing to do back home. Would it lead to questions she didn't want to answer?

"And?"

"And I love to spend my time with … animals."

"Animals? What do you mean?"

"Well, I love our dogs. I spend a lot of time playing with and taking care of our dogs. And rabbits. We have a lot of rabbits. And several turtles, and even …"

"It sounds like you have your own zoo back home. The naguals of Ocelotl would be proud. Which one is your favorite?"

"The dogs. I like that you don't have to be a nagual to make them love you. They are so eager to please, so loving and loyal"—her voice grew faster and slightly frantic—"they never judge you or expect anything from you that you can't give them. They love you no matter what."

Ahkin had opened his eyes and was looking at her with a strange expression on his face, almost like pity.

Her eyes stung as she remembered the pain of watching the ashes of her most beloved dog, Ona, smoldering in the embers of the sacrificial fire. She could still see her father's knife dripping with his blood. Mayana hadn't cared that it was the month of the dog, that the gods demanded the sacrifice. She had still tried to hide him, to keep him away from her father once he had told her what he intended to do.

At only eight cycles of the calendar, Mayana had not completely understood. Nor had she been adequate at hiding Ona. Her father had found him in her room not even ten minutes after she sneaked him out of the banquet hall. Mayana had thrown herself over the warm, dark body, her eyes locking with her father's as she begged him not to take her friend. She hated the pain of slicing her own flesh and didn't want Ona to experience it. She didn't want to lose him forever. Her screams and begging had attracted almost every member of the family until her mother literally had to restrain her as her father summoned a nagual. The man from Ocelotl controlled Ona to walk right out of her room without a backward glance. Mayana had sobbed and dug her claws into her mother's arms to escape.

The worst part was having to watch. Her father, believing she needed to learn the ways of their people, had forced her to sit and watch as he drew the blade across Ona's throat. As long as she lived, Mayana would never forget those dark glassy eyes and the feeling in her stomach as the light behind them faded. She had sworn to herself, then and there, that she would never sacrifice another animal. Her heart told her that something about the practice was not right. How could loving gods demand *this*?

Her extended family was so large that her turn as designated blood-letter did not come up very often, but she never stopped dreading when it did. When she was twelve, she had refused to the point of hysteria to sacrifice a lizard at their evening feast. Her father held her hand and forced it through the motions, while she fought him through gritted teeth. After it was over, the lord of Atl had slapped her cheek with such force that it knocked Mayana sideways onto the floor in front of every noble and family member gathered for the feast. It was the first and last time he ever struck her. Mayana's mother had rushed forward to stop her father from lifting his hand again, assuring him that next time, *next time*, Mayana would have matured enough to handle her responsibility.

That had been five years ago, and not until just days ago had her turn as bloodletter come up again. Her mother was no longer there to protect her from her father's anger, from his rage at what he probably perceived was Mayana putting all of their lives in danger. Mayana tried to under-stand, she tried to believe that something like sacrificing an animal could protect them from disasters. It hadn't protected her mother. Her mother always followed the rituals perfectly, and they hadn't saved her.

Ahkin's head tilted ever so slightly to the side as he studied her face.

"Your mind is somewhere else," he said, reaching up to smooth the creases in her forehead.

"I'm sorry," she said. "It's not important."

"You miss your family?" he guessed.

Mayana sighed. It was true, she did miss her family. She missed her brothers, her aunts and cousins, even her father. It was not what was pre-occupying her mind, but it would be a good answer to give.

"Yes," she said, not meeting his eyes. "I do."

"Well then, I am excited for when you get to see them again."

Mayana's breath caught in her chest.

"What? What do you mean, when I get to see them again?"

"I have an idea." His smirk was playful, teasing again.

"Will you tell me?"

"What will you give me to tell you?"

"Give you? I've already given you a doll. What more could you possibly want?"

He laughed and brought his finger to his lips as he pondered. "I know what I want ..." His hand slid suggestively up the skin of her leg and Mayana gasped.

"I can't give you that, so you will have to pick something else." Ahkin's hand froze on her thigh, and he made a great show of frustration as he growled at her.

"Fine, I guess I just can't tell you."

"You are going to drive me to insanity, my lord," Mayana huffed, the rate of her breathing steadily climbing.

Ahkin reached up and pulled Mayana's head down toward his own.

"I disagree, daughter of water. It is *you* who will drive me to insanity." And the world dissolved in the taste of his lips on hers.

CHAPTER

26

Mayana and Ahkin were both overheated by the time they left the steam bath. The cool night air soothed their flushed skin.

"I'm glad you came with me tonight," Ahkin said, snaking his fingers through Mayana's again as they walked through the darkened garden pathways back to her room.

"I'm glad I didn't hurt you when I threw that pebble at your head."

Ahkin lifted her hand and kissed it. "Me too."

"So, what happens tomorrow?"

"Tomorrow we have a ball game competition in honor of the selection ritual and then another feast at sunset."

"Will you dance with me?" Mayana couldn't wait to watch his beautiful body moving along with the beat of the drums again.

Ahkin sighed heavily, but then smiled. "As much as I hate dancing, I actually look forward to it with you."

A question quivered on the tip of Mayana's tongue like an arrow waiting to be released, but she bit it back. She would not press him.

"I would like to make an important announcement at tomorrow night's feast. One that I hope you will like."

Hope exploded through her chest at his words. Did that mean he was choosing her? Would she indeed live to see her family again like he promised?

She was afraid to give into the dreams that were forming in her mind's eye—dreams of a wedding and nights like tonight that were not hindered by the rules of the codex. Her cheeks burned at the thought.

Her joy was entirely complete as Ahkin pulled her in close for one last embrace. He pressed his mouth against hers, an air of promises hanging around them like the steam from the baths. He pulled away and kissed her one last time on her forehead before disappearing back into the dark garden.

Mayana mounted the steps to her room, biting her lip to keep the giddy giggle building inside her from escaping.

But as she entered, her body went numb and the joy drained from her heart faster than blood from the throat of a sacrifice victim. She was not alone.

Yemania stood before her, eyes red and puffy, an expression of horrified disbelief upon her face. Her expression screamed a thousand curses of betrayal without Yemania having to utter a single word.

Shame unlike anything Mayana had ever experienced burned deep within her stomach. She wished she could curl in on herself and never meet Yemania's eyes again.

"Zorrah said … but I didn't believe her … I didn't want to …" Yemania backed slowly away from Mayana, shaking her head.

"Yemania, I know what this looks like." Mayana held her palms out to Yemania in a gesture of peace.

"He's going to choose you, isn't he?" Her voice broke with the strain of her despair.

"I don't know, I think so? I—"

"We were going to die together. You promised me. We both knew our chances were slim and at least we wouldn't have to die alone. And now you're going to stand there and *watch*. You will be crowned empress and I … I …" She couldn't finish. The sobs that shook Yemania's body broke Mayana's heart into tiny fragments.

Mayana moved to embrace her but Yemania leapt out of her reach.

"How long do I have, Mayana? When will he announce his decision?"

Mayana folded her hands and dropped her head, tears flowing freely down her cheeks.

"When?" Yemania screamed at her when Mayana didn't answer.

"Tomorrow." Mayana's voice was barely louder than a whisper. "I think he might be making an announcement tomorrow night."

"And you think he will choose you?"

"I—I do." Mayana sank slowly to her knees.

Yemania's chest heaved as she drew ragged breaths, but when she spoke again, her voice was quiet and resigned.

"Well, it is done then." She turned on the spot and left, pushing the blue curtain of Atl aside. Before she disappeared back into the hall, she turned to face Mayana one last time. "I hope he knows the real you, what you really believe about the codex. If he is going to choose you, he at least deserves to know the truth." And with that, she was gone.

Mayana felt as though her heart might cleave in two. Still on her knees, she hunched forward, hands clenched as she fought against the burning sensation in the back of her throat. She rocked slowly back and forth, unable to stop the tears from pouring.

Her heart had been so full, so complete, only moments before. Mayana was ashamed to admit it to herself, but she had forgotten about Yemania in the excitement of her time with Ahkin. She had only thought about what his decision would mean for her, not for everyone else.

Maybe she was selfish after all.

How could she stand to watch Yemania sacrificed when she could barely stand to watch a bird? Mayana had never seen a human sacrifice before. The practice only happened in Tollan. The smaller city-states sent any enemy warriors they captured to the Temple of the Sun as tributes to Ahkin's father and to the gods. She had to find a way to save Yemania. She didn't know how, but she would talk to Ahkin, convince him somehow.

When she had enough strength to gather some of her composure, Mayana forced herself to crawl to her bed mat and collapsed into the furs. She couldn't wait to lose herself in the oblivion of sleep.

Without warning, a piercing, burning pain shot through Mayana's right calf. It was as if she had been shot by a blow dart—a flaming blow dart. Mayana let out a high, uncontrolled scream. The pain was excruciating, and before she could react, it struck again, and then a third time.

Throwing the furs off herself, she scrambled to her feet, trying to get away from whatever was stinging her.

The movement of the blanket revealed the jointed black body of a scorpion. It rattled across the stone floor, its stinging tail hovering over its beetle-black head.

Mayana stumbled back, the burning sensation in her lower leg spreading, throbbing with each beat of her frantic heart.

The scorpion was as large as her hand at least. It scuttled toward her upon its many legs, as though determined to continue its attack.

Mayana screamed again and backed herself into her baskets of clothing, stumbling over them and falling onto her backside. Her hands groped among the crinkly woven fibers and soft clothing until her fingers closed around something solid and metal. She lifted the hideous half-sun headpiece her aunts had packed for her and brought it down with a sickening crunch on top of the scorpion's shining, dark shell.

Heart thundering, Mayana sank back into the mess of clothing and shattered baskets, arching her back and gritting her teeth at the pain surging through every nerve of her body. What kind of scorpion had that been? How had it gotten in her room? More importantly, was it poisonous?

Mayana could feel the skin of her leg swelling and stretching tight where the barb had pierced her skin. The burning sensation continued, but now Mayana started to notice a throbbing in her head. Her ears felt as if someone had stuffed them full of cotton. The tips of her fingers started to feel numb, and nausea roiled her stomach.

Definitely poisonous, then. She had to get help immediately. The poison was already flooding through her system, especially with having been stung three times. She tried to push herself to her feet, but her arms were made of water, and her legs were no better. Mayana wobbled dangerously and fell hard on her side.

Terror sharper than the scorpion's barb pierced her heart. If she didn't get help, she was going to die. All her dreams for the future seemed to crumble through her fingers like sand. It couldn't end like this. It wasn't fair.

Mayana thrust out a hand and clawed at the woven mat beneath her, dragging herself forward. The door. She had to get to the door.

"Help!" Her scream ripped through her dry throat.

Using her good leg, Mayana continued her clumsy, sluggish movements across the floor. Whimpers and cries of pain escaped her with every inch she gained. She was almost to the curtain. Her tongue was numb and swollen, and her head felt like a heavy stone. She wanted more than anything to just stop moving. But she couldn't. Not if she wanted to live to see the morning.

With each strain of effort, Mayana could feel her strength fading. She wasn't going to make it. She would die here on the floor and Atanzah would find her body in the morning.

The edges of her vision started to go dark, but she continued to fight. Mayana pushed back against the darkness, back against the pain and exhaustion, but it wasn't enough. Her fingertips were just inches from the blue fabric of the curtain when the last of her strength left her and the world faded to blackness.

27

"My lord, I mean you no disrespect, but you seem—distracted." Yaotl, the commander of the Jaguar warriors, knocked the prince to the ground with an almighty sweep of his thick arm. Ahkin landed hard on his back, the wind whooshing from his lungs as his shield and macana sword skidded across the dirt. His pride seemed to leave along with his breath.

"What do you mean?" Ahkin coughed and rubbed his chest as he clambered back to his feet.

Yaotl lifted his wooden eagle helmet and mopped back the sweat that drenched his heavily lidded brow. Ahkin was pretty sure the older man had never smiled a day in his life.

"Your sparring is usually cleaner than this. You are sloppy."

"Let's go again." Ahkin shifted his shoulders up and down. He steadied his footing and lifted his shield and the flattened wood club inlaid with sharp edges of obsidian.

"No, I am afraid I would damage your pretty face before your wedding. Enough melee. If you insist on practicing, we can work with the bow."

Ahkin lowered his shield. Yaotl had trained him since he was a little boy and knew him better than anyone besides Metzi. As the most elite member of the Jaguar warriors, Yaotl officially possessed the title of fiercest warrior in the entire Chicome kingdom. He had captured more enemies than any other soldier—the fastest way for any peasant to rise to the status of nobility. The noble families bid and competed for the best warriors to sponsor their sons through training, but as the son of the emperor, Ahkin had secured the best mentor available. He had followed in Yaotl's shadow, learning and watching and eventually emulating him on the battlefield.

Yaotl was dressed in accordance with his status, a jaguar coat draped across his shoulders and his headband adorned with red, blue, and yellow feathers. His massive stature made him intimidating and fearsome even to Ahkin, who had seen the man in battle on many occasions.

Ahkin himself had captured only two Miquitz enemies, but he was well on his way to achieving the level of respect Yaotl commanded.

"You have decided which girl to marry, then?" Yaotl retrieved two large bows from a nearby basket along with a quiver of flint-tipped arrows.

"How do you know that's where my head is?" Ahkin grabbed the long wood bow strung with animal sinew and nocked an arrow. The back of his neck warmed at the thought of discussing women with his mentor.

"You may be the prince, but you are still a man, and nothing distracts a man more than a woman."

"Are you married, Yaotl?" Ahkin had never thought to ask him, after all these years.

"I am, my lord," he grunted in response.

"And … when did you know? That your wife was the girl you wished to marry?"

"I had known her since we were children. We grew up in the city together. I watched her turn from an awkward child into the beautiful creature she is now, and there is no one on Ometeotl's creation who knows me better."

"Hmm." Ahkin tensed his arm as he pulled back the bowstring and released the shark-tooth arrow toward the trees. It whistled past the trunk of the tree he had been aiming for. Ahkin lowered the bow with a frown.

"It happens to the best of us." Yaotl ripped the bow from his grip, a wide smile spreading across his face.

Yes, perhaps it did happen to the best of them. Ahkin rubbed the back of his neck, dumbfounded that Yaotl had actually smiled for a change.

Speaking of his own wife seemed to be the one arrow that could pierce through the general's toughened skin. "Fine, I think I need a break for the time being. How is the situation faring at the borders?"

Ahkin sensed the tension harden in Yaotl. There was something his commander was hiding. Did he think he could not handle it?

"What? What have you not told me?"

"I did not wish to add to the burdens already plaguing you until I have a plan of action to recommend."

"I am the future emperor. I need to be made aware of any and all situations." Ahkin crossed his arms over his chest and glared at his mentor. "I know you care to protect me, but I am no longer just an apprentice."

Yaotl considered him for a moment before consenting.

"Forgive me, my prince. The Miquitz seem to be more … restless than usual. They have conducted more raids for human sacrifices over the last few weeks than they ever have in the past. I wonder if they are planning a massive ceremony of some kind. What is most unusual is that they seem to be taking peasants and farmers as well as warriors."

Ahkin pinched the bridge of his nose. *Several* raids? Peasants and farmers too? How many Chicome citizens had been captured without his knowledge? Ahkin slapped his palm against his forehead. He had been too busy running his hands over the smooth curves of a beautiful girl to ask about the state of the kingdom, and now his people were paying with their lives. Perhaps he was as young and foolish as everyone else seemed to think.

"Where is this happening?"

"Millacatl, mostly. Just outside the maize fields at the base of the mountains. I think the passage there is the easiest way for them to come down into the valley."

"And you are unsure how best to proceed?"

"My first instinct is to attack them. Head on. Capture their warriors, sacrifice them to Huitzilopochtli and show them the might of the Chicome. Show them that your ancestor was not only the god of the sun but also the god of war." Yaotl's voice was a growl.

Ahkin's heart thrummed with pride, like a drum in battle. Yes. He would show the Miquitz exactly what they could expect from his leadership. Maybe he could convince himself of that in the process.

"Send the notices to our armies. I want a battalion ready to depart in two days for Millacatl."

"With pleasure, my prince."

Yaotl inclined his head, but then jerked his face up, ears pricked like a dog catching a sound.

Ahkin recognized the hurried slapping of sandals against stone. Yaotl stepped in front of the prince, a living shield, but it was an unnecessary precaution as Atanzah huffed into view. Her round face was ruddy and shining with a sheen of sweat.

"My—my lord. I had to come right away." Atanzah's hand yanked at her shawl to keep it from falling off her shoulders.

Apprehension settled over Ahkin like a morning mist, making the back of his neck tingle. What more could go wrong today?

"One of the princesses was stung by a poisonous scorpion."

Ahkin's stomach writhed as if he had swallowed a snake. "Who?" he asked, though the feeling in his stomach told him he already knew the answer. The gods were determined to punish him for his weakness.

"The daughter of Atl, my lord."

Mayana. All thoughts of the Miquitz, of the sun dying, of losing his parents faded as her face swam before his eyes. *No. Not her. Please let her live.* She had been the only ray of hope and light piercing through a dark cloud cover. He needed her.

"Is she ...?"

"She is still alive, my lord." The darkening clouds gathering in his mind thinned.

"Where is she? What happened?"

"The daughter of Pahtia found her on the floor of her room, minutes from death. She healed her as best she could before summoning Coatl. The girl is resting in Coatl's quarters as we speak."

Relief as warm as a bowl of pulque spread to the tips of Ahkin's fingers.

"Yaotl, please proceed with our plans for notifying the warriors to prepare for battle. I need to—"

"Go." Yaotl nodded toward the hallway. "Your mind is already with her anyway."

Ahkin gave his best soldier an apologetic smile before sprinting out of the courtyard, leaving Atanzah to shuffle along behind him.

CHAPTER

28

Ahkin ran up the steps to the royal residences, taking two at a time. When he finally reached the doorway of Coatl's room, he wrenched the red curtain aside without bothering to announce himself.

Mayana was lying on a woven mat with a cushion propped under her dark hair. Her head thrashed from side to side, eyes closed and brow damp with perspiration. The breaths escaping her lips sounded ragged and harsh. Ahkin didn't understand. Hadn't Atanzah said she was healed? Why did she still seem so ill?

Coatl sat hunched at her side, holding her still as he applied some kind of salve to the massive swelling on her lower leg.

"Coatl!" Ahkin meant his voice to sound forceful, authoritative. Instead it trembled with anxiety. "What's wrong with her? What … what's happening?"

He rushed forward and cradled Mayana's head in his hands as her eyes rolled and fluttered under her eyelids, unseeing. He rubbed a thumb gently across her warm cheek, panicked at the fever scorching her skin. Her head continued to loll between his hands, and the muscles of her arms and legs twitched as though she were being shocked by a lightning fish.

"It's the poison." Coatl frowned down at her form.

"I thought your sister healed her," Ahkin shouted, confusion mingling with his fear and making him unreasonably furious.

Coatl turned to face the prince, his eyes full of repressed impatience.

"She did, my lord." He drew out the title like stretching tree sap. "But you see, when you heal a wound, as my sister did, with poison still coursing through the body, it does not exactly help."

"What? What do you mean?" Ahkin's gaze fell to the wound on Mayana's leg. A fresh gash oozed blood into a bowl positioned beneath her calf. The blood of the goddess Atlacoya, the blood of the girl he wanted to marry.

Coatl let out an impatient sigh. "I am draining the wound and attempting to draw out the poison with the power in my own blood." He lifted his palm to show the prince his own small cut. "It has spread extensively throughout her system, as I am sure you can see." Coatl motioned toward her twitching arms.

"Will she be alright?" Ahkin's heart raced as he attempted to read every grimace on Coatl's face. Anything that might give him the answer he sought.

Coatl pursed his lips, his brow furrowing. "I think so. We will have to see if she survives the night, I think, before I can know anything for sure."

"I will stay with her until she is completely healed." Ahkin reached for her hand and held it steady within his own.

"Of course, you will." The healer sighed.

Ahkin narrowed his eyes dangerously. "Watch your impertinence," he snapped.

"But of course, my lord." Coatl's voice became as slick and sweet as agave syrup. "I only live to serve you."

Ahkin shifted his shoulders uneasily. What had become of his friend who loved to play tricks on the servants and flirt with the girls Ahkin was always too afraid to talk to? Coatl had changed much in the recent months. He had always been proud, even when he first arrived at the palace years ago. He boasted how he could heal any and all ailments, how no one in Pahtia possessed the sacred ability of the god Ixtlilton as powerfully as he did. That was why Ahkin's father had requested he come to the palace of Tollan, to train as the royal family's personal healer. He certainly had lived up to his self-proclaimed reputation. At least, until the night Ahkin's father died. Not even Coatl could be everywhere at all times.

But recently, in addition to being prideful, he had grown disrespectful, as if he himself were a god and not just the descendant of one. Coatl was a wild pup in need of a stern hand. What had caused the sudden change?

"Ahkin?" Metzi's melodious voice came from the doorway. His twin pushed aside the curtain and entered with cautious steps, hugging her arms around her chest as if trying to stop herself from shaking. Her eyes roved over Mayana's sickened form and her hand slowly lifted to cover her open mouth.

"Oh, my gods, it's true," she said, her eyes filling with tears. "Will she survive?"

"We are not sure ..." Coatl began, but Ahkin interrupted.

"Yes," he said with finality, as if the decision were entirely up to him. "She will. I know Mayana. She is strong. She honors and loves the gods deeply. Surely they will spare her life."

"How well can you know someone after three days?" Coatl snorted, so quietly Ahkin wasn't sure he was even meant to hear. Ahkin clenched his teeth, but Metzi's soft hand on his shoulder calmed the fury coursing through him.

"What happened to you, Coatl? We were like brothers. Now you'll hardly look at me, and speak to me as though you're angry at me. Is this because I haven't chosen your sister?"

Coatl didn't respond, merely kept working as though Ahkin had not spoken.

"I came to fetch you, brother," Metzi cut in. "The high priest wishes to speak with you."

Ahkin growled in frustration. He didn't want to leave Mayana's side, and yet he still had responsibilities to uphold. How could the world around him keep going on as though nothing had changed—especially when the entire future he had planned was crumbling in his hands like ill-formed pottery? Why couldn't the world stop for him until he knew for sure that she would be alright?

Ahkin pressed a kiss to Mayana's warm, moist hand and rose, still shaking, to his feet. "Please watch over her for me, Metzi. I hope she will one day be your friend and sister."

"I will," Metzi said breathlessly, moving her hand to her heart as though it were aching.

"You will love her," Ahkin said.

"I already do." Metzi gave Ahkin a reassuring smile and rushed him out the door.

CHAPTER

29

Mayana had no idea what had happened. She didn't know where she was or how she had gotten there.

When she was little, she remembered trying to chase after her older brothers as they played in the river, but the water would slow her down, tugging at her legs and refusing to let her move as quickly as she wanted to. She would lift her knees high, sloshing against the force holding her, but she was never fast enough, could never quite reach them.

That's how her brain felt now. Blurred colors and shapes danced just out of her reach, and no matter how hard she pushed, she couldn't get a handle on them. Her thinking felt as thick as cold honey. And the pain. Oh gods, the pain.

Every nerve in her body throbbed and pulsated, as if her veins had been replaced with prickly cactus spines that pierced her skin whenever she moved. At the same time, her fingers and lips and toes were numb, and it was the most perplexing sensation to feel both too much and nothing at the same time.

Bits and pieces of her memory came back to her. Images of the scorpion arching its tail, the feel of its shell crunching beneath the helmet, crawling across the floor and trying to scream for help, all flashed beneath her eyelids. It was a miracle she was still alive.

Was that Ahkin's voice? She wanted to find it, to listen to it and catch a glimpse of the smile that made her stomach turn inside out. Actually, maybe it was better her stomach stayed as calm as possible. Nausea overwhelmed her and the burning in her throat and nose told her that her stomach had already suffered enough trauma as it was.

There was a warm pressure on her fingers, someone squeezing her hand, saying something to the blurred shapes wading through the bright bursts of light that broke her vision every time her eyelids fluttered. It was like trying to watch something on the other side of a curtain buffeted back and forth in a wind.

Then the warm hand was gone, and relief flooded through her. Her body was too hot already, and the warmth had been uncomfortable. She tried to focus on something else, *anything* else to distract her from the sensations of the poison coursing through her. She wasn't dead yet.

She would keep fighting.

Mayana pictured the faces of her brothers, remembered Chimalli's playful teasing and Tenoch's boyish, mischievous spirit. She imagined her father and how his face would glow with pride like the rising sun when he heard that Prince Ahkin had chosen her as his empress. She just had to survive to get there.

Most of all, she focused on reliving those moments with Ahkin in the garden. She remembered the sensation in her stomach as he kissed her for the first time, and she tried to replace the nausea with the memory of that feeling. She imagined his eyes, the way they had filled with such desire as he lowered his head toward her. The feel of the cool water contrasted with the warmth of his skin.

But then, like poison seeping into her mind, her thoughts turned to guilt and shame. She had let Ahkin believe she saved the jaguar out of some desire to honor the calendar and the rituals with even more devotion than was necessary. She never once corrected him. That was the whole reason he noticed her in the first place. Would he have given her the same attention if she hadn't acted to save it—supposedly out of a desire to *honor* the gods?

She didn't know where she stood anymore. Ever since she'd lost Ona,

Mayana had almost resented the gods for their demands. Her father viewed all life as a gift from the gods and the sacrifices as just giving those lives back. But why did it hurt so much?

Her confusion was what had encouraged her to study the original texts in the first place, and that's how she noticed the difference between the older texts and the new. She tried to bring it up to her father once, but she stopped when the look on his face suggested his eyes were going to burst from their sockets. Fine. She got the message clear enough. Do not question the codex. Ever. Do the rituals and stay quiet. Which she had … with the exception of the animal sacrifices.

Then there was Yemania. And Yoli. Even the other princesses, Itza and Teniza, whom she didn't really know as well. She didn't want to sacrifice them. Their loss of life wasn't fair. Why gift them with life in the first place—beautiful young lives with so much still to give—and then demand it back?

Zorrah, on the other hand, could give her life back as soon as possible, as far as Mayana was concerned. She wasn't stupid. She knew exactly how a scorpion had ended up in her bed, of all places. Zorrah had tried to kill her before she even made it to Tollan, though she wasn't sure why the animal princess had targeted her before she became a threat.

Mayana would confront Zorrah as soon as she had the chance. She may hate sacrificing, but that didn't make her weak. It took great strength to question her entire society's way of life. Mayana's chest burned in anger and determination.

She was strong. Stronger than anyone gave her credit for.

The haze cleared slightly, and her eyelids slid open. She was not in her room anymore. She turned her head slightly to get a better look at her surroundings and the movement sent a wave of pain through her temples.

She groaned loudly at the ache, almost wanting to slip back into her semiconscious twilight.

"Is she … awake?"

Mayana recognized the woman's voice, clear and beautiful as a bell. Was that the prince's sister? Metzi?

"I don't know." That was the smooth, disdainful voice of Coatl.

The colors she was seeing sharpened, as if she had blinked away tears. Mayana could make out a white cotton dress and the sheen of gold jewelry framed with long, dark hair. Definitely Metzi.

Coatl had his back to Mayana, the tanned, strong muscles of his back puckered with red lines like ... fingernail scratches? He too wore white cotton wrapped around his waist. He turned to face her. A gold pendant with a glittering ruby like a drop of blood glinted on his chest.

Confusion hit her over the head like a spiked club. What ... what were they doing? Why were they standing so close together? *Were his arms around her waist?* Mayana wanted to say something but her tongue was swollen and dry as sand.

"She's awake! She saw us!" Metzi's usually pleasant voice suddenly shrieked, like one of the irritating jungle birds back home that screeched into Mayana's window far too early in the morning. She winced.

Before she could make sense of what she had just seen, before she could ask a single question, something cold and wet was pressed against her face. The fabric covered her nose and mouth and smelled so strongly of some kind of herb that it overwhelmed her senses. Suffocating terror gripped her, but she was too weak to even lift a hand to fight. Her nose burned and her eyes watered at the strong scent. Her vision faded at the edges as her strength gave out. Her body relaxed, and she drifted back into the welcoming arms of darkness.

"You wished to see me, Toani?" Ahkin tapped a knuckle against the golden doorframe.

The slow shuffling of feet and the clattering of numerous beads announced Toani's approach from the depths of the temple. Ahkin always wondered how the old man had the strength to march up and down the hundreds of narrow steps of the Temple of the Sun.

Toani shifted the bloodred cloak upon his shoulders.

"Follow me," he said. Ahkin couldn't help but notice that he wasn't smiling.

Toani turned on the spot and several of the massive feathers of his headpiece smacked across Ahkin's face. The priest probably didn't mean to disrespect him, right? Ahkin gritted his teeth and followed the priest toward the study chamber behind the altar, the holy room where the texts of the codex were stored.

"Atanzah informed me about the unfortunate circumstances regarding one of the princesses," Toani's voice floated back to him.

Ahkin's stomach clenched. He didn't need to be reminded.

"Yes, the daughter of the lord of Atl was stung by a scorpion."

Toani nodded sorrowfully. "Was she of particular interest to you?"

Blood rushed to Ahkin's cheeks, so he was grateful Toani walked ahead of him and could not see.

"Yes," he said tersely. "I had actually hoped to announce her as my choice at this evening's feast."

"And you think it a coincidence the girl you had chosen has been struck?"

Confusion clouded his thoughts at the question. "What … are you insinuating, Toani?"

"Sometimes the gods act in mysterious ways." Toani's voice trailed off as he disappeared through the doorway. Ahkin followed a little reluctantly.

The light of several flaming torches illuminated the room, but its high walls always made Ahkin feel like he was sitting at the bottom of a well. Detailed carvings and paintings depicting the gods and people of the various ages stretched high above his head. The musty scent of old paper mingled with spices hung in the air. The chamber was cool and still, as though the wind itself were being quiet and respectful.

The original holy books of the codex lay stacked neatly on a low, carved stone table. Number charts and a Chicome calendar stone sat beside them. The fig-bark paper used for the codices were long continuous sheets, painted with colored pictures detailing the Chicome's histories, their rituals, and explanations of the calendar. Unfolded, each sheet could run the length of the stone table and even onto the temple floor. When Ahkin was a boy, his father showed him the careful ways to open and fold the codex papers to preserve them.

Toani led him to the table and pulled several charts and star maps toward them.

"What exactly do you want me to look at?" Ahkin studied the pictures and lines arching across the paper.

"I have the plans finished for your father's celebration of life. I have been studying the signs, and I believe that tomorrow would be the best time to begin his burial. His tomb has been finished for several years already, of course, and I would recommend you begin construction on your personal tomb the moment you are crowned. These things can take many years to complete, and as your late father showed us"—Toani heaved a heavy sigh—"we never know when our journeys will begin."

"Tomorrow works well. I am planning to leave the following day as it is."

"You are leaving, my lord?" Toani blinked his tiny, ancient eyes at the prince.

"I will lead a battalion of Jaguar and Eagle warriors to confront the Miquitz outside the fields of Millacatl. They have been capturing peasants and warriors alike, and I intend to repay the kindness."

Toani pursed his lips. "That may be wise. I continue to track the sun's movements across the sky, and it seems to grow ever weaker, setting earlier and earlier each night. The people will soon notice, my prince, and begin to panic. Perhaps a sacrifice of several Miquitz captives will give the Seventh Sun some of the nourishment it seeks."

Ahkin couldn't help but notice that Toani did not seem convinced of his own suggestion. Ahkin wasn't even convinced himself. He knew the real reason the sun was struggling. He wasn't strong enough. His blood was too weak. Still, it couldn't hurt to try. Either way, he would not stand for the Miquitz violating Chicome borders. He could not stand the thought of peasants and farmers disappearing into the night, dragged up into the mountains by the death demons.

Ahkin forced confidence into his voice. "Hopefully we will bring back enough for the sun to gorge itself on Miquitz blood."

CHAPTER

31

The burial ceremony drew citizens from every corner of the Chicome Empire. The high priest laid Ahkin's parents to rest in the elegant tomb his father had built in preparation. Alongside them rested numerous tributes of food and riches and the bodies of a servant and a dog to serve his father during his journey through Xibalba. Ahkin himself placed the carved mask of jade upon his father's face, so peaceful in his eternal slumber.

And his mother, beautiful even in death, would forever sleep by his side while their souls completed the journey through the underworld together. Despite the assurances and praises of the priest, Ahkin still couldn't subdue the part of his heart that screamed against his mother's actions. Was what she had done truly necessary to please the gods? He feared they sensed the weakness within him, his lack of faith in what they demanded.

Metzi had stood nearby as the tomb was sealed, silent tears streaming down her cheeks, a look of staunch determination on her face. Even Metzi could not ease the ache of loneliness gnawing at his spirit. After the Nemontemi, she would be sent to Ehecatl to marry the oldest son of their lord. She wasn't happy about it, that much he could tell, but he also knew she would do what was required of her. She understood responsibility as much as he did.

The other princesses watched silently, chins dipped in respect, but they were already spirits to him. There but not there at the same time. Ahkin could only think about how he wished Mayana was by his side.

He imagined her slipping her hand into his and warming the coldness seeping through him. Then, at least, he would have known that he did not have to face an unknown future alone. Maybe with her help he could find the strength to save the sun. Coatl said she was improving every time he went to visit her, but he feared he would have to leave before she awoke.

The next morning, the army prepared for the departure to Millacatl. In Coatl's room, Ahkin pressed his lips against Mayana's limp fingers. He would return to her. He had to.

Ahkin turned to Coatl, his eyes pleading.

"Tell me her condition is improving?"

Coatl did not meet his eyes but continued mixing some pungently scented combination of herbs and paste in a stone bowl. "I am confident she will make a full recovery, my lord."

"How can you be sure? I would have thought she would be awake by now."

"I am purposely keeping her sedated. Her muscles need to relax after the trauma her nerves experienced. You can see she is no longer twitching. And feel—her fever is gone."

Relief coursed through Ahkin as he checked the temperature of her cheek one more time. Slightly cooler.

There was a long moment of silence, in which the only sound that could be heard was the rhythmic grinding of Coatl's pestle.

"Coatl, have you ever …?"

Coatl paused, and turned to stare at the prince with wide, disbelieving eyes.

"Really? We are going to talk women? We haven't done that since we saw fourteen cycles of the calendar." He turned back to his work.

"You're right. You're probably not the best one to ask anyway, considering the women of Tollan always flocked to you like flies to honey."

He watched Coatl's mouth tick up in a half smile. It was almost like having his old friend back for a moment.

"You were always too busy smashing skulls or looking at the stars to pay attention to the ones fawning over you. Besides, I'm more handsome than you are."

"Perhaps, but I am a prince, and that must count for more than a pretty face." Ahkin forced out the playful jibe. He spoke with a confidence he did not feel—he would not let Coatl see the true depths of his self-doubt.

"Being a prince doesn't mean you know how to warm their beds as well as I do. The codex prevents you from gaining that experience, whereas I am as free as an eagle."

Ahkin snorted. This was the Coatl he remembered. They had grown up in the palace together since they were fourteen. What havoc they had caused, playing tricks on the servants and driving his father to fits of rage with their antics. He still remembered Coatl convincing his father that it was a monkey that had dropped that piece of fruit on the commander's head during a banquet. Ahkin had never had the confidence that Coatl did. How Ahkin had envied him.

"So where are you leading your pack of wild animals off to this time? Ehecatl giving us trouble again?"

"No, I'm taking the Jaguar and Eagle warriors with me to Millacatl. The Miquitz are attacking peasants and farmers there. Yaotl thinks they may be preparing for some kind of massive sacrificial ceremony, but if I have any say, they will not sacrifice Chicome blood for their rituals."

Coatl bent down to Mayana's leg and spread the greenish-yellow paste across the still-swollen flesh of her calf.

"Send those death demons back to the depths of the underworld."

Ahkin grasped his old friend's shoulder briefly.

"I promise I will, as long as you make sure I have my future wife to return to."

Coatl said nothing as he wrapped a new bandage around Mayana's leg. Ahkin regretted his words. Perhaps Coatl was still bitter about his sister not being chosen.

"I don't know what happened between us, Coatl, but I will always consider you my brother. Thank you for saving her."

The healer closed his eyes briefly, as though Ahkin's words caused him pain.

"It is my job, my lord."

Ahkin turned to leave, not wanting to press whatever wound Coatl was trying so hard to keep hidden.

"I know it is. But I still thank you."

CHAPTER

32

Coatl had not been the most talkative companion since Mayana woke up that morning. Had she not been entirely consumed with the feeling her leg was about to fall off, she might have actually said something to him. He explained where she was, how she had gotten there, and why her body felt like it had been trampled by deer hooves. But he made no jokes that made her blush, no suggestive comments that made her skin crawl. Not that she was complaining. It was just … unnerving. Like there was a tension hanging about the room she couldn't get a handle on. Coatl wasn't being himself.

So, she said nothing.

Instead, she bit her lip to keep from screaming as he wrapped her lower right leg with clean white cotton and warned her to come back if she started feeling dizzy or nauseated again. He asked her what she remembered from the last two days, and she wasn't entirely honest. She told him it was all a blur, that she remembered nothing specific after collapsing onto her bedroom floor.

She still wasn't sure if what she had seen between him and Metzi was real or the result of her addled brain creating hallucinations. It could have easily been either. Still, she couldn't help but notice that Coatl had been very keen to get her out of his chambers, and she didn't object.

Mayana knocked softly on the stone doorframe of Yemania's room. With only six more days until the start of the Nemontemi, her time was limited to make amends with her friend. Ahkin wanted his wife chosen before the un-lucky last days of the calendar year. The red cotton curtain fluttered slightly, and Yemania's brown eyes peered through the gap along the edge.

"It's me. Can I come in?"

Yemania's eyes darted back and forth several times before disappearing behind the curtain.

Mayana dipped her chin, her heart sinking for the briefest of mo-ments before Yemania heaved a great sigh and wrenched the curtain aside.

Mayana's heart took flight like a bird from the jungle canopy. She jerked her head back up, wanting to launch herself through the doorway and wrap her arms around the other girl. Instead, her fingers merely twitched at her side as she took in Yemania's crossed arms and defensive pose.

"What?" Yemania's sharp voice cut through her like an obsidian blade.

Mayana gulped. Why did this have to be so difficult? Why couldn't Yemania just understand? "I—just wanted to thank you. For—for saving my life. You didn't have to, and you did it anyway, even after ..."

Yemania's arms relaxed ever so slightly.

"Well, you weren't supposed to die alone in your room. That wasn't part of our agreement either."

Mayana gave a watery laugh, rubbing her nose and sniffing loudly. "Thank you for making sure I honored our agreement. You are a talented healer."

"Well, I shouldn't have healed your skin with the poison still inside, but at least you didn't die on the spot."

"You need to give yourself more credit, Yemania, you saved my life."

Yemania shrugged. "I love healing. I actually always wanted to start my own business selling remedies and cures for the commoners who don't get royal healers. I will never get to live that dream now that I am sen-tenced to die, but it looks like I have a little more time to imagine it, at least for the time being."

The wind flew out of Mayana's lungs. "What do you mean, more time? What happened?" She dug her fingernails into her palms.

"You didn't hear?"

"Hear what?"

"The prince left yesterday morning to lead an army to the maize fields at the foot of the Miquitz Mountains. Just outside of Millacatl."

Mayana's head throbbed, like the scorpion poison had somehow found a way back into her body and was slowly killing her heart and her vision all at once.

She stumbled sideways, and her shoulder slammed against the door-frame.

"How did you not know?"

"Yemania, I just left Coatl's room. I barely have the strength to stand as it is. The first thing I wanted to do when he gave me permission to rest in my room was come talk to you. He told me what you did to save me."

Yemania studied her with a look almost like pity.

"I'm sorry you didn't get to say goodbye to him."

Yemania could not have said anything more painful. It reminded her of how much she missed Ahkin and worried for his safety, but also of how guilty she still felt about their sudden romance. A romance that essentially doomed Yemania to die alone. How could she do that to the friend who had just saved her life?

"Yemania, I can't let you be sacrificed." Mayana stomped her foot in stubborn determination and immediately regretted it as searing pain lanced up her calf. She stumbled back onto the doorway and pushed herself back to standing.

Yemania studied her through narrowed, and slightly amused, eyes. "Oh, you're not going to *let* me?"

"Yes! If I'm going to be empress, then surely I can ..."

Yemania held up a hand to stop her.

"Mayana. I know where you are going with this. You cannot save me. My death will honor the gods and bless Ahkin's coronation. You would be risking the success of his reign to even suggest withholding blood from the Mother goddess over your own selfish desires. You would bring a curse upon us all. If you truly want to help me, then reject him. Say no. Let us begin our journeys through Xibalba together."

Mayana resisted the urge to cover her ears with her hands. She refused to consider the possibility of losing Yemania. "No. I can ask him to spare you. He will be grateful you saved my life. He'll listen to me."

"You think he would defy the gods?"

Legend said that when the volcano at Papatlaca erupted and destroyed the Third Sun, that the pressure and tension had been slowly building for years. Mayana was the volcano. Years of repressing her doubts and frustrations with the rituals and suffocating rules laid out in the codex, of suffering under the crushing disappointment of her family, of having to watch the blood of innocent creatures spilled over and over again without her being able to stop it suddenly erupted from her like liquid fire.

"I am *tired* of being silenced. I do not believe the gods demand these rituals from us."

Yemania froze, her mouth slightly open, but she did not back away. Mayana continued to vent the words that had built up pressure inside her heart from the moment her father had killed her dog and she had gone to read the texts for herself in the temple.

"I think they were created by our own people to give us some sense of control in avoiding the end of our world. But it isn't up to us! We do not have the power to prevent an apocalypse. The gods alone have that power. Am I the selfish one? Am I the one dishonoring them, when we minimize the sacrifices they made by thinking *our* actions can save us? We are not honoring them. We are negating what they did by taking our salvation into our own hands. We have fallen more in love with our rules than with the gods themselves!"

Mayana's chest heaved and she raked her hands through her hair as she tried to calm her breathing. The fire within her cooled, like lava solidifying in the fresh jungle air as the earth released it from its depths. These thoughts had churned within her for years, ever since she saw the ritual codex sheets that seemed much newer than the original creation accounts and histories. How had no one ever questioned before? Maybe they had just been silenced too, forced to obey and not question.

"How ... how can you even say such things?" Yemania's lip trembled and her eyes shone with silver.

"I will show you." An idea suddenly formed in Mayana's mind. She would show Yemania the codices, show her that there was something different about the ritual sheets. If she just saw in person, maybe she would understand.

Mayana grabbed her hand and dragged her out into the hall. Her leg throbbed, but she ignored it in her desire to be vindicated.

"Where are we going?" Yemania's cold hand went limp within her own, like she was already giving up.

"I'm taking you to see the codices. I want to show *someone* that I'm not just crazy, and I have my reasons for questioning the rituals."

The fear that shone within Yemania's eyes and the passionate energy coursing through her own veins made Mayana wonder if perhaps she was crazy after all.

She didn't know why this was suddenly so important to her, but she needed validation. Mayana needed someone to see her for who she was— that she wasn't a heretic. Then Yemania would understand, and she would let Mayana save her.

CHAPTER

33

If Mayana thought climbing the stone steps of the temple in Atl had been exhausting, it was nothing compared to ascending the stairs to the Temple of the Sun. The height was dizzying, and Mayana half expected the peak of the temple to pierce right through the clouds.

Yemania was reluctant to follow, but Mayana kept a firm grip on her hand, partly to force her to keep up and partly to steady herself, as the pain in her leg ached with each step. Mayana was being stubborn, she knew it in the depths of her heart, but she didn't stop. She would make Yemania understand.

"What exactly are you hoping to accomplish here?" Yemania panted. Sweat beaded into little crystal droplets on her forehead, glistening in the blistering heat of the Seventh Sun. They passed lower-level priests and commoners bringing tributes or requests to the gods.

Mayana forced her foot up another step, the toe of her sandal catching on the edge and making her stumble. "I want to show you the reason why I started to question the rituals."

"I thought you've never been to Tollan before." Yemania frowned.

"I haven't. But our codex sheets in Atl, the second city, are the oldest copies of the original sheets in Tollan. I am sure they are the same."

"I don't see how any good can come from this …"

Mayana groaned in response. "Just humor me for a few minutes. I'm trying to save your life, Yemania."

Yemania did not respond, keeping her eyes focused on her own feet.

Finally, *finally*, they crested the final step. Mayana turned around to face the sprawling city of Tollan. The gold-and-white stone buildings stretched across the entire surface of the volcanic plateau, broken only by the dense greenery of trees growing between the structures. Birds flitted between branches, and the occasional small brown blur of a monkey darted across rooftops.

A large plaza spread out below them, bustling with a busy marketplace. The citizens of the capital carried out their daily business, trading at stalls or chasing small children through the crowds. Mayana smiled at the life that throbbed within the winding city streets like the blood of a great animal, the temple sitting at its heart.

"It's spectacular." Yemania's wide eyes roved the details of the city.

"Come on." Mayana looped her arm around Yemania's. She dragged her away from the edge and toward the shadowed depths of the temple. A large brazier burned within a square firepit, continually kept alive by the actions of the high priest. The codex stipulated that the flame never be allowed to die, lest the people of the Chicome die along with it.

So many rules to stay alive.

The many rooms interspersed throughout the towering columns housed the residences of the Tlana priests, supplies for religious ceremonies, and effigies of the gods themselves. If it was anything like the temple in Atl, one of these rooms would contain the codex texts.

Mayana was just thinking how surprised she was that they had not encountered another soul, when a Tlana priest materialized from behind a red pillar thicker than a tree trunk. He rattled out in front of them, bells and beads dangling from his neck and wrists. Long sloping dark feathers framed his face and red paint covered his wrinkled eyes and nose. He resembled an angry crimson turkey. Mayana stifled a giggle and bit her lower lip.

"Can I help you ladies?" His voice was deep and sorrowful.

Mayana straightened her spine and forced her tone to remain as cool and respectful as possible.

"We wish to study the codices."

"With what authority do you have access to our most holy texts?"

"We are daughters of nobility, descendants of the gods themselves. Through my veins runs the blood of Atlacoya and through hers, the blood of Ixtlilton. These holy texts account our ancestors, and it is our desire to see them."

The old turkey's eyes appraised her up and down with suspicion. He did not speak for several long moments, and Mayana was sure he was about to refuse them when he gave a low bow and swept his arm to the side to allow them to pass.

"Thank you." Mayana inclined her head.

"You will find the texts in that room there." He pointed a finger at a door toward the back of the temple hallway.

"Quick thinking," Yemania whispered, and clutched Mayana's hand. They sedately made their way toward the door, both resisting the urge to turn and see if the priest was still watching them. Mayana wasn't entirely sure they were allowed to be looking at the original holy texts, but she had to admit she had sounded pretty convincing, even to herself.

Yemania stopped suddenly as they entered the doorway of the room where the codex texts were kept. Mayana jerked back, caught by her arm that was still looped through her friend's.

"What is it?"

"I've just … never seen the actual sheets of the codex myself. Not in person." Yemania's voice shook with a combination of awe and terror.

"I only have once in my life." Mayana's mind flashed back to that night after Ona's sacrifice.

"How did you get to see them?"

"I—no one except my mother knew. I think she felt the same way about sacrifices but hid it a lot better. She encouraged me to study the texts, so … I sneaked up to the top of our temple and saw them for myself."

"Why did you want to?" Yemania cocked her head to the side. The gesture reminded Mayana of Ona, and a twinge of sadness rippled in her gut.

"I wanted to see for myself if the gods demanded all the rituals we follow." Mayana rubbed her nose and sniffed. She took a deep breath, deciding she wanted Yemania to know everything, why she couldn't accept the rituals and sacrifices as a way of life. Squaring her shoulders, she looked Yemania full in the face.

"When I was young, I could never keep up with my brothers. I was the only girl, and I was so often alone. My mother would notice, I think, how lonely and left out I felt. She … she gave me Ona. He was a beautiful dog, black as a dark night with eyes like almonds. He was smooth and warm, and he became my dearest friend, one of the only ones I had at times."

Mayana lifted her gaze. Yemania was watching her with polite curiosity, but also with a tinge of pity behind her eyes.

"When I had seen eight cycles of the calendar," Mayana continued, "my father decided that Ona needed to be sacrificed in honor of the month of the dog. It had been a difficult year for the family, the rains a little more sparse than usual, and he insisted that a sacrifice of great value was necessary. Sacrifices are supposed to be painful, as I'm sure you already know, to show our dedication to the will of the gods above our own. But I wouldn't let him. I sneaked Ona out of the evening meal and tried to hide him. It didn't work …"

Mayana would spare her friend the details of her anguished cries, her father's fury, and her mother's guilt.

"Ona was sacrificed, and my father forced me to watch. I … struggled with the decision. With what my father called 'necessary.' I had always been taught that the gods were loving, loving enough to die for us. I couldn't make sense of how gods who died for us could demand repayment for their love. Ona gave love unconditionally. He never expected anything in return. So, I decided to see for myself."

Mayana pulled her arm out from Yemania's and nervously fiddled with the ends of her hair. She slowly walked to the intricately carved stone table where the various sheets of the codex were neatly stacked in their precise order.

She glanced up at the high ceiling, tall and narrow with carvings and paintings of the gods looking down on her and watching her every movement.

Reaching out and pulling the top sheet from the stack on the far left, Mayana motioned for Yemania to join her.

"These are the oldest texts we have."

Yemania studied the pictures without words, colorful splashes across the yellowing paper.

"The creation accounts," she whispered.

"Look at them. See how they are pictures alone without any kind of hieroglyph? And notice the paper itself, it is a different material than the sheets in these other stacks." Mayana waved a hand absently to the right side of the table.

"So?" Yemania furrowed her brow at the creation codex.

Mayana slowly unfolded the sheet, showing picture after picture of the stories they had all been taught since childhood. How Ometeotl, both male and female in one, the duality, had created the other gods and the world. How her son, Quetzalcoatl, created the first people, but they suffered in the darkness without a sun. How Ahkin's ancestor, the brother of Quetzalcoatl, gave his life to birth the first sun and save the first people from their sufferings. How the first people were subsequently destroyed by water after a god's wife was stolen. How the gods wept for the loss of their beloved creations.

Mayana ran a finger over the image of her ancestor, the goddess Atlacoya, distinguishable by her blue dress and hair flowing like a river. The next image showed her stabbing herself with a knife of obsidian and hurling herself into the depths of Xibalba. From her blood, the Second Sun was born, and the bones of the people were brought back to life.

And so the sheet continued, outlining how each of the suns was destroyed until their sun, the Seventh Sun, was born from the blood of Tezcatlipoca, and the bones of their people given life to live as the Chicome, the seventh people.

"I know these stories, Mayana, we all do. I don't understand why you think the rituals are no longer needed from—"

"But look at these," Mayana interrupted her, pulling a sheet from a stack on the right. It was noticeably brighter, lighter in color than the creation accounts. There were still some pictures, but this sheet now showed mostly hieroglyphs, detailing instructions for a ritual to cleanse the body.

Yemania frowned. "They're different."

"Yes," Mayana breathed. "They are obviously newer, which makes me believe these were written and given to us by men, not the gods."

"And if the rituals aren't given by the gods ..." Yemania curled her lip as if she had bitten into a chili pepper.

"This is why I struggle with following them so meticulously. Nowhere in the creation codex sheets does it call for repaying the blood the gods paid for us. There is no debt to be paid. It was selfless love that saved us. Sacrifice is the ultimate form of selflessness, and sacrificing yourself for others is the ultimate act of love."

Mayana traced her finger again across the form of Atlacoya. The goddess had loved her people enough to die for them. The tears that rose in Mayana's eyes surprised her. The knowledge that Atlacoya had loved them enough to die for them, that the Mother had loved them enough to let her daughter die for them, was almost overwhelming.

"I honestly don't know what to think about all of this, Mayana. I'm sorry, but it's just a lot to process." Yemania carefully folded the pages of the codex and placed it back where it belonged.

"Thank you for listening to me at least," Mayana said. "It's more than anyone else in my life has done."

Maybe it was hopeless to think that Yemania could be convinced to believe as she did, but when Yemania glanced back at the holy pages there seemed to be an intense war waging behind her eyes.

CHAPTER

34

Tlana priests, carrying effigies of the gods, marched along the jungle trade path. The volcanic plateau beneath Tollan disappeared behind them. Ahkin led the contingent of nobles and Jaguar warriors, but his mind was not on the procession. He had left without saying goodbye to Mayana, and a feeling like a heavy stone settled at the bottom of his stomach. What if she died before he returned?

The news of the coming battle had gone out to the main plaza of Tollan and a small army had been mobilized over the past two days. There were only about four hundred men aside from the regiment of fifty elite Jaguar and Eagle warriors accompanying them. Yaotl assured Ahkin that their numbers were more than sufficient for securing the border from Miquitz raiders. They were not facing the entire army of the Miquitz, or else they would have summoned soldiers from the other city-states within the empire as well.

At their backs, the thundering of hundreds of feet and the clatter of beads and bells on the warriors' costumes were almost deafening. Ahkin gripped the sides of his golden chair, wishing he could just jump down and run away from them all, away from the prying eyes and expectations. Away from the eyes of the gods that were surely punishing him. Several royal naguals from Ocelotl, draped in furs of various wild creatures and adorned with fanged helmets to match, bobbed along beside him on the shoulders of their own servants. The slinking bodies of jaguars and wolves followed behind their masters, their jaws itching for the flesh of the death demons.

With the well-maintained roads and the small size of their army, Ahkin expected to reach the outskirts of Millacatl by dawn the next morning. Metzi would have to raise the sun for him until he returned, but she hadn't seemed to mind the responsibility as much as he thought she would. Still, Ahkin wanted this campaign over with as soon as possible. He wanted to make Mayana his wife, endure his coronation and the sacrifices of the other princesses, and then they could begin their life together. He would have appeased the gods. Then the rules of the codex would not hold him back from showing her how very much he wanted her. Dare he say—loved her?

His mind flitted back to the night with her in the bathing pool and he shifted uncomfortably in the chair. He needed to focus on the coming battle.

"Are you alright, my lord?" Yaotl's deep voice came from somewhere on his left.

"Yes." Ahkin cleared his throat and did not meet the eyes of his general.

"You will come home to her soon, and when you do, you can come back an accomplished warrior. Sacrifice one of the demons to the gods in her name and make her proud." Yaotl, wearing his warrior costume, looked as menacing as a prowling jungle cat. The jaws of the beast he had slain opened wide so that the cat appeared to eat his head as the teeth of it crowned his brow. The gold-and-black speckled paws rested on his shoulders.

"I will capture another tomorrow. Mark my words, Yaotl." Ahkin slammed a fist onto the armrest, sounding more confident than he felt.

"I do not doubt it, my lord. Though you will have to capture many more if you ever plan to break my record."

"We will just have to see." Ahkin gave him an impish grin.

Yaotl didn't smile in return. "We will just have to see if you can get your lady love out of your head long enough to focus on the battle itself."

"Don't make me remove your title." Ahkin lifted an eyebrow while Yaotl's lips ticked slightly upward, not quite a smile, but close. His mentor was silent for several more beats of a heart, but then his face turned grave.

"I only half jest, my lord. Make sure your head is fit before we reach Millacatl. Distractions are not welcome on the battlefield, and we cannot afford to lose you."

Ahkin frowned and did not respond. Yaotl was right. Ahkin was well trained. He had captured two warriors already, and his skills were acknowledged as superb even among the Jaguar warriors. Plus, he had an advantage over everyone else because of his heritage. But if he did not get his head in the proper place, none of it would matter.

———

After a full day and night marching, the army of Tollan broke through a line of trees and were greeted by the expansive rolling fields that lay at the foot of the dark mountains. Acres of fields and orchards produced every plant and food imaginable around the stone city perched upon a small grassy knoll. Though made of stone instead of gold, Millacatl rivaled Tollan in wealth. The abundance of food and plants provided the city-state with the most luxurious of fabrics and dyes, and the fact that they grew the empire's currency within their cacao groves had established them as important allies. Sure enough, upon their arrival at the city gates that night, the lord of Millacatl greeted them with bowls of cacao and an overly extravagant feast in honor of the coming battle.

They sacrificed an eagle upon their altar to grant the warriors swiftness and cunning, and Ahkin lost himself in the preparations. This was one area in which he knew he excelled. Weapons were inspected, costumes and wooden armor adjusted. Ahkin sparred with many of the Jaguar warriors under Yaotl and had them on the ground within minutes. The strength flowing within his muscles and the exertion of the exercises focused his mind, and he was ready.

Come dawn the next day, the death demons of Miquitz would be sent to the gods of the underworld they worshipped. He would make them pay for capturing farmers and peasants from his empire, for taking him away from Mayana, and he would offer *their* blood as sacrifice to the gods.

Ahkin brought his macana sword down upon the shield of a sparring Jaguar warrior with such force that the man staggered and fell onto his backside. The obsidian edges of the wooden sword embedded themselves in the shield. Despite Yaotl's warnings, Mayana filled Ahkin's thoughts. A righteous anger coursed through him as he thought of losing first his parents and now potentially his bride. The gods were not being fair. Instead of being by her side, making sure she healed, he was here, preparing to fight the pestilential death demons. Again.

Shame quickly replaced the anger. If he continued to question them, the gods would probably punish him even more. Ahkin placed a foot on the shield and forced it back to pry the blades loose.

"Yield," the warrior cried, scrambling back onto his feet.

From across the courtyard, Yaotl gave an approving nod as he lounged with nobles and the lord of Millacatl. Then he motioned for Ahkin to join them.

Panting heavily, Ahkin wiped the sweat from his forehead and made his way toward the group.

"We would like to discuss our strategy for tomorrow," Yaotl whispered roughly in his ear as Ahkin crouched low on an empty reed mat. A servant offered him a bowl of warmed cacao before he even had time to ask for one.

The general turned his attention to the nobles gathered. There were twelve naguals from the royal family at Ocelotl, the leader of the Eagle warriors, plus five priests and the lord of Millacatl with his three oldest sons. Ahkin still could not believe the man had ten children, though Teniza currently resided in Tollan. His own parents had constantly lamented that they had only him and Metzi, but as in every other aspect, the gods blessed the lord of Millacatl with abundance. Every head turned to face Ahkin, who stiffened and hastily lifted the bowl to his mouth and motioned with his hand to Yaotl, directing their attention back to him.

His heart thrummed like a battle drum. He was not yet accustomed to the faces of the leaders he admired looking to *him* for direction. Every battle-planning meeting Ahkin had ever attended, he lingered in his father's shadow, watching and observing, but always respectfully silent. He had assumed there would be many more meetings to practice voicing his opinions before leadership was dropped into his hands. Until now, Ahkin had always preferred calculating and mapping in the privacy of his own mind. As eyes turned expectantly toward him, his neck grew warm. Could they all still see the little boy behind his eyes? The one trying desperately to pretend he could live up to his father?

For the time being, he would rely on the guidance of his general and mentor, and he was grateful for Yaotl's willingness to fill that role.

"The raiders are camped at the base of the mountain. Our spies estimate that they number a little over two hundred," Yaotl rumbled.

"Why so few?" The lead warrior of the Eagles narrowed his eyes in suspicion.

"This is not an invading army. They hide in their mountain cities and continue to poke at us like a child pesters a slumbering dog. It is time we awaken and bite."

"Do we know their purpose in capturing my people?" The voice of the lord of Millacatl boomed with the authority of a city-state high priest and patriarch used to demanding attention and receiving it. The commanding presence, combined with his towering height, slightly intimidated Ahkin.

But just as plants lived off of light, Millacatl and Tollan were dependent on each other. Wealth, stature, and power were nothing without a sun, and Ahkin and his sister alone still owned that respect. Ahkin sat up a little straighter.

"My prince, would you care to explain?" Yaotl offered.

Ahkin cleared his throat and willed his voice to remain calm and collected. "We do not yet know why they are targeting your peasants. It is my hope that in capturing some of their warriors, we may question them and gain some answers. It is possible that news of my father's death has reached them, and they are testing our resolve in the wake of the tragedy."

"They likely question the strength of our empire with such a young and inexperienced emperor about to ascend the throne." The lord of Millacatl snorted in disgust.

Dismay filled Ahkin's chest, as though he were an impostor who had finally been discovered. This man saw the little boy Ahkin was trying so desperately to keep hidden. Perhaps the lord of Millacatl assumed that if Ahkin chose his daughter, he would hold a great deal of influence over him. Rebellion flared within him. It was fortunate Mayana had sealed off his heart from the other daughters. He would not grant this man any more power than he already wielded.

"I will show them on the battlefield just how afraid of me they should be," Ahkin growled. Behind the lord of Millacatl's back, the corner of Yaotl's mouth ticked up.

The lord waved his hand dismissively, and Ahkin wished he could use his sword to wipe the smug smile off the man's face.

"Speaking of battlefields ..." The lord looked down his nose at the young prince. "How fares the battlefield of the heart? Have you selected a wife yet?" His voice remained casual, but Ahkin could sense the tension simmering just under the surface.

"I have." Ahkin avoided his eyes. "I was unable to announce my decision before the battle and I plan on making my selection official the moment I return."

"Excellent." The lord lifted his bowl in the air for more pulque, though his cheeks were already crimson from the drink. "I am confident the prince will make the best decision for the well-being of the kingdom and not follow a childish impulse of passion one would expect for his age." He lifted the newly filled bowl in Ahkin's direction as a salute before bringing the bowl to his lips.

The rage pulsing through Ahkin's veins surged, and he leapt to his feet. Did everyone have to remind him how young he was? How inexperienced? The look of surprise on Lord Millacatl's face so mirrored that of his sons on either side that Ahkin remembered this man was still a father. A father probably afraid that Ahkin had not chosen his daughter. The thought calmed his anger. He knew too well the pain of losing family to the rituals. They were about to go into battle and the last thing they needed was to be fighting amongst themselves.

"Excuse me, I wish to continue with my practice." Ahkin turned on the spot and motioned for the Jaguar warrior he had been sparring with previously to follow him. The warrior let out an exhausted huff, eyes darting to Yaotl as though asking to be saved, and shuffled his feet to follow the prince back to the center of the courtyard.

CHAPTER

35

Mayana had never told anyone about her revelations regarding the codex texts. She expected to feel immensely relieved, as if she were putting down a weight she had been carrying inside her soul for years. But for some reason, when she and Yemania left the temple, a sense of dread settled into the pit of her stomach. Her secret was not something so petty as Coatl and Metzi sharing passionate trysts throughout the palace, but something that truly put her life in danger. Not only did she risk the prince discovering she was not as religious as he thought, but she was in danger of offending the religious leadership.

As they left the shadowed rooms of the temple, the hairs on the back of her neck rose. She lifted her gaze from Yemania's face to find the high priest of Tollan, a priest of even higher status than her father, watching her from a distant doorway. His rank was evident from the adornments of feathers and beads he wore around his neck and the headdress that dwarfed those of the Tlana priests. She had never seen the high priest before, only heard of him spoken about back home. His wide, wrinkled face contorted into a frown as they passed, and something about the knowing look in his dark, deep-set eyes unnerved her. They had been alone in the rooms with the codex, hadn't they? There was no way he could know what she and Yemania had discussed.

Yemania did not notice the high priest as she muttered about wanting to enjoy the palace's food before she died, and Mayana tore her eyes away from the ancient face.

"Yes," Mayana said. "I'm starving. Let's go."

Back in Mayana's room several hours later, the remnants of flatbread and various fruit cores piled in a wooden bowl in the corner, Mayana stretched out her injured leg. She hissed as the bandages pressed against the throbbing skin and she wished she could smash the scorpion all over again just to feel the satisfying crunch of its shell. The exertion of the climb up the temple had aggravated the swelling, but she didn't regret their trip at all.

"You never did tell me what happened. How did you know to come find me?" Mayana remembered the edges of her vision going dark but didn't remember anyone else being in the room.

"I heard you," Yemania said simply. "You screamed for help, so I came."

"But you were so angry with me. I had just …" Mayana couldn't say the words out loud.

"I don't hate you because the prince likes you. I understand why he does." She bumped her shoulder teasingly against Mayana's. "Well, mostly. Does he know how you feel about the rituals? What you think about the codex?"

Mayana couldn't meet her eyes. She busied her fingers with the edge of the bandage around her calf.

Yemania clucked her tongue. "He doesn't know, does he?"

"No." Mayana jerked her hands away from her leg and pressed her fists into her eyes. "No, he doesn't know. He thinks I saved the jaguar because I was overly concerned with honoring the calendar."

Yemania blanched. "Mayana. You're … you're basically lying to him."

Mayana brought her knees to her chest and wrapped her arms around them, dropping her forehead and hiding her face in the little bubble of darkness she created for herself.

"I like him, Yemania." Her words sounded muffled as she spoke into her legs.

"Well, I think we all like him. I mean, he's handsome, he's smart, and good gods the man can dance."

Mayana gave a weak chuckle. "He hates dancing."

Yemania was silent for a moment. "Did he tell you that?"

Mayana nodded, her face still hidden.

Yemania heaved a sigh. "I will probably regret asking this, but what happened after the feast that night? Where did you go with him?"

Images flashed within Mayana's mind's eye. Ahkin tipping up her chin and kissing her for the first time, his voice whispering "Don't ever hide yourself from me." The feel of his warm body against hers in the cold water. The taste of his lips as she ran her tongue along them. The feel of his hair as she ran her fingers through it.

The blood rose in her cheeks as she remembered the way she had stopped his hands mere inches from the fabric around her chest, and his groan of frustration. How she had wanted more than anything *not* to stop him. To let his hands caress the parts of herself she never let anyone else ...

"You're blushing." Yemania's blunt interjection brought her back to the present.

"Sorry ..."

"Zorrah says you ... uh—" Yemania bit her lip.

"No. We didn't do *that*. Gods, Yemania, you think I would do that just to make him pick me?" Mayana swore her cheeks burned even hotter.

"So, you didn't?"

"No!"

"I didn't think so. Not really," Yemania said, her voice barely above a whisper.

"And why would you believe Zorrah anyway? I'm fairly certain a scorpion didn't get into my room by accident." Mayana fluffed the pillow beneath her with a little more force than was entirely necessary.

"Did you kiss him, though?"

Mayana froze. She couldn't lie to Yemania, not now. Besides, she had already told her the prince was probably going to pick her. "No. Technically he kissed me."

Yemania's hands flew to her mouth. "How did that happen?"

"Well ... we kissed in the hallway. And again in ... one of the bathing pools in the pleasure garden."

Yemania sucked in a loud breath.

"And then we sat in a steam bath for a while and just ... talked. We talked for hours, actually."

"You love him," Yemania said. It wasn't a question.

Mayana squirmed. "Can you truly love someone you hardly know?"

"Fine. You are falling in love with him, aren't you?"

"I think I might be. It's hard to tell. It was one night together and then this happened." She gestured to her swollen calf. "And now he's off fighting death demons while I sit here and wonder if he's even going to come back."

To her surprise, tears pricked at the back of her eyes. She cared for him, perhaps was falling in love with him, but what did that matter if his godly blood drained itself out on the jungle floor? Or worse, if he were captured and taken to Miquitz as a sacrifice to the gods of the underworld?

"If you truly care for him, then you have to tell him the truth," Yemania said. She folded her hands in her lap and stared at Mayana with a deep sadness in her eyes.

"If I tell him the truth, he won't ... like me anymore. He won't pick me." Mayana's voice trembled with suppressed emotion.

"Maybe not." Yemania shrugged. "But he will find out eventually. That is not a secret you will be able to hide forever. Not unless you can accept the rituals as they are and decide you can do the sacrifices. Including the sacrifice of the rest of us."

"I cannot watch you die," Mayana said through gritted teeth. "I won't. Not for rules created by men."

"Then we will likely die together anyway." Yemania turned her face toward the open veranda, where sunlight poured in through the vines covering the opening.

"Does the light seem ... off to you?" Yemania asked suddenly, her mouth falling into a frown.

"What light?" Mayana turned her head to face the entrance to the garden.

"The light of the sun."

Mayana studied the beams piercing through the room. She pushed herself back onto her feet, wincing as she put her weight on her bad calf, and hobbled toward the vines. The sun was definitely far too low for the time of day, and in the fading yellow band of sky along the horizon, the bleeding comet seemed to shine a little brighter.

CHAPTER

36

A conch-shell horn broke the silence of the early morning. The warriors of Tollan slithered out of the trees like spirits of the night just as the sun's face broke above the distant horizon. Ahkin said a silent prayer of thanks to his sister for her blood sacrifice back in the capital.

Every sense in his body awakened and came alive as he prepared himself. The world around him came into sharper focus, just as it did before every battle. Colors seemed brighter, sounds louder, smells stronger. His muscles twitched as anticipation raced through his veins; he was anxious for the battle to begin so that he could free the peasants and return to Mayana as soon as possible. He may not be a great emperor—his faith was not as strong as it should be—but at least he knew his place on a battlefield.

Across the tall grass field shimmering with a fine layer of mist, the Miquitz raiders' camp stirred to life in response to the call of the horn.

From this distance he could not see where the captives were being kept, but he knew they were still alive. The Miquitz would wait to sacrifice them in their temple.

Ahkin lifted his arm high in the sky.

"Bows! Wait until they are making their way across the field. We do not wish to attack the camp directly and risk Lord Millacatl's peasants."

The group of men armed with bows and slings readied themselves but held their weapons. Ahkin narrowed his eyes as the enemy raiders gathered along the edge of the field. They wore inky-black warrior costumes accentuated with random splashes of bright color, but Ahkin shivered at the defining characteristic of the Miquitz warriors. Human finger bones rattled from their shields and their quivers were filled not with arrows, but with sharpened bones from enemy arms and legs. Painted across their black clothing were the forms of skeletons. He could not see their faces because they were whitened to resemble skulls or covered with actual fragments of skulls.

Their silence as they assembled brought to mind an army of the dead rising up from the depths of Xibalba itself. Ahkin couldn't wait to send them where they belonged.

As he studied them, something did not seem right. There were barely a hundred. Hadn't Yaotl estimated there were twice as many? Where were the rest of the demon raiders? Had they already disappeared into the mountains with their captives?

The Miquitz suddenly let out an almighty scream, raising the hair on Ahkin's arms and causing the shoulders of the warriors beside him to shift uncomfortably. A few nervously glanced at their neighbors, but they held their positions. A burning surge of pride raced through him, and he turned back to face the skeleton warriors.

The death demons charged like wild spirits escaping the underworld.

"Now!" The scream ripped through Ahkin's throat as he slashed his arm downward.

Arrows and spears fired a rain of wood and obsidian upon the coming enemy. Many fell, but many more continued their charge through the tall grasses.

Ahkin lifted and then lowered his arm again, signaling a second volley of projectiles across the misty distance and sending even more skeleton warriors to the ground, hopefully to Xibalba.

Yaotl signaled the drummers, who beat a frenzied rhythm not unlike the music he and Mayana first shared a dance to. His heart had hurtled into his rib cage on that occasion too, though for entirely different reasons. Ahkin suppressed a smile and reached a hand down toward his macana sword. Tied to its handle was a small doll the size of his thumb wearing a tiny blue-and-yellow dress. He squeezed the soft body in his hand as the warriors beside him released their own battle cries. He said a silent prayer to Ometeotl to protect him so that he could see Mayana again.

The readiness for battle raced through his blood and his muscles ached to move, but he had to wait. Yaotl never let him join the first wave of Jaguar and Eagle warriors. As talented a warrior as he might be, his blood was still more valuable than any of the others around him.

The conch-shell horn cried out through the chaos for a second time, and the warriors beside him surged forward. The thundering of feet reminded Ahkin of the powerful booming clouds of a fierce storm. The vibrations rattled his bones.

The hulking forms of jaguars and wolves controlled by their nagual masters sprinted out to meet the Miquitz first, and several demons fell under the flash of teeth and claws. Growls and roars of beasts now blended with the booms of the war drums and the yells of warriors.

The smell of bodies and blood filled Ahkin's nose and he leaned forward, anxious to join his fellows in the melee, to show his people that while their emperor may be young, he was fierce. He would make them proud to follow him.

The horn sounded a third time as the Chicome gained the advantage over the Miquitz. The numbers were obviously making a difference. Ahkin released his own ear-splitting cry and launched himself forward.

A mass of bodies writhed in front of him, black skeletons grappling with the brightly adorned Eagles and Jaguars. He caught a glimpse of massive Yaotl knocking down two warriors with a single sweep of his arm before he turned and landed his giant foot on another's chest. Ahkin smiled at the sickening crunch of ribs as he sprinted toward them.

Before he reached the melee, Ahkin ran a finger across his own blade, exposing his blood to the crisp morning air.

Where Yaotl had mass and girth as his greatest weapons, Ahkin's skill lay in his speed and agility … and his godly abilities. His father had taught him the human eye only saw what it did because of light, and by manipulating that light, Ahkin could control what people saw. By bending light, he could even make something disappear altogether. He bent the light around himself, willing it not to strike him.

In his enemies' eyes, he was no longer there.

Ahkin tightened his hand around the leather handle of his macana sword, savoring the soft yet sturdy grip. Bringing it high above his head, he leapt like a monkey from a branch and brought his sword down into the back of a warrior that had been charging toward Yaotl.

"You finally made it, my lord. It's good to see you … or not see you, I should say." Yaotl turned to see the Miquitz warrior fall without obvious explanation.

"You could at least smile, Yaotl. That was a relatively good joke," Ahkin teased.

Yaotl grunted and smashed his fist into another face.

Ahkin whirled on the spot and worked his way through the remaining warriors. His feet squelched in the red-tinged mud of the field as he brought down blow after blow. Sometimes he allowed himself to appear for a moment before bending the light again, confusing the death demons and increasing the sense of fear as they realized he could be anywhere. Soon, a trail of bodies littered the ground in his wake.

He released the light and showed himself to a particularly vicious-looking raider who had an Eagle warrior on his knees by the topknot of his hair, a blade of obsidian mere inches from his throat. His sudden appearance distracted the death demon, whose eyes went wide beneath his partial skull mask.

He dropped the Eagle warrior, backing slowly away. "The prince! The prince is here!"

Instead of engaging him as Ahkin expected, the man ran at a full sprint back toward his camp continuing to scream, "The prince!"

A tingle of unease fluttered through his stomach along with confusion at the warrior's odd behavior. He let it shake him for only the length of a heartbeat before he bent down to help the Eagle warrior back to his feet.

"Thank you, my lord."

Ahkin grunted in response, shoving the man back toward the battle.

Something barreled into him from behind, knocking the wind from his lungs and slamming him to the ground with a force that brought stars of light sparking across Ahkin's eyes. The warm, sticky body of a giant wolf lay prostrate across his stomach, arrows of bone protruding from the dark fur on its back.

Ahkin couldn't breathe beneath its weight and he shoved at the body of the beast with every ounce of strength he possessed, one hand still firmly gripping the handle of his macana sword.

A shadowy figure appeared above him, a bone-white spear in his hand. The spear lifted into the air and Ahkin lifted his sword to block the blow, the tiny bloodstained doll bouncing against his curled fist.

The warrior's eyes, a black band of paint across them, widened in surprise and focused on the small doll tied to the handle. His head cocked ever so slightly to the side, making a tiny bone earring rest against his cheek as he studied the doll that had no place on the battlefield. In that moment of hesitation, a spear burst through the man's bare chest, splattering blood across the carcass of the wolf and Ahkin's face.

CHAPTER

37

"You know, you could have hidden yourself," Yaotl growled, shifting the dead wolf off of Ahkin's legs and helping him wriggle out from beneath it.

"How, exactly? Even if I had bent the light around me, he already knew where I was."

"So, you were going to just lie there?" Yaotl thundered.

"I was going to defend myself." Ahkin raised his own voice in return, lifting his macana for emphasis.

Yaotl's eyes focused on the bloodied worry doll and he let out of bellow of frustration. "Get the girl out of your head!"

Ahkin took a step back, his eyes narrowed. "It just saved my life," he said defensively. "It distracted him."

Before Yaotl could respond, a fourth horn blast demanded their attention.

"That's ... not ours, is it?" Ahkin studied the concern evident on his general's face and took it as confirmation.

At the sound of the horn, every death demon left fighting turned away from the battle and sprinted full force back toward the mountains like a pack of black deer.

"What ...?" Confusion clouded every thought running through Ahkin's head as the enemy retreated.

"Get behind me, and bend the damn light so no one can see you."

"Why?"

"My lord, something's not right." Did he sense a hint of fear? Ahkin had never heard anything like it in his mentor's deep voice.

He immediately stepped behind Yaotl's mountainous form and concealed himself between the beams of morning sunlight now bathing the field.

Every warrior that was left of the Chicome stood transfixed and staring as a single dark-cloaked figure emerged from a tent at the Miquitz camp. The figure's head was entirely smooth, bearing not a single strand of hair, and the skin was painted ghostly white. He slowly glided forward. The black paint around the man's eyes covered the entire socket, making his face resemble a skull with burning dark eyes. His smile was accentuated with even more dark paint, making it seem twice as wide as a normal human mouth.

Ahkin's heart thrashed within his chest, something urging him to run as far from the battlefield as possible.

The figure swept his arms wide, revealing a bare chest and a necklace of bone beads and shining black raven feathers.

"Prince of light," the skeleton man called in a high, clear voice. "I know you are here."

Yaotl muttered a string of curses under his breath.

Several warriors around Ahkin took involuntary steps back, their gazes darting back to the trees behind them. Ahkin didn't blame them; he was half considering bolting for the trees himself.

"There is no use in hiding behind your general, dear prince. I feel your life force, even if my eyes cannot detect you."

Yaotl's muttered curses turned full volume as he took a step to further shield Ahkin from this ominous new arrival. He called out in his deep voice, "I do not know what you want with the prince, but I know your people rely on the sun as much as we do. You play a dangerous game, skull man."

The unusually wide smile of the man just spread even wider. Nausea rolled through Ahkin's stomach.

"I merely wish to speak with him." His voice was eerily calculating and calm, almost amused.

"No." Yaotl's yell carried through the tense silence.

"What do you want with me?" Ahkin stepped out from behind his mentor and allowed the light to fall upon him once more.

The warriors around him gasped and moved in closer, trying to form a human shield between Ahkin and the skull demon.

"My dear prince Ahkin, it is a pleasure to *see* you at last." He flourished his hand into an exaggerated bow.

"Who are you?" Ahkin demanded.

"I am Tzom, high priest of Miquitz and speaker for the gods of the underworld."

Ahkin stiffened his spine. He had heard rumors of the priests of Miquitz ... of what they could do. They were capable of possessing the spirits of the living to control them and allowing the spirits of the dead to possess their own bodies. They dealt in the magic of the soul, a power long-forbidden and long-feared by the Chicome.

Almost as if in response to his thoughts, the light faded from Yaotl's eyes. His mouth and features went slack, and before Ahkin could respond, Yaotl's thick arms wrapped around him and held him in place like a parent restraining a screaming child.

Ahkin strained against his mentor's hold, but he was no match for Yaotl's strength. His remaining Eagle and Jaguar warriors rushed forward, spears and macana swords drawn, but clearly torn as to how to proceed. Were they supposed to attack Yaotl?

"Stop!" Ahkin commanded them. "I will not have his blood on our own hands."

"Oh, relax, my dear prince." Tzom chuckled softly. Bloodlust raged within Ahkin's veins and he longed to shred the white skin off of the high priest's face for possessing Yaotl and using him like this.

"I have no desire to hurt your men any further. I will even ..."

But Tzom's words were cut short as vines shot through the ground at his feet and snaked themselves around his arms and legs.

His wide, eerie smile turned to a grimace as the skull man clawed at the plants attempting to restrain him.

The arms around Ahkin slackened, and Yaotl shook his head like a wet dog.

Without hesitation, the general scooped Ahkin up into his arms again, shielding him from the view of the death demon, and whistled through his teeth. Feet thundered against the ground as they ran for the cover of the jungle trees, leaving the frustrated shrieks of the high priest of Miquitz behind them still wrestling the vines pulling at his limbs.

As soon as they reached the cover of the trees, Ahkin caught sight of the lord of Millacatl, a bleeding palm outstretched toward Tzom.

"I can restrain him for a little while longer," the lord of Millacatl said through gritted teeth. "Fall back to the city and station the naguals at our borders. I think the demons will retreat back to the mountains for now."

Ahkin threw Yaotl's arms off him and faced the lord of Millacatl. "Did we save the peasants, at least?"

"No, my lord," the lord of Millacatl said with an edge to his voice. "Half of the demons escaped with them into the mountains and we accomplished nothing except spilling our own blood on the jungle floor."

With a strained breath, sweat beading on his brow, the lord dropped his hand and the vines in the distance retreated back into the earth.

Ahkin's heart flipped as he realized Tzom was gone, along with the other death demons and the peasants Ahkin had failed to save. The lord of Millacatl turned his back on them and stormed back toward the city.

Yaotl placed a hand on Ahkin's shoulder, which he shrugged off rather roughly.

"You did all you could, my lord."

"Did I, Yaotl? Because as far as I can tell, we accomplished nothing." Ahkin threw his macana sword at the ground with enough force to split a man in two. He rubbed his eyes and pinched the bridge of his nose. Another failure. Another example of his youthful inexperience and weakness. Was there anything he could do right as an emperor?

"Not so, my prince."

Ahkin looked up at Yaotl's words, trying not to let himself hope.

Yaotl jerked his head toward the empty battlefield. "We captured three of the death demons to take home for our trouble."

Ahkin rubbed the back of his neck. At least they had that. And at least now he could return home to Mayana.

PART 3

CHAPTER

38

Mayana paced the length of her room three times before throwing her hands in the air with a great sigh of frustration.

He had to be home soon. Metzi had announced at breakfast that a raven had arrived from Millacatl with a message declaring the warriors would return by evening.

She hadn't said Ahkin was among them, but surely if he wasn't, she wouldn't look so relieved.

The sun was already setting, again far too early for this time of year, but that meant they should be home soon. They could even be home already. Would he come to see her? Should she try to go see him?

At the midday meal, the other princesses had seemed restless too. Teniza, the towering daughter of Millacatl, had finally snapped at Yoli's morbid musing about how they would likely be sacrificed. The two girls bickered through the rest of the meal.

"You are a beanpole with no brain!"

"You love death so much, why don't you just marry a prince of Miquitz!"

Mayana dropped her forehead onto the low stone table and waited for it to stop.

She never had to deal with issues like these with five brothers at home. At least if they were upset with you, they could just punch you and be done with it. Mayana was not used to the way women interacted with one another.

The one princess who always remained relatively aloof was the storm princess of Ehecatl. Anytime Mayana came upon her, Itza was deeply involved in prayer or meditation. She had heard rumors of Ehecatl's piety and devotion to the gods, but Itza seemed to be interested in little else. Twice Mayana had tried engaging her in conversation, trying to thank her for blowing away the smoke after the jaguar incident, but she had never spoken more than three words since then, so Mayana just gave up.

At least she had Yemania, and she planned to ask Ahkin about sparing her life the moment he returned. She also thought about taking Yemania's advice and telling the prince how she *really* felt about the codex rituals ... but she just couldn't bring herself to do it. Perhaps part of her wanted to see how he reacted to her suggestion of saving Yemania. If he took that well, maybe he'd be more understanding. If he didn't, then ... Mayana would just have to figure out what she would do later.

She had to find something to do to pass the time until Ahkin returned, or she would go crazy, and sweating out her anxiety in the steam baths seemed like a good idea.

"But it's so late," Yemania complained.

"Please, I just need to do something other than sit in my room and stare at the wall." Mayana made her eyes as big and pitiful as possible.

"Fine." Yemania sighed. She grabbed a woven white towel from her own baskets of belongings and followed Mayana out into the hall.

They rounded the corner and Mayana, so relieved to finally be *doing* something, didn't notice the other person heading the opposite way until she smacked against a hard-muscled chest. For a wild moment, she thought it was Ahkin finally home at last, until she recognized the brown curly hair of Coatl as he stumbled back away from her.

"Coatl? What are you doing in the residence halls so late?" Yemania asked.

Coatl's cheeks were flushed and his eyes darted around as though expecting to see more than just his sister and her friend. His nervous energy reminded Mayana of a skittish deer cornered by hunters.

"I was attending to the princess. She has been complaining of headaches and I offered her a remedy."

Yemania perked up at the mention of remedies. "Did you try offering her chalalatli root? I've found that to be really helpful."

"Yes, actually." Coatl shuffled his feet. "I remembered when you used that remedy for Mother. It really seems to be helping."

"I'm so glad." Yemania beamed. Mayana's heart swelled at the pride she could see practically glowing off her friend. She must be a truly gifted healer when her lack of confidence did not stand in the way.

"I should probably get back to my work." Coatl fingered the ruby pendant hanging around his neck and refused to meet their eyes. Just as he had when Mayana awoke in his chambers, he seemed to want to be rid of them as soon as possible.

"Alright." Yemania's smile faltered slightly. "It was good to see you, brother."

Coatl returned a smile that was tight and pained. He did not acknowledge Mayana's presence whatsoever before he marched past them.

"He has certainly seemed distant lately," Yemania mused as they continued toward the steam baths. "Do you think he's worried about me being sacrificed?"

"I imagine that's a great sadness for him. But that won't happen if I have anything to say about it." Mayana laid a hand on Yemania's arm. Yemania looked as though she wanted to respond but thought better of it.

Steam engulfed them when they finally entered the low stone room, but it appeared that they were not the only ones seeking solace in the steam bath.

Metzi lounged across the stone bench that encircled the room, her long dark hair sprawled around her head like an ebony halo. She sat up on an elbow as they entered and greeted them with a playful smile. Sweat beaded along her forehead and shoulders and dripped down her bare back and chest.

"Good evening, ladies. Come to enjoy the healing powers of the mists as well?"

Yemania bowed her head in respect and squeaked an inaudible response.

"I hope your headache is improving," Mayana said, taking a seat across from Metzi.

"My headache?" Metzi's eyebrows drew together. "Oh, yes. I'm sorry.

The healer gave me a root tea that worked so well, I almost forgot I had it."

"Chalalatli root, my lady. It has many anti-inflammatory properties." Yemania sat up a little straighter. "It's a remedy my brother and I often used at home."

"That's right, you are Coatl's sister." Metzi cocked her head to the side and appraised her. "I imagine you must be exceedingly gifted to come from the same line as Coatl."

"Thank you." Yemania dropped her gaze to the floor with a sweet, satisfied smile.

A snort sounded from the doorway, and all three girls looked up to find Zorrah and Teniza standing with towels in their hands as well.

"So much for a peaceful evening," Teniza said out of the corner of her mouth.

Metzi gave the comment no notice. "Join us, ladies, this will be fun for me to get to know all of you. It's important for the royal line to be familiar with the noble families of the empire." She motioned for them to come in. "In fact, I have an idea."

The prince's twin disappeared for several minutes into the hallway. Teniza and Zorrah tentatively took seats as far away from Mayana as possible. Mayana crossed her arms across her own bare chest and refused to look in their direction.

"I've sent a servant for the other two princesses to join us." Metzi reentered the steam bath and clapped her hands together in a satisfied way. "Let's all play a little game, shall we? I have always loved games. A way to ease the tensions and let me get to know each of you better. I can even report back to my brother. An unofficial third task."

Mayana couldn't help but notice a gleam of mischief sparkling in the princess of light's eyes. What were Metzi's real intentions? She seemed the type to subtly remind everyone who held the true power in the room.

Yoli and Itza finally joined them, both looking thoroughly disgruntled at having been roused from bed to sit in a steam room with the other princesses. Yoli tapped an impatient foot and glared at the prince's sister. Itza's eyes were lowered in apparent meditation or prayer, but her lips were tightly pursed.

Metzi didn't appear fazed in the slightest. On the contrary, she seemed to feed off the negative energy as though it were a challenge—a challenge to prove her superiority.

"Here is my game. I want each of you to tell me one thing about you that is true and one thing about you that is a lie, and I will try to guess which is the lie. It's a game Ahkin and I played together all the time as children, and I always won. He's nowhere near as good at reading people as I am. In fact, there isn't much I'm not better at than he is." She wiggled a teasing eyebrow.

Zorrah and Teniza exchanged significant glances, but neither responded, probably too afraid of offending the prince's sister. Mayana was willing to bet that Yoli would be raising her obsidian shard toward her eyes if she had it with her.

"Let's start with you, Lady Teniza. Millacatl always seems to think it should come first anyway." Metzi was still smiling, but everyone stiffened at the obvious insinuation behind her words. Mayana bit back a laugh.

Teniza straightened her spine and tilted her nose in the air. "Fine. I will tell one lie and one truth. I have many boys back home falling over their feet at the chance to marry me, and I prefer deer pelts for my bedding over rabbit furs." She folded her woven towel neatly across her lap.

Metzi snorted. "That's obvious, and completely expected. Your answers show your desire to impress me, even with the lie of what bedding you prefer to flaunt your wealthy status. Deer pelts are needlessly extravagant. What insecurities are you hiding behind that pretty face that you feel the need to work so hard to maintain your facade? Do you really feel you have no worth aside from your beauty and wealth?"

Teniza drew back as though Metzi had slapped her. "Excuse me?"

"I told you I have a gift for reading people." The prince's sister tilted her head and smiled sweetly at Teniza. Something about the smile churned Mayana's stomach. She was clever, but what she had just done to Teniza bordered on cruel, like a child who liked to tease others but never knew when it had gone too far. Tears glistened in the corners of Teniza's eyes, and Mayana's heart lurched in response.

"Maybe Lady Teniza is just being careful. She doesn't know us well, and to share such intimate details …" Mayana opened her palms to Metzi, an offering of peace.

"I don't need you to defend me, daughter of water," Teniza spat at her. "Fine, you want some real truth? I left the man I really love behind, knowing that I must marry another or perish. My father gave me no choice in the matter, and if I don't survive, my real love promised to join me in the underworld." Her voice cracked slightly at the end. "If I win, I must marry a man I don't love, but if I lose, I will kill the one I do love with my failure." With that, she wrapped the towel forcefully around her heaving chest and stormed from the steam bath. All of the air seemed to leave the room in her wake, making it hard for Mayana to breathe. She couldn't imagine being in a position like that.

Metzi's smile widened. "That's more along the lines of what I had in mind. Who would like to go next?"

Zorrah and Yoli both narrowed their eyes, glowering at Metzi as though she were a dangerous snake dangling from a tree branch.

"Lady Zorrah? Would you like to play my game?"

Zorrah rose slowly to her feet, but her hands curled into fists at her side. "No, thank you, Lady Metzi. My life has been nothing but a series of games to prove myself, and forgive me if I have had enough of them. May I retire back to my room?"

Metzi nodded. "I expect nothing less from a city whose people treat each other like the beasts they command. But like a proper wolf, you know to submit when faced with an alpha."

Zorrah bared her teeth but did not respond. Instead, she turned to look down upon Mayana and said, "I also know how to sense the weaknesses in those who are below me."

Mayana stiffened as the animal princess swept past her and followed in Teniza's footsteps.

Metzi let her breath out in a huff. "Well, now that they are gone, we can have some real conversation, can't we?"

Mayana glanced at Yemania and noticed that her eyes were glassy with tears.

"Come now, girls, we all know that the only way to deal with bullies like Teniza and Zorrah is to stand up to them. There is nothing more satisfying than knocking the pedestals out from under those that think they are above everyone else."

The corner of Yoli's mouth curved up. "Your majesty does make an excellent point."

Mayana still didn't know where she stood. She didn't at all approve of the way Metzi had just treated Teniza and Zorrah, and yet at the same time, it *was* slightly satisfying. Disgust immediately flooded through her at the thought. Zorrah and Teniza, despite their faults, did not deserve to be treated in such a way. If her mother had taught her anything, it was that just because others may treat you poorly, it never gives you the right to treat them poorly in return.

"Please. I truly would like to get to know you girls better, to get to know your families and your city-states. It is a princess's responsibility to be familiar with the intricacies of the empire." Metzi's lower lip pouted, her demeanor now light to the darkness it had been moments before.

"What do you want to know?" Itza's sharp voice commanded from the corner of the steam bath. She fixed the princess of Tollan with a shrewd, calculating look.

"From you, daughter of storms, I would love to hear more about your home, as it is soon to be my own. What can you tell me of Ehecatl?"

"You will find it very different from your life here in Tollan."

Metzi leaned forward as though waiting for Itza to continue, but she didn't.

"And that is all? What about your family? Your brother, my betrothed?"

"We prepare for Quetzalcoatl's return." The diminutive wind princess studied her nails intently.

"I know that. But how so?"

"I am sure you will see when you get there."

Metzi slammed her hands against the stone bench beneath her. "Why is everything with you storm lords so vague and mystical? Never a straight answer. It's maddening."

Itza rose gracefully and inclined her head to each of them. "I would like to finish my evening prayers now, if you don't mind."

Metzi waved a dismissive hand, obviously too frustrated with the daughter of Ehecatl to continue her questioning.

"Does that mean we can all go now? Since the game doesn't seem to be going anywhere?" Yoli rose to her feet.

Metzi laid her head back down on the bench and rubbed at her temples with the tips of her fingers. "If that is what you wish, daughter of fire. My headache does seem to be returning."

Mayana and Yemania took that as a cue to leave as well. They made their way toward the door of the steam baths, but before they could leave, Yemania hesitated.

"Your majesty?" she whispered nervously.

"Yes?" Metzi did not open her eyes as she continued to rub little circles against the side of her head.

"Would you like me to send for more chalalatli root?"

"Thank you, daughter of healing, but I will probably summon Coatl back. It seems to be worsening. I do appreciate your thoughtfulness." Her voice strained with sudden exhaustion and fatigue.

"I hope you feel better," Mayana added before grabbing Yemania's wrist and leaving the princess of the sun to herself.

CHAPTER

39

Mayana stood frozen at the entrance to her bed chambers. Zorrah had apparently sent a monkey into her room and ordered it to go berserk. The musky scent of the beast still hung in the air. All of her baskets had been upended and most of her clothing torn to bits. Her door curtain hung half off its rod and all of the creams and makeup her aunts sent along with her now decorated her walls like a painted pot. Mayana just laughed at the pettiness. At least there were no more scorpions … for now.

Flumping onto the many rabbit furs on her bed mat, she threw an arm across her eyes. The steam baths were supposed to be relaxing, but tonight they had had the opposite effect. At least they had been a distraction. Dear gods, if she did not hear something about Ahkin soon she would—

"You expect me to honor the codex and wait until we are married with you sprawled out across a bed like that?"

Mayana's breath caught in her throat and she sat straight up. Her eyes roved the messy room until she saw him, leaning casually against the frame of her doorway and fingering the lopsided curtain.

"I must admit, I thought you would be a little cleaner than this." His mouth ticked up into a crooked smile and Mayana swore her heart would stop right then and there. His eyes took in the paint- and cream-smeared walls, the shredded baskets and clothing across the floor, and he chuckled as her cheeks flushed.

"I—it wasn't *me*—there was a monkey—"

"What did you do to make it destroy your room?"

"More like what did I do to its master ..." Mayana growled. She moved to push herself up and hissed at the pain in her leg, buckling slightly as it gave under her weight.

Ahkin rushed forward and caught her in his arms before she fell.

"Thank you. It's just still a little sore when I put pressure on it." Mayana tucked her hair behind her ear and refused to meet his eyes. She waited for him to steady her and then step away, but he didn't.

He didn't let her go.

Instead, he gently turned her around until they were face-to-face, her hands splayed across the bare muscles of his chest. He still held her firmly, but she was sure she'd collapse anyway if she met his eyes.

She lifted her gaze to peer at him through her lashes, and the desire that raged within them came to the surface as he crushed his mouth against hers.

And then she did collapse. But this time, he collapsed with her, and his arms guided her gently onto her bed mat. The mostly bare skin of her back tingled at the warmth of his hands and the smooth, soft feel of the rabbit furs. He smelled like sunlight, if that even had a smell, and like something distinctly male. He shifted his body as he towered over her, letting his weight fall and yet also holding himself up on his forearms so he didn't overwhelm her. But Mayana didn't care, she *wanted* the weight of his body overpowering hers. She snaked her arms around his chest and ran her fingers over the muscles of his shoulders. She dug in the tips of her fingers, trying to pull him closer to her.

He groaned in response and deepened their kiss. She could taste the urgency between them as they explored each other's bodies with their hands, learning every curve as though they were afraid they would be separated again.

The urgency behind their movements reached an almost fevered pitch until he broke their kiss and leaned his forehead against hers. His breath came in heavy pants, and Mayana let out a small giggle she couldn't hold back.

"I missed you," he said, his voice deep and husky.

"I guessed as much." She planted a small kiss on the tip of his nose. "I missed you as well."

"Can we just be married now?"

"Is that your way of asking me?"

Ahkin froze, as if he had just realized something. "I haven't asked you yet, have I?"

Mayana was sure an entire swarm of happy bees took flight inside her stomach.

"Well, I am assuming, considering where your hands are at this very moment." Mayana raised her eyebrows at him. Ahkin just smiled playfully and gripped her even tighter.

"Well. Then I guess I have an important announcement to make tomorrow evening. Oh! And your surprise!"

"My surprise?" Mayana cocked her head.

"Yes, I had planned … then the scorpion …" Ahkin slapped a hand against his forehead before he turned to face her again. "How are you feeling, by the way? I was so afraid for you when I left. Coatl assured me you were recovering, but I was terrified I'd never see you again."

The bees in her stomach buzzed excitedly.

"I'm alright. I mean, I'm still sore. Coatl says most of the poison has worked itself out of my system and that the swelling just lasts for a week or two."

Ahkin kissed her hard. "Never do that to me again."

"Well, have a chat with the princess of Ocelotl if you wish to avoid me dying by scorpions or jag—" Mayana bit her tongue, not wanting to touch the topic of the damned jaguar.

A shadow crossed over Ahkin's face. "What do you mean?"

"I'm fairly certain the scorpion was not in here by accident."

"If that is the case …" He started to push himself up, but Mayana wrapped her arms around his chest and pulled him back down.

"No, deal with it later. I've been sitting here wondering if you've been captured or killed on a field and now you're here. I'm not letting you go until I am thoroughly convinced you are alive."

The shadow faded and was replaced by a teasing grin.

"And you are not yet convinced I am alive?" He grabbed her hand and placed it over his chest, where his heart thudded against her fingers.

Mayana laughed. "Fine. I'm convinced, but don't go. Please."

Ahkin lowered his body back onto hers and buried his face into her neck.

"Thank you." A satisfied smile crossed her face as she traced her fingers through the hair on the back of his head.

Ahkin made a sound of contentment in the back of his throat and turned his head so that his nose brushed her cheek. They stayed like that for minutes, hours, days. Mayana lost track. She could easily fall asleep.

Ahkin's breathing did eventually slow to the point that Mayana thought he was asleep, but then he jerked slightly and traced his lips from the edge of her jaw back to the corner of her mouth.

"Can I ask you something?" She wanted to distract him before they lost themselves again.

"Anything," he breathed against her cheek.

"Do we have to sacrifice *all* of the other princesses?"

Did she imagine him stiffen? He was quiet for a long time, and the bees inside her stomach suddenly turned angry, swarming around and making her feel sick. She shouldn't have asked. She must have crossed a line. Was he angry with her now?

Ahkin propped himself up on his elbows and frowned at her. He didn't look angry, but not entirely happy either.

Mayana bit her lip and chewed it.

"Well, it's just the only reason I'm alive right now is because of Yemania."

"Who?"

"Yemania. The daughter of Pahtia." Mayana tried to pretend it didn't pierce her heart that he didn't even know her name. "She found me and saved me, even when letting me die would have improved her own chances. I feel as though I owe her my life, and I wanted to know if there was any way we could save hers ..." She let herself trail off, as she could see the answer in his eyes before he gave it.

"Mayana, it is what the rituals dictate. The princesses are to be sacrificed to bless our marriage and my reign as emperor. I'm going to need every blessing I can get. It's hard to do as the gods command sometimes, I understand that better than anyone, but do you think it wise to test their favor? To go against ...?"

"Of course not!" Mayana sensed the conversation was not going at all as she had hoped. "I ... I care about honoring the codex above all else, of course." She was a wretched, selfish person after all. The bees now repeatedly stung the inside of her stomach. Why couldn't she just tell him the truth?

"I am not willing to risk the success of our life together." He pressed his lips to the fingertips of her left hand.

"Me either. It was a stupid suggestion. I'm sorry for even bringing it up." She pushed his head back against her neck and he nestled in, unable to see the tears pooling in her eyes.

That was not the answer she had been expecting. Now what was she going to do to save Yemania? Letting her die was not an option in Mayana's mind. She would do *something*.

CHAPTER

40

Mayana knew that it was long past the city's curfew, but she wasn't going to send him out of her room now. Especially once he decided to send a servant to fetch them some fruit to enjoy. She savored his company after fearing she'd never see him again. "Tell me about the battle. Was it strange for you to not have your father there?"

"You know, it was. As usual, you are the only one who notices things like that." Ahkin sank his teeth into a banana and gazed at her in wonderment.

Her cheeks burned, and she looked down at her own food, pretending to be busy selecting which berry she wanted to eat. "So, what happened?"

Ahkin considered her for a moment. Mayana could practically see the memories flitting around inside his eyes.

"It's hard to describe to someone who has never been in battle." Mayana could tell he didn't want to talk about it.

"It's alright. I respect your decision not to talk about it if you don't want to." And she meant it. She didn't want to stir up things he'd rather forget.

Ahkin gave her an appreciative smile.

"I just … didn't accomplish what I wanted. The Miquitz escaped back into the mountains with the captives and I'm sure they will be sacrificed." He dropped his head into his hands. "I feel like I've failed."

Mayana's heart twisted at his words. She couldn't imagine the pressure to prove himself and gain the confidence of the empire. She had no idea what to say to him to ease the burden.

"I believe in you," she said softly. "I think you'll be one of the greatest emperors the Chicome have ever had."

Ahkin scoffed. "And how do you know that?"

"I can read people well," Mayana said. "And you care deeply about doing what's right, about taking care of your people. And you are strong, more than just physically. You are clever and shrewd, but not unkind. You are born under the sign of the earthquake; you have the power to move mountains if you choose."

Ahkin stared at her with his mouth slightly open. He tackled her back onto the furs, wrapping his arms around her.

"If I will be a great emperor, it will be because of the empress by my side."

Mayana screeched and held the berries above their heads.

"You're going to squish my fruit." She shoved playfully at him. But Ahkin just held her tighter and gave her a quick, wistful kiss.

"I cannot wait to marry you," he said.

"Fine, the berries be damned." And she dropped the bowl with a clatter onto the ground, fat, succulent berries rolling forgotten across the tile. There was nothing sweeter in this world than the taste of his lips on hers.

"You saved my life, you know." Ahkin brushed aside the hair that fell across Mayana's face. He cupped her cheek gently in his hand.

Mayana leaned into his touch and closed her eyes. "Really? How exactly did I do that?"

Ahkin reached a hand into the wrap around his waist and withdrew a tiny bloodstained doll.

"Ack! What did you do to it?"

Ahkin chuckled as Mayana snatched the doll from his palm.

"It's covered in blood and dirt." Mayana clucked her tongue and gave him an exasperated look. "Leave it to a boy." She sighed.

Ahkin held up his hands toward her. "It's not my fault. What do you expect when you take a doll into battle?"

"You took it into battle with you?" Mayana let her eyes widen in disbelief. Why would he do such a thing?

"Well, I couldn't take *you* with me, so she was the next best thing."

Mayana pinched the doll between her thumb and forefinger and held it out away from her, her mouth puckering in disgust.

"Well thank goodness you couldn't take me with you, if this is what you did to a beautiful little doll."

Ahkin shrugged.

"Give me your knife," Mayana said suddenly, holding out her hand to him.

"What? Why? I hardly think being dirty means you need to end the poor doll's life. She has so much more to live for."

Mayana rolled her eyes. "Just give it to me."

"Don't you have your own knife?"

"I do," Mayana shook her hand impatiently, "but it's over on the table. Let me use yours."

Ahkin slipped the dark blade out from his waistband and flicked it into the air. The blade spun several times before he caught it by the tip and offered her the handle.

"Show-off." Mayana snatched the dagger from him.

She gently pricked the tip of her finger. She handed the dagger back and then pointed her finger toward a water jug against the wall. The water came to her like a dog greeting its master and she forced the stream to settle into one of their empty food bowls. She reached for the little doll and carefully removed its soiled dress.

Ahkin nudged her, a playful smile spreading on his face. "Shouldn't you ask her to marry you first? At least set up an arrangement with a matchmaker?"

Mayana smacked him on the arm. She pretended not to, but she loved the way Ahkin teased her. It was as if she was experiencing a happier, less surly side of him that others rarely got to see.

She dropped the dress into the water and began washing the dirt and blood from the fabric.

The water in the bowl clouded to a murky reddish brown while she scrubbed. Finally, the dress was relatively clean, and she set to work on the tiny woven face.

"Well, that's going to be a bit dirty from here on out, I'm afraid." She wrung out the excess water and used her ability to dispel the dirty water out into the garden. "But at least now it doesn't look like a sacrifice victim."

"Thank you." Ahkin took the doll back and tucked it into his waistband next to his knife.

"Oh, you didn't tell me how it saved your life." Mayana folded her legs beneath her.

"I know she doesn't look like much, but this little worry doll is quite skilled with a macana sword—"

Mayana clicked her tongue impatiently.

"Okay, fine. Actually, I had her tied to my sword for luck, and as I was trapped underneath the body of a fallen wolf, she distracted a death demon long enough for someone to kill him before he killed me."

"She distracted him?" Mayana dug her nails into her palms.

"Well ..." Ahkin leaned back on his elbows. "Not many warriors are accustomed to seeing a doll on the battlefield. It was a little out of place." He gave her a crooked smile.

"I'm glad she was able to help with more than just handling your worries."

Ahkin's smile faltered. "I do have plenty of those."

"Is there anything I can help with?"

Ahkin leaned forward and brushed his lips briefly against hers. "This is enough," he said.

"Are you worried about the kidnapped peasants? The empress selection?"

"All of it." Ahkin rubbed the back of his neck. "I failed to save the captives. The lord of Millacatl and who knows who else think I am too young to lead them. I have to ship off my sister to Ehecatl to appease their issues with Tollan's leadership, when she's the only family I have left. One of the princesses I'm hosting in my home tried to kill the girl I wish to marry. I have to sentence five girls to death just so that I can marry you.

Ill omens are filling the skies. The Nemontemi starts in three days and an eclipse is set to happen next month, and that's if the sun even lives that long anyway."

His words came out rushed, the desperation behind them barely concealed. Mayana's heart clenched as though a fist were squeezing it. So many burdens he held on his shoulders. It broke her to see him struggle under the weight of so many worries alone.

Leaning forward, she wrapped her arms around him, pulling him into an embrace. She didn't know the words to say. She only knew she wanted to show him he wasn't alone.

His arms mimicked hers, holding her close, and he buried his face into her hair.

She didn't know how long they sat on the floor of her room, holding on to each other as if their embrace could stop the world itself from falling apart. Maybe part of her believed it could.

Something he said crept back into her mind and made her pause. He had mentioned something about the sun not lasting until the eclipse. She pulled away, keeping her hands on his shoulders, searching his eyes for answers.

"What did you mean when you said, 'if the sun even lives that long'?"

Ahkin gritted his teeth. "Have you noticed the sun setting earlier and earlier each day?"

Mayana thought back to the orange light streaming into her room, Yemania commenting on how strange the light was shining for that time of day. Then she remembered the sun setting too early when she first arrived in Tollan. Even the first night she learned of the selection ritual had seemed to stretch on forever.

"Actually … yes. I have. What does that mean?"

"We don't know for sure yet. The high priest tells me my blood might not be enough to raise it anymore. That maybe the blood of the sun god has become so diluted it's no longer enough to sustain its journey across the sky. It would make sense to me. I must not be strong enough to raise the sun properly."

Mayana's face crumpled. Something about that didn't feel right.

"Are your abilities affected at all?"

"What do you mean?"

"Do they seem weaker to you?"

Ahkin thought for moment before answering. "No. I can still bend light and make it obey my every command. I can bend it around myself to the point I disappear completely."

Mayana's eyes were as round as the moon. "I—didn't know that."

"Know what?"

"You can make yourself disappear?"

Ahkin shrugged and removed his knife to prick his finger. In an instant, his form shimmered and disappeared entirely.

Mayana gasped.

"I'm still here. You just can't see me without light bouncing off my body and returning to your eyes."

He came back into view as Mayana blinked her eyes rapidly.

"Your blood seems strong enough to me," she said weakly. "Can you promise me something?"

"Anything."

"Don't ever use that to spy on me while I'm changing. Promise?"

"Once we're married, I'm confident that won't be necessary."

Mayana's toes curled at the thought, but she wouldn't let him change the subject.

"I don't think that's the reason the sun is setting earlier," she said.

Ahkin wiped the drop of blood off his finger. His eyes were downcast. "It would make sense to me," he said.

Mayana fixed him with eyes full of profound sadness. "You are so ready to believe you are not enough," she whispered.

"What if I'm not?"

"No one can convince you that you are, aside from yourself." She tapped him playfully on the nose.

Ahkin sighed heavily but didn't argue. He stretched himself out across her bed mat and patted the furs beside him. Mayana scooted forward and then wedged her back against his chest, fitting into him perfectly as he draped his arm across her, drawing her in even closer.

It was a glorious warm sensation, like the world was safe and he would protect her from whatever came. And she believed he would, even if he didn't think he was capable.

His breathing slowed into the rhythms of sleep as she herself drifted in the same direction. The last thought to cross her mind was that tomorrow the selection ritual would be over, and he would announce to the entire Chicome Empire that she was to become their empress.

"My lord!"

Atanzah's screech of surprise cut through the dark peace of the night. Ahkin sat up so abruptly that Mayana, who had been lying with her head on his chest, fell to the ground with a thud.

She winced as she rubbed the side of her head. He planted a quick kiss where it had hit the ground before turning to frown as his matchmaker. "Atanzah, what is the meaning of—?"

"It's time to raise the sun! We couldn't find you. You were not in your room …"

Ahkin was on his feet before Atanzah could finish her thought. He reached a hand down to Mayana and lifted her to her feet alongside him.

"Come with me," he told her. He wanted her to see the most important ritual of all. With her appreciation for the ways of the gods, it would be something she'd enjoy.

"Am I allowed to?" Mayana glanced at the matchmaker as though she could give her permission.

"I don't see why not." Atanzah sighed and shoved them out through the doorway. "But afterward, let's have a little chat, my prince, about what is appropriate in terms of staying the night with ladies to whom we are not bonded before the gods."

"No!" Mayana blanched. "We didn't—that's not what—we just—"

"I do not need to know any details, my lady. The gods know the truth and that is what matters."

Ahkin prayed this did not lose Mayana favor with Atanzah. After all, they were not allowed to be married if the matchmaker did not approve the match. He had already commanded her to contact Mayana's family in anticipation of announcing her selection. The matchmaker had been thoughtful and quiet, but she carried out his commands without voicing concern.

Ahkin suppressed a laugh at the look of horror on Mayana's face. She was so beautiful, especially when she was embarrassed. He wove his fingers through hers and pulled her forward.

He couldn't wait to raise the sun. Today was going to be one of the most important days of his life. He would start it with her by his side, a symbol he hoped would be significant.

Ahkin also couldn't wait for the surprise he had planned for her that evening. No matter what else he failed at, he would succeed in making her happy. Ahkin could already imagine the joy upon her face when she noticed her father and brothers waiting for her at the banquet. They would be so proud of her and so relieved to know her life would be spared. The lord of Atl had lost his wife, so he was certain the lord would appreciate not losing a daughter as well.

Atanzah cleared her throat. "We are a tad behind schedule, my lord. Might we go a little faster?"

Mayana let out an adorable laugh as they broke into a run—down the steps leading to the royal residence halls, out through a botanical courtyard, and toward the pillars of the grand entrance. Her leg finally seemed to be healing. He assumed he had her friend, the princess from Pahtia, to thank for speeding up the process.

They sprinted across the main avenue toward the temple. He leapt onto the stairs of the pyramid, taking two at a time as Mayana stumbled to keep up. Atanzah had stopped at the foot of the steps and stood doubled over, her belly pressed against her knees as she gasped for breath and waved at them to go on without her.

The sky was inky black and tinged with pink and yellow along the distant mountain range where the sun remained hidden and waiting.

The stars themselves guided their steps as twinkling light reflected off the smooth golden stairs.

Once they reached the top, Ahkin respectfully slowed his pace. The high priest waited with his arms folded. The deep frown on his face bordered on a grimace as his eyes flitted to Ahkin's hand where it held onto Mayana's.

He could hear her panting breath beside him, and she took a slight step behind him under the flaming gaze of the high priest. Ahkin didn't blame her. Toani seethed with fury at the sight of them.

"I am sorry I was late. I assure you it was an accident, and—"

Toani turned on his heels and marched toward the altar. Ahkin stiffened at the cold rebuff, making a mental plan to speak to Toani in private after the ritual.

Mayana squeaked, but he snaked a reassuring arm around her waist and guided her toward the altar. Toani stood partly covered in shadow beside it, glaring at Ahkin and waiting for him to begin.

Ahkin ascended the steps to the altar and lifted the ceremonial knife. He sliced his palm, and the papers on the altar absorbed the drops like dry earth soaking up a summer rain.

He collected the papers in his hands and dispersed them into the brazier fire. The moment the strips of bone-white paper shriveled into dust, the sun blinded them all with its welcome radiance.

Mayana's lips were parted in awe, and her skin glowed in the light of the new dawn. Ahkin silently thanked the Mother goddess for her gift to him in the form of this glorious creature. Mayana turned to look at him, her eyes shining with pride and wonder, and the sun itself paled in comparison to the brilliance of her smile.

Toani stepped between them, demanding Ahkin's attention.

"My lord, I wish to speak with you. Immediately." The priest lifted his chin, gazing down at Ahkin in a way that made him feel like he was in trouble for something.

Ahkin bristled, but he had no desire to anger the priest who had provided him with so much welcome guidance in the past. He dipped his chin in acquiescence.

"Alone."

Ahkin opened his mouth to protest, but Mayana's soft voice interrupted him. "My lord prince." She gave a small bow. "I will return to the palace and begin my preparations for the day. Perhaps we can see each other again before the feast this afternoon."

"That is a splendid idea, the temple is no place for a princess," Toani said without looking at her. He waved a dismissive hand in her direction.

Mayana gave Ahkin a placating smile and a playful wink before turning to descend the temple steps.

Ahkin frowned at Toani the moment she disappeared from view. "I would like an explanation for why you treated your future empress with such disrespect."

"That poisonous snake is not deserving of the crown of the empress and least of all my respect. She flouts our very way of life and endangers the entire empire as a result." Toani spat the words as though the taste of them burned his tongue.

Ahkin took a step back. Such vehemence was unusual from the usually peaceful and pious priest.

"You do not know Mayana as I do." Ahkin's voice rose along with his temper. "I lo—"

"Do not say you love her." Toani held up a hand. "You are barely a man, my prince. You do not even know what love is. You do not know the pain and depths of suffering that true love can bring to the heart. You are deceived. You do not know this girl as you think you do. I overheard her speaking with one of the other princesses and—"

"I am the one to make this decision. No one else." Ahkin never dreamed he would yell at his high priest like this. The insinuation of his youthful inexperience stung like salt in an already open wound.

"You have always followed your head above your heart, my prince. I beg you to—"

"I will not stand here while you insult me and my future wife. I assure you, Toani, you do not know her as I do."

Toani relaxed his face and his shoulders, not in defeat, but more in a manner of resignation. "So be it." Toani inclined his head, his voice dangerously soft. "I assume you wish to announce your decision this afternoon?"

"I do." Ahkin hated feeling like a spoiled child.

"Then, might I make a suggestion for the midday sacrifice?"

Ahkin didn't understand the direction their discussion had turned. Why was Toani suddenly talking about sacrifices?

"Uh ... alright."

"Why don't we have the daughter of water lead us in this afternoon's sacrifice to bless the meal? As the future empress, her position as a spiritual leader in the kingdom is a vital one. What better way to introduce her to the kingdom as your choice than through honoring the gods?"

Ahkin considered Toani's suggestion for several moments.

"That's a wonderful idea, Toani. I am sure Mayana would welcome the opportunity to lead us in a sacrifice. She can show you what a capable spiritual leader she will be for our kingdom."

Toani's lip curled in a way that did not entirely ease the worry churning inside Ahkin's stomach. "Might I make a further suggestion?"

Ahkin gave a noncommittal grunt.

"Why don't we refrain from telling her until the feast? Have it be a final test of sorts. See how she can handle the stress of having to perform a religious sacrifice without time to prepare."

Ahkin didn't see the harm in such a request. He often had to be able to perform rituals or sacrifices as situations arose. It seemed a fitting way to end the selection ritual.

"The final task," Ahkin mused. "What is the sign for today?"

"Today is the day of the dog, my lord." Toani's curling lip broke into a wide, unnerving smile.

"I think that will work well." Ahkin folded his arms across his chest, satisfied at their agreement. Something nagged at the back of his mind, but he ignored it. He knew that Mayana had a passion for dogs, but with her level of dedication to the rituals, it shouldn't be an issue.

Toani bent forward in a sweeping bow. "I agree, my prince. A dog will be perfect."

CHAPTER

42

Mayana had a sinking feeling in her stomach as she jogged down the steps of the Temple of the Sun. Something about the way the high priest glared at her, as though she was a hissing beetle he longed to squish beneath his sandal, made her fear to leave Ahkin alone with him.

Why would the priest have such disdain for her? She'd never spoken to the man before in her life. She was a daughter of a noble lord, a descendant of the gods the man proclaimed to serve.

A sudden thought occurred to her, and Mayana's foot slipped on one of the smooth steps. Her feet flew out in front of her and she landed hard on her tailbone. She slid down several of the stairs, the edges biting into her back and rattling her teeth as her body jolted.

Adrenaline raced through her, and Mayana threw out her hands to stop herself from sliding down the rest of the steps on her backside. Her fingers slipped across the gold but eventually found traction and the movement stopped all at once.

She ached everywhere, and her heart thundered away beneath her ribs. Stupid stairs on these stupid gargantuan pyramids. Why couldn't the builders have made the stairs wider? Did they have to be so narrow?

Mayana fought the urge to cry as embarrassment, anger, frustration, and fear all melded together into a burning mass inside her stomach.

The fear from her fall was still nothing compared to the fear of the thought that had caused her to lose her focus in the first place. She had considered the possibility that Toani had overheard her conversation with Yemania in the room with the codex. She hadn't seen him anywhere, but unseeing eyes do not always equal unhearing ears.

What choice did she have now if he had? What would he do? What would happen to her? Mayana shuddered at the thought. She reminded herself not to jump to conclusions.

Her confidence as bruised as her backside, Mayana rubbed a hand across her throbbing elbow and slowly made her way back toward the palace residential rooms.

———

"So, he came to see you?" Yemania's tone sounded casual, but Mayana knew better.

Mayana nodded and threw another bowl of water against the scorching-hot wall of the steam bath. The water splashed across the surface of the dark-gray stone and hissed as it vaporized. Wonderful warmth seeped into her skin when the cloud engulfed her, though it did little to ease the bone-deep chill that filled her from within.

Yemania draped a white cotton towel across her lap while Mayana lay down on the low stone bench with an arm over her face.

"You don't look too excited about it."

"Well, after we woke up this morning ..."

"*We* woke up this morning? As in, you woke up together?" Yemania tittered into the silence like an angry little sparrow.

Mayana dropped her arm to roll her eyes at the daughter of healing.

"Good gods, we didn't do anything, we just fell asleep together, that's all."

"You didn't do anything at all?"

Mayana didn't think it was possible for her cheeks to get any warmer than they already were in the steam room, but apparently it was.

"Well ... we did some things, but not what you think."

"Do you respect *any* of the rituals in the codex?"

Mayana bristled at the comment. She crossed her arms over her bare chest and glared at the ceiling above her.

"I do, in fact. I am the one who has stopped it from going any further, for your information."

Yemania sucked in a breath.

"Well, I think he would have stopped before that point too," Mayana added, "I mean, he's far more devoted to the rituals than I am. But that rule ... I don't know. Maybe I'm afraid, or maybe I feel like it's better to have some level of promise from someone before giving over so much of yourself ... if that makes any sense."

Yemania considered her for a moment.

"Well, maybe you aren't a complete heathen," she said with a smirk.

"I'm not a heathen." Mayana frowned. "I love the gods. I want to honor them as much as you do, I just have different ideas about how that can be done."

"Well, I'm not the one you need to convince. I'll likely be dead tomorrow anyway." Mayana could tell Yemania was trying to be flippant, but her quivering lip betrayed her.

"Yemania ..."

"Did you tell him?" Yemania interrupted. "Did you tell him why you really saved that jaguar? What you really think about the codex?"

Mayana bit her lip, and Yemania threw her hands into the air with an exasperated sigh.

"I tried. I was going to, but I asked about sparing you from the sacrifice and his reaction was so bad, I was afraid to."

Yemania squealed like a frightened wild piglet and her hands flew to cover her mouth.

"You didn't." Glimmers of silver shone in the corners of her eyes.

"I told you I was going to," Mayana said, crossing her arms again defensively.

"That's so disrespectful, Mayana, and I don't want the prince to think that I am not willing to do my duty."

"He doesn't think that." Mayana waved a dismissive hand.

"I am willing to do what I must to bless the reign of our emperor, and

I wish you would too. If he truly is to be your husband, you owe your devotion to him, not yourself."

Mayana pinched her face together. She was tired of being called selfish. Disrespectful. A heretic. She knew in her heart that those weren't the reasons she questioned the brutality of her people's traditions. Sacrifices didn't sit well with her heart, in the same way that chili peppers never sat well in her stomach. It was something more, something she couldn't control ... she didn't know how to explain it. She was exhausted from trying to for so long. She had tried by showing Yemania one of her reasons, and that had been a mistake. Now the priest likely labeled her in the exact same way as everyone else.

So Mayana let out a sigh and didn't respond. She didn't know how to show everyone that she wasn't being selfish, at least not about this. She doubted she would ever be able to.

They sat in silence for several more minutes, until Yemania finally changed the subject.

"So, what happens this afternoon?"

Mayana turned her head on the bench to look at her. "We need to get ready for another feast."

Yemania chuckled. They had talked at length about how many feasts they had attended since arriving in Tollan. Typically they were reserved for bloodletting festivals in both Atl and Pahtia, so it seemed a little excessive to have a feast every day. But perhaps here, with so many nobles and important members of society constantly visiting, feasts were just a normal way of life.

Mayana laughed along with her. "Ahkin did say he had a surprise for me at this feast, so perhaps that will make it a little more exciting."

"He's making his selection this afternoon. I bet that's what it is," Yemania said quietly, fiddling with the edge of the towel on her lap.

"I think it's something else ... but yes, I do think he will make the announcement at the feast."

"Well then." Yemania took a deep breath and slapped her hands on her thighs before rising to her feet. "This may very well be my last feast in this world, so we better not be late."

Mayana's heart twisted at Yemania's words, but she had no idea what to say, so she said nothing. Instead she gave Yemania a weak smile and followed her out into the hall. The much colder air assaulted her skin. Mayana wrapped a towel around her shoulders and shivered.

If only they could stay in the steam bath forever. Babies sometimes overstayed their welcome inside their mother's bodies, not wanting to be born into the world outside. Mayana could understand the feeling. Sometimes she wished she could be spared the realities of the world too.

After an hour of servants painting designs on her arms and face, selecting the right outfit from what was left of her thoroughly demolished baskets, and draping herself in jade jewelry from Atl, Mayana was finally ready for the midday feast. Her room was still a disaster from the monkey invader, but at least *she* appeared put together.

The bees in her stomach were buzzing again, anticipating the end to this selection ritual. She was also excited to see what Ahkin's surprise for her was going to be. Would it be a wedding present? What kind of presents did emperors give to their wives? She couldn't even begin to imagine.

"Can it only have been two weeks since we arrived?"

Yemania stood in the doorframe exactly as she had the first night Mayana arrived in Tollan. Just as on that first night, she twisted her hands in front of her, shoulders slumped. "It feels like it's been much longer, doesn't it? I always knew it would be over before the last days of the calendar. It's such an unlucky time," Yemania said.

"I figured it would be over by then too." Mayana sighed. Rising to her feet, she wove her arm through Yemania's and the two noble daughters joined the others gathering in the hall.

"You look particularly done up for this time of day," Yoli commented, taking in Mayana's brilliant blue loincloth skirt and the beaded fabric tied around her chest. Jade dangled from her ears, neck, and wrists, an homage to her home in Atl. "Jade for water, right?"

Mayana nodded and adjusted her headpiece so that the turquoise feathers better framed her face. "Obsidian for Papatlaca, right?"

Yoli grinned and bit the dark ring of stone protruding through her lower lip. Yemania gave a snort of disgust, but Yoli just wiggled her eyebrows.

"You scare easily, daughter of Pahtia. How do you heal if you are so weak-stomached?"

"I do what I have to," Yemania whispered under her breath.

Mayana liked both girls, obviously for different reasons, so she intervened before any claws were drawn.

"The prince is back, so he should be dining with us."

Yoli gave her a knowing smile, and Mayana shifted her shoulders uncomfortably.

"Did he tell you that in your room last night?" Yoli cocked her head to the side in an amused sort of way.

Mayana swallowed hard.

"I—I—don't know what you—" Mayana tripped over her words, but Yoli just barked a short laugh.

"I don't care, daughter of water." Yoli nudged Mayana with her shoulder, so roughly that Mayana almost fell into the wall. "As I've said before, I am already at peace with my fate. I just have to admit that I did not see you as the type to invite the prince back to your room."

Teniza of Millacatl whirled around to face them, her towering frame making Mayana feel like a small child. The princess's face burned red, her curled hands tense at her sides. "You invited him into your room?"

Mayana frowned. This was getting way out of hand. The other princesses were making assumptions that frankly insulted her.

Zorrah appeared through the curtain and stood beside Teniza, her arms crossed over her chest. Mayana couldn't help but notice that her arms covered her more thoroughly than the bits of jaguar pelts she was wearing.

Both Teniza and Zorrah blocked the hallway, the jealously and rage billowing off of them like heat from the brazier at the top of the temple.

Mayana straightened her spine in response. She tried to remember that Teniza had a boy back home whose life she was trying to save by being chosen. Remembering that blunted the edge of Teniza's harshness. Mayana took a deep breath to calm the anger she could already feel boiling beneath the surface at Teniza's insinuation. "Yes, he stayed in my room last night, but nothing happened." She kept her voice level, calm.

Zorrah bared her teeth like an angry monkey. "You know, in Ocelotl we have a word for a beast that all the males like to …"

Something inside her flared red hot and Mayana lunged, but Yoli was between them faster than Mayana could believe possible. The fire princess wrapped her arms around Mayana, pinning her arms to her side. Mayana struggled, but Yoli's grip was firm.

"Stop." Her whisper was harsh in Mayana's ear. "She lost. We all know it. She is trying to provoke you."

"You're one to talk of provoking, daughter of fire." Teniza directed her condescension at Yoli.

"I will snap you, you towering beanstalk," Yoli growled back.

"Please," Yemania cried desperately, hugging her fists to her chest as though her heart ached. "This might be our last meal together and I don't want to spend it like this."

"Our last meal together?" Teniza's voice now reached the high pitch of a shrieking bird. "Of course, it is. No one else even stood a chance." She rounded on Mayana. "You demanded his attention from the beginning. I don't even know how you did it. Did your family threaten him? Is that it? Choose our daughter or we will kill you all with drought? I honestly can't see why else he would have spared you a second glance." Teniza's dark eyes roved Mayana up and down as though she were a disgusting worm. Mayana's throat constricted. She was not used to how mean girls could be. She would rather take a fist from one of her brothers any day.

"No," Zorrah purred, prowling around Yoli and Mayana like a jaguar. "She has him fooled. She has you all fooled. My family has seen exactly who she is. Every time one of my uncles came back from her city they would scoff at how the lord of Atl let his daughter spill a few tears and get away with not doing her duty. We would tell stories and laugh about the weakling princess whose father coddled her, at how quickly she would die in the survival matches in Ocelotl. Mayana is nothing more than a spoiled brat whose father turns a blind eye while she spits upon our ways. She doesn't care for the gods or the rituals, or anything but herself and her own comfort."

"Then why was she such a threat to you?" Yoli scoffed.

"The weak always have a way of attracting the powerful. They arouse that desire to protect something so fragile and sweet. My uncles warned me that if she could manipulate the lord of Atl, there was no doubt she'd manipulate the prince right into her hands. And she has. She has lied to all of you, especially the prince."

Yoli's arms around her stiffened, but Zorrah continued, a wide, wicked smile spreading across her painted face. "Tell them, Mayana. Tell them the real reason you saved the jaguar."

Mayana's arms trembled from the effort of keeping herself calm. Yoli slowly released her, her brow furrowed in confusion.

"She saved the jaguar to honor the calendar." Yoli's gaze never left Mayana's face as she spoke, but Mayana was having difficulty meeting her eyes.

Zorrah laughed softly. "Yes. To honor the calendar. The calendar specifies sacrifices for meals and special circumstances like weddings. My demonstration of my power was neither, and so a specific animal for the day or month was not necessary. But Mayana is so *devout*, of course, she insisted on honoring the calendar even when it wasn't required. Am I right, Mayana?"

Mayana stared determinedly at the floor. She would not lie, but she would not let Zorrah bait her like a fly-trapping plant either.

"I don't understand." Yoli turned back to face the animal princess, her gaze darting back and forth between Zorrah's haughty form and Mayana's dejected stance. "Why else would she have acted the way she did?"

"Let's go. I'm starving." A forceful, authoritative voice from behind them all cut through the tension. Every head swiveled to see Itza glaring at them. Mayana so rarely heard her speak outside of quoting the codex or muttering prayers, she was momentarily taken aback by the power radiating from the girl's fiery eyes.

"Go," she commanded, lifting her chin defiantly at them. Teniza turned on her heel with a huff and marched away from them, while Zor-rah gave another sneer and prowled after her.

Yoli, Mayana, and Yemania remained rooted on the spot like ancient trees, staring at Itza with expressions ranging from disbelief to mild awe.

Itza didn't seem fazed. Her crackling gaze collided with Mayana's, and Mayana took a small step back. It was as if a delicate butterfly had sud-denly revealed it had a sharp stinger.

"You need to hide it better," Itza snarled.

Mayana's heart leapt into her throat with such force she was afraid she would choke on it.

"W-what?" Mayana sputtered, forcing her heart back down where it belonged.

"You are not the only one who believes as you do, but if you do not learn to play the game more carefully, you are going to lose it."

And with that, Itza swept past them, and Mayana swore she could feel the air sizzling with energy.

Yoli shrugged and followed after her, while Yemania fixed Mayana with a terrified expression.

"What just happened?" Yemania grabbed her arm and dug in her nails. Mayana reached out and loosened her constrictor-like grip.

"I'm not exactly sure." Mayana couldn't take her eyes off the storm princess as she swept around the corner. Itza had said that Mayana wasn't the only one who believed as she did ... did that mean there were oth-ers who questioned the codex as well? Was that the reason Ehecatl and Tollan were always on such tense terms? Perhaps why Metzi had been promised to marry Itza's brother in an attempt to strengthen their ties? Her father's words about everything being political floated back to her along with Atanzah's approving smile toward Itza days ago ... what if the matchmaker preferred Itza to marry the prince?

"Yemania, what do you know about Ehecatl?"

Yemania bit her lip. "Well, you know the healers are involved in all of the city-states, so I've heard from some of my family members ... that they worship the gods differently than we do. They ... they don't agree with how the sacrifices are carried out."

"What does that mean exactly?"

"I don't really know. That's all I've heard. That they don't want to be under the rule of Tollan any more because of how we worship the gods."

"So maybe I'm not alone in what I believe after all." Hope blossomed in Mayana's heart at the thought.

"That's what I'm afraid of," Yemania whispered to her toes.

CHAPTER

44

What happened with Itza almost distracted Mayana from wondering about the prince's surprise. As the princesses neared the banquet hall, a low rumble of hundreds of voices greeted them. Mayana's breath hitched. There was a large crowd gathered this afternoon. Mayana hadn't taken the time to think about what an ordeal Ahkin's announcement was going to be. It made perfect sense that every noble and guest within the palace would want to be in attendance.

The moment they passed through the hanging curtain, a wave of sound washed over them. Mayana took in the crowd, larger by far than it had been the night she'd had to demonstrate her abilities. Every corner of the cavernous room was filled with people sitting on mats and benches, servants with bowls and trays weaving throughout like leaf-cutter ants following predetermined paths. At the head of the room on the raised dais sat Ahkin himself, lounging on the golden sun throne with the most distinguished guests seated around him. Metzi sat immediately to his left, leaning in to whisper to Coatl with her hand lightly perched on his forearm. Coatl's mouth was pressed into a thin line as he took in her words. On Ahkin's other side, the high priest Toani and Ahkin's Jaguar general were watching the girls enter with shrewd eyes. There were other prominent figures Mayana was starting to recognize ... the feathered headdress of the head of the Eagle warriors, the bloodred robes of the Tlana priests, the jaguar pelts of several naguals from Ocelotl.

Atanzah stood behind Metzi and Coatl, and Mayana noticed that her usual excitement seemed to have been quelled, as though she was not looking forward to whatever was coming. Mayana squirmed internally at the matchmaker's lack of enthusiasm. But beside them, where the empty mats waited for Mayana and the other princesses, sat another small group of people draped in fabrics of dark blue with matching feathers, and jade jewelry adorning their warm, tanned skin.

A shriek of surprise escaped through her throat and her hands flew to cover her mouth. Her family was sitting up there waiting for her. Well, a few of them. Her eyes roved over Chimalli's wide smile, Tenoch's frantically waving hand, and finally her father's face, beaming with pride like the sun. The rest of her older brothers were pointing at her and mouthing teasing remarks. Her aunts and cousins must all be back home, but just the sight of her father and brothers was enough to make her heart feel as though it were swelling to twice its normal size.

Mayana threw her tear-filled eyes to Ahkin, gratitude and adoration seeping from every pore of her body. She mouthed a silent "thank-you" to him, which he received with a nod and his own glorious smile.

The prince had given her the greatest surprise she could ever imagine. To see her family again, and to have them watch as he chose her as his empress. For as long as she could remember, Mayana had wanted to make her father proud. She wanted him to look at her with the same satisfaction in his eyes as when he watched Chimalli practice his skills as a warrior, or Tenoch as he quoted lines from the codex.

She had always felt like a disappointment—the only daughter in a brood of strong, capable sons. The only one who was, in his eyes, too weak to handle the requirements of the codex. As much as she wanted to make him proud, she was forever trapped in that battle between fulfilling his wishes and the desires of her heart. Today, he would know that she had done something right. She would no longer be the embarrassing daughter of the lord of Atl. She would be the future empress of the Chicome Empire. The one the prince chose above all others.

"Is that your family?" Yemania gently touched her shoulder from behind.

"Yes," Mayana breathed, trying to keep herself from crying with how overjoyed and fulfilled she felt.

"I am happy they will be here to see you succeed." It sounded as though she meant it. Mayana's heart twisted again as she thought of her friend, her friend who did not deserve to die. She shoved the thought away, knowing she could not find a solution at this moment. She would have to try to figure something out later tonight. She had managed to think of a way to save the jaguar, after all. She was sure she'd think of something to save Yemania before the wedding and coronation.

The princesses reached the dais, and Mayana immediately threw herself into her oldest brother's arms. He smelled like maize and peppers and every other smell that reminded her of home. He buried his face in her hair, and Mayana clung to him as several tears escaped. She broke away as Tenoch tugged at her skirt and swept him into her arms. She planted kisses all over his face and he squirmed away.

"Ugh, Mayana! I am excited to see you too, but you don't need to kiss me like a baby."

"You are a precious little baby to me," she said, and covered his cheeks again. He shoved her away and she dropped him back to his feet. Her eyes found her father's and her throat constricted as she took in the familiar lines of his face, the gray strands dusting the darkness of his hair like ashes from a fire.

The lord of Atl cleared his throat and gave her the quickest, most awkward hug she had ever experienced, releasing her as though she might bite him. Mayana gave him a teary chuckle and placed her hand on his cheek.

"I missed you," she said. Her father gruffly pulled himself away from her hand and blinked his eyes furiously. Were those tears? Actual tears from the lord of Atl?

"Well, I did tell you I'd see you again, so ..." He cleared his throat again and shifted his shoulders uncomfortably. Mayana wanted to throw herself into his arms, but he would never allow such a thing with so many people watching.

Mayana caught a glimpse of the other princesses now sitting on the mats before her. Yemania's eyes appeared as wet as her own, while Teniza and Zorrah both seethed in silence. Yoli merely looked bored, but Itza met her gaze and held it with a smile playing about her lips.

A warm hand slid around her waist and she jumped. Turning on the spot, she faced Ahkin, who had come to greet them. The hall around them continued to buzz with talking and laughter as Ahkin reached out a hand to greet her father.

"Lord of Atl, thank you for responding to Atanzah's invitation. I anticipate this to be an exciting evening for us all as we begin our marriage negotiations," he said.

Her father bowed and then firmly clasped the prince's hand. Mayana tried not to giggle at the thought of her stoic father negotiating and planning a wedding with whatever extravagance Atanzah would likely suggest.

"Thank you, my prince, for including us in this historic event. We could not be more proud of our daughter." Her father's eyes fell upon her, and a true smile broke through his normally reserved demeanor like light breaking through storm clouds.

Ahkin hugged her tightly to his side and Mayana's cheeks burned in response. "Come," he whispered in her ear as he wove his fingers through hers. "Let's begin the rest of our lives together."

Mayana looked to her father, who motioned with his head for her to follow her future husband. Mayana bit her lip and obeyed. She squeezed Ahkin's hand tighter as they stood in front of his throne.

So many faces, all watching her with hungry expressions of expectation. Not letting go of her hand, Ahkin turned to face the gathered nobles and guests. Silence swept the room quickly and completely.

"Welcome to the feast this evening. After my father began his journey in the underworld, I did not feel prepared to handle the responsibilities he left upon my shoulders. I no longer fear to shoulder those responsibilities on my own." He lifted her hand to his lips and pressed a quick kiss against the back of her palm. "I began the selection ritual with equal apprehension, not sure what I was looking for other than someone to help us continue the royal bloodline of Huitzilopochtli. Now, I know I have found the other half of my duality. As the creator, Ometeotl, has both male and female aspects, wholly complete, I now feel that I have found the half that will make me complete as your emperor. Pending the approval and negotiations between my matchmaker and the noble family of Atl, I would like to introduce everyone to my future wife and your future empress, Mayana, daughter of Atl and descendant of the goddess Atlacoya."

Ahkin turned to face her, his eyes sparkling with excitement and passion. "For when water and light come together, it makes something beautiful. Mayana, you have brought color and life into my cold gray world, and I can't wait to see what the gods have in store for our future together."

And then he kissed her. In front of everyone. In front of her *father*. Mayana wanted to laugh, to cry, to hide all at once. Instead, she lost herself in the feel of his lips and the roaring cheers and calls around her were silenced as the world consisted of no one else. They were the only two people in the empire.

A throat cleared loudly and Mayana reluctantly pulled away to find the calculating eyes of the high priest upon them. He was a thundercloud hovering over their sunlit meadow.

His deep frown and cruel eyes sent a thrill of apprehension through her, as though an invisible hand was drawing a finger down the length of her spine. Intuition told Mayana that she would not enjoy whatever came next.

"My prince." His voice was as cold as his eyes. "Are we ready for her final test?"

A feeling like cold water suddenly filled her lungs, extinguishing the warmth that had burned there moments before. What final test? And why was the priest smiling at her like a wolf at his prey?

Ahkin smiled encouragingly at Mayana and waved his hand toward one of the naguals sitting to the right of the throne. He saw panic flicker in her eyes, so he gave her another quick kiss.

"Don't worry, Mayana. Toani just thought it would be a good idea for you to lead us in the sacrifice before dinner, that's all." He tried to force as much reassurance into his voice as possible.

"As the spiritual leaders of the empire, we will have to do this sort of thing all the time. It's not any different from what you do at home during your family's bloodletting feasts." He shrugged to show her she had nothing to be afraid of.

Mayana's eyes darted to his face, to her father's, and then to the daughter of Pahtia.

The daughter of Atl trembled like a cornered animal. Poor thing. She would get used to the pressure of large crowds eventually. He rubbed a reassuring hand over her upper arm as the nagual rose to his feet.

"No, really, my lord, I think it would best if you …" Her voice was quiet and frantic, and Ahkin had to lean in to hear her.

"I know there are a lot of people, but I know you can do it. As long as the blood gets into the fire, there isn't anything else that can go wrong. I promise."

"What am I sacrificing? A bird?" Mayana's gaze darted around as though looking for the beast, and Ahkin's heart wrenched at the pain on her face. Why was she so upset? Was she really that nervous?

"No, it's the day of the—"

"*Dog?*" Her pupils contracted with fear as her eyes took in the smooth dark-haired body of the beast the nagual summoned into the room.

Her chest heaved with shallow breaths and she wiped her hands on her skirt. She looked like a young warrior about to enter his first battle.

The nagual directed the dog to sit at her feet—its head only reaching her hip. A fat pink tongue lolled out of the side of its panting mouth.

Ahkin studied her face and suddenly worried that she was going to be sick. Her normally flushed cheeks were pale, and when she took a step forward, her legs shook beneath her.

He chanced a look at her father, to see if he was worried for her health as well, and to his surprise the lord of Atl appeared just as frightened as his daughter. The man's hands were balled into fists and his eyes bulged as he stared between the dog and his daughter.

Mayana's eyes rose to her father's face again and filled with tears. Ahkin didn't understand the reaction the lord of Atl gave her as he clenched his jaw and mouthed what looked like "please." It was as if they were having a private, entirely silent conversation.

Ahkin let himself focus on her brothers, all of whom became suddenly preoccupied with their sandals. The daughter of Pahtia fanned herself with a chubby hand as though about to faint.

Confusion and doubt crept into his consciousness like a silent hunting spider. Something was not right.

"Do you need a blade, daughter of water? Do you have your own or shall I provide one for you?" Toani practically sang with mirth, his eyes dancing with amusement. Ahkin stiffened. Whatever was going on, Toani seemed well aware of it, and worse than that, he appeared to be savoring it.

"I—I—have my own." Mayana gave her head a little shake and leaned down to pull a blade with a jadeite handle from the feathered cuff around her ankle. Ahkin couldn't help but admire the regality of the deadly-looking weapon. It would do the job nicely.

Ahkin released a breath as she tightened her grip on the blade and crouched down low. Thank the gods she was going to just get it over with. This shouldn't be such an ordeal. Mayana ran her free hand over the dog's head, scratching behind its ear. The dog closed its eyes lazily at her touch. The tenderness in her gaze as she looked at the dog pulled at something inside his chest. The image of his mother flashed before his eyes, though he didn't understand why. Suddenly, there was a small part of him that didn't want her to kill the dog, but such a feeling was heresy. He silenced it immediately.

The lord of Atl shook his head, and Toani leaned forward eagerly.

"Let us begin, my dear. The food is waiting." The priest gave her a smile that did not reach his eyes.

Mayana gave a small nod and slowly raised the blade toward the soft skin under the dog's jawline. She continued to run her fingers over its head. The beast was completely oblivious to the fate that waited inches from its neck.

The blade paused. Ahkin's fingers twitched, aching to grab the blade from her and finish the sacrifice himself. Why was there so much tension around this single act? It was a basic meal sacrifice. It should be over by now and he should already be enjoying the spiced deer meat that filled the hall with its tantalizing aroma. Mayana should be sitting by his side, enjoying the meal and their coming future along with him.

Mayana lifted her eyes to meet his. They were swimming with tears and she bit her lower lip in a pleading gesture. *Why didn't she just do it?*

"I'm sorry," she whispered, her voice trembling as much as her hand holding the blade.

"What—Why are you sorry?" Ahkin looked to the lord of Atl, who now pitched himself forward with his head in his hands. "Just do the sacrifice, Mayana. Please."

"I can't." The tears spilled over and she lowered her gaze to the dog, still scratching its ear. She rose to her feet and lowered the blade to her side.

"I don't understand. Do you feel sick?" Ahkin could feel the heavy stares of the crowd upon them.

"She's not sick. She won't do it, my lord." Toani ripped the blade from her hand. "Just as I expected."

Ahkin did not like to be made a fool. He already felt like enough of one on his own. "Obviously everyone here seems aware of that fact except me, and I demand to be told what's going on. Now."

"My prince, I tried to tell you this morning. This deceitful creature had her claws so deep into your heart that you were not willing to listen. I knew that showing you would be the only way to convince you of her *heresy*."

Toani glared at Mayana. To his surprise, Mayana did not cower under his stare. Instead, she defiantly lifted her chin and met his gaze. Tear trails still glittered on her cheeks, but she said nothing.

"Mayana," Ahkin's voice turned pleading. He needed her to deny whatever Toani was accusing her of. "Please. Just show him—"

"I can't, my lord. I ... I don't believe in the sacrifices."

Ahkin took a step back as though she had slapped him. Perhaps that would have been less of a shock. Angry hissing voices filled the hall like a violent wind. "How can you not believe in the sacrifices? They are commanded by the gods." His voice rose despite his efforts to remain calm.

"I don't believe they are, my prince. I believe that the codex that details the rituals was written by men and not the gods."

Toani pushed himself in before Ahkin could respond.

"This heretic questions the validity of our texts, and her actions jeopardize the safety of this empire and the lives of all who live within it. I told you before, I cannot allow such a demon to lead this empire by your side."

Ahkin slowly began putting the pieces together. She had refused to allow the sacrifice of the jaguar, she had asked to spare her friend from the sacrifice that would bless his reign. Her family's reaction to the dog sacrifice. It all made sense. How could she not have told him something so vitally important? How could she have let him believe she was devoted to the gods? She wasn't devoted to them at all. She blatantly disregarded their holy instructions. The instructions his mother had followed to the point of taking her own life. She had *lied* to him.

Ahkin took several steps back. It was as though he was seeing her clearly for the first time.

"Why didn't you tell me?" The room was just the two of them again, only this time, his feelings toward her could not be more different.

"I wanted to, I just—" She reached out a hand to him. The tenderness and heartbreak in her eyes made his stomach turn. How dare she act heartbroken. *Her* heart was not the one shattered by this revelation. The worst part was that he had been questioning the rightness of his mother's death since it happened, fighting his own hesitation with it, convinced the gods were punishing him for his lack of faith in the rituals. And here she was, not attempting to silence the doubt as he did, but fully embracing it.

"You just knew I wouldn't choose you? Is that why you lied to me? You were trying to save your own life?" Was he shouting? He should probably be showing more decorum than this.

He saw it now. He saw what Toani had been trying to tell him this morning. He was in love with the idea of Mayana, not the Mayana who stood before him.

"I have had my own doubts at times, Mayana. But I have pushed them away for the sake of the empire. To do what is best for my people. But you? You embrace your feelings, no matter the cost to anyone else. That is selfishness that I never thought you were capable of. I don't even know who you are." He had been a fool. A fool for not seeing the truth about her, a fool for falling into the trap of first love. Maybe the lord of Millacatl had been right about him after all. He was a young, inexperienced child. He should have made a decision based off politics and logic. How could this have happened to him?

"That's not true. I have been nothing but myself with you. Aside from my beliefs about the rituals ..."

"And I am supposed to believe you?"

"Yes." She stomped a foot. "Every moment we've spent together, I have adored your strength and intelligence—"

"Stop." Ahkin turned away from her. He could not hear her say these things. Not in front of so many spectators. She didn't believe in the rituals. She didn't care that they protected the entire empire. A sick wave of nausea rolled through his stomach. "You are essentially saying the rituals do not matter. The rituals that my mother followed when she took her own life. Are you saying that was unnecessary? Are you saying her death was pointless?"

Mayana let out a sound like a whimper, agony written across her face.

"Ahkin." Metzi was beside him, her smooth hand upon his shoulder. "Please, calm down. She fooled us all. It's not—"

"She didn't fool us all. He knew." He waved a hand at Toani. "She obviously knew." He pointed toward the terrified-looking daughter of Pahtia, glimpsing a triumphant smile on the face of the animal princess as well. "Only Ometeotl knows how many others saw the truth that I did not."

"Ahkin, please, let me explain." Mayana fell to her knees before him with her palms splayed.

"I do not want to hear anything more you have to say. You deceived me. You made me think you were something you obviously aren't. You made me fall—" He couldn't let his heart go there. "I need some air."

He threw off his sister's hand and pushed past Toani and Coatl, who had both moved toward him.

The room suffocated him with its heat. He needed to get outside, away from staring eyes and deceitful young women. From the shame crushing his very insides. He couldn't even bear to look at Yaotl. How ashamed of him would the general be? Would *everyone* be? He had let Mayana get into his head, and it had nearly cost him everything.

Ahkin slammed a fist through a curtain and a servant carrying bowls of pulque squealed and tumbled to the floor. Sticky liquid covered the floor and his feet, but Ahkin kept moving. He didn't even mutter an apology.

Where should he go? He couldn't go to the gardens. The memories of their time in the bathing pools stung like salt in a wound. He wished he could speak to his father, but Emperor Acatl was gone. He couldn't give Ahkin counsel anymore. He couldn't guide him down the right path. He couldn't even ask his mother to explain the infuriating ways of women.

His feet carried him toward his father's tomb. He hadn't even realized it was where he was going until he stood before the elaborately carved pyramid structure beside the Temple of the Sun. He pushed aside the heavy entrance stone and stepped into the darkness. The sun had yet to set for the evening, though it was still too low in the sky, so Ahkin sliced a small cut on his finger and bent the light to follow him in.

The beams of late-afternoon sunlight clung to his hands as if he were holding a torch. He stopped before the sealed entrance where his father's body lay. He didn't want to speak, didn't want to do or feel anything at all.

Ahkin slumped against the door to the tomb, letting his back slide down against the hieroglyphs carved into the surface. He wished his father was still alive. He wanted to let *him* handle the situation with the dying sun, the Miquitz capturing captives, the skeleton priest. He wanted his father to tell him who to marry so that he could just obey and not worry about making the decision for himself.

And his mother. She would know how to comfort him. But instead, she was gone because of the very rituals Mayana was proclaiming were not right. Why did that small part of him sing in agreement? Blasphemy. It was blasphemy even to have such a thought.

Ahkin leaned his head back and slammed it against the stone. He had no idea how to proceed. Part of him wanted to hide in the tomb forever and just let the sun die, but he knew he couldn't. He had wanted Mayana to stand by his side through everything that loomed before him. She was supposed to be his source of strength—his reason to keep fighting.

Maybe he wasn't strong enough to be the emperor. He obviously wasn't strong enough to raise the sun properly. How would he ever be able to father children and bring them up to do a job he couldn't even do himself? Weak. He was weak. And foolish. Too foolish to see that she wasn't even being honest with him. And yet, despite it all, he still loved her. That part of him that knew it was wrong for his mother to take her own life called out in kinship with Mayana's soul, and it terrified him. He wasn't even strong enough to silence his heart which still screamed for him to run to her.

Perhaps it was best Mayana never discovered how weak and foolish he truly was. For once, he was grateful his parents weren't here to see him fail.

The Chicome deserved so much better.

Still on her knees before the throne, Mayana stared down at her open, empty hands. Ahkin was gone and the silence in the room screamed a thousand accusations at her. She couldn't do it. She couldn't kill that dog that looked so much like Ona. And her father had been there. Her brothers. Not only had she humiliated herself in front of the entire empire, she had humiliated her family along with her.

When she lifted her eyes, she searched for her father's face. He wouldn't meet her gaze, and she could tell it was deliberate. Instead, he was gathering her brothers to lead them out of the banquet room. They were leaving. She was already dead to them.

Panic rose in her chest like water filling her lungs. She would never see them again—this was the last time, and she needed to say goodbye. To apologize. To tell them she loved them one last time. Even Chimalli kept his eyes on the floor as he followed their father out toward the courtyard. Only Tenoch met her gaze, and the pain and heartbreak within them as Chimalli dragged him forward by the hand shattered her heart into a thousand tiny pieces like volcanic glass.

"I'm sorry," she mouthed to him. His face crumpled into an anguished sob as he disappeared behind the curtain.

"You have brought this on yourself, demon woman." Toani's cold voice raised the hair on her arms. Mayana got shakily back to her feet. She would not respond.

She had to find Ahkin to explain. The sun had not yet set. There was still time to find him. But where would he go?

Metzi had stepped in front of the throne and held her arms aloft to demand attention.

"This afternoon's feast will be postponed. The food will available in the courtyard and will be properly blessed with a sacrifice if you care to take some before returning home. We look forward to seeing everyone at the games tomorrow morning, where we will be sacrificing several of our Miquitz captives."

Mayana barely registered her words. They were doing a human sacrifice tomorrow morning? She would not enjoy watching that, but she had more pressing matters to address. She must convince Ahkin to forgive her. She had to get him to listen. She cared about him far more than he realized, even more than she realized until he turned and left her on the floor.

The anguish she now found herself in had less to do with losing her own life than with losing him. Of course, she was terrified of the idea of being sacrificed, but she couldn't imagine Teniza, or Zorrah, or anyone else in his arms. Pressing her lips against his …

No. Absolutely not. He could not choose another princess. Her heart belonged to him now and she knew his belonged to her too. He just needed to see that not everything about her was a lie.

"Move along, daughter of water. Slither back into your hole and wait for fate to claim you." Toani dismissed her with a wave of his hand as the masses of people clambered to their feet.

"You fought for what you wanted," Mayana said to him, defiantly lifting her chin. "And so will I."

The priest narrowed his eyes at her but said nothing. Mayana strode past the other princesses without looking at them. She would not be ashamed for being who she was, and she wasn't going to let them make her feel that way either. The hundreds of eyes in the room burned into her with condemnation, but she would not take that condemnation into her heart.

"Mayana …" Yemania's soft, panicked voice reached her ear, but

Mayana ignored her. She didn't have time to explain. She wanted to find Ahkin and she wouldn't stop until she did.

Stumbling out into the courtyard bathed in golden orange light, Mayana squinted toward the dying sun, trying to think of where Ahkin might go. The gardens, maybe? Ahkin had said he needed air. Her feet propelled her toward the back of the palace.

A stitch in her side ached as she ran, and she had to remind herself to breathe. By the time she found the tiled path at the garden entrance, the sky had faded from golden to a smoky indigo with the crescent moon peeking just above the distant mountains.

Ahkin had mentioned the sun fading, and with it already growing dark so early, Mayana worried he was right.

She raced through bushes and around pools, looking for some sign of glinting gold amongst the foliage. But nothing. He wasn't here, and darkness gathered around her like a suffocating cloak being pulled over her head.

Mayana crouched on the ground and hugged her knees for stability. Where else could he be? Was she allowed to visit his private quarters? Would servants prevent her from getting close? Well, she could at least try.

She rose back to her feet and heard the distinct snapping of twigs nearby. She froze, not wanting to deal with talking to anyone until she saw Ahkin. She scooted herself into the shadow of a large tree, determined to stay hidden until whoever was rushing through the garden passed.

"You don't think this was way too early? It won't look suspicious?" a familiar voice was saying. Smooth, lazy, and utterly recognizable. What was Coatl doing in the gardens?

"We don't have time to be subtle anymore. This is the perfect moment."

Was that Metzi's voice? Instead of dancing with melody as it usually did, her tone sounded harsh and cold, like the edge of a blade. Mayana chanced a peek around the trunk to see them hurrying up the path, Metzi clutching her hand to her chest.

"Let me heal it before we get inside." Coatl reached for her hand.

Metzi hissed at him. "No, I want to go back to my room as quickly as possible. With the stupid feast canceled, there are too many people wandering the halls. We can heal it once we are alone."

Coatl grumbled a response that Mayana couldn't quite make out, though she thought she heard something like "Miquitz." She tucked her hair behind her ear, listening hard. Why would Coatl be talking about the death demons?

"I'm not discussing it again. You should have thought about that before you agreed to take care of my father for me. Our deal with the death priest is already done." Metzi's voice finally faded along with the hurried slapping of their sandals against the stone tiles.

Mayana's pulse pounded inside her ears. She couldn't have heard them correctly. The splashing water of the waterfalls must have distorted their words because it sounded like ... But no. There was no way.

Coatl had said something about it being too early, that they had done something that would seem suspicious ... and Metzi was cradling her hand against her chest. An injured hand. Didn't Metzi's blood possess the same power as her brother's? If she could raise the sun, then surely her blood could set it as well—set it far earlier than it should be setting. With a gasp, Mayana realized that Metzi was the reason the sun appeared to be dying. It wasn't an apocalypse at all. And she had Coatl "take care" of her father? What deal with the death priest?

Fury burned within Mayana's chest. Metzi certainly had the ability, but why would she do such a thing? Why would she want everyone to think the sun was dying? To have her own father killed and maybe even to conspire with the Miquitz? She knew the ruling family had a history of ruthlessness when it came to the throne, but she thought such practices had died out long ago.

Mayana didn't need to guess why Coatl was involved. He obviously loved her, and from her hazy memories of that morning after the scorpion sting, Metzi loved him too. She also needed him to heal her hand each night.

Now Mayana *really* needed to find Ahkin. She had to tell him everything. The emperor had been murdered by his own healer—and his own daughter. The sun wasn't dying after all. Metzi was sneaking out each evening and pulling the Seventh Sun below the horizon at earlier and earlier times. Mayana wondered if it had something to do with Metzi being sent to Ehecatl.

But would anyone believe her? Especially now?

Mayana just needed to find him. The desperation inside of her chafed like wet sand against her skin, rubbing her raw and not allowing her to think about anything else.

As she had guessed, the servants wouldn't let her anywhere near his quarters, though they assured her he wasn't there anyway. Mayana wasn't sure she could believe them, but she didn't have a choice.

After an hour of searching the shadow-filled halls, Mayana dejectedly decided to go back to her own room. Perhaps Ahkin was looking for her and she wasn't where she was supposed to be. Yes, that would make sense. Maybe he was waiting for her in her own room, waiting to talk about what happened.

Mayana was nearly sprinting by the time she reached the entrance to her room.

She shoved the still-lopsided curtain aside, her smile wide and expectant—and there *was* someone waiting for her in the room.

But it wasn't Ahkin.

Zorrah stood before the hanging vines that led out to the garden beyond with a curling lip and a monkey perched on her shoulder like a personal guard.

CHAPTER

47

Mayana was clenching her teeth so tightly, her jaw ached.

"I don't care why you're here. Get out of my room." Mayana held the curtain open and jerked her head toward the hallway.

"No, I don't think I will." Zorrah's smile was taunting. On her shoulder, the yellow-faced monkey fiddled with a golden necklace in its nimble fingers. It brought the jade pendant to its mouth and chewed noisily on the precious stone.

"Take your filthy little servant out of here and give me back my necklace."

"Why?" Zorrah pulled the pendant from the monkey's grasp and the creature shrieked in frustration, greedy little fingers reaching for its treasure. "I don't think you'll be needing it much longer."

Mayana balled her hands into fists at her side. She knew exactly why Zorrah was here. This girl from Ocelotl had tried to kill her on more than one occasion, and now she came here to gloat about the fact that Mayana would never be empress.

"I was going to send in another scorpion, but what's the point now? He isn't going to choose a sacrilegious little worm like you. You showed us all exactly who you are, and I didn't even have to do anything. You sealed your own tomb." Zorrah tilted her head as though amused.

"I must admit," she continued, "when my uncles warned me of your beauty and charm, your ability to manipulate others to feel sorry for you,

I was almost worried. But we all knew where your heart truly was. My uncle watched you sob like an infant over your pet dog, and he watched your father let you get away with not doing sacrifices just by shedding a few tears. You don't have the courage or the strength to do what's necessary for the people of this empire."

Mayana tried to block out her words, but even the blood rushing in her ears still could not silence Zorrah.

"You are the epitome of selfishness, and now it cost you the prince. He'll probably choose Teniza and you can die knowing that she'll give him everything you couldn't. Or maybe he'll choose me and see what only the princess of animals can show him in private."

Mayana wasn't exactly sure when she made the decision to attack Zorrah, but it was made. Perhaps the stress and desperation had stripped her down to nothing more than an animal like Zorrah, pulled away her patience and compassion like petals off a flower.

Mayana ripped the dagger out of her ankle cuff and—in a blinding flash of fire glass—her palm was soaked in blood. Every water jug along the wall, every fountain inside her room and in the garden outside, exploded.

The water rushed around her, a swirling mass of transparent glass, a giant turning whirlpool with Mayana at its center. The power of it made her feel like a goddess—a terrifying goddess whose wrath would now be suffered. Her godly heritage flowed through her, overwhelming any sense of fear. She could destroy Zorrah if she wanted to, and oh, she definitely wanted to.

Mayana shoved her arms out in front of her, and the water followed the movement of her hands, shooting out from her like a geyser.

The rush of water caught Zorrah in the stomach and threw her backward. She landed on the ground with a surprised shriek. Her monkey spun across the stone floor, buffeted by the streaming torrent of water.

Zorrah was back on her feet in an instant, a feral snarl escaping her lips. Her own dagger in her hand, the animal princess mimicked Mayana and sliced her palm, crimson now dripping from her body along with the water.

Zorrah lifted her bloody hand in the air and a flock of birds rushed through the vines of the entrance to the garden, surrounding her in her own wild whirlwind.

"Two can play that game, daughter of water," Zorrah snarled, and she unleashed the birds with a thrust of her fist.

Like a thousand tiny blow darts, the birds assailed Mayana, their beaks and claws shredding her skin wherever they found it.

"Don't hurt the poor little birdies," Zorrah cooed as Mayana shielded her head with her arms.

Rage rose within Mayana like an almighty wave, and with a sweep of her arm the water surrounded her body—encasing her in a transparent spherical shield.

She threw out a hand and shot another wave of water toward the princess of Ocelotl, but this time she kept the water low to the ground. Growing up playing in the rivers of Atl had taught her one thing: moving water had great power. Six inches of water moving fast enough could knock a grown man off his feet.

Sure enough, the current beat against Zorrah's ankles and she could not stand. She was instantly knocked to the floor as her feet swept out from under her.

Something cold and dark settled over Mayana. She forced more water over Zorrah, until the animal princess herself was encased in a glittering sphere of water. She thrashed around inside of it, unable to claw her way out, great bubbles escaping from her mouth as she foolishly released the air from her lungs. Mayana laughed and tightened her control over the mass of water.

"Mayana!" Yemania's screech from the doorway broke her concentration. The water surrounding Zorrah collapsed in a cold rush across the floor. The animal princess coughed and sputtered, her soaked form sprawled across the stone. She was a vicious drowned cat—on edge and waiting to lash out. Her chest heaved, and she narrowed her eyes dangerously at Mayana.

"You will regret that, you heathen." Zorrah reached toward the doorway to the garden and this time, several smooth, muscular snakes slithered through the opening. Their forked tongues lashed out at the air. The vivid green color of their scales made Mayana think of living vines as piercing yellow eyes fixed on her.

"Stop! Please." Yemania burst into the room, utterly helpless as the snakes glided toward Mayana.

Mayana summoned the water back to her and trapped one inside a floating silver orb, but the snakes had separated. Two more still moved toward her from opposite sides.

A wall of fire rose between her and the snakes, as quickly as though dried tinder had been placed along the stone.

Mayana turned toward the doorway and found Yoli, her face fierce, holding an outstretched hand dripping with blood.

"Let the real fun begin." She laughed. Mayana swore something dark and primal stirred within Yoli's eyes as she glared at Zorrah. "I've been waiting for a chance to tame that wild spirit of yours, animal princess."

Zorrah hissed and jumped back to her feet, water streaming from her long dark ponytail down her back. Her hands curled into claws.

"Is the kitten scared to play with fire?" Yoli's dark eyes smoldered. Flames rose up her arms and engulfed her as though she were a living torch. Yemania scrambled back against the wall, eyes darting between them as if she weren't sure who to be more afraid of.

"No." Mayana held up a hand toward Yoli. "She tried to kill me. I want to deal with her on my own."

"I don't like people who think they can use their power to push others around." A dangerous rage seethed within Yoli, and Mayana worried that, like a volcano, she was waiting for a moment to release it. Her heart ached as she wondered what suffering Yoli must have experienced to give her such a deeply rooted anger. She had never thought to ask.

Something snaked around Mayana's ankles and dragged her to the ground. Growling in frustration, she twisted around to see vines wrapped around them. She clawed at the vines, bits of thick green plant matter bunching under her fingernails as she tore at them.

"I won't let you hurt her just because she saw the truth of who you are from the beginning." Teniza materialized through the hanging vines now too, standing beside Zorrah.

Yoli shot a tongue of flame toward the vines. "We all know why you hate Mayana, you twig. It was supposed to be you. You couldn't buy his heart with all your money and influence, and you hated her for that. You think you're so much better than the rest of us." The vines were burnt clean through. Their grip around Mayana slackened, and she kicked them off.

Yemania curled into a ball against the wall, crying "Stop it, stop it," with her hands over her ears. Mayana felt as if her heart would cleave in two.

"How could I compete with someone so flippant about the rules of the codex? No wonder you had no shame in seducing him into your bed. That's the only real reason he chose you." Teniza spat the words at her with as much venom as one of Zorrah's snakes.

Mayana lunged to close the space between them. She would rip those tiny little flowers right out of Teniza's hair. She heard Yoli's delighted yell behind her. Mayana was not alone as she hurtled toward Teniza and Zorrah.

A whirlwind erupted between them, and all four princesses were thrown back against the walls. The fierce power of the wind held them in place, beating against Mayana with such force that she had difficulty turning her head to see where the wind was coming from.

Itza stood beside Yemania with her arms spread wide, her face contorted in concentration as she held the battling noble daughters in place. Mayana was momentarily dumbstruck at how someone so tiny could wield such intense power. She immobilized all four of them with the deadly force of a hurricane.

"That's enough." Her voice was eerily calm. "You are all fools if you think the selection ritual is your biggest concern."

"What are you talking about?" Zorrah hissed between her teeth, struggling against Itza's gale.

The pounding of feet in the hall broke the tense silence. At least ten Jaguar warriors burst through Mayana's curtain. Their weapons lowered, and their faces fell slack at the scene before them—Yemania curled against the side wall crying, Itza on her feet and holding Yoli, Mayana, Teniza, and Zorrah against the wall with swirling winds. Blood and water soaked the floor, which was littered with the charred remains of the snakes and Teniza's vines. Itza didn't answer. She just released them all at once. Mayana fell to the ground in a crumpled heap and gasped for breath.

Ahkin's general, the head of the Jaguar warriors, entered the room in formidable silence.

He glared at them all, though the disgust on his face was particularly apparent when his eyes fell on Mayana.

"I don't know what's going on in here, but you are shaming your families and the gods themselves with your behavior. You will each return to your room and stay there. I will be placing guards throughout the halls and the garden to make sure no one even thinks of disobeying me. You will all be ready for the sacrificial games tomorrow, and we will not tell the lord prince about whatever this is." He waved his hand around the room.

Mayana wiped her running nose with her arm as the other girls filed out of her room. Zorrah and Teniza both gave her looks that spoke plainly of their desire to skin her like a rabbit carcass. Yemania had to be half carried by an uncomfortable-looking warrior. Itza didn't look angry, just disappointed, as she shook her head at Mayana and left for her own room.

The general turned to face Mayana, crossing his massive arms across his chest.

"He really loved you," he said. His frown deepened the lines on his face. "I don't know why, but the last thing he needed was a broken heart on top of everything else. I hope you realize the pain you've caused him. If you truly love him as you claim, then leave him alone. You've done enough damage as it is."

The air within Mayana's lungs whooshed out as he left, a fist closing around her heart. The general had managed to do far more damage with his words than Zorrah ever could have done with her beasts.

He was right. She had hurt Ahkin. Deeply. She hadn't been honest with him. She had *let* him fall in love with the Mayana he wanted to see. She hadn't stopped him because she wanted to be that girl. Or, at least she had thought she wanted to be that girl.

The Mayana he wanted would have sacrificed the dog in front of everyone—would have silently and obediently submitted herself to the rules forced on her by others. That wasn't the true Mayana. The true Mayana loved and cared for humans and beasts alike, longed to honor the gods through celebrating their loving sacrifices, not by paying back some supposed blood debt.

If she really cared for Ahkin, was it best just to let him go? Or should she continue to fight for him? Either way, regardless of what happened between them, he still needed to be warned about his sister. Maybe she should have told the general when she had the chance.

Somehow, Mayana would expose Metzi for what she truly was ... even if it was the last thing she did before Ahkin sacrificed her to bless his marriage to another.

CHAPTER

48

Ahkin wasn't sure how long he sheltered in the darkness of his father's tomb, but he could not hide forever. How embarrassing to feel like he needed to run to his parents when life got too hard.

When morning came, he did his duty to raise the sun and focus on the future. The past was the past. He could do nothing with it but learn from it. He would sacrifice the Miquitz captives today and learn why they were capturing peasants. Then he would decide what to do about Mayana.

He was furious with her for not being honest with him. But he also couldn't pretend that a part of him didn't to want to run to her room and hold her and never let go. To agree with her that the rituals were brutal and awful. But the gods would never forgive him if he did such a thing. Not everything about her had been a lie—that he knew in his heart. But was it enough? Would the empire support his choice of a wife who dishonored the gods and risked bringing disaster upon them all?

Ahkin knew his people. The empire was in a continual panic about the next apocalypse—the next disaster. Their only comfort came from the rituals, from the patterns that promised to keep them safe. To ask them to accept an empress who didn't agree—Ahkin shivered at the thought.

He couldn't have her become empress, but the thought of sacrificing her to the gods was equally unbearable. He would just need more time to think about it.

"All three of the captives chose combat instead of voluntarily submitting themselves to the gods," Yaotl informed him when he arrived at the arena. Tiered stone benches rose around a pit of sand with a single round stone platform at its center.

When a criminal was sentenced to die for his crimes, he had the option of gladiatorial combat to earn his freedom. Of course, the chances of survival were incredibly slim. The victim was tied to the stone platform and given a single weapon to fight against four Jaguar warriors. The criminal was given his freedom if he survived, but Ahkin had never seen the Jaguars defeated.

The Miquitz captives chose that option anyway. He respected their decision. Warriors until the end.

The crowd of onlookers trickled into the seats until a sea of faces surrounded them on all sides. Toani stood by the altar at the back of the arena, where a bowl of flames awaited the hearts of the victims.

The princesses filed in to his left, taking their seats along the bench behind the stone throne where he would watch.

His eyes flickered to Mayana, who was obviously trying to get his attention, then forced himself to look away. He hadn't made any decisions yet, and he didn't want to give her false hope.

How would Mayana handle watching a human sacrifice, having never been to Tollan to see one before? He took a deep breath. They were about to find out.

Several Jaguar warriors led the first of the sacrificial captives toward the round stone platform. The man wore the dyed black costume he had fought in at the battle at Millacatl, painted to resemble a skeleton. A thick stripe of black face paint had covered his eyes at one point, but it was mostly smeared now.

Two Jaguar warriors held the captive in place by his arms while a third tied a rope around his waist. The man's eyes darted side to side like those of a cornered beast, and he flinched as he was handed a shield and a dull wooden club.

Ahkin rose to his feet and raised a hand for silence.

"You have been captured by the Chicome Empire and will now be sacrificed to the goddess Ometeotl to honor the sacrifices made by her divine children." His voice was deep and powerful as it echoed around the arena, far steadier than he felt. He moved to sit back down.

"Wait, my lord," the captive yelled out to him, pulling against the bonds that held him to the platform.

Ahkin froze. He furrowed his brow and straightened back up. What could this man possibly want? He took several steps forward, scrutinizing the sacrificial victim before him. "Is there something you wish to say?"

"Yes," the man gasped. "You must listen, prince of light, the fate of our world depends on you."

Ahkin tensed and took a step toward the man. Something about his desperation was unnerving. Metzi fidgeted beside him.

"What do you mean?"

"We had to lure you onto the battlefield. Our priest insisted that if we did not capture you and sacrifice you …"

"Are you not aware that you and your people rely on the power of my blood as much as the Chicome? You need the sun to rise as much as we do."

"Exactly." The captive fell to his knees, dropping the shield and club to the ground and opening his hands toward the prince. "We will all perish without the light of the sun, and the Seventh Sun is dying. The next apocalypse is upon us all. Surely your holy scholars have read the signs in the heavens."

Ahkin swore loudly and looked around the arena. The faces of the people betrayed their shock and fear. Panicked whispers swept through the crowd like an angry wind, gathering strength until the whispers turned into yells and screams. Ahkin had prayed the people of the empire would not notice the sun was dying until he had figured out a plan to save them. Maybe he was foolish for hoping he had more time. He knew they would notice eventually, and their reactions would incite empire-wide chaos.

The sound of a conch horn cut through the cacophony of voices, bringing the attention of the audience back to the arena floor. Ahkin nodded toward Yaotl, thanking him for his timely intervention, and raised his arms toward his subjects. He had to keep them calm to protect them from themselves.

"It is true that the sun sets earlier and earlier each night, but we have not given up hope that we can find a way to save the seventh people. As we speak, my priests work tirelessly to divine the secrets of the stars for a way to avoid—"

"There is only one way to save the sun," the high-pitched and panicked voice of the captive interrupted. The man strained against the ropes. "You are the only way."

A silence fell over the arena, thick and tense. The weight of every set of eyes upon him, Ahkin felt acutely aware of how hard his heart was throwing itself against his ribcage. A terrible thought had formed in his mind. His blood was the only way to feed the sun …

"The sun needs the blood of the gods, and the blood of the sun god himself stands before me." The captive said the words so softly only Ahkin and those closest to him could hear them.

The air whooshed from Ahkin's lungs. Flashes of images swirled in his mind, condensing into a larger picture that Ahkin had not considered before. It was as if he had been putting every ounce of his strength into studying a single star, only to realize that the star was part of a much larger constellation.

The first sun had been created from the blood of his ancestor, the god Huitzilopochtli. He was no longer here to die for them, but his divine blood still walked this earth. Ahkin stared down at his wrist, at the bluish lines that pulsed beneath the skin. The veins that flowed with the blood of Huitzilopochtli. Toani had said that he worried that the god's blood had become so diluted over the years that the drops of his blood on the sacrificial papers no longer contained enough power to keep the sun alive.

But … what if the answer was that the sun needed more? Would all of his blood, spilled like his ancestor's, give the sun the strength it needed? Ahkin was not a god, but the apocalypse had not happened yet. They didn't need to create an entirely new sun. Maybe the blood of a demigod would be enough to prevent theirs from being destroyed.

He would have to die. He would have to give his life as a sacrifice for the lives of his people. He would need to be as brave as his mother. That would be enough to save the sun. Metzi could raise it each morning after he was gone. Thank Ometeotl he had a sister to fulfill that responsibility after he was gone. His eyes found her looking at him with deep concern etched onto her beautiful features. Metzi was strong, and with the storm prince of Ehecatl by her side, he was sure she would make an excellent empress.

The answer was so obvious, Ahkin was surprised he hadn't seen it before. Perhaps he hadn't wanted to see it because he had been too focused on Mayana. So much foolish time had been wasted trying to find a wife, when in reality he wasn't going to need one at all.

A determined calm settled over him. He could never be the ruler his people needed anyway. Ahkin hated floundering in indecision or chaotic emotions. He just wanted a plan. He wanted to know what had to be done so he could quiet his mind and focus on the task at hand.

"Yaotl," Ahkin said quietly.

"No, my lord. I know where your thoughts have gone, and I don't think—"

"What are we discussing?" Toani had crossed the arena to join them.

"Ahkin is thinking that sacrificing himself will save the sun." Yaotl crossed his arms across his chest, exasperation clear in the set of his wide mouth.

"The sun is dying." Ahkin surprised himself at how calm he was able to keep his voice. "My blood nourishes the sun. It makes perfect sense."

Toani's deep eyes bore into Ahkin's. Ahkin could practically see the pieces coming together inside the priest's mind before the weathered face crumpled in pain.

"I am so sorry, my prince." Toani's sad eyes shimmered slightly. "But I see the same solution. I am afraid it may be the only way. Your blood is no longer strong enough. The gods must be demanding more."

Ahkin took a deep breath, his suspicions confirmed. He was not enough. Not unless he had the courage to follow the gods with the same devotion as his mother. A true test of the strength of his faith.

"Well, what are we waiting for then? Toani, how do we proceed?"

Yaotl looked as though he wanted to object, but the warrior bit his tongue when Ahkin gave him a sharp look.

The priest pondered for the length of several heartbeats. "Huitzilopochtli was the first of the gods to give his own blood to create a sun, and he threw himself into the pit of Xibalba."

"I think I would prefer that to a gladiatorial sacrifice, to be honest." Ahkin gave Yaotl a pained look. "I would not ask you to kill me."

Yaotl harrumphed but kept his opinions to himself.

"Then you will hurl yourself into the depths of Xibalba. I recommend stabbing yourself first to make sure a sufficient amount of blood is exposed before you fall."

The content of the conversation momentarily stunned Ahkin. Here they were discussing how he was going to take his own life. This certainly wasn't the direction he had expected the day to take. Why had it taken the word of a captured Miquitz soldier to finally make him realize? Not that his decision was based on the soldier. Ahkin felt the truth of his words deep inside his bones. He wasn't strong enough to lead his people; he hadn't even saved those peasants from the Miquitz. His faith in the gods hadn't been strong enough; a secret piece of his heart rejected the gods' demands for his mother to take her own life.

"Won't my blood spill when I crash into the floor of the underworld?" Ahkin asked, internally flinching at the morbidity of the thought.

"Oh no. You will not hit a floor when you fall." Toani frowned. "The first level of the underworld is the Sea of the Dead. Those who enter must escape the jaws of the sea monster Cipactli. If they are devoured, they will never reach the shore to finish their journey through the other layers of the underworld. Only through proving your worth in the various trials of each layer can you earn a place in a paradise."

Ahkin's stomach clenched. "How … encouraging." He had studied the codices on the layers of creation, but not extensively. He wished he had more knowledge to prepare him for what he was about to face.

"Well, living bodies do not usually enter directly into Xibalba. It is their souls that enter, after their bodies decompose and release them. But if you choose to die in the manner of your ancestor, entering the underworld with your heart still beating and in your physical body, you will face Cipactli."

"Then I will do what I must. My death will bring salvation to our people either way. Whether or not my soul survives the journey through the underworld and makes it to a paradise is my own concern." Ahkin spoke far more confidently than he felt. He wondered briefly what history would say about his short reign. He hoped he would be remembered for being brave enough to do what was necessary. Hopefully he would be remembered for having the same devotion his mother had.

"What do we do with the Miquitz captives, my lord?" Yaotl interrupted, bringing Ahkin's attention back to the skeleton man still tied to the stone platform.

"Actually," Ahkin was struck with a sudden idea, "see if their priest will trade them for the lives of the peasants they captured. Make sure the death priest knows that I will have done my duty and given my blood." Another star in the overall constellation burned into existence. He understood now that the whole reason the Miquitz were capturing peasants was to gain Ahkin's retaliation—to get him onto the battlefield so they could capture him. They knew his blood would save the sun.

"Let's gather at the entrance to Xibalba, and then I will make my announcement to the nobility." He let his gaze drift toward the bench, where the princesses watched him with concern. Mayana was leaning toward him, her face pleading, but he quickly diverted his eyes. Whatever she had to say to him now would be meaningless. It would only lead to more pain. In many ways, his heart was still hers despite everything that had happened, despite what he knew to be reasonable, but it didn't matter anymore.

"I'm ready," he said, more to himself than to his two most trusted advisors. The longer he waited, the harder this was going to be. "Let's go."

CHAPTER

49

"Where are we going?" Yemania asked. She turned her head to look around the crowd filing out of the sacrificial arena as though someone there could tell them.

Mayana pressed in close beside her, foreboding churning her stomach. Now everyone thought the sun was dying. Not a soul aside from Coatl and Metzi, and now Mayana, knew the truth about why the sun was setting earlier. And though she knew who was responsible for setting the sun, she still didn't know *why*. How could Metzi think this would save her from going to Ehecatl?

All around them, the air crackled with frantic energy. Whispers and nervous glances toward the sun dominated the scene. Mayana felt the nervousness seep into her. Her pulse pounded behind her ears.

When most of the city had dispersed out onto the cobblestone streets of Tollan, she caught sight of Atanzah. She was waiting for them at the entrance, motioning with a wrinkled hand for the princesses to gather around her.

"The prince has requested the presence of the nobility and religious leaders at the pit of Xibalba. He wishes to make an important announcement."

Yemania stumbled, her knees giving out beneath her. Mayana reached out an arm to steady her.

"This is it," she whispered to Mayana. "The prince has made his decision and he will sacrifice the rest of us."

Mayana pursed her lips. "I'm not sure that's what this is about."

"Yes, it is." Yemania wailed like a woman in mourning. "We're going to be thrown into the pit of Xibalba."

"Who would he even pick? He hasn't spent any time with anyone but me," Mayana said.

"He's not choosing you." Teniza's usually beautiful face scrunched in a sneer from across the circle of gathered girls. "So, you and Yemania can die together like you planned."

"Ladies, please." Atanzah held up a hand between them. "I do not know what this is about either, but I am sure the prince will inform us when we are all gathered."

Mayana wanted to barrel through the crowd, push them all aside until she found Ahkin. Even if he chose another princess, he still needed to know what she had seen in the garden. He needed to know that it was Metzi who was setting the sun. The Jaguar warriors, posted outside both entrances to Mayana's room, had kept her isolated until they had escorted her to the arena this morning. She had paced her room all night, trying to no avail to find a way past them. Mayana had eventually decided to tell him after the sacrifices, but no one expected the ceremony to end so quickly. No one expected the captive to announce to the city that the sun was dying.

The princesses wound their way through the palace halls and into the expansive pleasure gardens. Mayana tried not to look at the pool where she and Ahkin had enjoyed each other's company, and yet her eyes were drawn to it all the same. Her chest constricted at the memories of his warm body pressed against hers in the cold water, the feel of his slick hair beneath her twisting fingers. Mayana drew a tremulous breath and focused her attention toward the back of the garden, where the edge dropped into terraces and then the cliff face.

On the final terrace, the stone platform kissed the cliff's edge, the same she and Ahkin had visited that night in the gardens. Ahkin had told her that a massive sinkhole waited on the jungle floor at the cliff's bottom, leading not into the earth, but into the underworld itself. Supposedly this was where the sun god had sacrificed himself to create the very first sun. Huitzilopochtli had spilled his own blood and then hurled himself into the abyss. His brother, Tecuciztecatl, the god of snails, had been jealous, and threw himself into the underworld as well. But the world could not handle two suns, so the gods threw a rabbit into the face of Tecuciztecatl, and he became the moon instead.

Mayana supposed that was the story depicted by the hieroglyphs adorning the sides of the platform and the pillars. A small crowd of important nobles and religious leaders had already gathered around the platform, where Ahkin stood with the high priest. Mayana studied his face but couldn't decide what she saw there. Was he angry? Afraid? Something in the way he clenched his jaw told Mayana that he wanted to get whatever ritual this was over with as soon as possible.

Fear spider-walked down her spine. Could he be making the selection for his wife? Surely not without the matchmaker's approval. Unless ... had he already gotten approval for someone else and she didn't know? He still refused to make eye contact with her, and that knowledge only enhanced her anxiety. If he was making his choice now, he wasn't choosing her. At least her family was not here to watch.

She reached for Yemania's hand and squeezed it. Her friend returned the gesture as they gathered in front of the platform. Sweat beaded along Mayana's hairline in the humid air, and she found herself wishing for a breeze. The sun sat relatively high in the sky, blazing down upon them as though punishing them for not sacrificing the blood of the Miquitz captives. The mingling scents of noble perfumes and so many hot bodies gathered together made her wrinkle her nose.

Ahkin stood just ahead, elevated on the stone dais, close enough to hear her if she yelled. Mayana chewed her bottom lip, wondering if she should indeed call out to him, but he looked determinedly at his sandaled feet, his jaw still clenched tight.

"My lords and ladies, I thank you for your understanding in this rather sudden change of events." Toani raised his arms to call for silence, the crimson sleeves of his ceremonial robes sliding down his withered wrists. Mayana resisted the urge to snort.

"As many of you heard in the arena just moments ago, there is evidence to suggest that the sun does not have enough energy to continue its journey across the sky." Toani motioned toward the flaming disk raining heat down upon them all.

Mayana looked around for Metzi, curious how she was pretending to handle the supposed revelation. She stood beside Coatl, though still keeping a careful distance from him. Her hands were clasped in front of her, her head bowed in mock concern. Coatl looked exceedingly uncomfortable. His eyes darted from the floor to Ahkin and back as though he had some kind of tic, like he was regretting whatever was about to happen. Mayana guessed from his behavior that this plan, whatever it was they were hoping to accomplish, was Metzi's idea.

"We have decided that the best course of action to prevent the death of the sun is to offer it a substantial sacrifice of godly blood, the substance that birthed the sun in the first place."

The fear that had been slowly sneaking down her spine suddenly sank its teeth into her flesh. To her left, Yemania whimpered. They were going to sacrifice the princesses. Her heart threw itself against her ribcage as though it was determined to escape before it could be cut away and thrown into the pit of Xibalba.

"No, they can't do this," Mayana said quietly, fighting back at the traitorous tears that were now pricking at her eyes. On her right, Yoli straightened her spine in a regal manner to welcome her fate.

"You are so selfish that you would spare your own life to doom your empire to the next apocalypse?" Teniza said coldly from in front of them.

"Or she just hopes that the rest of us can die to save the sun and she can live happily with the prince like she originally planned." Zorrah joined in the verbal assault.

Mayana clenched her hands into fists. "You are all fools," she started to say.

Itza looked up from her whispered prayers to hiss at her as the prince stepped forward. "You don't know what his plan is yet, so how about we wait to see what he has to say?"

Mayana stubbornly clamped her teeth together. These princesses were infuriating. How could she have always wished for sisters?

"Yemania," she whispered quickly to her friend. "Listen to me, I don't know what's about to happen, but Metzi and Coatl are secretly together. I saw them in the garden. They killed the emperor and are secretly pulling the sun down each night. I need to tell Ahkin. He has no idea. This isn't about me."

Mayana didn't think Yemania's eyes could get any wider than they already were.

"How do you know? Are you sure?"

"I'm positive. Yemania, you know your brother has always had great ambition. Think about it. Ahkin has to know—"

Ahkin cleared his throat and drew an obsidian blade from his waistband. Itza was right. They didn't know what ritual he was performing yet.

"My ancestor, Huitzilopochtli, gave his life to create the first sun. The blood of the gods has saved us each time our world was destroyed, and now, I am hoping that his divine blood can save us from another apocalypse."

Mayana heard the words that Ahkin was saying, but they didn't seem to make sense. Why was he talking about his own blood?

"I have made the decision to sacrifice myself. With my blood, the sun will be nourished enough to ..."

"No!" The scream ripped through Mayana's throat before she even considered holding it back.

Every head swiveled to face her. The high priest looked highly affronted, the other princesses looked embarrassed, and Ahkin ... oh gods, Ahkin's face was painted with grief and disappointment.

"Ahkin, you can't—"

"You will hold your tongue, you insolent snake!" Toani cut across her before she could finish.

"But, it's not—"

"Mayana ..." Ahkin looked at her, the pain so evident upon his face that it broke her heart and stole the breath from her lungs. "You have shamed yourself enough already. Just leave this be."

Mayana gasped as though she had been punched in the stomach. She let her gaze circle around the faces glaring at her and caught Metzi's eye in that instant, blazing fury evident in her expression. Mayana realized that this was exactly what Metzi wanted. She *wanted* Ahkin to sacrifice himself. If he did, the only descendant of the sun god left to rule was …

"No, listen to me, Ahkin …" Mayana pushed forward, trying to get to the stone platform, but the bodies around her pushed her back, as unyielding as a thicket of trees.

"Listen to her!" Yemania found her voice and let it join Mayana's in protest.

"No, Mayana, you listen to me. You dishonor the gods and spit upon the traditions of your own people. I, unlike you, care more about the lives of my people than my own comfort. I have the courage to do what is required of me." Ahkin wasn't looking at her now. He turned away to face the gaping hole in the earth.

Mayana was almost to the platform, her fingertips mere inches away as she writhed against the crowd.

"Please—" she screamed in frustration. "Just wait—"

She was helpless, powerless. She was running through water again, chasing after her brothers and never able to catch them. Tears slid down her cheeks and she growled at the nobles blocking her path. The bodies jostled aside just enough to let her through, but Ahkin turned his back to her and lifted his knife.

"Stop!" Mayana broke through the line of people and slammed against the platform. The stone edge jutted into her stomach and she gasped. Mayana dug her nails into the carved surface to haul herself up, but she was too late.

The blade flashed in the light of the Seventh Sun and Ahkin plunged the blade into his own stomach.

Mayana screamed as crimson blood, the blood of the sun god, the blood of the prince she loved, oozed from between his fingers and dropped like red rain onto the surface of the stone. She clawed her way up, stumbling to her feet just as Ahkin turned to look at her.

"I think I still would have chosen you," he said quietly, his lips trembling.

And then, Ahkin spread his arms wide, his body soaked in the divine blood of the gods, and let himself fall back into the blackness of the sinkhole.

His body fell so slowly, tipping over the edge like a terrible nightmare. Mayana lunged toward him, but she wasn't fast enough.

Toani closed his arms around her waist, hoisting her back away from the edge, but Mayana twisted against his restraint and shrieked like a feral cat. She ran her nails along the high priest's face. Rage and fear and her own sense of powerlessness poisoned her blood like the scorpion sting, overwhelming her nerves and turning her into some kind of wild beast.

Suddenly, she was not the only one fighting. Yemania was there, her nails digging into the priest's flesh as she pulled at his hands.

"Let her go!" Yemania shrieked. "She understands more than you ever will!"

The priest screamed and finally released his grip, his own common blood now glistening on his cheeks and hands. Mayana's body slammed onto the ground, but she pushed herself back up, simultaneously reaching for the blade stashed in the cuff around her ankle.

It was the blade her brother had given her, the blade he had said was for an empress. Everyone around her thought she was the worst possible candidate, too selfish and concerned with her own will above the will of the gods, but she knew in her heart that wasn't true. In fact, she was about to do the least selfish thing she could possibly imagine.

She turned toward Yemania, and her friend's eyes shone with a new-found courage. The daughter of Pahtia now stood with outstretched arms like a barrier between the crowd and Mayana, holding back whoever might interfere. Pride flooded through Mayana at the sight of Yemania standing up to so many.

"Do what you must," was all Yemania said, and it was enough.

"Thank you, Yemania."

Without hesitation, without grimacing at the pain or flinching at the sting, she drew the blade across her hand. The red comet in the sky seemed to flare a little brighter, as if it knew her plan and urged her on.

The moment the blood appeared, she sprinted for the edge. She didn't slow or miss a step as she hurled herself into the open air and into the pit of the underworld.

The cold air bit against Mayana's skin as she fell. Tears streamed out of her eyes as she strained them for some sign of Ahkin's falling body, but the daylight had already receded above her and the darkness around her felt unnatural. Otherworldly.

How far was she going to fall? The darkness pressed in like a mass, like dark water that would fill her lungs and drown her. The fall seemed to last an eternity. She gripped the dagger in her hand as tightly as she could, the only solid thing she could hold on to.

Mayana tried to scream Ahkin's name, but blackness and air swirling around her prevented her from making a sound. Just when she thought she must be falling to the center of the earth itself, the darkness thinned. A dull gray light opened at her feet, and she plunged into what looked like swirling storm clouds.

Her stomach in her throat, she wrapped her arms around herself against the droplets of cold mist that pricked at her face like thousands of tiny cactus spines. The clouds rumbled angrily, as though she had disturbed them as they slumbered, and the overwhelming sound of it rattled her teeth.

The world around her flashed with light and she tried to scream again, sure that lightning would strike her as she fell and burn her into an ember. More rumbling of thunder through the mist shook her deep within her bones.

Without warning, she broke through the bank of clouds, and a massive gray ocean writhed beneath her. Its glittering surface, reflecting the flashes of lightning above, rushed toward her. With hardly any time to prepare herself, she plunged into the water feetfirst.

Icy water enveloped her as she dropped like a stone in a lake. Bubbles now mixed with a different kind of darkness as the pressure of her descent squeezed painfully against her ears.

Mayana kicked out with her legs, grateful to the depths of her soul that she knew how to swim. Salt water burned its way through her nose and throat, overwhelming her sense of smell and taste. Salt everywhere. She reached out her hands, kicking and pulling herself upward. Her lungs screamed in protest, but the stinging on her palm reminded her of the bleeding cut on her hand. She willed the water around her to obey and push her up. A geyser of water caught her within its current and forced her back toward the surface.

Cold wind finally swept across Mayana's face and she gasped, gulping in as much air as she could. Before she could think too hard about where she was, she focused all her strength into feeling the water, reaching out with her divine sense to locate where Ahkin had fallen. As if she were a jungle bat using sound to judge her location, she sent out a small burst of water in every direction, feeling for where the current met an obstacle.

Behind her, several yards away, her current of water ran up against something, so she turned herself around. Blood coated the surface of the turbulent water, a further indication.

She pushed out her hands and swept the current of water around his body to pull it toward her. It wasn't until the warmth of his body pressed against her own that she finally let out a choked sob.

"Ahkin? Ahkin!"

She turned his face away from her, wrapping her arms around his chest and tipping him back so that his head lolled against her shoulder. It was a technique her father had showed her when helping someone incapacitated in the water, to take advantage of the human body's natural buoyancy. She wished she had thanked her father for all the things he had taught her, but she'd worry about that later.

She continued to will the currents to keep Ahkin afloat. She turned his face toward hers, trying not to look at the gaping wound in his abdomen.

"Ahkin," she pleaded, slapping his rough cheek. "Please, please, wake up."

His heart still beat faintly beneath her hands, but how long had he been in the water?

Mayana moved a hand to his throat and a coolness across her skin told her that water had gotten into his lungs.

Panicked, she willed the water to come out, the blood from her hand spreading on his chest. Water poured from his mouth. His muscles tensed, and she turned his head to the side as he retched, sending more of the blood from his stomach wound into the already red-stained current around them.

She held him tight, listening to him cough and gag up the last of the water.

He turned his head to look at her. Of all the emotions to flicker across his face once he realized who held him, anger was the last Mayana expected.

"What in the name of the Mother—?"

Mayana frowned.

"Before you lecture me on how disrespectful and selfish I am, let's get to shore, shall we?" Her voice came off more sharply than she meant it to, but she was already exhausted from the effort of keeping them both above water. They had only the time until her skin healed, or else she would have to reopen the cut on her palm.

A small wave slapped against her face like a cold hand and she spat the salty water out of her mouth.

"Can you see anything?" she asked him. She didn't like the blue color of his lips or how his usually sun-kissed skin was starting to pale.

"What are you doing here, Mayana? You were supposed to live."

"Well, I'm here and I need to save us."

"No, we need to save *you*. Then you can let me die in peace." He winced as he twisted to look around them. "That way." He lifted his arm and pointed to their right before groaning and letting it drop again. "I see a ridge of dark mountains in the distance. There must be land." Ahkin gritted his teeth.

"Where are we, anyway?" Mayana panted as she turned to face the same direction. She looked up at the dark clouds obscuring the world above from view. It was hard to believe that falling through a simple sinkhole could throw you into an entirely different realm of creation.

Ahkin leaned his head back against her shoulder. He was starting to shiver.

"The Sea of the Dead." His voice sounded weak, tired. "It's the boundary that separates the layers of the underworld from the mortal world and heavens above. The in-between."

"The Sea of the Dead," Mayana repeated. That at least explained why the water tasted so strongly of salt. Nothing could live in the Sea of the Dead ... nothing except ...

"There is something else to that legend I'm forgetting," she said.

Ahkin hissed in a breath as he tried to move, a hand shooting to his stomach wound.

"Cipactli. I'd like to avoid him if we can."

It was one word, but it was enough to bring back nightmares from her childhood, nightmares she had after hearing the stories told around dinner fires about the beast that devoured the souls of the living who tried to enter the realms of the dead.

Most of the legends agreed that he was a giant crocodile with a fish tail and the legs of a toad—who also happened to have an appetite so insatiable that he had an extra mouth at every one of his joints. That many more mouths to avoid if they had to escape him. Her pulse quickened at the thought.

She turned around, as though expecting to see him prowling toward them, but so far, all she could see were the whitecaps and gray waves of the turbulent sea.

"Where is he?"

"I don't know," Ahkin said sharply. "But we better get to shore as soon as we can, especially with how much blood I'm getting in the water. I'd rather die on shore where my soul won't be devoured."

"Too bad I'm from Atl and not Pahtia," Mayana grumbled, eyeing his wound again.

"Thank the gods you are from Atl, or I would be dead already. Just focus on getting us to shore." His voice was starting to sound feebler.

The cut on Mayana's hand was hardly bleeding anymore thanks to the rushing salt water. Taking a deep breath, she deepened the cut and willed the currents to push them toward the black mountains on the horizon.

She kicked along with the current, which carried them like a river might carry debris down the side of a steep mountain after a heavy rain.

Out of precaution, she sent out continual surges of water in every direction, feeling for some kind of obstruction, a warning that Cipactli was approaching.

Ahkin wasn't much help, mostly because he couldn't swim, but also because when he moved the wound gushed even worse. Mayana didn't know what they would do once they reached the shore. She couldn't heal. They had no supplies with them. All she had was the dagger from her brother and the clothes on her back.

An idea hit her like the lightning still flashing across the dark, swirling clouds above them. She stopped swimming momentarily and shoved her dagger underwater to where her long loincloth skirt tangled with her kicking legs. Mayana pulled the dagger through the long fabric until a strip longer than her arm came free.

"Angle yourself toward me if you can," she told the prince, and he obliged as best he could.

Mayana's fingers were numb with cold as she fumbled to tie the fabric around his waist, securing the gaping hole against the elements.

"Hopefully that can staunch the bleeding for a while."

Ahkin nodded but didn't respond. Mayana's stomach twisted. He looked so pale.

She sent out another pulse of water around them and froze. Terror gripped at her heart like the claws of a beast ... which was exactly what was approaching.

Mayana had felt her current run up against something massive, something headed right for them.

She forced the water to push them faster, so fast that Ahkin cried out at the sudden rushing movement of the current. Mayana just focused on pushing them toward the shore, on keeping Ahkin's head above the water. She couldn't think about what lurked within these waters, or she'd freeze from panic and never be able to force herself to keep going.

An ear-splitting roar shook the waters as a massive head thrashed out of the sea behind them. Mayana had never seen anything like it. It was as if a scaled brown-and-green volcano had just erupted out of the seafloor and thrust toward the heavens. The head of the biggest crocodile in existence, large enough to swallow the stone temple back in Atl whole, turned toward them, yellow eyes the size of the sun.

Mayana screamed and Ahkin turned to see what she was seeing, his arms still gripping her for dear life in the endlessly deep water. Mayana didn't think it was possible for him to grow any paler than he already was, but as he took in the form of Cipactli, it looked as though every drop of blood had drained from his face.

"Go," he breathed.

"I can't, the shore is still so far away. We'll never make it."

Ahkin squeezed her shoulders, fixing her with an intensity in his gaze she had never seen before. "If anyone can get to that shore, it's you. I know you can. Leave me behind."

"No," Mayana groaned, fear and desperation choking her. She forced the water to push them as fast as she could, but it was like trying to make honey flow faster down the side of a tree. It would only move so fast.

An almighty roar shook the waters more effectively than an earthquake. Mayana hoped her ears weren't bleeding from the intensity of the sound. They were definitely ringing. She kicked her legs even harder, moving with the water as though it flowed through her like her own blood. The shadow of the mountains in the distance grew larger. They were close enough now to see the frothing waves crashing against the jet-black volcanic beach.

Faster. *Faster.*

Mayana made the mistake of turning to look behind her and found herself fixed by the glowing orbed eyes of the beast not even twenty feet away.

The truth crashed over her as another salty wave slapped her in the face. She wasn't fast enough.

CHAPTER

51

"I can't do it, Ahkin. We won't make it." Mayana panted with exhaustion, struggling to draw in salty breaths.

"Leave me and get to the beach." His hand snaked up her arm and gripped her shoulder.

Mayana gritted her teeth.

"That's not an option," she hissed at him, spitting bloody water out of her mouth.

"Mayana ..." His voice was so frail, as if every word was costing him enormous effort. His body shook against her own, shivering from the cold water and blood loss. "I need to die to save the sun. Besides, I'm not going to survive even if we make it to the beach."

"Yes, you are." He had to. She couldn't do this without him. She wouldn't.

"You're so stubborn."

"And I stubbornly refuse to let you die."

He gave a weak chuckle and leaned his forehead against her cheek. Mayana turned and pressed her lips against his clammy skin. They were just going to die together.

Cipactli opened his massive maw, a gaping hole with darkness even blacker than the sinkhole they fell through. She immediately understood the legends of him swallowing the stars and every creation the gods tried to make before being banished to the Sea of the Dead. Gray water churned around the pointed teeth—teeth as long as her body—lining his elongated mouth like those of the caimans she had seen waiting for fish in the river back home.

The looming darkness settled into her heart as Mayana realized they were going to die. There was no escaping him. She had fought so hard, so very hard, against the darkness that had hovered over her since she found out about the selection ritual. Death had marked her from the beginning, her own personal apocalypse, and there was no one to sacrifice their life for her. A dry sob escaped her throat and Ahkin nestled his head into the crook of her neck. Why did it have to end like this?

As she faced the darkness of the monster's mouth surging forward to devour her, a glimmer of light caught her eye, just above Cipactli's head. It was the form of an elderly man, transparent and glittering like a crystal of quartz. A spirit—just beginning his journey through Xibalba. Mayana remembered the legends that allowed the spirits of the dead to avoid the great crocodile. They soared high above the waters of the Sea of the Dead, safely above the guardian appointed to protect the realm of the dead from living trespassers. Jealousy stabbed at her chest. Her soul and Ahkin's would never get the chance to begin their journey through the underworld if Cipactli swallowed them. They would fester forever in the belly of the beast along with every other creation he devoured.

She wished they could float high above his head like the spirits. Because like any other crocodile, he was confined to the water ...

"Ahkin, hold on tight to me," she screamed, slicing her blade across the palm of her other hand. Blood. More blood. She wasn't sure if her idea would work. It was crazy, bigger than anything she had ever tried before. How much of her blood would she need?

Mayana had been practicing floating orbs of water for the past two weeks, for fun, to give water to Xol and the other servants, blasting them apart to make mist and rainbows. Whenever she summoned the water toward her, it always floated through the air like a shining silver snake, *like a shining silver spirit*. She and Ahkin couldn't fly like the spirits, but she could make the water around them fly.

The water swirled with dark crimson stains, a beacon to Cipactli but also the source of the power that just might save them. Mayana focused all of her strength, every ounce of her concentration, into forming the water around her and Ahkin into a sphere, a floating mass big enough to lift them. Slowly, they began to rise into the air like a seabird hovering above the surface of the water.

Ahkin dug his nails into her skin as he realized what she was doing. "How are you—?"

But Mayana didn't answer him, afraid that if she lost her focus they would plummet back into the sea.

Another earth-shattering roar echoed across the waters, vibrating inside her chest like a drum. Cipactli must have realized they were out of his reach. Mayana didn't look down to see how far above him they hovered. After the length of several heartbeats, she felt them sinking, and her stomach jolted. No, they couldn't sink back down, not when they were so close to escaping the monster. Maybe more blood was necessary to suspend so much water? Sometimes, when her father had to divert whole rivers, he would bleed to the point that he almost passed out. They were not full gods after all—they did not possess the same level of strength as their divine ancestors. They were still part human—demigods—and limited as to how much blood they could afford to lose before it killed their human bodies.

Mayana needed more, so she forced the blade across her lower arm, just as Yoli had done at her demonstration two weeks ago. Biting her lip at the pain of it, she let the blood pour out into the water, now almost completely red from her and Ahkin's losses.

Stay up, she begged the mass of water. *Stay up. Stay up. Stay up.*

She made the mistake of looking down. Terror like she had never experienced in her life almost shattered her concentration. He was so big, so *other* compared to any creature she had ever seen before. His head was indeed that of a crocodile, massive and scaled, with the same deadly ridge of teeth and soulless predatory fierceness in his eyes. But giant clawed hands were swiping toward them, far more human than they should be. More razor teeth lined the mouths in the crooks of its elbows. Spikes as long as spears scattered along his back and thrashing tail.

"Can he jump?" Ahkin asked, his eyes skyward. He was smart to avoid looking too closely at the monster.

"I don't know. I don't think he can unless he swims back down first." Mayana hoped so, anyway.

Her head was so heavy, but another roar of rage from Cipactli reminded her why she was fighting so hard, losing so much blood. The next roar of the beast sounded far enough below that she felt safe to move them toward the volcanic beach.

Forward, she willed the water to move, following behind the spirit of the old man that had passed over them.

"You're doing it ... Keep going ... We are almost there," Ahkin whispered encouragements to her, still gripping onto her tighter than a sloth on a tree branch. Every word hissed through his teeth like an exhaled breath, the life seeping out of him as fast as it was seeping out of her.

The beach came closer, a crescent of dark sand in the craggy black cliffs. Jagged rocks like curving fingers protruded through the frothing gray water of the cove, splashes of seafoam and mist contrasting against the volcanic backdrop.

From this height, Mayana caught a glimpse of expansive dead fields atop the cliff, gray and lifeless—stretching out to more black mountains far in the distance. There were no trees, no structures, only sporadic, gnarled remains of charred black trunks hunched like broken old men on the pockmarked landscape. The smell of sulfur and death, like rotting flesh, grew stronger and stronger the closer the shore came.

Mayana's stomach lurched, her mouth full of salt from both the blood and the seawater. They started to drop toward the beach. She didn't have the energy to keep them up any longer. The orb supporting them careened toward the sand like a massive drop of rain. She was so dizzy, as if her head and lungs were filling with the bloody seawater.

Now that they were no longer above the sea, she released her hold over the water like a breath. With a sound like a wave sliding over sand, the mass of water crashed against the beach in an explosion of black dust and blood. Mayana lay sprawled on her back, feeling as though she had run a thousand miles. The muscles in her legs burned like coals and her lungs heaved with the effort to pull in more air. She rolled on her side as she retched and heaved, but nothing came up. She longed for fresh water to wash the taste of salt from her mouth.

Mayana rolled onto her back and threw an arm over her eyes, only to pull it back as it covered her face in more warm stickiness. Only then did she finally look down. The fabric wrapped around her chest was no longer blue, but a deep purple from being stained with so much red. The tattered remains of her loincloth skirt were the same color, the feathered cuffs around her ankles limp and soaked like drowned birds. She wedged a toe beneath them one at a time and eased them off over her feet, the metal edges scraping against the sand.

Her eyes lifted to the water, where Cipactli seethed behind the fingers of rocks jutting up from the depths offshore. With a final rumble deep inside his massive body that sent the water over his back trembling, he slowly sank beneath the waves, obviously accepting that he would have to wait for another meal.

Even if they had outswum Cipactli, Mayana had no idea how they would have negotiated the turbulent water offshore. The pounding surf would have smashed them against the rocks.

It was a miracle they survived.

Mayana propped herself up on a shaky elbow, turning to face Ahkin. He also sprawled across the sand on his back, his chest rapidly rising and falling. The fabric tied across his stomach was even redder than her clothing.

She almost cried out with joy. But the look on his face made the cry die in her throat.

Her shoulders slumped. "We made it."

"Do you ... have any idea ... what you've done?" Ahkin panted, eyes as filled with rage as the monster prowling out in the water.

Her own temper flared. "I've just saved both of our lives. Weren't you just cheering me on as we escaped?"

"I didn't want you to die! You were supposed to be safe. It was supposed ... to be me. Only me," he said. Mayana imagined he would be screaming at her if he had the energy to raise his voice above the faint whisper. "Those who venture here rarely return. I've only read of a few who survived. Now you're going to die too, Mayana. I was the only one who needed to die."

"You're such an idiot." Mayana flopped herself back down onto the sand, rolling her eyes.

"Excuse me?" Ahkin struggled to lift himself but gave up. "I am the emperor. You cannot ..."

"*Don't ever hide yourself from me.*" Mayana threw his own words back in his face. That night in the garden was a lifetime ago. Literally, now. "Well, here I am—and I think you're a blind fool."

"I swear to Ometeotl, if you insult me again ..."

"You'll do what? Bleed on me? Too late," she said savagely as she fingered the ruined fabric of her skirt.

Ahkin gritted his teeth and turned away from her.

There were several minutes of fuming silence. Finally, Ahkin pounded a fist against the sand, sending the black fragments of rock flying into the air.

"My sacrifice was supposed to save everyone, and you were going to live a long healthy life without me."

"Your sacrifice would have accomplished nothing." Mayana forced herself up and inspected the gaping wound in her forearm. She gagged, and Ahkin laughed rather cruelly.

"Right. Because you don't believe in the sacrifices." He let out a condescending snort.

"No," Mayana snapped back. "Because it's your lovely twin sister that's working with the Miquitz and lowering the sun each night to make it look like the sun is dying."

Ahkin stared at her, opening and closing his mouth like a catfish on the deck of a boat.

"You're lying."

Mayana ripped another strip of fabric off her ruined skirt and wrapped it slowly around her arm, wincing as the salt water stung the wound.

"I heard her. In the garden last night. Coatl was with her and"—she hissed as a sharp stab of pain shot through her arm as she tightened the fabric—"he healed her hand after. They're worshipping the goddess of lust together, by the way, in case you missed that too while you were busy pretending to be a god."

"It's not true." He threw his head back on the sand.

"Just because you wish something wasn't true, doesn't mean it isn't."

She was furious at him. Furious that he was stubbornly sticking his head in the sand rather than admit he was wrong about his sister. He just didn't want to admit he had almost killed himself for nothing.

"Well, it won't matter, anyway." Mayana wiped her running nose and started to shiver despite the warm, humid air. Sand clung to her skin and scratched against her as she moved.

They had made it to the beach, escaped an endless eternity in the belly of Cipactli, but they were still two living souls, clinging to life on the shores of the land of the dead.

CHAPTER

52

Ahkin glared at the dark clouds swirling overhead. The darkness around them lightened somehow, like a pale morning when the sun waited below the horizon for him. He had no idea where the pale gray light in this god-forsaken place came from, considering somewhere far above the clouds should be a ceiling of rock, not the sky of a different layer of creation. But Xibalba was its own world. A world for the dead.

Day and night reversed themselves in Xibalba, and this was Xibalba's night. While the sun lived in the world above during the day, it died each night and made its own journey through the underworld. Its light would not reach them until the sun set above. Maybe the moon was traveling through the underworld somewhere far above them, casting that ghostly glow from behind the clouds.

"I'm going to look around," Mayana announced.

"Do … whatever you want." Ahkin continued to pant, feeling weaker and weaker as his blood dripped down his sides into the dark sand. He was furious at her for daring to suggest Metzi could do something so selfish. For ruining his plan and sentencing herself to die as well.

She stomped away several yards and then turned back to face him.

"Just know that letting yourself die isn't going to save anyone. Now that you're gone, Metzi will steal your throne and stop setting the sun early." Mayana spat the words at him before she stalked away toward the cliff behind them.

Something roared up inside his chest and almost escaped through his mouth, but he bit it back. Whatever attack he longed to throw at her, he didn't have the energy to do anything more than whisper, so it wouldn't do his rage any justice. What he longed to say needed to be yelled, preferably with his arms thrown in the air in frustration.

So instead, Ahkin sighed and lolled his head to the side. He had never had an injury this severe, and he was secretly afraid to move. He was so cold, colder than he had ever been in his life. Part of him wished the fire princess had jumped in after him so she could make a fire to keep him warm. Or even the princess of Pahtia to heal the wounds in his abdomen.

His body shook violently, his extremities practically burning from the cold. Ahkin wiggled his fingers in an attempt to force feeling back into them, but the effort was exhausting.

Yes, Mayana had saved him from Cipactli, but he was still inches from death anyway. He refused to believe what Mayana claimed about his sister. What would happen when the last of his lifeblood leaked out onto the sand? Would his spirit simply leave his body? Would it still be enough of a sacrifice to save the sun?

Well, despite how angry he was at her, Ahkin refused to leave Mayana alone in this place, so he would fight until he couldn't fight anymore.

After a while the crunch of shifting sand announced her return.

"Did … you find … anything?" His words were now stretched between his shallow panting breaths. Ahkin knew better than to hope, but he asked anyway. A dry cough ripped through his throat.

"Other than sand and rocks? No. I think there's a path leading up the cliff face, but I'm not leaving you here defenseless while I explore."

"I can … defend myself." Ahkin tried to reach for his knife before he realized it was gone. He must have lost it when he fell into the sea. His fingers groped at his empty waistband and his hand flopped pathetically back onto the sand like a dead fish.

"Clearly." Mayana huffed.

"Look, I'm sorry … for being so angry … it just wasn't … supposed to be … like this."

"Stop talking so much. You don't have enough energy." Her voice softened, and she pressed her fists into her eyes. "But I know what you mean. Nothing turned out like it was supposed to."

"My father … should still be alive. My mother never should have taken her own life." Maybe it was because he was dying that he didn't have the strength left, but he couldn't stop his eyes from burning. Hopelessness hovered over them like a shadow. "I wasn't even supposed … to be emperor … yet."

"You didn't want to be emperor?" Mayana settled down beside him, drawing her knees to her chest and hugging them tight.

"Not yet … I wasn't ready."

Mayana gave a hollow laugh. She probably related—her entire life shifted course with his father's death too.

"I really cared about you, you know." She turned her head to face away from him, but he was sure her cheeks were flushed.

Ahkin's heart swelled. "I meant … what I said … before I fell. I still … would have chosen … you."

"Except that no one in the empire would have let you." She still wasn't facing him.

"It still … doesn't matter."

"You're right. It doesn't matter because you still would have tried to kill yourself, even if you had chosen me."

"I don't … want to fight … right now, Mayana." Ahkin inched his hand toward her. "Please … I just want you to know … how much …"

"You can't leave me. Please. Ahkin, don't leave me here alone." She closed the distance between their hands and squeezed his fingers, as though she could hold his spirit back. It shattered his heart to hear the desperation and fear in her voice, and it only strengthened his resolve to hold on as long as he could.

"Oh, don't worry, dear, he won't."

Ahkin's stomach shot into his throat and Mayana shrieked before scrambling toward him like a sand crab.

"Who is—?" he started to ask before Mayana let out another scream.

"*Yoco?*"

Yoco? That name meant nothing to him. He tried to turn his head to get a look at the new apparition on the beach. His first impression was of a withered old owl. He took in the form of a hunched woman with wrinkled skin hanging off her bones like dried animal hides. She was dressed in swirling patterns of white and black, with hair to match. The faint smell of incense teased his nose.

Yoco was sitting cross-legged on a large rock behind them, her fingers working furiously with some small colorful bundle of fabric. Ahkin recognized it as a worry doll like the one Mayana had given him. In fact, there were hundreds of worry dolls spread around her on the rock, as though she had decided to take up shop here on this beach on the edge of Xibalba.

"You … know her?" Ahkin breathed toward Mayana.

"I—she—that's where I got your worry doll from," Mayana said distractedly as she continued to stare dumbstruck at the old woman.

"Yoco—how did you get here?" Mayana asked, her eyes as wide as the full moon.

"I can go anywhere I want, dear child." The shriveled figure lifted the doll to her craggy, broken teeth and gnashed at a dangling thread before spitting it out onto the ground and holding up the finished doll to survey her work.

"Perfect. Relatively." She picked up another bundle of fabric and started fiddling with it.

Ahkin furrowed his brow, his head pounding from working so hard to make sense of what he was seeing.

"Who … are you?" he finally managed to ask.

"I am the duality, son of the sun. The light and the dark, joy and pain, the Mother and the Father in one." She gestured to her swirling white-and-black tunic dress. He recognized the colors of white and black from a symbol in the codex sheets …

"The duality? You mean … you are—?"

"You know me as Ometeotl, Mother of the gods, although technically I am the Father of the gods as well, you know. Everyone seems to forget that part …"

"But you're an old woman," Mayana said, pursing her lips.

"To your eyes, perhaps. I am whatever I need to be, and right now, you are both sorely in need of the Mother's guidance and stern hand." She chucked the latest doll onto the surface of the rock with the others, not even looking at Mayana and Ahkin.

Ahkin's chest tightened at the mention of needing a mother.

"What … do you mean … stern hand?"

"We'll get to that." Ometeotl waved an impatient, wrinkled hand. "For now, let's take care of these injuries, shall we? Before I need to pluck your spirit from the air and bring it back to your body."

With two fingers between her withered lips, she gave an ear-splittingly loud whistle. A distant bark answered, echoing toward them. A bark? She was summoning a dog?

Mayana cocked her head to the side, a deep frown upon her face, and Ahkin tried to shift to see what she was looking at.

Bounding toward them came a black dog, smooth and sleek with a tuft of shaggy hair atop its thick head. Its large ears protruded upward, with the ear on the left slightly bent out at an awkward angle. A giant pink tongue flopped out of its mouth as it frolicked toward them across the sand.

"*Ona?*" Mayana's hands flew to her mouth, and Ahkin frowned a little. How did she know the names of everyone they were meeting down here?

Tears glistened in her eyes as the dog leapt toward her, knocking her onto the sand and dragging its pink tongue across every inch of her face and arms and hands. Mayana was sobbing now, tears streaming down her cheeks as she attempted to embrace the erratically wiggling form, which seemed too excited to hold still for very long. Its whiplike tail lashed across Ahkin's arm and he drew it back with a hiss. Who was this dog?

Ometeotl gave another sharp whistle and both of Ona's ears perked upright. He sat patiently on the sand beside Mayana, facing the Mother goddess as though waiting for instructions.

"Yes, I am gifting Ona to you to help on this journey. Every spirit needs a guide through Xibalba, and dogs usually make the best companions, don't you think?" Ometeotl clapped her hands together and held them against her chest in a loving gesture.

"Thank you," Mayana managed to choke the words out through her shuddering breaths as she tried to calm herself.

"He'll also come in handy for another reason." Ometeotl snapped her fingers several times and motioned toward Ahkin.

The dog—*Ona*, he heard Mayana call him—sauntered lazily toward him. He bent his smooth black head toward the wound on Ahkin's stomach and began to lick. The warm, rough tongue pulled at the skin, and Ahkin cried out in pain before trying unsuccessfully to move his body away from the dog.

The moment the dog lifted his head, Ahkin peered down at his stomach—at the wound—but the wound was gone. There was nothing but the tanned, muscled plane of his abdomen. Ahkin had seen dogs lick their own wounds to promote healing, but never anything like this.

"I might have given him a few gifts of his own for the journey." The Mother goddess smiled with a proud gleam in her eye.

Ahkin sat up, running a hand over the newly healed skin. His head still swam with dizziness from the loss of blood, but his body could now slowly replenish it without losing more.

He lifted his awed gaze to Mayana, who was staring at the healed skin on her own hands and arm, twisting them around and flexing her fingers.

They were still trapped on the shores of the underworld, but now they were no longer bleeding to death, and they certainly were no longer alone and without hope.

Mayana could not believe that Ona was here, or that her beloved dog had just healed the gashes on her hands and arm. As if she needed any other reason to feel overwhelmed with joy at seeing her long-lost friend.

"I have a feeling his gifts will come in handy. Ah, speaking of gifts …" Ometeotl rummaged in the folds of her dress and withdrew a long golden chain. A small jade skull no bigger than Mayana's palm dangled from the end. Glittering blue sapphires filled the skull's eye sockets, but its little mouth gaped open and empty. It was beautiful, yet something about it sent a cool shiver across her skin.

"This, Mayana, is the Amulet of Atlacoya. It was a gift I gave to my daughter to end the flood that destroyed your first sun. I now gift it to you."

Mayana took the gift with shaking hands and secured it around her neck. The skull felt cold against her skin.

"In addition to the amulet, I want to give you something else that will prove essential." Ometeotl lifted one of the tiny dolls off the rock and tossed it gently toward her.

Mayana caught the thumb-sized doll in her newly healed hand and opened her fingers to study it. It wore a little yellow dress, embroidered along with edges with tiny green reeds.

"What does this do?" she asked.

Ometeotl looked at her over her beaklike nose. "It's a doll. It doesn't do anything."

"Oh." Mayana flushed and tucked the doll into the fabric around her chest. Really? How could a simple tiny doll "prove essential"?

"I have gifts for you too, prince of light."

Ahkin sat up straighter and swayed a little.

"Give it some time. Ona has the power to heal flesh wounds, but nothing more. Your body will recover its blood soon enough. And you're going to need it." The Mother goddess waved a shriveled hand, and a shield materialized on the sand. The wooden disk was sanded smooth and had a thick leather handle, but its most prominent feature was a carved golden sun inlaid with hieroglyphs and a skull staring up from its center. The golden symbol shone with a subtle hue, almost as if the carved sun radiated its own light like its true-life counterpart.

Ahkin leaned forward and fitted the shield to his arm, thrusting it outward to take out an imaginary enemy. He flexed his fingers with an impressed smile upon his face.

"That is the shield of my son Huitzilopochtli. It has seen many battles and will protect you well."

"Thank you, great Mother." Ahkin's face shone with boyish excitement as he studied the detailed surface of the carved golden sun.

"And your second gift"—she withdrew what looked to Mayana like a large walnut from her dress—"will also be essential to your survival."

The Mother goddess gently handed the walnut to Ahkin. His shrewd eyes studied the shell with skepticism.

"You humans can be so narrow-minded." Ometeotl threw her hands in the air in frustration.

Ahkin's cheeks reddened and he muttered an apology.

"Thank you for the gift," he said, bowing his head.

Ometeotl clicked her tongue impatiently and motioned toward the shell. "Look inside, child."

The color in his cheeks deepened, and Mayana recognized a flicker of pain across his face at being called a child. With a thumb and forefinger, he eased the shells apart and shook it over his palm.

A tiny white worm, no larger than Mayana's smallest finger, wriggled out from between the two halves and landed in Ahkin's outstretched hand.

He immediately hissed as the worm bit him, leaving a perfect tiny circle of blood. His hand jerked, and the worm dropped into the sand.

"No, idiot boy, leave it in the shell. I just told you to look at it." The Mother goddess snatched the shell back and scooped up the worm from the dark sand. She returned the worm to its confinement and handed it back to Ahkin with suspicious eyes, as though she wasn't sure whether giving him the worm was the smartest idea after all.

"Why a worm?" Mayana asked, thoroughly confused as to how it could possibly be essential to their survival.

"It is time you learned to stop questioning the gods at every turn and trust that sometimes I might know better than you." Ometeotl pressed her mouth into a thin line, deepening the creases in her chin.

Mayana sucked in a breath, and tears stung her eyes at the reprimand.

"I do not mean that unkindly, my dear. You understand far more than most of your people." She shot a sideways glance at Ahkin, whose spine went rigid. "But you both still have much to learn."

"I am sorry, Mother Ometeotl." Mayana dipped her head respectfully and Ometeotl's face softened.

"You remind me of her." The goddess's eyes suddenly shone bright in the pale gray light surrounding them. "Such stubbornness, yet such softness at the same time. That is the power of water within you, persistent enough to destroy mountains, yet gentle as tears from the heavens."

Mayana didn't know how to respond, but luckily the goddess seemed too lost in thought to notice.

Ona trotted over to Ahkin and licked the wound on his hand from the worm, leaving behind freshly healed pink skin. Ahkin ran his healed hand across the dog's head in thanks.

Ometeotl finally heaved a sigh and steadied her shoulders.

"Water, doll, shield, worm, and—oh, yes." She clapped her gnarled hands together and an animal-hide bag overflowing with dried corn and maize kernels appeared on the ground at her feet. "You will also need sustenance for the next few days. You have exactly five days until the end of the Nemontemi. The last days of the calendar are considered so unlucky because they are. The spirits and evils of the underworld are able to escape as the entrances between the layers of creation are opened. Once the new calendar year starts, the layers will close, and I'm afraid the price to escape would be too great for either of you to pay."

"So we have to escape in five days or we will be trapped here?" Ahkin repeated, as though reciting battle plans.

"And die, yes," Ometeotl said matter-of-factly. "That's why I'm not giving you more than enough food for five days. If you do not escape before the end of the year, well, you won't be needing the food much longer anyway."

Mayana let out a terrified squeak, and the Mother focused her eyes back on her.

"Can't you just … send us back to our world? Can't you just save us?" Mayana knew what the answer would be before the goddess answered.

"Of course not. I have many purposes for the journey you are about to undertake. You will learn most of them as you go, but there is one reason in particular I need you to make this journey."

A thrill of foreboding snaked up Mayana's spine, and a clever smile pulled at the goddess's mouth.

"Remember, my dear, how you paid for the doll you gave to your prince?"

The thrill solidified into pure fear in the pit of her stomach. She nodded.

"You owe me a favor, and I am now calling upon you to honor that favor."

Mayana clenched her hands into fists to stop them from shaking. "How may I serve you, Mother of creation?"

"You will retrieve the bones of my son, Quetzalcoatl, from Cizin. I want you to return them to me at any cost. I will use them to resurrect him in the caves of creation." Her eyes bore into Mayana's with such intensity that Mayana blinked and looked away.

"Who is Cizin?" Mayana racked her brain for any memory of his legends.

"The Dark Lord of Xibalba. His throne is made from the jade bones of my children." Ometeotl's voice trembled with emotion at the mention of the sacrificed gods.

"We will get them," Mayana whispered to her feet.

"Very well." The Mother looked satisfied. "That takes care of that. Now to the part every mother dreads." Her eyes were full of pity, not anger, but it still chilled Mayana to her core. What did she mean by "the part every mother dreads"? Were they about to be punished for something?

Ahkin moved closer to Mayana and gripped her elbow tightly, angling himself in front of her as though hoping to take the brunt of whatever was coming.

"Well, since you volunteered, Ahkin, let's start with you, shall we?"

Ahkin took in a sharp breath beside her, as if he was bracing himself.

"You, Ahkin, along with the majority of your empire, have come to care more for the rituals than for the gods themselves. More than for *me*."

Ahkin opened his mouth to argue, but the goddess silenced him with a look.

"Rules do not honor the gods. They honor yourselves. You put your faith more in your own ability to be holy than in the love and sacrifice I made for you. I suffered the pain of losing my children, and you continue to offer me more pain and suffering."

Ahkin rubbed the back of his neck. "I—am sorry. How can we best honor you and the other gods?"

"You know, what I want more than anything … is your hearts."

Ahkin's hand shot to his chest.

Ometeotl ducked her head and pinched the bridge of her nose.

"Not your literal hearts. Humans …" She sighed and mumbled to herself for several moments.

"I want your *love*, your *adoration*. I do not want you to honor me with death. I have had enough of death and loss. Honor me with singing, with dancing, with your gifts. Honor me with *life*."

"But I thought the sacrifices honored the sacrifices you made—"

"Do you think I want to be reminded of my losses every day? My children who died to save you all did so because they loved you, as I do. You are our creations. But you dishonor their sacrifice by thinking you need to continue to pay a price that they already paid for you. I know you creatures. You like predictability, you like safety, but you also like control. You want control over your own fate by thinking your rules will save you. You are placing your hope in the rules, not in me and my divine purpose."

Mayana could not believe the words she was hearing, and neither, it seemed, did Ahkin. He stared at the Mother goddess as though she were an impostor, as if this were all a great trick.

Mayana, on the other hand, savored each word of the Mother. The doubts and frustrations that had always plagued her heart were finally given freedom. It was as if leeches had been slowly sucking the life out of her and now had been removed.

Mayana had been right. The gods, at least the Mother goddess anyway, did not want sacrifices. She *didn't* want more pain and suffering. Why hadn't the Mother made her will known before now? How could she have allowed this to continue for so long?

"I was right?" Mayana exhaled, a hand over her own heart now. It beat frantically beneath her fingers, as if it were dancing in celebration.

"Of course. I made you. I put the truth within your heart so that you and others like you could show the truth. It is within everyone's heart, but you are attuned enough to listen."

Mayana suddenly frowned.

"But—why me? Do you have any idea how much I have suffered because I haven't submitted to everyone around me?"

"For exactly that reason. You are not the type to submit. You have water within you, enough water to help wash the mud from the eyes of my people. Like this one." She jerked a thumb at Ahkin.

Ahkin stumbled back to a rock and slumped against it, his head in his hands. When he looked up again, his fingers pulling his short hair in all directions, he looked as though he had been told the world had burned down around him without him noticing.

"I—don't understand. Are you saying that the sacrifices, the rituals, aren't … necessary?"

"They are not how I want to be worshipped and honored. No. Your blind dedication to them allowed you to be fooled into handing over your empire to your twin sister—who did deceive you, by the way."

His head drooped, and Ometeotl again faced Mayana.

"While he sorts that out, I also want to address a concern I have with you."

Mayana's joy shriveled like a grape in the sun.

"You are strong and stubborn and stand for what your heart tells you. I have watched you closely, as I have all the noble daughters of my descendants. But my darling daughter of water," the Mother goddess smoothed the folds of her white-and-black dress, "you put your own heart above even my own. You think you know better than the gods, and that will be your downfall unless you trust me. Before your journey ends, you will have to make a choice that will destroy your world or mine. The Seventh Sun may not have been dying after all, but the next true apocalypse is quickly approaching. The bleeding star I placed in the skies is indeed a dangerous omen, and the skies will continue to proclaim my warnings. The world could end again very soon. I hope you will have the strength to trust me."

Without warning, the goddess rose shakily to her feet, gathering the remaining dolls into her arms.

"You must begin your journey now. Ona will guide you, but you face many dangers and trials ahead. At least you both have what you need to survive."

"Thank you for our gifts, Ome—" Mayana began before the Mother goddess waved her down.

"I do not mean your gifts, though certainly those will help."

"What do you—?"

"You have what you need because you have each other." Her crinkled face broke into a wide, joyous smile.

"Nothing makes me happier than creating two souls for each other and seeing them find their way together. You are dualities of each other, heart and mind, passion and duty. You will both teach each other what the other needs to learn."

Ahkin lifted his head out of his hands again.

"We—were created for each other? You mean I was destined to choose her all along?"

"Oh no, son of the sun, just because I created her for you and you for her does not mean that is your destiny. You must still choose. Free will is the gift I gave to all humanity. I know what is best, but you still have the freedom to ignore me. But I do promise, as Mayana must come to learn, that not trusting me often comes with dreadfully painful consequences."

Mayana blinked, and she was suddenly staring at empty black stone. The goddess was gone.

Ahkin turned to look at her, confusion, pain, fear, desire, so many things swimming in his eyes at once it was a miracle he was not drowning in them. Perhaps he was. The pleading posture of his body made him look so lost. Did he want Mayana to tell him what to do?

Mayana felt just as lost. They were supposed to travel through the levels of the underworld, somehow steal the bones of Quetzalcoatl from the Lord of the Dead, and find their way back to the mortal world before the end of the calendar year? That, and the next apocalypse was truly coming and Mayana would make a decision that could save or destroy them all?

Her stomach suddenly rolled with nausea. How was she supposed to do this?

Mayana slumped down on the rock beside Ahkin, afraid that if she opened her mouth at all, she would be sick.

Ahkin didn't say anything to her, but instead slid his hand over hers and wove their fingers together. He squeezed her hand so tightly it hurt, but she returned the pressure with equal intensity.

A lifetime ago, she had gripped the handle of her knife as the only steady thing in a world shifting beneath her feet. Now, his hand would be that anchor.

Mayana didn't have any idea what they were facing or what they would have to endure, but she did know that she wouldn't have to walk through hell alone.

Perhaps together, water and light could bring color into a world succumbing to blackness.

I have always been fascinated by Mesoamerican history, and when my family moved to Mexico, I knew I wanted to set the story in a fantasy world roughly based on the diverse ancient cultures of South and Central America. As the daughter of a research librarian, I began doing what I love to do best: research! I started scouring through original sources for inspiration, and after reading the origin myth of "The Five Suns," this story began to take shape. Though the Chicome Empire is a fantasy, I did try to remain true to various historical details whenever possible. That being said, I did take some creative liberties to tell Mayana's story. For example, the original myth states that we are living in the age of the Fifth Sun and not the Seventh Sun. I also changed some names for the sake of continuity. Xibalba is actually the Mayan name of the underworld, as opposed to Mictlan, which is the Aztec version. As far as I am aware, the Aztecs also did *not* practice the self-sacrifice of a wife upon the death of her husband. Just as with ancient Egyptian culture, sometimes servants and animals were buried with their ruler to serve them in their journey through the underworld. The Aztecs were a highly ritualized culture, which I felt would be the perfect foil to a heart like Mayana's. She is ordered to follow certain practices because they are accepted as truth, even though she knows they are rules created by man. In so many ways, it mirrors some of my own personal spiritual struggles.

The Aztecs were a syncretistic society, often adopting the myths and practices of the societies they conquered. For this reason, there are many different versions of various mythologies. Ometeotl is an example of a highly debated deity. Some scholars believe the Ometeotl did not exist, while other sources refer to Ometeotl as the original creator couple. I chose to use Ometeotl as the Mother/Father creator. Duality, or balance between opposites, is such an important concept in Mesoamerican thought. I wanted her/his character in the story to really embody that important element. That is also why I wanted Mayana and Ahkin to be dualities of each other, a balance of heart and mind.

The issue of human sacrifice can also be highly controversial when discussing the religious practices of ancient Mesoamericans. Western culture likes to represent harmful "bloodthirsty" stereotypes that do not do justice to the deeply spiritual practices. In my story, I wanted to make sure that the religious context was explained. When citizens of various genders and ages were sacrificed, it was considered a great honor. The Mexica believed that the gods sacrificed themselves in order to create mankind and the sun itself. Blood held the power of fertilization. Because of their belief in duality, you cannot receive without first giving. They believed that the offer of blood was an act of thanks for the origin sacrifice and a way to offer a gift in exchange for life-giving sustenance. This was sometimes done through animal or human sacrifices, but also through ritual self-sacrifice of blood. Usually, self-sacrifice included pricking oneself with a sharp instrument such as a stingray or cactus spine. Because of their belief of the power held in blood, it made sense—for the sake of the story—for blood to hold many forms of power. This is why my magic system is so closely tied to the idea of bloodletting. It is not meant to encourage any kind of self-mutilation but was chosen in recognition of the specific historical practice.

Though there is much evidence for human sacrifice, there is also much debate around the scale to which the practice was performed. It is often believed that the Spanish priests exaggerated claims of numbers in order to support their own agendas. In reality, societies all over the world practiced killing for religious purposes, including those same European churches that burned countless people at the stake to "purify" their souls. The Aztecs also did not kill indiscriminately during war. The purpose of many battles was to *capture* enemies that would be later sacrificed for a specific religious purpose, as we see in the story with the Miquitz soldiers in Tollan. The ritual of the noble daughters being sacrificed to bless the emperor's reign was fictional, but sacrifices were often performed during important ceremonies or times of the year. So, for me, it made sense that an important sacrifice would be performed to initiate the reign of a new emperor.

If you would like to learn more, I highly recommend the book *Handbook to Life in the Aztec World* by Professor Manuel Aguilar-Moreno. Thank you for taking this journey with me, and I can't wait to share the next part of Mayana and Ahkin's story with you!

Lani

ACKNOWLEDGMENTS

In writing this book, I channeled so many of my own emotional and spiritual struggles. Like Mayana, I am fortunate to be surrounded by loved ones who challenge me to face difficult questions and continue to love me as I wrestle through them. First and foremost, I want to thank God, for teaching me the true meaning of love and sacrifice and showing me unending grace. And I want to thank my mother for not only instilling a deep love for books in my heart, but for showing me what it means to be a strong woman. Mom, you taught me to never give up and to always pursue your dreams, no matter the obstacles that stand in your way. Without those lessons, I am sure this book would not exist.

Samantha Wekstein was my superhero agent, brainstorming ideas and helping me get this book out into the world. I am so grateful that you fell in love with this story as much as I did. Thank you for helping me navigate the publishing waters and being willing to patiently answer my never-ending questions. The amazingly talented editors Betsy Mitchell and Courtney Vatis polished this manuscript until it really shined. I know it wouldn't be the story it is without both of you! I am still amazed at the beautiful cover and artwork done by Kathryn English. You took my vision and not only made it come to life, but blew my expectations out of the water! To Josie Woodbridge, Lauren Maturo, Greg Boguslawski, Jeffrey Yamaguchi, Mandy Earles, Rick Bleiweiss and everyone else at Blackstone

Publishing for taking a chance on a young debut author. You all made my dreams come true. I am so lucky to be with such a talented and successful publishing house!

There are so many people I want to thank for reading early versions of this book, and I know I will probably forget some, but I will do my best! *DEEP BREATH* Here we go. To my sisters, Hana and Noelle, thank you for letting me talk your ears off about story ideas and being my cheerleaders through the whole process. To John for sharing your love of Mexico with me and being such an amazing father to our family. To Kevin, you are the other half of my duality and you always will be. To Raelyn and Zach, thank you for being patient with mommy during all those hours I spent on the computer writing (and to Beverly, Dale, Becky, Dan, Julie, GG, and Uncle Fat for helping watch them with Mommy's crazy schedule!). A special thank-you to my critique partners Angie Howard, Marilyn Allison, and Dana Lange; Erica Cruz, Rachel Scott, Tanager Haemmerle, Angela D'Ambrosio, and Margo Kelly for reading my earliest drafts. To Bethany Kaczmarek for teaching me so much about writing and editing. To my first beta readers Brittany Salling, Melissa Kirscher, Matt Moncrief, Brian Coultrup, Alaina Henry, and Meg Alberda. I am so grateful for the feedback of the incredible readers at Writers House: Sarah Grill, Nikki Sinning, Christopher Cappello, and Hannah Sutker. To Merrie Destefano and Rachel Marks, thank you for believing in me and giving me the courage to believe that I could really do this "author" thing. To all the wonderful authors who were willing to read and give blurbs about this story before it was even published. You are ALL rock stars for helping me walk through this process!

And lastly, thank you reader for joining me on this journey and letting me share the crazy world I made up in my head! I can't wait to see where else this journey takes us!